D1590520

ODETTE'S

A Quality Men's Club

by Bridget Finnegan

DURHAM, NH

Bridget Finnegan is an author, designer and illustrator.
This is her first novel.
She lives in seacoast New Hampshire with her partner
Mike Cleary.

bridgetfinnegan.com

Follow Bridget on Instagram: @bridgeedawdle
Follow Bridget on Facebook:
www.facebook.com/authorbridgetfinnegan

Published by Dawdle Publishing, LLC
Copyright ©2021 by Bridget A. Finnegan

ISBN 9781955072007

To all the fabulous women who
made this book possible.

Especially:

Lorna Albertson
Leslie Barrett
Angie Bloom
Suzanne Cornellius
Shawn Finnegan
Colleen Flaherty
Pam Joplin
Dolores Leonard
Erika Mantz
Kitty Marple

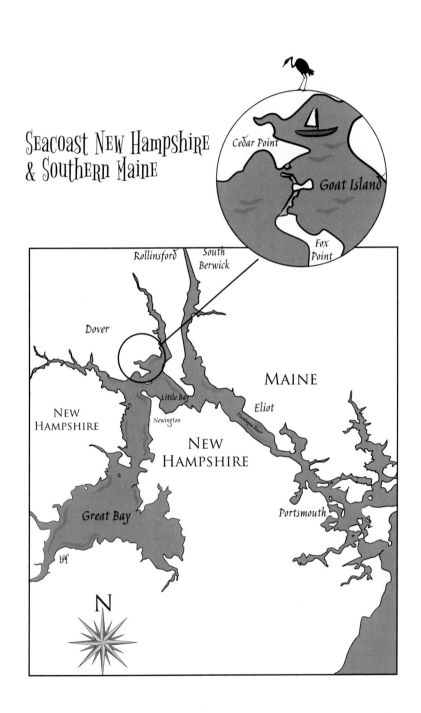

Seacoast New Hampshire & Southern Maine

Cedar Point

Goat Island

Fox Point

Rollinsford

South Berwick

Dover

MAINE

Little Bay

Eliot

Newington

Piscataqua River

NEW HAMPSHIRE

NEW HAMPSHIRE

Great Bay

Portsmouth

N

The Isles of Shoals

MAINE
NEW HAMPSHIRE

Duck

Eastern

Shag

Mingo

Appledore

Malaga

Smuttynose X

Cedar

Lunging

Star

Seavey

White

Fall 1854

The old madam was spitting mad when they left five years ago. Now here Odette sits in the front parlor of their home—seemingly a world away but really only a few blocks from the whorehouse.

"You'll be back," she had warned. "All the girls come begging sooner or later. You and that little shit bastard you're carrying won't be able to find any respectable man to take care of you."

"That's just the thing. I won't need a man." Jessamyn flipped her long brown braid and answered with a confidence that she didn't feel. She had been earning more as an investigator than as a whore lately but still she was unsure.

"Well, don't think that you can just come back here any old time you want. I need girls who are reliable. And you tell that bitch Sarah that she better grow eyes in the back of her head. I might just tell the authorities about how she arrived on my steps in the first place. Those scars are a dead giveaway."

She was bluffing. At the time Odette had girls of all colors working for her. All of them had run away from something. It was way too much of a risk to her livelihood to invite the closer look of a slave catcher.

"And you better not be taking any of those fancy French garments that I so generously provided for you and Sarah while you were here. You really are ungrateful little shits."

Jessamyn's eyes rolled. "Cruppers, Odette. Those are about as French as you are—made out of cotton sateen from the mills in Dover. I'm pretty sure that Sarah and I won't be needing your ridiculous underthings. Anyway, if you recall, you docked our pay for those pieces of ticky tack. You wouldn't know French silk if you were being strangled with it." She told herself to shut up. The goal was to get out of here with the least amount of drama. They were only moving to Holt Street—not Canada.

The old madam's stream of tobacco lands with a splat about a foot away from the brass spittoon adding a new pattern to the cheap Oriental carpet.

"I won't miss that." Jessamyn thought as she and Sarah walked out the front door of the finest whorehouse in Portsmouth.

And now here Odette sits. Five years later and she's looking to hire Jessamyn and Sarah.

Sarah couldn't stomach the thought of meeting with the old madam, so she and Jonah left to dig for clams on the mudflats as soon as the coach arrived.

Jess doesn't offer tea and sits opposite the old woman in a wingback chair.

The five years have not been kind to the madam. Her once milky skin is now pockmarked and ruddy. She looks like a large pincushion in her silk dress.

"You've done very well for yourself Anastasia—I mean Jessamyn. J. Jakes discreet Inquiries seems to have taken off. I heard that Captain Pritchard even gave you this house," she says as she waves her hand around the well-appointed room. "It was his mother's, right? You must have serviced him really well," she chuckles.

Even though the house was payment for locating a shipment of stolen goods for the captain's company—Jessamyn says nothing in response to the baiting.

"Why are you here, Odette?"

"It's Suzanne. She's missing," the old woman responds.

After five years, Jessamyn still feels the sting of Sweetness's rejection.

"Why would you care about her being missing? She must have been more trouble than she's worth lately—with the opium."

"I've grown to care about her like a daughter."

Jessamyn frowns. Odette was quick to toss out any girl who wasn't meeting her quota. Sweetness must have still taken clients even though she was out of it most of the time. "When was the last time you saw her?"

"Yesterday."

"Why do you think she's missing?" Jess asks. "Maybe she's with an overnight customer."

"Since the poppy started, she hasn't really left the house. All of her clients come to her—and she wouldn't have scheduled an overnight without telling me," she adds as an afterthought. "Essie saw her yesterday afternoon in a buggy with Dewitt Taylor headed towards Newington."

"Taylor? That sadistic crupper. Didn't he try to strangle Daisy?"

"That's him, yes," the madam replies.

"I thought you threw him out after that."

A customer had to be pretty bad for Odette to ban them. To this day Daisy speaks with a raspy voice.

"Yes. He hasn't been around."

"Could Essie be mistaken?" Jess asks tucking a tendril of hair into her bun.

"No, she was sure. She had her own encounter with him. He scared the shit out of her. She came running home to tell me as soon as she saw him."

"Did they see her?"

"She says not," Odette replies. "She says that she hid behind a tree."

"If they headed through Newington," Jess muses, "they probably stopped at the Goat Island Tavern. The bridge is the only way across Little Bay. I'll ride up there this afternoon and see what I can find out."

"Thank you." The settee groans as Odette lifts her herself up.

"I charge $10 per day plus expenses," Jess says doubling her usual rate, "and I'll need a deposit of $25 in advance."

"What do you mean, Jessamyn? I assumed that you would want to find Suzanne as much as I would—you were so close and all."

Jessamyn's mind goes back to the time Odette caught her and Sweetness together. She didn't care that they were lovers. She was infuriated that two of her whores were engaging in an activity that wasn't making her any money.

"That's ancient history. This is my business. It's how Sarah and I earn a living."

"Is Sarah your new girl?" Odette asks with a smirk.

"No. We're family. Even after working for you she still prefers men."

Odette scowls and yells for her driver. "Tot! Take me home and bring Miss Jakes $25. Be sure and wait for a receipt."

CHAPTER 2

Jack comes barking to the front door. Sarah and Jonah must not be far behind. The boy tracks mud across the faded Turkish carpet as he chases the terrier through the parlor into the kitchen waving his clamming fork. "Momma! We have a whole bucket full! Sarah let me dig them up."

Sarah hates clamming. Jessamyn keeps scolding her for tricking Jonah into doing chores she dislikes.

"That's wonderful, Nah. We'll have them for dinner. Momma's going to Newington for work this afternoon and I'll probably stay over."

"So, you're taking the old lady's case, huh? What happened? Did she lose something up that enormous derriere of hers?" Sarah, dressed in workman's boots and pants, walks into the kitchen.

"No," Jess says. "Apparently, Sweetness is missing."

"Missing? That girl's been out of it for so long I wouldn't say she's been on this earth for a while now."

"That's certainly true. This is a little different. Essie saw her in a buggy headed to Newington with Dewitt Taylor."

"Oh dear. I thought we were rid of that mutton nob. Why in God's creation would Suzanne go with him?" Sarah asks.

"More importantly, why would Odette care?" Jess replies.

"There must be something more here," Sarah says twisting her curly hair between her slender fingers. "The old lady must be up to something and I bet it's about money."

"That's all she really cares about," Jessamyn agrees.

"Who's Odette?" Jonah asks with eyes big as saucers.

The two women exchange glances. They're always forgetting that they shouldn't talk about cases in front of Nah. He is smart for his five years and remembers everything they say then repeats it verbatim to his friends. It's hard enough for him to keep pals when their parents find out about Jess and Sarah's past.

"Honey, why don't you take Jack next door to the widow Markwart?" Jess asks. "Come right home after she gives you your cookie."

"Oh!" he replies with a frown. "I always have to leave when you're talking about something good."

"Don't worry, Nah," Sarah laughs as she puts the bucket next to the sink. "Your momma and I will save the interesting topics for you."

Jonah rolls his eyes as he leads the terrier back through the fancy parlor out the front door.

Jess watches them leave. "That dog spends more time over here than at home. Maybe we should think about getting Nah his own pet."

"Are you joking, Jess? This is perfect. A dog without any of the care or feeding. Besides, Mrs. Markwart seems to enjoy visiting with the boy."

"I hope so," Jess says. "Maybe she can watch him for the afternoon. I was thinking that you might check in with the girls at Odette's to see if you can find out anything more about Sweetness."

Sarah replies, "Sure. I'll do that after I review the land deeds for the

Baxter case and maybe stop by the Athenaeum."

Jessamyn smiles. Sarah's favorite place in the world is the Portsmouth Athenaeum—the old private library in the center of Market Square—a wealth of book knowledge just waiting for her to discover. She's been going every week for the last five years.

"You don't think you'll be home until tomorrow?" the younger woman asks as she cleans up the muddy trail left by the boy and the dog.

"Well, it's just over seven miles to the tavern," Jess replies dumping the bucket of clams into the lead-lined sink. "If I find out anything I may need to continue on. That is assuming I can figure out where they went, I'll keep following them. I could be gone even longer than just tomorrow. Either way I'll find a way to get word back to you."

Jessamyn pumps water into the sink and scrubs the clams while Sarah stokes the stove. A few potatoes out of the root cellar and a few leaves of lettuce from the glass box in the garden and they'll be ready for supper.

"Mrs. Markwart is so ancient!" Jonah yells on his way into the house. "Momma, did you know that she has almost 50 years? How does anyone get to be that old?"

"Don't die?" Sarah answers with a smile.

Jonah's eyes grow wide again. "How old are you, Momma? You're not going to die, are you?"

"Stop teasing your brother, Sarah. To answer your question Nah, I'm 27 and your sister is 20. We have many more years in us, I think."

He seems overwhelmed by this information and sits quietly for a few minutes as Sarah peels the vegetables.

"Keep an eye on those potatoes, Sarah. I'm going upstairs to get my things together for the trip," Jess says.

Jessamyn changes from her dress into men's riding clothes in the room she shares with Jonah. She would wear comfortable clothes all the time but has found that people respond better to her questions if she's in a dress. There's something about a woman in pants that causes men to panic. She packs up a dress, corset and petticoats just in case she needs them.

"What a pain in the crupper. Lady wear takes up too much room." She unpacks it all and throws it onto the faded blue wingback chair near the bureau.

She catches a glimpse of herself in the discolored framed mirror above the dresser. Her brown hair is astray—her bun lopsided with half of it falling down her back.

"I need to do something about that." She pulls all of the pins out of her hair before she brushes it and quickly works it into a braid extending to her waist. She picks up the gray men's hat she usually wears in the garden and places it on her head.

"Much better."

She looks at Jonah's bed and notices that his stuffed doll has sprung a leak of cotton. "I'll need to fix that when I get back," she says to herself.

Sarah smiles at her as she passes through the kitchen. "I like the hat. It suits you."

Jess nods and leads Jonah to the barn where she saddles up their black gelding, William Henry Harrison. She leaves blonde Buttercup and the wagon for the others.

"There now, Willie," she coos into his ear as she puts the saddle onto his back. Nah feeds the horse a carrot and he nuzzles the boy's neck in return.

"That tickles, Willie!" Jonah laughs.

"Nah, will you please run upstairs to Sarah's workroom and find me two large sheets of paper?"

They built a room in the loft of the barn as a studio of sorts for Sarah's bird studies. Drawings are pinned up covering the walls. A bird skeleton lays flat on a table with an array of seashells and feathers. A small wood burning stove sits in the corner next to a ragged settee covered with an old patchwork quilt.

Ordinarily Jonah is not allowed in this space. He tiptoes in and picks up two sheets from the stack on Sarah's table.

The stairs creak as he returns and hands his mother the paper. She folds them up so they fit into her saddle bag.

"I just need to tie it all to Willie and I'll be all ready, Jonah."

"Can I help?" he asks—eager to show off his new knot tying skills.

"Of course, Nah, remember how I showed you—around the tree and through the rabbit hole."

"You're silly momma," he says as he rolls his eyes. "There's no tree and no rabbit. There's just string."

He ties the saddle bag and races for the house. Jess chuckles as she unties the mess he's made and starts over. "He's really not much for knots, is he?"

She pats Willie's nose, gives him a kiss then leads him into the sunny small garden between the house and barn.

"Don't worry Mr. President, I'll be back in a bit and we'll be on our way."

Jess notices some late season carrots in the garden and pulls them up. Jonah and Sarah can have them while she is gone.

Her daughter has set the simple wooden kitchen table—they never use the fancy dining room—except to lay out papers from whatever case they are working on.

The steamers taste salty and delicious even without the butter that Sarah forgot to buy on her way home from the library the other day. Nah's appreciation of the mollusks has grown since his sister taught him how to dig them up a few weeks ago. He slurps them happily while Sarah and Jess make a plan for the week.

"So once I have the documents for the Baxter case do you want me to put them in the mail or have a courier take them to Boston?" Sarah asks.

"I think the mail will be fine," Jess replies. "There really isn't anything confidential in them. They just confirm the details of the original contract."

"It will be nice to get the final payment," Sarah says. "We could sure use the money."

"Amen to that."

CHAPTER 3

J essamyn hugs Sarah and Jonah goodbye and checks her saddlebag to be sure that everything is in order before heading on her way.

"Be nice to your sister while I'm gone, Nah."

"Brodie says that Sarah can't be my sister."

"Why is that?" Jess asks.

"He said because she ain't the right color."

"First of all," Sarah says, "never say that word 'ain't.' Only unsophisticated country people say that word. Second of all, do we have the same last name?"

"Jakes? Yup."

"That means we're family. You tell that pipsqueak Brodie to mind his own business."

Jessamyn laughs. "Remember, Nah? I told you that Sarah and I chose to become a family."

She was able to adopt Sarah officially and change her name even though she's only seven years older. She's carefully building a documented history with their new identities. Of course, there was a little finessing of the paperwork to make it go through.

Sarah and Jonah walk next door to Mrs. Markwart's house as Jessamyn leads Willie to the front of the house on Holt Street.

The sun is warm on Jess's back. Even though it's October, it feels more like an early September day. She looks back at the white clapboard house that they have called home for the last five years. "I suppose the place looks a little run down. At the very least the front door could use some new black paint," she mumbles.

She spies her neighbor across the street, Reverend Hobson, just as he leaves the rectory behind the stone church.

"Hello Jessamyn."

She tips her hat. "Reverend Hobson."

"Headed out of town?"

"Well, you know..." She prefers that the preacher knows none of her business, so she doesn't elaborate.

The reverend has spent much effort over the last five years trying to shame Sarah and Jess into attending services.

"Pray tell your business today?" he asks.

"Well reverend. Nice of you to ask." But of course, it's not. It's just plain rude. "I'm actually headed to Market Square to meet with my pastor, The Right Reverend Howard Bunford Cheney. He's been offering my family spiritual guidance at the West Church."

"Ah, Cheney." Hobson grimaces at the sound of his rival's name and raises an eyebrow in disdain. They have been in a Puritan Holy War for years over patrons—their two parishes being only a few blocks apart. Jess takes great pleasure in needling the clergyman. She might even have to attend services at the West Church one Sunday just to irk her neighbor.

Not that Reverend Cheney is any less onerous as far as she can see. He's just a little farther away—a half a mile to be exact.

Putt, the caretaker, emerges from the church with a bucket and a mop. His eyes light up when he sees her.

"Hello Miss Jess. How are you today?"

"Better now that I've seen you, Putt. You've improved the state of company exponentially."

The red-haired giant shows his gap-toothed smile. "I don't know what that means Miss Jessamyn, but I'm glad to hear it."

She whispers to the young man. "Psst. How much is he paying you, Putt?"

"Paying me? You mean like money? The reverend don't pay me. I get to live in his shed for free."

She makes a mental note. Another reason to dislike the reverend.

"I don't know why you talk to that simpleton," Hobson says as he follows her down the road.

"All creatures are equal in the eyes of God, aren't they reverend?"

He scowls and walks away.

Instead of heading west towards Newington straightaway she trots a few hundred yards towards downtown for the benefit of the skeletal man.

It will take her a couple of hours to reach Newington. She plans to arrive later in the day—early enough to have daylight to look around and late enough to not seem suspicious about staying the night. Early travelers typically would cross the tavern bridge and keep heading to the larger town of Dover where there are many more options for supper and lodging.

The sun is low in the sky as she passes through the town center which is really just a white church and the small town hall. She says hello to a woman using the carved step rock to mount her saggy, cream-colored horse.

A few minutes later she crosses the bridge—a beautiful span with stone arches—from Fox Point to Goat Island. She deposits a penny in the toll box and approaches her destination.

The tavern is a two-story yellow clapboard house with a small barn and an outbuilding. The nearest neighbors, the Bunkers, occupy a farm across a second bridge to Cedar Point.

Smoke from the fire reaches her nose—it smells like oyster stew cooking. There's a horse tied up on the side of the building. No sign of a buggy or wagon. If Suzanne and Taylor were here, they aren't anymore.

"Hello!" Jess calls as she opens the front door.

She hears giggling from the back room and decides to take a seat at the table by the stove rather than intrude upon a private moment. The pot of stew simmers on top. Her stomach growls. It feels like a long time since dinner. The tavern is known for tasty, hearty fare. She makes a mental note to take some of their bread back to Nah and Sarah.

The room is plain but tidy with whitewashed walls, pine floors and modest adornments. A braided rug lies in front of a faded peach settee situated under the stairwell near the kitchen door.

A pink, round-faced, blonde woman stumbles into the room adjusting her apron followed by a tall, sandy-haired man in working man's clothes. He nods and darts out the front door.

"Hello. May I help you?" the woman asks.

"Yes please. I'm Jessamyn Jakes. I'm hoping for a room for the night."

"Yes ma'am. I'm Mrs. Simpson. You can call me Matie. My husband, Samuel, will be right out to stable your horse. It will just be a few moments while I get your room ready. There's cider warming on the stove if you'd like some while you wait."

Jess ladles herself a mug of the warm cider and settles in at the table. She pulls out the paper from her bag and sharpens the tip of her pencil with her knife, carefully tossing the shavings into the front door of the stove.

She notices a portrait on the wall of a distinguished looking couple in their Sunday best.

"Interesting painting," she says as Matie walks back in the room.

"My parents. That was their wedding portrait."

The innkeeper stands at the bottom of the stairs rubbing her belly absentmindedly.

"The room rate is two dollars a day. That includes supper and breakfast. Payment up front." She looks down. "We've had some problems collecting in the morning lately."

Jess replies, "That sounds fine," and hands over the money. "Say, a friend of mine was on her way through here yesterday."

"Hmmm. A couple came through last night. The woman was a blonde frail thing."

"Yes, that sounds like her. Was her name Suzanne?"

"I never caught her first name. Lafferty was their last name. Sorry to tell you but your friend looked poorly when she was here. She and her husband only stopped because she was ill. He took her right upstairs. I brought some food up for her when he came downstairs to drink ale."

"Did her husband say anything to you?" Jess asks.

"Nothing. He just grunted at the ale and stew. It seemed best to avoid him—I'm sorry if he was your friend—he was a bit out of sorts. I made my husband bring him a second helping when he called for it."

"No, I don't really know him. His wife was my friend from years ago."

"Ma'am, your horse is in the barn for the night." A heavyset bald man in a dark workman's coat fills the front door.

"This is my husband, Samuel," Mrs. Simpson's eyes never leave Jess's face.

"Very nice to meet you, Samuel," Jessamyn nods at the couple. His wife's face relaxes into a smile. "I'll just drop some things in my room and take a walk around the island before supper."

Matie shows her up the stairs to one of two small bedrooms.

"I do love my husband," she says quietly once they are in the room.

"It's none of my business, ma'am. I don't judge others." Jess smiles.

"We have an understanding."

The innkeeper seems to want to explain but Jess would prefer to keep the conversation on the case.

"Really ma'am—back to your guests. Did you see them again?"

"What? Oh no, I came in from the barn around midnight and heard the front door shut. I looked outside but didn't see anything. Then later, before first light, there was a series of bumps—like someone was dragging a bag down the stairs and out the door. They were gone when we rose at dawn."

CHAPTER 4

Sarah avoids the main streets in Portsmouth as she makes her way to Odette's. She'll never feel totally safe with the crowds even though it's been nine years since she arrived here. She has too much to lose now to do something stupid. Luckily, Portsmouth is a rough seaport town with people from all over the world. There are lots of women and men of every color. Still, it pays to be careful.

She stops to straighten her bonnet and smooth her simple yellow dress before she enters Odette's via the back entrance into the kitchen.

"Sarah!" Moira, the round smiling cook looks up from her table. "I haven't seen you in an age. Granny, take these biscuits to the oven and keep an eye on them while we chat."

A small dark-haired girl of about ten picks up the tray and scurries off to the oven behind the house. Her oversized shoes slap the stone floor as she makes her way.

"Granny? That's a strange name for a child," Sarah says.

"Her real name is spelled G-r-a-i-n-n-e—pronounced 'grawn-ya.' Nobody can pronounce it except for me so now she's just 'Granny.'"

"At least she doesn't have a whore name."

"Yet—that will come soon enough. So, what's up, lamb chop? Usually Jess comes to pick up any new tidbits of information. Why are you here?"

"She has other business today. I'm here because Odette came by our house. She wants us to look for Suzanne."

"Oh, monkey balls." Moira rolls her eyes and hands her a cup of tea.

"What do you mean by that?"

"Sweetness hasn't been right in the head since you and Jess left. The opium has just made it worse. I'm not sure that looking for her is worth your time."

"Was she meeting her numbers?" Sarah asks blowing on the tea to cool it before taking a tentative sip.

"Hell no. I've no idea why Odette hasn't tossed her out before now. She's not one for sentimentality."

"She says that Suzanne is like a daughter to her," Sarah replies.

Moira spews tea out of her mouth across the worn wooden counter top. "Are you kidding me? That's the funniest thing I've heard all day."

"We thought that sounded like periwinkle piss. So, why does she care if Suzanne left?"

"Who knows? Maybe the old rumors are true," Moira says as she rolls out the next round of dough.

"Are you talking about the stories about Odette's stash?" Sarah asks. "Do you really think she has a chest of jewels and coins hidden somewhere?"

Moire says, "Well, I suppose it would explain a lot if Sweetness stole it. What I don't understand about that theory is why would Odette stick around here if she was sitting on a pile of money?"

"Good point." Sarah nods. "I have to admit that for the three years I was here I dug through every orifice in this house and didn't find a thing."

"Orifice? Jesus, Mary and Joseph, you are getting smart. What the hell is an orifice?"

"A hole," Sarah replies laughing.

"Why not just say hole? Seems kind of unnecessary to fancy it up like that. Whatever you call it, you and every other girl has done the same. None of them ever left for something better except for you and Jess, so nobody must have found anything. If there is a treasure somewhere it must not be in this house."

Moira's right. Most of the girls who left Odette's ended up in the less desirable houses on Water Street such as Sally Lightfoot's or The Randy Piddock.

"Who knows?" Sarah continues. "Did any of the girls have much to say about the day Suzanne went missing?"

The servant girl walks back in the kitchen with the hot biscuits. Moira sees Sarah lick her lips.

"Granny, pack some of those up for Miss Sarah to take with her."

"Yes ma'am," the small girl replies.

"And take a few for yourself. They'll be no talking of this to the girls or to Miss Odette, Granny."

"Yes ma'am." She grins, wraps the biscuits and hands Sarah her bundle.

"Now be a love and go to Fogarty's cart to buy some pickled eggs. We're near out and Odette likes them for dinner."

Granny smiles shyly and walks out the door.

"She's very young," Sarah observes. "When is that old bag of snakes going to auction off her cherry?"

"She wanted to do it this year, but I think we've talked her out of it. With more Irishmen coming every day she'll get more cash the longer she waits—a sweet young lass like that."

Sarah shudders at the memory of her own auction. She hadn't even started her monthlies yet.

"So, what have the girls been saying?"

"Mostly that Odette hired Dewitt Taylor to take Sweetness away to get rid of her."

"That does sound like something she would do," Sarah says settling down on the familiar worn stool.

"The afternoon girls will be coming down any minute for their shift. Why don't you stick around? You can ask them yourself."

One of the reasons Odette's has been so successful is that it's organized like a factory—complete with shifts. Odette charges customers more who want to see a particular girl off hours—not that she shares any of the additional profit. Higher earning ladies are rewarded with the better shifts. Of course, in a seafaring town who's to say what the good time slots are? Ships arrive at all time of night or day. Sometimes it's busiest at 5:30 in the morning.

There's not a lot of longevity in the whore business. Sarah only recognizes two of the five girls that wander in for tea. Essie and Daisy hug her. All the girls have inexpensive cotton lace corsets with cheap metal stays over faded shifts. A few wrap themselves in tattered floral shawls. The others hover near the stove to keep warm.

"Well if it isn't the bitch who got away," a tall buxom redhead calls from the doorway. She's dressed better than the other girls with French undergarments and a silk green robe that matches her eyes.

"Hello Savannah," Sarah says blandly.

"Hello Désirée," the redhead replies.

"It's Sarah now, Sarah Jakes."

"Sure—sure, it is," Savannah says as she thrusts her hip out. "What are you doing here? The old lady always said you'd be back sometime. I guess she was right. Are you working this shift? You'll need to change out of that potato sack and freshen up your mutt face."

"Give it a rest, Savannah," Moira interrupts.

"Aren't you a little long in the tooth for this work?" Sarah replies. "I've seen cows with perkier tits than yours."

"Savannah is still one of the top earners," Moira says, trying to keep the peace. The truth is that she has one regular client every Wednesday who is so afraid of exposure that he pays Odette four times the going rate. Only Odette and Savannah know who he is.

"Sarah is here to look into Sweetness's disappearance," Moira continues.

"Why?" Savannah asks. "Who cares about that bitch leaving?"

Sarah can tell this conversation is a big mistake. She's going to be better off speaking to Daisy and Essie alone. "I'm an old friend of hers and I'm worried about her going off with Taylor."

Daisy stiffens with the mention of Taylor's name.

Savannah rolls her eyes. "If you're so concerned about Sweetness, where the hell have you been for the last five years?"

"I think it's time you girls assembled in the front parlor," Moira says. "Odette will be off her chump if any of you are late."

With the cook's warning they slowly make their way to the front to start their day.

Sarah taps one of the girls on the shoulder."Essie, do you have a moment to speak?"

She looks shyly from under a mop of black curls. "I guess so."

"I understand that you saw Suzanne and Taylor together the other day."

She retreats behind her curls. The only thing visible is her pale nose.

"I...I guess I did."

"Where did you see them, Essie?" Sarah asks quitely.

"Near the docks—you know—Water Street," she answers retreating behind her hair.

"So Essie, you didn't see them leaving town headed west in a wagon?"

"Oh wait! That's where I saw them. Yep. On their way somewhere far away or something. In a wagon."

"So where exactly were you?" Sarah asks.

"Watching them leave town. In a wagon," the girl replies nodding.

It's obvious to Sarah why Essie never achieved her dream of becoming an actress.

"Thanks Essie! You've been so much help." Sarah gives her a hug.

She smiles and sighs with relief that their talk is over.

When not working the girls sleep in a dormitory style room in the basement of the house. There they each have their own old sailor chest with a padlock for a few personal belongings. The girls call them the "Life Before" or "libee" chests. The relics of their previous lives are kept away from prying eyes. Every girl gets a new name and a new backstory when she enters the house. Sarah's alter ego, "Désirée," was supposed to be from New Orleans where her daddy was a pirate and her mother was a Creole princess.

Odette crafts the biographies and the names according to the whims of her customers. She always has a country girl like Daisy, a southern belle like Savannah, and some variation of French royalty like Esmé—who much to Odette's horror—became "Essie" almost immediately. One poor girl was dubbed the "Nubian Princess" and was supposed to speak in some made up African language even though she was born in Portland.

Everything outside the libee belongs to the house. When a girl leaves Odette opens the chest with her master key and takes what she wants of anything that is left. The rest is distributed to the remaining girls in order of their earnings. Everything happens in that order. From picking clothes to shifts to bathing times—everything.

Sarah slips downstairs to the dormitory. She can hear Odette bellowing instructions to the girls starting their workday. A schooner arrived from New Bedford last night so they're in for a lot of customers. She shudders with the memory of those days. Barely enough time to clean up between clients. It's a miracle she and Jess emerged without any long-term effects. It's due to Jess's diligence in insisting that Odette purchase the highest quality condoms from New York and that all the girls use them. A certain Mrs. Goldstein of Brooklyn made so much money manufacturing johnnies for Odette that she was able to buy her own brownstone.

In spite of all that, little Nah was conceived.

The girls who just came off shift are already sleeping under tattered woolen blankets. Four small high windows provide the only light. She makes her way to Suzanne's libee. It takes her less than ten seconds to pick the lock.

When she lived here she knew what was in every single one of these chests. Some of the girls had letters which Sarah couldn't read but assumed were from long departed family, husbands or lovers. Others contained inexpensive jewelry, plain or homespun dresses and other artifacts from their lives before Odette's.

Sarah's chest contained only one thing—a hand bill advertising a reward for a missing house slave named Esther. It was the first thing that Jess taught her to read.

Five years ago they looked at the likeness one last time and burned it in the fireplace of their new home on Holt Street. Jess thought it was just too dangerous to keep around.

She opens the chest under Suzanne's bed. The contents are largely the same as the last time she looked eight years ago—velvet ribbons, bits of yellowing lace, and a broken fan. The only new item being a small opium pipe.

"Now why would Sweetness leave the pipe behind?" she asks herself.

The only thing missing—the small prayer book with a ripped leather cover.

CHAPTER 5

H e only has ten cents to his name. Enough for a shave or a drink. What he really wants is a whore. One he could squeeze the life out of as he put it to her. One dime wasn't going to pay for that. He toys with the idea of grabbing one of the mill girls and taking her out of town. He sits and nurses his drink as he watches a pair of the Megeso Mill private detectives walk the neighborhood. With the Dover police turning out to be such a sorry lot, the mills have taken the law into their own hands.

The private security force is modeled after the highly effective Pinkerton's of Chicago. The mill owners know that Ma and Pa Farmer are not going to send their daughters to work in Dover if it isn't safe. They even run company owned brothels—sad, functional affairs—nothing compared to the raunchy selection on the coast.

There's no private police force in Portsmouth. The shipbuilders don't give two nickels about the safety of farmers' daughters.

He wasn't starving. He'd stolen that loaf of bread from the old farmhouse with the carved cow head on it. He beat a hasty retreat before he could look for whiskey when he heard rustling upstairs.

Nursing his drink, he contemplates his next move. Maybe he should just get the hell out of New Hampshire. Boston would be an easy place to go unnoticed as he earns himself a living. He imagines there are many fine houses to break into.

There has to be lots of disposable women there too.

A pack of mill girls giggle as they walk by the front door.

"Bitches," Taylor says under his breath.

"Excuse me sir?" asks the freckle-cheeked bartender.

"Those girls there. They think they're so much better than any of us."

"Whatever you say, sir," the bartender says moving away.

"Always laughing at the likes of you and me," Taylor says wiping his nose on his dirty handkerchief and taking a swig of his drink.

The bartender knows it's time to cut him off—not because he's drunk but because he can see that he's nearly out of money.

"Say friend. You seem like you have a beef with someone. Maybe you should talk to them about it." Or at least get the hell out of here. The young barkeep heads to the back room and Taylor grabs the whiskey bottle on his way out the door—not bothering to leave the dime he owes.

His wagon is where he left it in the alley. The broken-down horse whinnies at him. Taylor swats him.

"Shut the hell up! Maybe I should just dump this rig and ride you to Boston." He takes another look at the saggy nag and decides that he's better off with the wagon.

At the top of a hill and he is greeted with a view of rolling farmland all the way to the Salmon Falls River glistening below. South Berwick, Maine, lies just on the other side. The swaying amber grasses lull him into sleepiness.

He pulls off the road and tucks the wagon behind some bushes so he can take a nap.

CHAPTER 6

The sky turns pink as a seal enjoys the last bit of the sun's warmth atop a rock pile.

Jess walks halfway across the wooden drawbridge from Goat Island to Cedar Point. What the bridge lacks in grace is made up with strength. The water rushes below with furious power. It's so loud that she doesn't hear Mrs. Simpson call her name until the woman is right beside her.

"Sorry to startle you, Miss Jakes."

"Jessamyn, please. It's so loud I didn't hear you walk up."

"This is quite the bridge," Mrs. Simpson starts. "Twice a day Great Bay empties and fills back up around this island. All that water coming through a pretty small hole. That's why it's sixty feet deep here."

"Really?" Jess replies. "That deep? It's hard to believe."

"Yes. Maybe it's my imagination but sometimes I think I can feel the bridge move under my feet."

"All that oak and granite seems pretty solid."

"Yes. I actually didn't come out here to talk about the bridge," the young innkeeper says.

"You really needn't explain about your relationship with your husband,"

Jess replies.

"I need to tell you," Matie replies. "I don't want you to get the wrong idea about me—about us. Besides, I need to tell someone and you look like the type of woman who can keep a secret."

Jess smiles. "Of course, but only if it will make you feel better."

Matie wraps her shawl around her shoulders and begins, "I am the second Mrs. Simpson. Samuel was first married to a woman named Anne."

Jessamyn smiles and nods.

"They tried for many years to have a child to no avail. Finally, one day Anne announced that she was pregnant."

"Uh oh," Jess mutters.

Matie blushes and looks down. "Yes. She also told him that she was leaving. She had fallen in love with a Canadian trader and was moving to Manitoba."

"Oh dear," Jess replies.

"Samuel told me all of this when we were courting. He also told me that he wants a child more than anything else. We've been trying for ten years— ever since we bought the tavern. He's a smart enough man to recognize that the problem was his and not Anne's—or mine."

"Most men wouldn't have accepted that knowledge."

"I know. Samuel is special," the innkeeper says.

"He must be," Jess exclaims. "It's funny how men claim they can't father a child when a whore comes up in trouble but it's the wife's fault when they can't sire a child."

Matie gives her a strange look.

Jess changes the subject. "So, how did Stephen come into the picture?"

"He was a guest who stayed with us one night over the summer. He was looking for employment and we hired him to help with the tavern. He day-dreams sometimes—but he's mostly a good worker."

"And pretty to look at."

Matie blushes. "That's true. I love his soft blonde beard."

A large flock of starlings swoops along the bay and rises to pass directly over their heads. The whoosh of their wings temporarily drowns out the sound of the rushing water. The cloud dances around the sky across Little Bay and towards the Piscataqua River.

"I wish Sarah were here," Jessamyn says.

"Sarah?" Matie asks.

She smiles. "My daughter. She's interested in birds. She would have loved that. I'm sorry to interrupt you. You were telling me about Stephen."

"After a month or so Samuel asked Stephen to join us in the sitting room after dinner. He poured us each a glass of the rum he saves for special oc-casions—then he poured us each a second one."

Jessamyn nods to the smaller woman.

"Samuel laid out an arrangement for Stephen," she continues.

"What sort of arrangement?"

"Stephen is to be paid $50 upon the delivery of a healthy baby."

After living at Odette's it's hard to surprise Jess anymore but she has to cough to suppress a laugh.

"I know it's strange," Matie says. "I'm no longer a regular scripture reader but this doesn't seem quite right to me."

"Oh, I don't know," Jess says. "My only concern is that after the child has some years behind him won't he wonder about all of this? What if he looks like Stephen? What are you going to tell him about his father?"

"That's the thing. After the baby survives to one year or if I am with child again Stephen is to leave and not return."

"An heir and a spare."

"Excuse me?"

"It's what royalty says about the duty of queens. They are to give birth to the heir to the throne and then another boy in case the first son dies."

"How do you know about royalty like that?"

Jessamyn smiles.

"Oh, I almost forgot," Matie says. "Something else happened when your friend was here. I didn't notice it until this afternoon."

"What was that?"

"My small bean pot went missing."

"Are you sure it disappeared while they were here?" Jess asks.

"I'm sure. I used it the morning of their arrival and it was put away in the pantry that afternoon. Samuel and Stephen know there will be hell to pay if they touch any of my kitchen things."

"Interesting."

"I wonder why they would steal a bean pot?" Matie asks.

CHAPTER 7

Sarah rushes to the deeds office to research the Baxter land estate case. She can skip the bakery now that she has the biscuits, but she wants to make time for her favorite weekly stop, the Atheneaum.

The repository has been around since 1817 and Capt. Pritchard is member number 346. He listed Sarah as a relative so that she can visit whenever she wishes.

She enters the double doors off Market Square into a grand, paneled room. Sliding ladders run along shelves filled with leather-bound books. She breathes deeply. Jess always laughs at the way she smells books. "It's like you're trying to inhale all the knowledge."

Old Reverend Cheney sits at one of the gleaming dark wood tables and smokes his pipe reading the latest news from Boston. He harrumphs as she passes.

She goes directly to the second floor where her friend, George Beaudette, works as a reference librarian. The walls of the small cluttered office are covered with bookshelves in complete disarray. Sarah teases him about it but he insists that he's able to find any volume in a few minutes. Somehow he has managed to squeeze in a small worktable as well. A pile of books sits waiting for her.

He smiles shyly over his glasses pushing his brown hair behind his ears. "Hello Sarah. I found a couple of tomes for you on the migratory patterns of the yellow crowned heron. You can even take them with you. Migration is not a popular topic with the membership."

"Thanks George. I'll read them this week," Sarah says as she takes three volumes out of her bag. "I really enjoyed the book about the songbirds of southern Italy. I can't say that I liked *Oliver Twist* as much—the fairy tale ending and such. It didn't seem very realistic to me. Nobody's life ends up like that—all tied up nicely with string."

She prefers nonfiction about birds as a general matter, but he always tries to slip other books in the mix as well. He has Thoreau's *Walden* and Charlotte Bronte's *Villette* on her pile for this week. Mostly he just wants to talk with her about more than birds.

George has never asked Sarah about her past. He heard from one of the shipbuilders about her time at Odette's but he makes no judgement about it. His own fisherman father died when he was very young, and his mother struggled to raise him and keep him in school. Sometimes money appeared without explanation. He learned to not ask too many questions.

One day she came home and told him to dress in his Sunday clothes and go speak with Mr. Quimby at the Atheneaum about a job sweeping up. That was ten years ago. Now, Stevie McGann does the sweeping up and George is the reference librarian.

It's his turn to take care of his mother now.

They live in a small set of rooms above Carbew's bakery on Wren Street and she happily spends her time with cross stitch and cooking. With their continued frugality he has even managed to accumulate a small nest egg on his librarian's salary.

Sarah sits at the worktable and starts where she always does with the oversized folio of *The Birds of America* by John James Audubon. She pulls out a large piece of paper and a pencil.

"What's the lucky bird this week, Sarah?"

"I think it will be the kingfisher," she replies.

"Ah, a fine selection. Are you wavering from your heron track?"

She laughs showing her pretty white teeth. George dreams about her smile every night.

"No, not at all. Did I tell you that I found a fresh dead heron and was able to do a series of close ups as it was decaying!"

"That's amazing." George is in awe of this girl. He never met anyone who was excited to find a dead bird.

She pulls out the large print of the kingfisher and begins sketching. First, she does a quick copy and then close ups of details like the eyes, feathers and beak. She makes notes alongside the drawings. With local birds she'll later add information about sightings and their environment.

She loves all birds, but her favorite is still the great blue heron.

She has spent hundreds of hours observing and drawing the majestic fowl. She and Jonah combed the area and discovered a hidden spot by the water where they can watch them wade on the mudflats. When the herons are engaged with fishing they're much more amenable to posing.

She's so absorbed that she doesn't notice George stealing glances at her as she works. He loves watching her. The cinnamon, heart-shaped birthmark on her cheek moves up and down as she frowns—trying to get some detail exactly right.

The church bells ring at 4 p.m. and jars her out of her trance.

"Oh mutton nob! I've got to get home for Jonah!" She springs up and fills her bag with the stack of books being careful not to crush the biscuits.

"Thanks, George!" she says on her way out the door.

"Will I see you soon?" he calls after her.

"I think so. Jessamyn has some more business for me so I'll be back in a couple of days."

"Goodbye, Sarah." He slumps back in his chair.

"Bye!" With that she darts down the back stairs into the alley.

CHAPTER 8

The regular closes the door behind him and Savannah lays back on the blue lacy pillows. She has about fifteen minutes before Odette comes and kicks her out of the room. Her shift is over and she should make her way back to the dormitory. First, she'll go down and eat her fill of the biscuits Moira made this afternoon. She shouldn't eat too many or she'll get fat. Of course, the customers don't seem to give a natty bit if she's fat. The regular seems to like the fact that her breasts are getting larger. He doesn't appear to care about her belly catching up to them.

Today was the same as usual with him. Starting with spanking—his bum, her riding crop. Sucking—her tits, his sour smelling bone box. Poking—his ass, her special-order French dingeedong. Wrap it all up with some dirty talk and more spanking. She barely has to touch his roly poly before he shoots his milt—it really is the easiest money she earns.

Usually, at this time of the week she's content. She's once again solidified her place as the top earner of the house and even has some extra cash to buy lingerie of her own—real silk and not that cheap sateen the rest of the girls wear. Her libee chest is filled with nice things.

It's that Désirée/Sarah that has her mood darkened. How is it that

Anastasia, or Jessamyn as she's currently known, has been able to leave Odette's and not ended up in the gutter? Sarah looked good. She didn't look at all like she was sleeping rough—she even still has those pretty teeth. How are they doing it all without a man to support them?

"Maybe it's time that I find myself some ticket out of here," she thinks. "If those two can become respectable in this town, anyone can." Not that she cares one monkey ding about respectability. She'll take money over that any day.

She toys with the idea of broaching the topic with the regular next time he's in. Maybe they can work out an arrangement. But can she handle ramming stuff up that wrinkled half moon for the rest of her life?

CHAPTER 9

Sarah wakes up with a start. It's Jonah staring at her from the side of the bed. He looks like he has been there for a while as he is shivering in the early morning air.

"You scared me half to death!" she say, "How long have you been standing there?"

"I miss Momma," he sniffles.

"It's OK, sweetie. She'll be home soon. Crawl in bed with me. You're freezing and it's too early to be up anyway."

Maybe she should have slept in Jess's bed last night. Jonah's still pretty little to sleep in his own room. He's so smart that she forgets that he's only five. He snuggles under the covers clutching his injured doll and asks, "Can you fix Mr. Soapy for me?"

"How about I show you how to fix Mr. Soapy so that you can keep him healthy forever yourself."

"OK. Sewing is kind of a girl thing but doctoring is a boy thing so I guess that would be all right." Sarah rolls her eyes.

She hugs him tightly and they watch the pink morning light hit the side of the white clapboard barn across the kitchen garden. It's way past when they should have gotten up, but the bed is so warm and comfortable.

"Why do you have a heart on your cheek?" Nah asks as he pokes it with his finger.

Sarah laughs. "I guess God must love me best, so he put it there to show the world."

He looks skeptical. "I'm hungry."

"How about we have a big breakfast this morning?"

"Bacon? Is it Sunday?"

"No," Sarah laughs, "but it is a special day with just you and me here."

"Well, OK."

They wander downstairs and use the privy beyond the kitchen garden before making breakfast.

Jonah goes out to get more wood for the stove as Sarah slices the bacon and puts it into the cast iron pan.

"What are we going to do today, Nah?"

"Shouldn't we wait here for Momma to come home?"

"Oh, we won't go far. How about we go to our favorite drawing spot and see if the heron is back?"

Jonah seems unsure but nods.

"Or, we could crawl back in bed and read books all day," she offers.

"I don't think Momma would like that. She's always telling me to be 'industous,' whatever that means."

"I think you mean 'industrious.' It means hard working or productive. Do you know how to use a dictionary?"

"What's a dictionary?"

"Oh, Jonah sweetie, you're in for a treat. Today I'm going to open a whole new world to you. Then we'll do some drawing and maybe some clamming.

Should we see if Jack is free to go with us?"

"Yes!" He starts to run out the front door towards Mrs. Markwart's house.

"Hold on there, Nah! We haven't eaten our breakfast yet."

He sulks back to the table. Ten seconds later he has a mouth full of bacon and biscuit.

Sarah goes to the parlor and retrieves the oversized dictionary.

"Now Nah," she says dropping the book on the table with a thud. "I think that you should endeavor to learn a new word every day. That way when you become an adventurer you can write about your exploits and become a famous author as well."

Nah looks at her with a blank stare.

He finally asks, "What's endeavor? Or exploits or author?"

"We'll start there," she laughs and they spend the rest of breakfast looking up those words.

They finish their food and Sarah puts the dishes in the sink.

"How about we fix Mr. Soapy next? You get him out of bed while I gather the necessary medical supplies."

Jonah races upstairs while Sarah retrieves the sewing basket from the parlor.

"Shall we give him a blue scar or red," she asks holding two spools of thread.

He furrows his brow. "Hm. I think blue. I wouldn't want him to think he is still bleeding."

Sarah threads the needle and pinches together the rip and begins to sew. "See Jonah how easy it is to perform surgery on Mr. Soapy?"

She hands him the doll and needle and he starts to mend his little friend. Sarah watches him as he works while she cleans up the dishes. His tongue slightly protrudes from his determined frowning mouth.

"I think I'm done, Sarah. Mr. Soapy is healed."

Sarah has to bite her tongue to keep from laughing. Mr. Soapy has multiple blue scars across his belly.

"That looks fantastic, Nah! He looks like he might need some recovery time. You better put Mr. Soapy to bed while we go to watch the heron fish."

He carries the doll upstairs, gives him a kiss goodbye and runs out the door to pick up Jack.

"Jess would kill me if she knew he was running around the neighborhood in his nightshirt," Sarah giggles.

CHAPTER 10

T he tavern bed is surprisingly comfortable and Jessamyn sleeps well. The two helpings of Matie's oyster stew and three tankards of ale probably help. She rises with the dawn and stops in the kitchen to say hello to her hostess who is chopping carrots and potatoes for tonight's dinner. The petite innkeeper hums to herself and rubs her belly. She stops as soon as she sees Jess and is flustered. "Oh! Good morning Miss Jakes."

Jess smiles at Matie as Stephen brings a load of wood for the cook stove. They all do seem like a vision of domestic tranquility—at least for now. Business arrangements involving sex rarely end well.

If she's not mistaken this one has reached the point of no return.

"Ma'am," he smiles as he goes back to the woodpile for another load.

"I'll be back shortly—just stretching my legs. Perhaps you could have my horse ready in about an hour."

"Certainly, ma'am." He nods at her with a slightly crooked smile and pushes his sandy hair out of his eyes.

"It's cold out there this morning," Matie warns. "We had the first frost of the season last night. Be sure to wrap up."

She smiles and thinks to herself, "Hopefully the Simpsons will get adorable children out of this."

It only takes five minutes to walk from the tavern to the eastern shore of the landmass. The pink sunrise illuminates steam rising from the water of the flat bay. It's hard to believe that this same water rushed under the bridge with such ferocity only a few hours before. Gulls shriek at each other over a dead crab on the exposed rock pile near Fox Point. "It must be near low tide," she murmurs.

The tavern is the only house on the island. There's not much else to investigate but an old garbage heap on the far side with broken crockery and glass bottles.

Only things beyond any usefulness end up here.

It looks like most of the pile is covered by a coating of spattered mud caused by a recent rainstorm. She leans closer in and notices that one section has been disturbed. Shards have been placed and dirt has been sprinkled over in an attempt to disguise some activity.

Half hidden in the pile is a small, perfect, brown bean pot.

"Not a chip on it," Jess observes.

She excavates the vessel and pops open the top.

She pulls out something wrapped in a clean cloth. It's a small leather-bound prayer book with a ripped cover. Inside in childlike handwriting, "Mabel Mary Collins, New Bedford, Massachusetts." Sarah had told her about such a book. It was in Suzanne's chest at Odette's. Was that Suzanne's name before? One of the unwritten rules of the house was to never tell anyone your birth name.

The lives before were best forgotten.

Jessamyn slips the book into her pocket and cleans the pot with seawater on the beach. She'll return it back to Matie saying that she found it along the trail. There's no need to give them more information than is necessary. You never know who might be asking about her after she departs. She goes back to the trash pile and kicks dirt over everything before walking back to the tavern.

Matie greets her in the front room pouring cider into mugs at the wooden table.

"We have bread and butter ready, and I'm working on some eggs and bacon for you, Jessamyn."

"That sounds delicious, Matie," she replies her stomach growling. "Perhaps I could get a cup of coffee to go with the cider?" she says as she hands the innkeeper the crockery.

"You found my missing pot!"

"Um yes, it was on the other side of the island. It was a little messy. You might want to wash it. I used seawater to get the mud off."

"Strange." Matie turns the pot over and over and opens the top cover to look inside. "Why would someone steal my bean pot and then leave it on the island?"

"Who knows?" She fingers the prayer book in her pocket.

Jessamyn intends to travel to Dover right after breakfast to ask around about Taylor and Sweetness. It's likely that they would buy supplies there as that's the closest town of any size around here. If they didn't stop in the mill town it will be hard to tell which direction they might have gone. They could have crossed the river into Maine and be headed for Portland or inland to Concord.

She returns to her room to pack her belongings taking a minute to flip through the prayer book. There are notations on nearly every page and underlined letters in pencil. Did Suzanne make these marks? What do they mean? Are they a code?

"Sarah will have this sorted in no time," she says to herself. Nobody's better at solving puzzles and riddles. That's why she always handles any investigation that requires the examination of documents or accounting.

"Miss Jessamyn, come quick!"

It's Stephen.

She runs down the stairs. "What is it?"

"A body! The farmer Bunker found a body across the water at Cedar Point."

She drops her saddle bag and runs across the bridge to the crowd on the shoreline. It's a woman. She can see that from here. She's lying on the rocks below the high tide line, twenty feet from the bridge.

A blonde woman.

Sweetness.

CHAPTER 11

Taylor sleeps better than he has in a while. He wakes in darkness and decides to stay where he is for the night. With no moon it would be hard to travel in the inky blackness.

When dawn arrives, he pisses in the woods and leads the horse and wagon back to the road where he sees Berwick Academy on the crest of the hill across the river. He'll head up there. Maybe he can find some food to steal.

A girl of about 12 years carries a bushel of apples across the bridge towards him.

Not a man of subtle actions, Taylor jumps from the rig and hits her in the face with the back of his hand sending the apples flying. She lies unconscious in the road and he tosses her into the wagon.

He covers her with a tarp, grabs the basket, picks up the apples and crosses the bridge into Maine.

Orla wakes up sometime later. She can tell she's in the back of a wagon but is unsure of what has happened. She just knows that she's in a heap load of trouble. When Da finds out that she lost the apples and the basket, he'll beat her to where she can't move for a week.

She hears the horse whinny and someone eating.

Apples.

The man driving the wagon is eating all of her apples. He stops chomping periodically to drink from a bottle of something.

The ride gets bumpier and bumpier. They must have gone off the road. She has no idea how far from home she is now.

The bottle must be empty because he tosses it into the back where is shatters. She can smell whiskey.

The wagon stops.

She hears a sound similar to a wounded animal and then the man descending from the seat.

She spies him through the slats of the wagon. He drops his pants. He must be really sick based on what's coming out of him.

Orla reaches for a piece of the broken bottle.

"God fucking dammit!" he yells.

She freezes. An awful smell fills her nostrils as she grabs the basket and makes a run for it. The man yells and starts to follow her but his pants are down and he's made a mess of himself.

She jumps out of the wagon and runs through the woods following the trail of freshly eaten apple cores.

"It's small wonder he's crapping like that. These apples are no good for anything but cider," she thinks as she runs past her own house, down the hill and crosses the bridge to her Aunt Fiona's. She can't go home.

Her aunt takes one look at her and drags her inside.

"What did your da do to you, Orla Flaherty?"

The girl bursts into tears.

CHAPTER 12

Soon Jess is there, pushing people out of the way. She sees a birthmark on the woman's pale shoulder. It's Sweetness alright.

The men on the shore turn her over. The cold water kept her body from bloating, but creatures have started eating at her face. Her one remaining eye stares into space. Purple bruises cover her body, especially around her neck.

Matie and Mrs. Bunker weep quietly on the bridge.

"Mr. Bunker found her. He was on his way to Portsmouth with a wagon load of butternut squash," Stephen tells Jess. He keeps averting his eyes from the body—even while he and Samuel pull Suzanne up onto the shore and cover her with a tarp from the wagon.

"I'll ride to Dover to get the sheriff," Samuel offers.

Jessamyn kneels in the dirt, uncovers Suzanne a bit and takes her clammy hand. "Oh Sweetness, what kind of nasty trouble did you get yourself into?"

Soon Matie kneels next to her and pulls her close. "It's OK, Jessamyn. She's with the Lord now. Nobody can hurt her anymore."

Jessamyn wishes she believed in the Lord.

Finally, Jess releases Suzanne's hand and the two women rise to return to the bridge. The men put rocks along the tarp to keep it from blowing off of the body and Samuel borrows the Bunker's gelding to fetch the doctor.

"Oh my!" Mrs. Bunker exclaims. "I just remembered that I had some bread stolen from my kitchen yesterday morning. I thought it was the dog. You don't suppose the killer…"

Matie's eyes open wide. "Oh my God! He was in our house. To think he stayed in the room next to ours. He could have killed us!"

Jess wishes that she could offer words that would comfort her companions, but she barely has it in her to nod in their direction.

The three women retreat to the tavern. It will be at least an hour and a half before the sheriff and doctor arrive.

Matie puts three glasses in front of the women and pours them rum.

Jessamyn takes the glass and downs it with one gulp. Mrs. Bunker nurses hers slowly and stares into space. They sit in silence thinking about the poor woman on the opposite shore.

The shock of the rum wakes Jess out of her daze. She starts to make a plan. Now that Dewitt Taylor is a murderer on the run he's probably long gone—unless he's a fool. A fool he is—a dangerous one.

She'll stay here to speak with the sheriff and then ride to Dover to see if there's any sign of the killer. That probably means another night at Goat Island. Somehow, she needs to get word and the prayer book to Sarah.

Stephen.

Maybe he can go to Portsmouth for her.

"Matie? May I ask a favor of you?"

"Of course. What do you need Miss Jess? Did you want another bit of rum?"

Jess smiles. "Thank you, but no. Could I possibly hire Stephen to take a note and a small package to my daughter in Portsmouth? Under the circumstances I think I'd better to stay here another night until the sheriff is done with his inquiries."

"Of course Miss Jess—anything. I'll send for him," Matie walks through the kitchen to the back door. She returns in a moment.

"Stephen will be in shortly. He's getting his horse ready."

"That sounds fine. Thank you. I'll need a few minutes anyway. Do you have some twine and sealing wax I can use?"

"Of course." Matie retrieves the items from the desk in the corner and hands them to Jess.

Jess takes the supplies up to her room and pulls a large piece of paper out of her saddlebag. She writes a note to her daughter.

Sarah,

S. is dead. I'm staying at the tavern to speak with the sheriff. I should be home tomorrow. Please use this book to say your prayers. Feed Stephen and let him sleep in your workroom if it's too late to return to Goat Island. Love to you and Nah. —J.

She wraps the book in the note, ties it with the twine and covers the knot with sealing wax. She presses the carved handle of her knife to make an impression.

She hears Matie giggle in the kitchen as she goes downstairs. Stephen must be in the kitchen saying goodbye. She stomps loudly on the bottom two steps so not to catch them mid-embrace. They appear in the parlor nervously adjusting their clothing.

"Here Stephen," Jess starts in. "I've written the address on the package—it's on Holt Street. Oh and Sarah and Jonah will feed you supper."

"Isn't Sarah kind of young to be on her own? I mean you don't look like you're old enough to have anything but a wee sprout," Matie asks.

Jess laughs. "You're right. She's my adopted daughter. She's just turned twenty. I also have a son who's five years old. His name is Jonah."

Matie looks wistful and rubs her belly. "You're so lucky."

Stephen looks at Matie. "Don't worry, I'll be back soon." He smiles as he mounts the waiting horse and makes his way to the coast.

CHAPTER 13

Sarah and Jonah return early afternoon after watching the heron fish from their hiding place near the mudflats. Sarah doesn't get much drawing done as the dog barks every time a bird comes near them.

Jonah's so excited to be home that he leaves the door open. Jack runs in and out and through the house finally ending upstairs on Nah's bed with Mr. Soapy in his mouth.

"You'd better grab that dog and bring him home to Mrs. Markwart," she yells up to Jonah, "and then change out of your muddy clothes before dinner." She pulls off her own dirty workman's pants and shirt and hangs them on a chair outside the kitchen door. Her shift falls to her knees. She takes the last of the biscuits out of the breadbox. "I'm sorry Jess. These are just too good to save for you."

"Are they really that delicious? Maybe you could spare one for me."

Sarah spins around. There's a light-haired, bearded man standing in the open doorway.

He has a sweet crooked smile. She's at a loss for words—a first for her.

"Are you Sarah?" he asks.

"Yes." Her face is warm and she feels naked with just her thin shift. She snatches her shawl off the chair and wraps herself in it.

"Hello Sarah. My name is Stephen Bailey. I work at the Goat Island Tavern and your mother sent me here to deliver you a package." He hands her the bundle.

"Can you wait here while I dress and read the note?" she asks.

"Of course." The smile returns to his face as he looks her up and down.

He rode hard to get here so he could quickly turn around and get back to Matie before nightfall. Now he isn't so sure that's what he wants to do.

He studies her face. She's a creamy mocha color with large brown eyes and a heart shaped birthmark on her cheek.

"I'll put a kettle on," she says as she tosses a log into the stove. She fills the teapot with leaves before going upstairs to change.

Her hands tremble as she cracks the familiar seal and opens the package. It's the prayer book from Suzanne's libee chest. Her eyes tear up as she reads about her death even though she didn't really like her—she always seemed to be one of those flighty girls without any sense. She flips through the small volume and sees the markings that she observed years ago. She understands what Jess means by praying. She'll decipher the information that Suzanne—or someone else—so carefully noted.

Sarah can hear Stephen downstairs. "And who are you, little fella?"

"That's Jack, Mrs. Markwart's dog," Jonah says with irritation in his voice. "He's a Jack Russell Terrier. That's why he's named Jack."

"He's a friendly one, isn't he?" the stranger says.

"I don't think you should be patting him without Mrs. Markwart's permission."

Sarah laughs as she pulls her damp shift over her head. The scars on her back itch as her skin warms.

"Are you Jonah?" Stephen asks.

"Yes, that's my name. Most people call me Nah. This is Mr. Soapy. He had surgery this morning so you can't touch him. He's still a little poorly. I think Jack just made some new holes in him."

"He looks like he was sewed up very well. Are you the doctor?"

"Yes. He's my first patient," Nah answers.

"Aren't you going to ask my name?"

"Momma says that I shouldn't talk to strangers," Nah replies.

Stephen erupts into laughter. What a funny little kid.

Sarah hurries into her corset and petticoats and goes down the staircase.

"Jonah. This is Stephen Bailey. He brought me a message from Momma."

"When is she coming back?" the boy asks.

"Soon sweetie, but not today."

He looks sad but is distracted by the stranger who—despite being told not to—continues to pat the dog.

"The note also says that we are to entertain Mr. Bailey if he should decide to stay the night," Sarah says. "What should we do with him?"

Stephen smiles.

"He needs to dig his share of clams and muck out the stalls," Nah answers sternly.

"I think I can do both of those things," Stephen offers.

"How about you take him to my workroom and make the fire? He'll need some warmth up there if he's staying the night—and take that dog back like I told you before."

"Mrs. Markwart isn't there. I knocked and knocked."

"I guess he's going clamming with us. Now you and Stephen go on and get the room ready."

With that Jonah leads the stranger through the kitchen garden, past the privy, into the barn and up the stairway to the loft.

Stephen lets the small boy boss him around, making up the settee into a bed and stoking the fire as the dog sprints around the room.

"Your sister is some kind of bird lover, isn't she?" the older man asks.

"What? Why would you ask that?"

"Well, for one thing there are about a hundred sketches of birds hanging around and there's a few stuffed ones to boot. And then there's that." He points to the bird skeleton on the table.

"Doesn't everyone have a barn like this?"

Stephen laughs. "Not exactly. Usually they're just filled with animals and old junk. Who is this?" He picks up a small bronze bust.

"He's Sarah's hero. He figured out some stuff about birds."

"Hm. This Charles Darwin must be special if Sarah likes him," Stephen muses.

CHAPTER 14

Strafford County Sheriff Tom Allgood pulls his wagon near the Cedar Point side of the bridge. He towers over the slight frame of Dr. Churchill who hops to the ground and goes right to Suzanne's body on the embankment. He's younger than Jess would have expected in a doctor. The Bunkers emerge from the farmhouse and greet the two men as she walks over the drawbridge.

"As I understand it, you found the body," Allgood says to Mr. Bunker.

"Yes."

The sheriff stares at him blankly and scratches his ample belly.

"So how did you find her?" Jess prompts the farmer.

"I'd finished loading the wagon with squash and started off to meet the boat on Fox Point. As soon as I got about halfway across the bridge, I saw her. I wasn't sure exactly what I was looking at—she looked like a wax figure or a doll lying face down on the rocks. I've never seen anything like it before. She must have drowned."

Jess moves closer to the doctor who carefully examines the marks around Suzanne's neck. He doesn't look up from his work but says. "I won't know for sure until I open her up but it looks like she was strangled and then dropped in the water."

"And you Miss," the doctor asks, "what is your connection to the victim?"

Jess chooses her words carefully. "She was an acquaintance of mine from Portsmouth. I don't know her real name, but everyone called her Suzanne."

"Where did she live in Portsmouth?" Churchill asks.

"Odette's."

Mrs. Bunker's eyes grow wide. "She was a whore?"

"Yes," Jess replies.

Mr. Simpson speaks up, "She stayed at our tavern two nights ago with a man claiming to be her husband. At least that's what they told my wife when they arrived—gave the names of Mr. and Mrs. Lafferty."

"Did you or your wife speak with them while they stayed with you?" the doctor asks.

The bored sheriff is distracted by a mink running along the shoreline. He pulls out his revolver too late. The animal is long gone before he can fire a shot.

"Not really," Matie answers. "She took supper in their room. Mrs. Lafferty, I mean Suzanne, was feeling poorly. Mr. Lafferty was a very unpleasant sort and I left him alone after giving him some stew and ale."

"Can you describe him?" the doctor continues.

"Surly looking with a black hat. Dark hair."

"Shouldn't you be writing this down?" Mr. Bunker asks the sheriff.

"Oh! Hey, I'm the law man around here," he says as he searches his pockets.

Jess hands him a piece of paper and a pencil from her bag.

Allgood grunts at her and scribbles a few notes on the paper.

"I have reason to believe that the man's name is actually Dewitt Taylor," Jess says.

The sheriff turns to her. "And how do you know that?"

Jess responds, "I was hired by Odette to locate Suzanne."

"Why would the madam hire you to find a whore?" he asks with a smirk.

"Because this is what I do—discreet inquiries."

He laughs and flails his arms. "Well then! Inquire!"

The doctor looks up from the ground with a frown. "Miss, kindly tell me your name?"

"Jessamyn Jakes," she replies.

"Miss Jakes, would you please accompany me and the poor Miss Suzanne back to my office? I think you would be most helpful."

"Certainly doctor. Let me fetch my horse from the tavern and I'll be right back." She retreats across the bridge.

The doctor carefully wraps Suzanne in the tarp. Mr. Simpson and Mr. Bunker help to gently put her in the back of the wagon. Allgood climbs aboard and they make their way up the hill towards Dover.

Jess catches up with them in front of the Bunker's red barn. She notices a painted wooden cow's head mounted above the hayloft door. "Hm. Strange. I don't think they have a dairy farm."

It's about five miles up a rut-filled dirt road to the center of Dover. They cross a rickety bridge that creaks under the weight. Jess lingers far enough back to hear their conversation but not close enough to participate. It doesn't matter anyway as the sheriff doesn't acknowledge her as he regales the doctor with stories of his illustrious career. She laughs to herself as she's pretty sure that Strafford County isn't quite the hotbed of dangerous criminal activity he's making it out to be—especially now that the Megeso Mill Police are around. The doctor remains silent but occasionally nods at the older man's stories.

After an hour or so they pull the wagon alongside a yellow house on the outskirts of town. The sign by the front door reads, "James Churchill, M.D."

They unload the body and bring it into the downstairs kitchen of the house. A metal table with sides and a drain takes up most of the space.

Allgood nearly drops Suzanne on the floor.

"Careful there, sheriff!" Churchill shouts. "Show some respect for the poor woman."

"Whatever you say Doc. I'll be back in a couple hours to see what you've found out. My stomach is grumbling and Durgan's is having a special on pie."

He brushes Jess to the side on his way out the door.

"I apologize for our esteemed sheriff, Miss Jakes. He's lacking social graces."

"Thank you, doctor, but he's not yours to apologize for. I do, however, appreciate you including me in your inquiry—and your kindness towards Suzanne."

"Not a problem. Do you want to stay as I work?" he asks as he puts a bucket under the drain. "It can be pretty unsightly."

Jess has seen an autopsy before so she knows what she's in for. The doctor unwraps Suzanne's face. She can't watch her former lover this way. She starts to feel faint.

"I don't suppose I will. I think I'll take the time to walk around town."

"OK. I'll have a few answers in an hour or so if you'd like to come back before the sheriff returns."

"Thanks doctor. That would be preferable."

CHAPTER 15

Dover, a town of about 10,000 people, is dominated by the cotton mills powered by the Cocheco River. The largest employer in town is the Megeso Textile and Fabric Company. You can tell the day of the week by the color of the river. A different dye for each day. The water glows with Thursday's green.

Jess leaves her horse at the doctor's office and walks towards the mills. The wind is at her back and propels her forward. She passes by a bakery, Durgan's and the post office. She's headed for the block filled with taverns and whorehouses. If Taylor was to stop anywhere, it would be on Franklin Street.

A redheaded bear of a man opens the door of Hornpipe's Pub and Barbers. He looks Jess up and down with her workman's pants and gray hat.

"C'mon in. I'm just opening for the day. The company requires that we wait until the lunch break is over. They don't want their mill supervisors drunk for the afternoon."

"Thanks. I'll take an ale, please." She'll need to pace herself. She can't have a drink in every bar on the strip or she'll be too drunk to find her way back to the doctor's office.

"Sure," the bartender pours her an ale from a tap of carved horn. He puts the drink in front of her.

"Thank you," she replies and holds the ale up. "Sláinte!"

He smiles as she takes a drink.

"Say, I heard that the mills own everything on this block—even the whorehouses? It that true?"

"Yep, that's the truth," he replies. We lease the properties from them with the understanding that we'll abide by their rules."

"Hm. Interesting. By any chance did you see a man of about mid-thirties yesterday driving a wagon? He might have been wearing a ratty black hat. He's a bit of a crupper."

"I don't think so, but I was off yesterday most of the day on account of my aunt passing away. My nephew, Patrick, was tending the store." He yells to the back room.

A young man emerges from the back with a case of bottles. "Yes Uncle?"

"Any lowlifes out of the ordinary come in yesterday, Patrick?"

"Just one," Patrick says. "A surly type. He smelled something fierce and he looked pretty rough. He had a fresh scratch on his cheek."

Good for Suzanne. At least she got one scrape in.

"Did he say anything notable?" Jess asks while pointing at her mug for a refill.

"Not really," Patrick replies wiping some mugs with a rag and hanging them on hooks along the wall. "There was one thing that was odd though. He kept raving about women. He was even eyeballing some of the mill girls and they can't be 15 yet."

"Raving, like how?" she asks.

"Like about what spiteful bitches—sorry ma'am—they are. He went on and on about it."

"Any idea which way he was headed?" she asks finishing her ale.

He shrugs. "I think he was going towards Maine."

"Why did you think that, Patrick?" his uncle asks.

"Well, he came from the south, so I assumed he was headed north. Oh, and the bastard stole a bottle of whiskey when I was in the back and ran out the door. He even took the dime that he put on the bar to pay for the first glass."

"Thank you, Patrick. You've been a big help," she says depositing a quarter on the bar.

He smiles and returns to the store room.

Jessamyn checks in at the brothels. She figures that if he only had a dime, he probably didn't have extra cash for a bit of basket making either. She's right. They haven't seen him.

On her way back to Churchill's office she stops in at Durgan's to get a quick bowl of something. The restaurant is filled with older men drinking out of mugs and eating apple pie.

Sheriff Allgood sits a table near the front holding court with his cronies. Suzanne is the fodder for today's story telling.

"So, everyone was just standing there with their thumbs up their asses. I saw what needed to be done and I jumped down the steep banking and grabbed that little filly around the waist and hoisted her to the shore. She was a pretty thing with long blonde hair."

A harried woman arrives at her table. "May I help you, miss?"

"What is the specialty of the house?" Jess asks.

The woman laughs. "I'm not sure it's special, but we have an eel stew that is very popular with King Chowderhead and his court over there."

Jess smiles. "Well, if it's good enough for royalty..."

The woman nods and retreats to the kitchen.

The sheriff drones on and Jess sits marveling at his ridiculous account and eats her delicious eel stew. She's relieved that the old bore didn't acknowledge her when she came in.

She pays the woman and wraps her workman's coat around her before heading out into the cold.

The leaves blow around the tiny front yards as she walks back up the hill. Hearing no reply to her knocks she enters the Doctor's front door and calls, "Hello!" She doesn't want to see Suzanne after the doc finished working so she remains in the foyer.

"Hello, Miss Jakes," Churchill says as he enters the front room. His apron is covered with blood. He removes it and uses a clean towel to wipe his hands.

"It seems that Suzanne was strangled. There was no water in her lungs. Her eyes, or what was left of them, showed signs of burst blood vessels."

"Poor Sweetness," she says under her breath.

"Excuse me?" asks the doctor.

"Oh. That was her nickname," Jess replies.

"Well," he starts, "Sweetness did manage to give her assailant a hell of a scratch. Even with her being in the water I detected a fair amount of flesh under her fingernails."

"A barkeep downtown saw Taylor and mentioned that he had a scratch on his face," Jess says.

"Sounds like your man, then," Churchill says. "Aside from what I've told you there isn't much else. I'll just finish up the paperwork and copy down the items that you might find helpful. It will just take a minute.

Jess's mind wanders as she sits in the doctor's front parlor watching the occasional wagon or coach lumber by.

Taylor. That creepy coward. Was it a sexual thing? After the encounter with Daisy they all thought he had a penchant for strangling women while shooting his milt. She said he was staring into her eyes as he clenched his hands harder around her neck.

"Miss Jakes?" Churchill interrupts her train of thought.

"Yes?" she says waking up from her daze.

"I'm sorry about your friend," he says handing her his report.

Her eyes tear up.

"Thank you, Doc."

"Would you like me to have the undertakers deliver her body to Portsmouth for burial?"

"A funeral? I hadn't even thought about that," she says.

He smiles at her and starts to reach out to pat her hand but recoils when he remembers the bloodstains on his fingers.

"I suppose so. Have them contact me when they have her ready." She writes her name and address down as the sheriff bursts through the door. He must have had more than a few ales at Durgan's. He sways as he walks knocking a marble bust of Hippocrates off of a side table.

Churchill sighs as he picks up the bust, dusts it off and returns it to it's rightful place.

"Lady, are you still here? I'd think you'd be well on your way what with all of the female detective work you must have to do." Allgood's belly quakes so hard with laughter that he gets a cramp and grimaces.

"Sheriff, if you would be so kind as to accompany me to the kitchen, I will give you the details of the autopsy."

"With that, I shall take my leave." Jess turns to the door ignoring the sheriff. "Thank you, doctor."

"Good day, Miss Jakes."

The last thing she hears is the sheriff vomiting in the kitchen. Autopsies don't go well with ale and pie. "I wonder if he'll tell that part of the story to his pals tomorrow," Jess whispers to Willie as she lifts the saddle onto his back.

She rides across the river to South Berwick to inquire after Taylor. They have no bars or whorehouses there, so she stops at Berwick Academy. It takes her while to locate anyone. Finally, she stops a groundskeeper and he tells her school is not in session this week. It seems unlikely that anyone has seen him.

"This was a waste of time," she says to Willie. "Perhaps I should take another look at Taylor and Odette's relationship when I get back to Portsmouth."

CHAPTER 16

J onah yells to his sister from the kitchen garden. "Sarah! I've got Stephen's bed all made for the night. Are we ready to go clamming?"

She's packed up the biscuits, leftover bacon, apples and cider for a picnic. She even has a pig's ear for the dog. She tucks the prayer book into her bag and hands Nah the clamming bucket.

"It's only a ten-minute walk to the beach with the best mudflats," she says as she greets Stephen in the kitchen garden. "The biggest clams are near the water opposite New Castle."

"Sarah, why are you wearing your Sunday dress?" Nah asks.

"Jonah, you know my work clothes are dirty," she replies blushing.

"But you always say that we can't get any more dirty so we might as well wear dirty clothes to start."

She glares at the boy.

Stephen seems oblivious to the banter and takes the bucket from the boy.

"My horse, Leonardo, seems quite taken with your blonde filly," he says.

"Her name is Buttercup," Nah offers. "Everyone loves her but she's Willie's girl."

"Willie?"

"William Henry Harrison," Sarah answers.

"I stabled him at the tavern for Miss Jakes," Stephen says." That's a funny name for a horse."

"He came with it," Jonah says. "He's named for some dead king or somebody like that."

"President, Nah. We don't have kings in America," Sarah scolds.

"Do we have them in New Hampshire?" the little boy asks.

Stephen laughs. Sarah raises an eyebrow at him.

"No sweetie. New Hampshire is part of America. We are a state and we have a governor."

"I'd rather have a king," the little boy responds.

"Well, you need to move to England. This is America where we elect our leaders. At least some people get to elect our leaders. Not people like me being a woman and not the right color, of course. Hard to say that I could do much worse than the pokers who vote now."

"Wow," Stephen says, "you sure talk a lot, Sarah."

She frowns. "Maybe you should start clamming now."

"OK, Stephen. This is where you start digging with your clam fork." He points to a mud flat about five yards away. "I can show you how."

"I think you better teach me." He spent summers on the water but lets Jonah instruct him. He sees Sarah watching him and she seems pleased that he is playing with the boy.

Jack tires of running around the mudflat and settles in next to Sarah.

"Oh dear," she muses. "We'll need to give you a rinse before we take you back to Mrs. Markwart. You're even worse than before."

Sitting on her favorite rock, she pulls out the prayer book and a set of blank paper cards. She flips through the book, page by page, to get an overview of what's inside. Suzanne, or someone, has made marks on every page and each margin is filled with letters and numbers. Sarah writes all of the margin notes onto each card then marks down the letters underlined on each page on their own cards. She realizes that she hasn't looked up for a long while when four muddy feet and a full bucket of clams appear right in front of her.

"Oh my! That's a lot of clams!" she exclaims. "I'd say that you taught Stephen pretty well, Nah."

She slips her things into her bag. "What do you say we eat our picnic?" She lays the blanket on the sand and the three of them settle on the beach. The warm sun makes it seem more like June than October.

Jonah takes off his muddy boots and wiggles his toes in the sand as they watch a pair of gulls fight over a sea urchin.

"They're so mean and nasty," Jonah observes.

"That's just the way they are," Sarah says. "If we didn't have the gulls the beach would be a lot dirtier. They clean it."

Sarah lays back on the blanket and closes her eyes. Jonah snuggles next to her. Soon they are both fast asleep.

Stephen studies her face. Smooth brown skin. Long eyelashes. Heart shaped birthmark on her cheek. A fly lands on her nose and she crinkles it slightly. He can't believe how his whole world has changed in the last five hours. There's no going back to Matie. It was a crazy business arrangement to father another man's child. He didn't see the harm when he'd agreed to help them.

He was also attracted to her.

Well, sort of attracted to her. Not like this—with Sarah.

What was he thinking? Now it all just seems wrong. Maybe it also has to do with Jonah. He's beginning to like this kid. He can't fathom having children that he has nothing to do with. Of course, it could also be the $50 that they were to pay him. He could use the money.

And Sarah. He watches her chest as she breathes. More than anything he'd like to run his hands over her breasts right now—maybe even up her thighs.

"And who, pray tell, are you?" A grating voice interrupts his fantasy.

Stephen jumps to his feet.

"Stephen Bailey, sir. Who are you?"

"I am Reverend Silas Hobson. I'm the caretaker of the souls in this town."

Sarah snorts and stifles a laugh.

Jonah stares at Hobson as he hides behind his sister. Momma has told him to stay away from the clergyman.

"Miss Jakes. Please convey to Miss Jessamyn that I fully expect you all in church on Sunday. I have an announcement to make and I wish all the residents of the neighborhood to hear it."

"Sure," Sarah says looking down to avoid his stare.

The reverend points his nose in the air and heads back up the hill.

Walking back to the house Stephen says, "So I'm guessing that you and Jessamyn are not regular church-goers."

She laughs. "You could say that."

"He seemed kind of insistent about you coming on Sunday. Why does he care so much?"

She looks down embarrassed. "He does seem somewhat obsessed with us. Of course, Jess antagonizes him. She takes sport in it."

He frowns. "You have a very strange family, Sarah."

"What do you mean by that?" she asks with a furrowed brow.

"Oh, I don't know," he stammers. "I mean you're just so interesting, that's all."

CHAPTER 17

Jess arrives back to Goat Island after sunset. She settles Willie in the barn before making her way through the murky darkness towards the lamp-lit house.

Mrs. Bunker sits with Matie and Samuel near the stove. An empty bottle lies on its side in the middle of the table.

"Join us, Miss Jakes." Samuel pulls a chair out for her in the front room. "I'll get another bottle."

"We've been sitting here trying to understand this," Matie says taking a sip of rum.

"How could we have had a killer in our house and not even known it?" Samuel asks.

"Could he have been in my kitchen?" Mrs. Bunker says resting her glass on her ample belly.

"Do you suppose that he strangled her in our guest bedroom?" Matie eyes grow large.

"I don't think so." Jess gives the answer she knows they want to hear. She needs to look more carefully around the bedroom before she can definitively say yes or no. The sheets won't provide much of an answer now that

Matie has washed them.

They sit and listen to the fire crackle in the stove.

"He must have thought that she would be out to sea by now," Samuel says after a while.

"Pardon me?" Jess asks.

"Taylor. He probably saw that ripping current and figured her body would be all the way to the Shoals by dawn. Not being from around here he may have been unaware of how unpredictable the waters of Little Bay and the Piscataqua are."

"He said he wasn't from around here. Maybe that was a lie also," Matie adds.

"I don't actually know where he's from," Jess says. "Tell me more about the water."

"Eddies form in each cove," Samuel continues. "The water can be going in opposite directions on the same part of the river."

"I noticed that the moored boats looked strange this morning. All pointed in different directions."

"It's tricky water. They say that a cork will take 10 days to make it to Portsmouth if you drop it off the bridge here. Back and forth it will go riding the currents—getting caught in the eddies."

"Wait a minute," Jess says. "Maybe he doesn't know."

"What do you mean?"

"He thinks that nobody will find Suzanne's body for a while—if ever. That means he doesn't think anyone is looking for him."

"I suppose that's right." Samuel takes a puff from his pipe.

"He'll know soon, though," Jess says. "The sheriff was telling everyone about it in Durgan's today. The word will spread like a whale oil slick."

Matie fetches some bread and bowls from the kitchen and dishes them each some soup. Nobody feels much like eating at first, but the warm stew is comforting, and they finish the pot.

"Well, I best be headed back to the farmhouse. Mr. Bunker will be back from town soon." She wobbles to the door.

"I'll walk you back," Jess offers. "I need some air."

"I'm fine," Mrs. Bunker says as she sways dangerously towards the fire.

"No worries. Really. I like a walk after supper."

Matie hands her a lamp and Jess takes the older woman's arm and leads her across the bridge.

"Mrs. Bunker. May I ask why you have a cow head on your barn? You don't appear to have a dairy farm."

"Oh, that's Peanut, Mr. Bunker's cow from growing up. I guess you never get over your first bovine."

"I guess not," Jess replies. "That must have been some cow."

Samuel and Matie are still at the table when she returns.

She nods to them as she enters the warm room. "I think I'll retire early and do a little reading in my room."

"Long day," Samuel nods. "We'll send up a bed warmer for you."

"Oh, no need. I'm so tired I'll barely notice the cold."

Jess looks carefully around the room but finds nothing out of the ordinary. There's no evidence of Suzanne and Taylor at all. She gets into the soft bed and pulls the brightly colored quilt over her. It's ice cold. She reaches for her socks and slips them onto her feet. "I can't wait to be home," she says to the pillow. Nah always crawls in her bed to say goodnight. He's a little furnace.

Jess hopes that Sweetness died here in this comfortable room and not outside. She hated the cold.

Jess always thought that her fragility masked the soul of a fighter. That's what was so strange. The opium. She didn't even like alcohol. She just drank it to numb herself like the other girls. Who knows. Jess was beginning to think she really didn't know Sweetness at all.

The estrangement started soon after that mysterious weekend with the customer at the Isles of Shoals.

That also marked the end of their relationship.

Jess always knew that she liked girls. Suzanne had seemed indifferent when she first met her.

One day there came a request for a ménage à trois. The customer picked Jess and Sweetness out from the lineup. They had these requests periodically, but most customers couldn't afford to pay for two whores. Plus, Odette added a special request surcharge to it.

Most of the time the girls put on a good show for the customer, but it was just playacting. She and Sweetness had never been together before.

The man started off telling them what to do to each other while he stroked his glister pipe with his hand.

"Kiss her toes while grabbing her sunshine. OK now stick your never land in my face while sucking her scone." Pretty pedestrian requests, so Jess started improvising. After a few minutes she realized that both she and Sweetness were completely ignoring the customer.

They got so involved that the man demanded his money back. Odette was furious. She was even more angry a few days later when Sweetness slipped into the blue room where Jess had just finished with a client. It was so strange feeling so excited in this house where all they had ever felt was dead.

Life suddenly had new meaning.

CHAPTER 18

Stephen is busy at the sink with today's haul. Water splashes everywhere as he washes the clams.

"For someone who doesn't know anything about clamming you sure know how to scrub them," Sarah observes.

Stephen laughs, "I may have understated my familiarity with the job."

"Thanks," she says.

"For what?"

"For letting Nah boss you around all day."

"Are you kidding?" he starts. "I learned a lot from the kid. For example, I had no idea that Mr. Zippy is such an amazing scientist and adventurer."

"You mean Mr. Soapy? He is a doll of many talents," she laughs.

He's really on to something. She seems to warm up whenever he's nice to her brother.

"So, Jonah says that you are some kind of bird expert," he says wiping his hands on a towel and putting the clams on the stove to steam.

"Me? Oh no. I'm just interested in them. They're fascinating. I mostly work with Jessamyn."

"What do you do?"

"We investigate and solve problems," she replies.

"Is that why she came to the tavern—to solve a mystery? Does it have to do with the dead woman?"

Sarah knows she shouldn't say much. "Maybe so."

"It was so sad." He shivers at the memory of her waxy skin. "I had never seen a dead body before this morning. It was awful."

"Really? Never? I've seen a lot. Probably more than most people."

He looks at her with an eyebrow cocked.

"Speaking of dead things," he says, "what's the story behind the bird bones in your room?"

"Oh!" she lights up. "I found a dead heron! It was so wonderful to be able to draw it up close. I did bunches of drawings of it before it really started to smell. I boiled him down so I could reassemble the skeleton."

Stephen looks at the pot on the stove hoping it's not the same one she used for the bird. She is a strange girl.

Wanting to get her alone he asks, "Could I see some more of your drawings?"

"I guess so. We'll have a little time after Jonah goes to bed. I can show you then."

"I would really like that," he says as he runs his hand along her arm.

She pulls away as Jack comes running through the kitchen from the garden. He doesn't look much cleaner, but he is certainly wetter. Water and mud splatter everywhere as Jonah chases him around the kitchen. "Sarah, I think I'm done washing the dog."

She laughs and wraps her brother in one towel and the dog in another.

"How about we let Stephen take Jack back next door while we get upstairs and put you in some dry clothes?"

"But what if he eats my cookie?" the little boy whines.

"I don't know Jonah. I think we may be able to trust him." She smiles at Stephen tossing him the towel. "It's the blue house next door."

Sarah lights an oil lamp and they climb the stairs. It takes a few minutes to brush the mud out of Jonah's hair. When they return downstairs Stephen is sitting at the kitchen table with two cookies in front of him.

"Two cookies!" Nah shrieks with delight. "How did you get two?"

"I told her that your doll was recovering from surgery and that he might need a cookie too."

They work on dinner together. A feast of clams, potatoes, carrots and even some lettuce from Jess's small greenhouse—it's probably the last batch of the year.

Sarah puts a pot of water to boil on the stove while they eat—some for tea and some for washing up.

"Where do you live, Stephen?" Nah asks with a mouthful of cookie.

"Goat Island in Little Bay."

"Do you have goats there?"

"No, we don't. There is a cow, though."

"Hmm." Nah frowns. "Why is isn't it called Cow Island if you don't have any goats on it?"

"I don't know, Jonah."

"Well, I think you should change the name or get some goats."

Stephen replies laughing, "I'll tell the owners your suggestion."

Sarah sits quietly and watches the man with Jonah until she suggests, "Let's clean up and play some games. I'll start with the dishes."

Stephen offers to dry so he can stand closer to her.

"I'll go get the cards," Jonah says as he scurries into the parlor.

Stephen leans closer to Sarah as he dries. She edges away from him until she can barely reach the wash basin. He takes a step backwards when Jonah emerges through the door.

"They're mostly all here. We're only missing the ten of hearts and the jack of diamonds—and maybe the 4 or 5 of clubs."

"We'll work around it," Sarah says laughing. "We could play in the parlor but it's warmer in here."

"I like here better than the fancy parlor," Jonah says. "It's too girly in there—all those lacy things."

"Here it is, then."

"Say, who are these old people? Your family?" Stephen points to a framed set of portraits near the pie safe. "The fancy writing here says 'Pritchard.'"

"Uh, no. That came with the house. The former owner was Mrs. Pritchard. That's her on the left."

"Hmm. Sturdy looking woman."

"I guess so," she replies.

Jonah insists on teaching them a game that he's invented. "It's called 'Rodeo.' Each player starts with five cards. Then I hand out five more. You can't look at your cards and you have to pretend to be a monkey."

"Have you ever seen a monkey, Nah?" Stephen asks.

"No. Sarah showed me a picture in a book."

The rules get more and more complex from there. Eventually a series of duck walks and silly faces are incorporated. Stephen wins that portion with his ability to stick his tongue into his nose.

"I don't know Nah. That was pretty complicated, little brother."

"But fun," Stephen says. "I haven't laughed that hard in a long time." He really does like the kid. He hasn't spent much time with children before.

The boy desperately wants to stay up later, but his eyelids droop until finally he curls up on his chair. Sarah carries him upstairs and tucks him into his bed. "Momma will be mad that we didn't scrub your teeth," she whispers to him as she gives him a kiss goodnight.

Stephen has put away the cards and placed his dirty cup near the last of the dishes. He's so excited to finally get Sarah alone.

"We should probably just collect some drawings and stoke the fire. I don't want to stay out there and leave Nah alone in the house."

"Of course." He's disappointed but picks up the oil lamp and follows Sarah out the door, through the garden and past the privy. He takes her hand and they go up the stairs.

"The stove is still warm," she says lighting another lamp.

"It shouldn't be too hard to get it going again. Why don't you pick out some drawings to show me and I'll tend to the fire."

Sarah picks up a stack from the shelf on the corner. He glances at her as she glows in the lamplight scrutinizing her work. He can almost see the curve of her breasts as she leans over the table. An image of her in her damp shift comes into his mind.

"I think these will do best. I want to show you the ones I drew from life and not the copies I made of James Audubon's prints."

She stands close to him and peers into the stove.

"It looks like it's going very nicely now. You should be warm enough tonight. If not, there are some more blankets in that chest over there."

He can smell her sweet breath. He reaches out and strokes the heart shaped birthmark on her cheek. His body responds to her. He moves towards her, but she steps away and picks up the stack of drawings.

"We should go back in. We've been out here too long," she says edging towards the stairs.

He can't walk back to the house like this.

"I'll meet you inside shortly. I need to do a couple of things."

"OK. All right, sure. I'll make some more tea."

She picks up the lamp and her drawings and walks to the stairs.

She pours the hot water carefully into the pot as Stephen comes through the door a few minutes later.

"There you are. I thought you might have fallen asleep like Nah."

"No, I just needed to use the privy," he lies.

"OK," she smiles and hands him a cup of tea.

"Thank you for letting me stay, Sarah." He takes her hand and brings it to his lips.

"Sure," she says. Her face flushes and she gently takes back her hand.

"These are mostly the ones I did of the dead heron," she says as she pulls away and spreads the drawings out on the table. The series includes the bird with his feathers and then she has carefully dissected him and done elaborate sketches at each stage.

He holds the oil lamp close to the drawings. He feels a little squeamish at the sight of the bird rotting away but the sketches are beautiful. "They are amazing. You are really talented."

"Thank you." Sarah looks a little puzzled by his praise. "You can have one if you like."

"Really?"

"Sure. Why not? Something to remember us by."

If Stephen has anything to do with it there won't be any reason to remember them.

He'll be around.

Forever.

Of course, he's felt this way before—more than a few times. This time is different—he's sure. She's so beautiful.

Sarah watches him study her drawings. He stares intently at the detailed rendering of the heron's eye. She feels a warmth in her vitals that is unfamiliar. She never felt anything like this when she worked at Odette's.

She starts to feel out of control. She needs time and space to think.

"Um," she starts, "I'm starting to feel tired and a little faint. I think I should retire upstairs."

"Are you OK? I can go out to my bed if you like."

"It's fine. Why don't you stay up as long as you like? I'll see you in the morning."

He starts to pull her towards him in a hug, but she holds out her hand instead. He takes it and looks into her eyes.

"Good night, Sarah. I am very happy to have made your acquaintance."

"Good night, Stephen."

She walks up the stairs and stops in her room to take off her dress, corset, petticoats and shift. She stands before her mirror in the candlelight. Her hands rub over her breasts and come to rest between her legs. For the first time she understands what it means to really desire someone. Odette's had taught her not to feel—to pretend to be somewhere else was the only way to get through it.

She pours some water into the bowl and splashes it onto her face. Slipping her shift over her head she gathers her cards and the prayer book and crawls into Jess's bed next door.

"I guess I'm in trouble for my lack of dental care too, Jonah."

Nah rolls over and mumbles something but then starts to snore quietly.

Mr. Soapy has been exiled to the end of the bed.

She's too wound up to concentrate on the book, so she extinguishes the oil lamp and lies in bed sorting out the day.

She feels like a completely different person from the one who woke up this morning.

CHAPTER 19

Jess rises at dawn to the sound of a rooster. She didn't see a coop here on the island so it must be from the Bunker farm across the bay. She pours some water into the basin to wash. It feels good on her skin. She'll be happy to be home. Maybe she'll even take a real bath.

She catches her image in the mirror. Her eyes are red. She looks exhausted. She was up too late thinking about Suzanne. Poor Sweetness.

Smells of bacon and coffee waft up the stairs. Matie is already up.

She dresses and makes her way out the back door to the privy. On her way in she sees the other woman rub her belly while stirring the porridge on the stove.

"Such nice people," Jess thinks. "I hope this all works out for them."

The sun is already melting the light coating of snow on the ground. It looks like it's to be another pleasant day. She thinks about a walk but wants to get an early start, so she returns to the warmth of the kitchen.

"The woman who was killed," Matie says.

"Yes? Suzanne?"

"She worked as a whore?"

"She did," Jess replies.

"That's so sad."

"It is."

"I've had troubles in my life. That could have been me." Matie's eyes well up. "I'm so lucky that I landed here with Samuel. My sister and I were nearly on the street after my aunt died."

"Many women find themselves in unfortunate circumstances. The lucky ones escape and have good lives," Jess says taking a sip of her coffee.

"It makes me appreciate what I have," she says as she strokes her belly.

"You're going to be a wonderful mother, Matie."

"You know?"

"It's not hard to tell. I am so happy for you both," Jess reaches out and squeezes her hand.

Matie smiles through her tears.

"I guess I better finish your breakfast so you can be on your way home."

"Thanks, Matie—for everything. I am very glad to have met you and Samuel."

After filling her belly with bacon and porridge sweetened with maple syrup, Jessamyn packs her belongings and goes outside. The tavern keeper has her horse waiting for her.

"Thank you for your hospitality, Samuel."

"Good luck to you, Miss Jessamyn."

CHAPTER 20

H e wakes up with a start. An eyeball stares at him. A wild turkey. He lunges for it. It might make for a decent breakfast. His stomach still churns from the apples. How long has he been lying here? By the look of the mess he's made he's been here for a while.

The horse is long gone. The wagon sits where he left it. He's covered with snow. He's lucky he didn't freeze to death.

Christ. The apples. He's never been that sick from food—or whiskey. He could kill that little bitch. She must have poisoned the apples to make him so sick.

He puts his hand to his cheek and recoils. That whore scratched him good when he caught her trying to escape. It was strange that she seemed to be coming back into the tavern when he caught her.

Now it's festering.

He finds a stream and attempts to clean himself. He starts with his cheek sloshing the water into the cut.

He takes off his clothes and washes everything as best he can. He lays them on a bush to dry.

"I can't stand around here naked until my clothes dry."

He pulls the tarp out of the wagon and wraps himself in it—shivering despite the warm sunshine.

He decides what he really needs is a plan.

The first thing he must have is more food—or whiskey—or both. By now that kid has probably screamed to high heaven and the entire town is probably looking for him.

By about midday he figures his clothes aren't getting any drier. They're stiff as a board and he jumps around to get them on. In the process he falls against the bush ripping the pant leg open.

"Shit!"

He wanders south for about an hour and comes upon a fishing shanty on the water. Waiting until darkness he breaks the back window to let himself in. It turns out there's no lock on the door anyway. The shanty has one room with a small stove and a pile of firewood and a small cot. He starts a fire in the stove and the structure fills with smoke. "There must be a nest of some critter in the chimney," he thinks. He opens the door and the smoke starts to dissipate. He hears a loud swoosh and scurrying feet.

"Whatever it was it's dead and burnt now."

His stomach growls.

"I wonder if it was edible?"

He's able to prime and start the small water pump. It's then that he notices a cabinet in the corner.

He's saved. It's filled with canned food. There are homemade glass jars of carrots, beets and eggs. There are even a few cans of sweetened condensed milk. He pokes a hole into the top of one and sucks the rich liquid into his mouth.

CHAPTER 21

Jessamyn is so happy to nearly be home that she doesn't even mind seeing Reverend Hobson standing on the street in front of her house.

He seems distracted by a petite figure standing next to him with two small carpet bags. The woman turns and smiles as Jess rides up.

Jess nods at the couple as she dismounts. "Hello Reverend. How are you today?"

"Excellent, Miss Jakes, excellent. May I present my fiancé, Miss Maryanne Twombly of Boston, Massachusetts."

"Fiancé?" Jess is stunned. The woman must be 20 years younger than the Reverend—and to top it off she's lovely with porcelain skin, blue eyes and dark brown hair pulled under her black hat. "Well, congratulations."

"It's so nice to make your acquaintance Miss Jakes. You're the first parishioner that I've met," the petite woman offers her gloved hand.

"I'm not exactly a parishioner," Jess says removing her gray hat.

"No, Miss Jakes chooses to worship across town at the West Church—when she does, that is."

"Oh, we'll have to see what we can do to change that," Maryanne says smiling with a tilt of her head.

Jessamyn can feel her face flush. Who is this woman? She can't be marrying that desiccated bag of twigs.

"Hi, Jess!" Putt calls as he comes out of the rectory.

"Hello, Putt."

"Welcome home! Sarah and Nah were having a lot of fun with their new friend yesterday."

"New friend? Oh, you must mean Stephen."

"Yes, I met Mr. Bailey yesterday also," the reverend adds. "Seems like a very nice fellow. Is he a suitor of Miss Sarah?"

Jess feels like she has come back to a strange community that looks sort of familiar—who are these people?

"Um. He's a family friend."

"Oh well, please wish him my…I mean our best." The old man puts his arm around his fiancé who stiffens at his touch.

"And who is this fine fellow?" Maryanne looks towards Putt.

"Oh, that's just Putt," Hobson says. "Never mind him. Let's go to the rectory so I can show you around."

Putt doesn't seem to notice the slight and resumes his raking, humming as he works.

Jessamyn watches the Reverend and Maryanne as they make their way to the house next to the church. There's no more familiarity between them although the older man seems to be trying hard to charm her. Maryanne turns and catches her staring. She smiles. Jess looks down. She's sure she's bright red again and is glad when the couple enters the yellow clapboard rectory.

Willie whinnies at her when she leads him up to the front door of her house. "Oh, sorry boy. I guess I'm not myself today." It's his turn to be confused when they enter the barn and he spies another horse in his stall.

"Cruppers! Is Stephen still here?"

"Momma!" Jonah comes running down the stairs from Sarah's workroom. She hears laughter upstairs. "Momma! Stephen is showing Sarah and I how to make birds out of folded paper."

"That sounds fun, Nah. Have you been having a good time with your guest?" she asks.

"Oh yes! Me and Sarah both. We were up all night playing cards and talking."

"If you consider going to bed at 8:30 p.m. staying up all night." Sarah walks down the stairs followed closely by the sandy haired man. "Stephen, you should probably move Leonardo out of Willie's stall."

"Oh, that's fine," Jess replies. "I can tie him up in the garden."

Willie stomps his foot and snorts.

"It's all right," Stephen replies. "I really should get going soon anyway. Matie—I mean the Simpsons—will be wondering where I am."

He walks upstairs to retrieve his things and looks one last time around the room. Sighing, he carefully folds the heron drawing and tucks it into his saddle bag.

"What the devil is going on?" Jess whispers to her daughter.

"What do you mean? You told us to entertain him," Sarah replies.

"I don't know. This looks like something more than that."

"Oh, don't worry," she laughs. "I haven't violated my vow."

"It's yours to break if you choose. I just want you to be careful."

Jonah starts crying as Stephen saddles up his horse. "Don't worry little man. I'll see you again soon. That is if your momma will let me visit when I come to the coast." Jess smiles but says nothing. There's too much happening for her to know how to feel about this.

As he's leaving, he turns to Jess. "May I ask you a question?"

"Of course."

"Sarah said that you are some kind of detective. Were you chasing that blonde woman and man?"

"Yes," she replies

"So, she wasn't a friend of yours?" he asks.

"She was a friend, but I was hired to find her."

"Wow—a lady detective!" he exclaims.

"Yes. A lady detective. Have a safe ride, Mr. Bailey."

"Thanks, Miss Jessamyn."

Jonah falls asleep immediately after supper. Jess and Sarah settle in with some tea in the kitchen.

"Poor Sweetness," Sarah shakes her head. "She wasn't the sharpest of sticks but even she should have known better than to go with Taylor. I can't believe that bastard killed her."

"It looks like he did," Jess says rubbing her eyes.

"Are the authorities looking for him?"

"They say so, but the sheriff of Stafford County seems incompetent. It won't be too difficult for Taylor to keep out of his way. Once he gets out of the local area, he may be hard to track. They won't care much about a dead working girl in Boston or Portland."

"That's certainly true," Sarah says.

Jess takes a sip of her tea. "Were you able to find out anything at Odette's?"

"The only thing missing from Suzanne's libee chest was the prayer book."

"Any luck with the markings?"

"Not so far but I've only just started. Is 'Mabel' Suzanne's real name? Was she from New Bedford?"

"I don't think so. She looked and sounded more like she was from the Midwest. I don't know for sure—even we never talked about our pasts."

"Interesting. Maybe we'll find out where she was really from when we unlock the secret of the book."

"One other thing," Jess says pouring more tea into her cup, "I'm pretty sure Suzanne couldn't read or write."

"Really?" Sarah replies. "Why wouldn't she ask you to teach her? She must have seen you tutoring me all those years."

"I don't know—embarrassed, I guess. She worked hard at pretending that she could."

"Why would she have a prayer book that she couldn't read? I never saw her pray."

"Me neither," Jess says shaking her head.

"So, who was Mabel?"

"Good question. Maybe you can write to the churches in New Bedford and see if they have a record of her birth. It might help to find out who her parents were. Would George have a directory for parishes?"

"I'll ask him."

Sarah smiles at the thought of another visit to the library.

"So, what else did you learn at the house?" Jess asks.

Sarah gets up to fill their teapot with more hot water from the stove and replies, "Moira said that nobody believes Odette gives a foozler's gill about Suzanne."

"We all can agree on that."

"Something strange happened."

"What do you mean?" Jess asks.

"Essie."

"What did she say?"

"First of all, she looked scared as a flap doodle in a harem when I started talking to her. All I was doing was confirming that she'd seen Suzanne and Taylor headed out of town together."

"Why would she be frightened of that?" Jess asks as she pours herself another cup of tea.

"Beats me, Jess. She told me that she saw them. She didn't say anything about a wagon or that they were headed towards Newington. That is until I mentioned it and she changed her story."

"So, somebody told her to lie. Who? Suzanne? Taylor?"

"My money's on Odette," Sarah says.

"Sarah, I bet that crupper skunk is playing us."

CHAPTER 22

Jonah sticks to his momma like a burr weed. Despite the Stephen distraction he missed her like crazy.

She needs to go see Odette so it's decided that after dinner they will all walk downtown, and Sarah will take Nah to meet George at the Athenaeum while Jess is occupied with the old madam. Nah has agreed to this arrangement for the sum of two cookies from Carbew's Bakery.

"You really need to stop bribing that child," Sarah says after Jonah goes looking for the dog.

"You're right, I'm not being a very good mother."

"It's not that, Jess. It's just that at some point it's going to get much more expensive than just two cookies. Soon it will be scones and you know where that leads."

"Cake?" Jess teases.

"Maybe. But definitely not muffins, Jess. You'll need to draw the line somewhere when it comes to baked goods."

"True. You have my permission to slap me if I am out of control."

Sarah wanders to the parlor. Freed up from Jonah, she spends the morning focused on the prayer book. She settles in on the blue wingback chair with her legs dangled over the side. First, she reviews her scribblings from yesterday. Sometimes a fresh look at old notes can open doors. Nothing jumps out at her. She holds the book upside down and sideways. Still nothing unusual pops. She looks at her notes from page one. The underlined letters are "ehgwosrfjngghuersvbnmkhgtysdgfj." No pattern to be seen there.

"Maybe the underlined letters themselves are not relevant. Maybe it's the placement of the letters on the page," she says under her breath. She counts the letters on page one until she hits an underlined "e." She writes "7" down on her notebook. The next letter is at position 11. She continues to mark down the positions of the letters until she has, "7, 11, 14, 27, 32, 38, 54." She tries another page and repeats the process until she has a stack of cards.

She spends the rest of the morning on it until she hears Jess and Jonah working on dinner in the kitchen.

"Any luck?" Jess asks.

"All I can say is that if Sweetness made this code up, maybe we were wrong about her being illiterate and not very smart. She has me stumped."

"Maybe we're investing too much into this. Maybe it has nothing to do with anything."

"But why would she go to the trouble of hiding it in the bean pot? It must have some significance."

"I would assume so," Jess agrees.

CHAPTER 23

T he closer he gets to Goat Island the more the hole in Stephen's gut grows. He has to tell the Simpsons that their arrangement is over.

He can't keep it together.

He can't get Sarah out of his mind.

He'll die if he can't have her.

They stop a mile from the tavern. Leo has a drink from a stream and Stephen settles on a rock.

He takes Sarah's drawing out of his bag and carefully opens it. The detail is beautiful. The delicate pencil strokes open a world that you can't see observing herons from a far. She really is talented. Way more than he is. All his training and he could never create something like this. He feels the same tinge of jealousy as when fellow student, Jackson Smythe, put his work up on the wall at the Academy. He couldn't stand to be inferior to that little prick.

"At least she's prettier than Smythe," he says to Leo.

He pulls out his sketchbook and tries to draw her face from memory. He struggles with the heart shaped birthmark on her cheek.

Imagining her neck and the curve of her breasts and adds them to his sketch. She looks at him from the drawing—beckoning him with her eyes. He adds details to her curly hair until the sunlight turns a deep orange and then dips behind the trees.

Leo nudges him and he takes a final look at his portrait. He's sort of satisfied with the likeness and starts to close his book. The thread holding the spine together snaps and the pages fall to the ground. He picks them up wiping off the dirt with his sleeve.

"I really need to get a new sketch book. This one is falling apart. Maybe when we get to Portsmouth, Leo."

The horse whinnies in response.

"I guess we can't put it off any longer—time to go to the tavern."

He saddles the horse in the dim light and makes his way the final mile to Goat Island. He can smell the cooking fire as he crosses the bridge. He'll certainly miss Matie's cooking. At first it was hard to get used to the earthy stews and robust bread. His palette was trained by Manon's French style cuisine at home. Appreciation of fine foods wasn't the only thing the petite French cook taught him.

The memory of their times together makes him ready to have another go at Matie before he tells her he is leaving. One for the road.

Leo walks directly to the barn and Stephen dismounts and takes off the tack and saddle. The stallion is agitated by the strange mare in the other stall. There must be a guest. Matie will be occupied making dinner, limiting the opportunities to slip away.

He considers saddling the horse and going right back to the coast when he hears the back door open.

Samuel's large figure blocks the light from the kitchen door.

"Stephen, is that you? C'mon inside! We've got something to discuss!"

"I'll be right there! I'm just finishing up with Leo."

He drops his bag into his small room off the barn and moves towards the house. Samuel has closed the kitchen door so Stephen opts to go to the front door to avoid Matie. He doesn't see the point of talking to her if there's no chance for fun.

A laughing, round man sits at the small table near the stove. He has one hand on the top of his bald head and the other clenched around the tankard of ale. He and Samuel quiet when Stephen enters, "Welcome home!" His boss bounds out of his chair and envelopes him with a big bear hug.

Matie comes running out of the kitchen. She stops when she sees Stephen. Her face lights up. He looks at the floor avoiding her gaze.

She knows immediately that something is different. She tells herself that it doesn't matter anymore.

"Stephen, could I speak to you in the kitchen?" she asks.

"Yes ma'am," he replies.

"Bring the rum in when you come back. We need to drink a toast." Samuel doesn't seem like he needs any more alcohol. It's obvious he and the guest have been at it the ale for a while. Stephen has never seen him drunk before.

As soon as he enters the kitchen, Matie takes his hand. "It's happened, Stephen. I think I'm with child! I've suspected for a while but didn't want to say anything until I was sure. The baby—our baby— will be here in January."

Stephen doesn't pay attention to the math. Matie knew that they conceived the first month of the blonde man's arrival on Goat Island. She said nothing and was surprised that he hadn't noticed her swelling abdomen.

She wraps her arms around him and buries her face into his neck. "Thank you so much. Samuel is thrilled."

"That's good news, Mrs. Simpson," he says unwrapping her arms.

She has tears in her eyes. "Stephen?"

"I think I'd better go out and light the stove. My room is bound to be freezing. Please tell Mr. Simpson how happy I am." He moves towards the door. "I'm pretty tired. I think I'll pass on the rum."

He makes his way to the barn and sits in the dark.

CHAPTER 24

Odette's is hopping busy. Moira greets Jess at the kitchen door. "Pepperell Shipbuilders launched a schooner yesterday and all the men received a bonus for finishing early." Granny scurries up and down the stairs with hot water for the girls to quickly wash between clients. Odette's is one of the few houses in town that offers this luxury.

It's even in the sales pitch when she greets customers. "We feature the cleanest girls in town!"

"I found Suzanne," Jessamyn says when Granny is out of earshot.

"Oh dear. The news can't be good. Did the opium finally get her?" The round cook asks as she rolls out a crust for a meat pie.

"She was strangled to death and thrown into Little Bay near the Goat Island Tavern."

"Oh, dear God. Poor Sweetness."

"Miss Odette will see you now," Granny tells Jess as she makes her way to the back door to dump the latest bucket of dirty water. She's strong for such a small girl.

Odette sits on a red velvet settee dressed in her favorite purple ensemble complete with embroidered peacocks. Jess wasn't in this room very much when she lived here as it was Odette's private office. Chinese red walls with a mish-mash of Oriental and Greco Roman decorations.

"Suzanne is dead," Jess reports.

"How?" the old woman asks.

"Strangled."

"By Taylor?"

"I believe so," Jess nods.

"Did you find him?" Odette asks looking towards the open door as if there may be eavesdroppers in the hallway.

"Not yet. But I will. He stopped in Dover afterwards for a whiskey but then disappeared. I don't know where."

"No stop at one of the mill-sanctioned houses?"

"No, apparently not," Jess shakes her head.

"Curious."

"What do you mean, Odette?"

"As we know, he's a man without any impulse control. If he had any extra money, he's likely to have roughed up one of the girls."

"I guess he didn't have any money," Jess responds. "It would have been lucky if he did. If he had stopped the mill security officers might have him by now."

Odette smiles slightly as she takes a pinch of snuff from a tarnished bronze box. "He'll be headed back this way, then."

"What do you mean?"

"Taylor is not a smart man. He'll come back to familiar territory. Keep looking for that asshole and when you find him, bring him to me."

"Not the police?" Jess asks.

"No. Bring him here first." Odette sneezes and the snuff residue stains her handkerchief.

"Anything in particular that you're looking for?" Jess asks.

"I just want to question him," the madam replies.

"OK. But we'll need to call the police as soon as we can."

"Trust me, they're so incompetent that it won't matter. Better for us to have spoken to him first."

She isn't wrong about that. The Portsmouth police force consists of twenty barely literate men—most of them customers of the brothels on Water Street. Funding is so bad that they don't have guns or even uniforms.

"Try Coxe's Boarding House first. That's where he was staying before he left with Sweetness."

"How would you know that? Why would he be staying there? That's more expensive than Finn's or Peabody's."

The madam dismisses the question with a wave of her hand and changes the subject. "Did you find anything interesting on Suzanne?"

"No. She was in the water. Her clothes were missing. The coroner thinks they're long gone by now. That is if she had anything on when she went into the bay in the first place."

"That's unfortunate." Odette squints her eyes at Jess.

She doesn't ask much else about Goat Island and certainly not the prayer book. She must have known about it as she routinely reviewed the contents of all the girl's libee chests. Maybe she didn't think it was important.

"Unless you have anything else, I'll go to Coxe's to see what I can find out."

"Remember, bring him here when you find him," Odette says dismissing Jess with a wave of her hand.

On her way out the door Jess notices an anomaly in the garish décor—a small map of the Isles of Shoals framed next to the madam's desk. "Curious," she says to herself.

After a five-minute walk to the boarding house, she finds Lily Coxe clean-ing up from dinner in the kitchen. The boarders sit in the parlor smoking.

"Good riddance to that one," the young landlady says. "He was right nasty. He left me with a disgusting set of bedding to clean up. If you find him, tell him he owes us the last week's rent. He slipped away in the middle of the night with my wagon and old Oatley, the nag."

"I suspect he owes money to a lot of people. Did he tell you anything about himself?"

"He used to come in and talk to me while I cooked. He said that he was about to become a very rich man."

"Really? Did he say how?"

"Yes. He said he was about to dig up a treasure. I didn't believe a word of it. I've met many a foozler who thought he was about to hit it rich. It seems to go with the territory."

"Did he say where the treasure was?" Jess asks.

"If he did, I don't remember. I'm pretty sure not. I was always trying to get rid of him, so I wasn't listening very carefully."

"Thanks for the information, Lily," Jess says as she turns towards the front door.

"Sorry that I wasn't much help, Jess."

CHAPTER 25

Stephen lies in his bed in the morning until he has the courage to face Matie. He doesn't like this uncomfortable feeling. Is it guilt?

He usually ends his affairs without a glance back—he barely remembers if Manon cried when he left.

He's leaving—hopefully today. He needs to get back to the coast. Back to Sarah—the new love of his life.

The room is frigid. The stove is freezing to the touch. He hurries into his clothes and walks across the frosty yard to the house.

The kitchen is warm and smells like cinnamon. She must have baked rolls for the guest.

"Hello, Stephen." She doesn't look up from her cooking.

"Hello, Matie."

"You're leaving, aren't you?"

"Yes," he replies.

She has tears in her eyes which are fixated on the bacon she is slicing. "I knew it would happen sometime."

"I'm sorry. I can't stay until the baby is born." He lingers holding his hat in his hands.

"Don't worry about that, Stephen. Here's your money." She hands him a leather pouch filled with coins. "You'll need it wherever you're headed—Portsmouth?"

"Yes."

"Jess's daughter?" she asks.

"Yes," he answers.

"I'm happy for you," she replies not looking up.

"Matie…I'm sorry…"

"Don't say anything, Stephen—just go. It would be best if you left as soon as you can. Samuel and I need to start our new lives. It will be easier if you're gone."

"Will I see him to say goodbye?" he asks meekly.

"No. I sent him to Dover early. He won't be back until tonight."

He looks at her.

"Matie, I'm sorry."

"Please stop apologizing. I can't bear it. You only did what we asked you to do. Goodbye, Stephen."

"Goodbye, Matie."

He packs his things. There isn't much. Just his drawing supplies and note-books. He opens the remains of his sketchbook and looks at his portrait of Sarah. Sighing, he saddles the horse and points him towards the coast.

arah and Jonah enter though the rear door of the Athenaeum so they can avoid the main reading room. She's not technically allowed in the library alone. She can only imagine what they'd say about Jonah.

"Hello, Sarah!" George's face lights up when he sees her. "And who is this fine fellow?"

Nah hides behind her skirts.

"This is my brother. Say 'hello' to George, Jonah."

He turns beet red, but gives George a small wave with his hand.

"Are you here to look at bird books with your sister, Jonah?"

"Nah. Everyone calls me Nah."

"Well, nice to meet you, Nah."

"Actually, George," Sarah starts as she pulls some volumes from her bag. "I'm hoping you can help me find a listing of churches in New Bedford."

"Hmmm. We wouldn't have that type of thing here, Sarah. What affiliation would you be looking for?"

"I'm not sure. Which one would use prayer books like this one?" She hands him the small volume.

"Oh, that would be the sister church to Reverend Cheney's. If you stop in across the street, I'm sure he could give you the address."

"Thank you, George."

She looks around for Nah.

"Mutton nob!"

"Don't worry Sarah, he can't have gone far."

They enter the front reading room and spot Jonah staring at a portrait of a sea captain on the wall. Thankfully old Cheney isn't sitting at his usual table. Only Mr. Dunwoody is in residence—asleep at a table in the corner with a line of drool making its way down his wrinkled chin and onto the newspaper below.

Jonah wanders off to inspect the objects in the curio cabinet across the room. He stares at great length at a jar with a two headed baby shark floating in liquid.

"As a matter of fact," George says to Sarah. "The gentleman in the painting there was from New Bedford originally."

Sarah leans in to read the nameplate.

"Captain Grievance Collins." Collins? It must be a coincidence.

"When was this portrait painted? He looks ancient."

"Well, he passed about five or six years ago so it had to be before that. He'd been here for at least ten years before that."

"How did he die?" she asks pulling her notepaper out of her bag.

"Well, they never found his body, but the conclusion was that he fell off the rocks at the Isles of Shoals and drowned. He went to the Smuttynose Hotel for the weekend and never returned."

"No witnesses?" she asks.

"The rumor was that he had a young woman with him, but she disappeared as well."

"Hmm," Sarah frowns. "I suppose her body was never found either?"

"Apparently not. A witness reported that he saw a young woman get into a wherry that night."

"Was there an investigation?" she asks.

"The witness was deemed a drunkard and Collins's housekeeper said that he was poorly. People speculated that the old man jumped into the water on purpose."

"Nobody investigated at all, George?"

"Well, since the Shoals are half in Maine and half in New Hampshire the two states argued about jurisdiction for a while and in the end neither really checked into it."

"How did the portrait end up here? Wouldn't his family want it?"

"No family apparently," he answers. "Mr. Quimby bought the painting at an estate sale."

She turns to the painting as tears come to her eyes.

"Sarah, are you OK?"

"It's just so sad. To die without anyone caring enough to even check into it."

George pats her on the shoulder. She shakes the tears away and asks, "Any of the members remember Collins?"

"Oddly no. Apparently, he didn't socialize much with others in Portsmouth. He mostly kept to himself."

"Hmm." She looks at the painting again fixated on the background.

"You've noticed. There's something odd."

She points at a small ship painted above his left shoulder. "You mean the ship and the map of the Isles of Shoals?"

"Yes."

"What's strange about that? He was a sea captain after all."

"He was a schooner captain. That ship is Spanish—a very specific ship."

Jonah has now sidled up to the snoring Dunwoody to investigate a coroded sextant sitting on the windowsill.

"Which ship?" Sarah asks.

"The Concepción from Cadiz."

"That seems very specific. How do you know it's that ship?"

"It happened to run into Smuttynose Island at the Shoals in 1813," he replies.

"Why would he care so much about a shipwreck that happened over 40 years ago?"

"I don't know. There were rumors about there being a treasure of silver."

Nah flies across the room. "Treasure? What treasure?"

"Missing Spanish silver from the Isles of Shoals," Sarah says winking at George.

"Were they pirates?" Jonah asks giggling. Dunwoody awakens, "What? What? Harrumph!"

"Shhhh Jonah!" Sarah says.

Dunwoody returns to his snoring.

"Do you have a book about this shipwreck? I'd like to maybe read it to Jonah. He seems to be interested in treasures."

Jonah nods.

"I think I might have something for you Nah," he winks at the boy. "I'll be right back with it."

"Thank you, George," Sarah smiles.

She takes a few minutes to sketch the painting. She makes short work of the seaman and concentrates on the background imagery. Jonah loses interest and returns to stare at the baby shark.

George takes her aside when he returns with the volume. "Mr Quimby just told me that there are some theories about the wreck that you should be aware of before you read the book to Jonah."

"Theories?"

"Well it seems that some of the Spanish sailors may or may not have been quite dead when they were buried on the island."

"Oh dear."

"Yes. Oh dear, is right."

Jonah is less enthusiastic about their second errand across the street at the West Church. The front door is unlocked. They enter and are surprised to see the shape of the Right Reverend Howard Bunford Cheney kneeling on the stone floor in front of the alter.

"Oh! Excuse me," she says. "I'm so sorry to interrupt you."

The old clergyman turns and faces her. His eyes are red like he's been crying.

Jonah hides behind her. She stands there motionless as the older man rises to his feet.

"I didn't mean to frighten you," the clergyman rises from the stone floor and brushes off his pale gray vestments. "I was simply atoning for my sins."

Sarah says nothing. Jonah is wrapped so tightly around her legs she nearly topples over.

"You're the young lady who frequents the Athenaeum, right?"

"Yes," Sarah looks down.

"Why do you always run through to the office instead of staying in the reading room?"

"Um. My friend George works there. He always has books to show me."

"Books about birds?"

"Yes. How did you know?"

"I've seen George collecting them for you. I was once looking for Darwin's *Journal of Researches* and he let it slip that you had borrowed it. Are you a fan of the boobies?"

Jonah giggles behind Sarah.

"The Galapagos boobies! Of course!"

"The blue footed are my favorite. Apparently, their mating dance is quite festive with the males showing the females their brightly colored feet."

"I've only seen them in Darwin's book. Most of the birds I know about come from Audubon's work."

"Ah yes, *The Birds of North America*. Shame he had to kill so many of them to do his studies."

"Oh! I didn't realize that. I guess I should have known. The detail is so fine."

Sarah unwraps Jonah and takes his hand and turns to go. "Sir, we're sorry to have bothered you."

"Wait. Did you want something in particular or were you just feeling inspired by the glory of God?" He smiles at them both.

"Actually sir, I was hoping that you would help me contact your sister church in New Bedford. I'd like to inquire about a parishioner there. Her name is Mable Mary Collins. We're trying to find out where she is now and maybe some details about her family."

"I'd be happy to help. I tell you what. I'll write to Reverend Bungie in New Bedford and report back to you as soon as I hear. I'll leave the information with George in case we don't cross paths at the library."

Sarah smiles.

"What is your name, girl?"

"I'm Sarah Jakes. This is my little brother, Jonah."

He tips his hat to the pair. "Well Sarah, I hope we have another chance to discuss birds."

"I'd like that sir," she replies.

CHAPTER 27

After checking out the boarding house Jess has a little time to kill before meeting up with her family so she walks to the bakery for some bread for dinner.

The tiny shop is nearly empty as it closes in early afternoon. There are just a few loaves left and the small woman in front of her looks like she might be buying the rest. She turns to face Jess.

Maryanne.

Jess's face flushes immediately.

The future Mrs. Reverend Hobson smiles. "Miss Jakes! I'm so happy to run into you—twice in one day no less—and here I am buying the rest of the bread. Please take a loaf with my blessings—or more accurately, my fiancé's blessing."

She passes the loaf to Jessamyn and as she gently lays her hand on the taller woman's shoulder.

Maryanne's eyes never leave Jess's.

"Excuse me ma'am," Mr. Jackson interrupts. "That will be a quarter for the lot of them."

"Of course." She hands him the coin and the two women walk out of the bakery.

"You came all the way here to buy bread? Why don't you just shop at Carbew's near the house?"

"It seems that the dear reverend made an enemy of Mrs. Carbew and she forbids him from buying from her. He's done without but I can't stomach breakfast without my tea and toast. Besides, I needed the walk."

"He has a tendency to do that kind of thing."

Maryanne laughs. "I can see that I have some bridges to mend—starting perhaps with you. Will I be seeing you in church tomorrow?"

Jess can feel her face flushing and a warmth between her legs that she hasn't felt since Sweetness.

"Uh, sure."

"God be with you," Maryanne says.

"And with you," Jess mumbles.

CHAPTER 28

I t takes Stephen the better part of the morning to make the journey back to Portsmouth. The money from Matie and Samuel will only last so long. The first thing he needs is a job.

He decides to check into the Codfish Inn—not the best in town but respectable, clean and rumored to have good food. He puts his belongings in his room and inspects himself in the mirror.

His blonde beard is far too long. He looks more like a long-haired sheep than a man.

He'll get himself cleaned up and purchase some new clothes before he ventures out to speak with potential employers.

Downstairs at dinner the innkeeper asks, "In town for business?" He brings cod cakes and refills Stephen's ale.

"I hope so. I'm looking for work."

"What kind of work? What can you do, Bailey?"

Stephen scratches his beard, "Well, I can draw well and am good at figures."

"Well then. Go to see my brother at Chapman's Shipyard. He's always looking for smart young men to work in the office. He's got plenty of muscle around the property. He's a bit shy on the brainy types."

"Thank you, sir."

"Elias Trask is the name, and my brother's Benedict."

"Thank you Elias. I will see him today. Oh, by the way, can you recommend a barber and a tailor for me?"

"I was going to suggest a little trim and refit for you," Trask says laughing. "Oh, and Benedict won't be at the yard until Monday. He's taken our mother to Boston to visit her sister."

"Thank you for the lead, Elias and the cod cakes were delicious."

"House specialty, my good man."

Two hours later Stephen emerges from the tailor with a new set of clothes—a deep blue suit with matching pants that the nice old man had made for another customer who passed away before he could take delivery. Luckily, he was nearly Stephen's size. The sleeves are a little short but the reduced cost couldn't be beat. He stops at the barber after and his beard is trimmed nicely. The barber offered to pull any troublesome teeth at the same time but Stephen declined.

"I hope Sarah likes this new version of me," he says eyeing his reflection.

He wanders along the harbor absorbing the activity of the waterfront. Street vendors display everything from vegetables, eggs, and household items. He stops at one wagon to review their selection of paper. They don't have any of the sketchbooks he likes but the hunched-over woman tells him she can order one from Boston for him.

He makes his way past multiple boat builders before finding Chapman's—it's bustling. The massive skeleton of a new schooner takes up the entire yard. Carpenters crawl over it like ants—measuring, sanding and cutting lumber for the hull.

Stephen settles in on a granite block and spends a few hours drawing the magnificent internal structure of the vessel and the men working on it.

CHAPTER 29

Taylor hears mumbling outside. He rolls over on the cot until they get louder and louder and he can't deny that they are voices.

"I told you I saw a light. There's someone in the shanty."

"Oh shit." He knew it was too good to be true. He had such a nice warm night and was hoping to spend at least one more before he headed back to Portsmouth. He was even planning on doing a little fishing in the morning. It feels kind of good to be off the whiskey for a bit.

He grabs his hat and coat and is out the back window before the owners enter the front door.

The woods are dark and it's getting cold. It's unlikely that he'll locate another building before morning, so he finds a crook in a rock and covers himself with leaves.

He's not that far from Eliot, Maine. He can catch a ride down the Piscataqua River to Portsmouth in the morning.

The bitch had died before she told him where the money was. All she said was that it was buried near Concord in a town called Gonic. He was beginning to think that wasn't the truth. Maybe she and the old fat madam were in it together—just trying to humiliate him—laughing at him as they sat on all that money or silver or gold or whatever it is.

Odette—that's who he needs to see—demand that she show him where the money is. He rubs his hands together wondering if they were large enough to fit around her fat neck.

He figures that he still has some time before the whore's body is found—if it ever is. He threw her off the drawbridge near the tavern. The water was rushing so hard that he's sure she's out to sea by now.

The apple girl.

That's another story. She must have squawked like a cat in heat.

Nobody knows him in that town. At least he has that going for him.

CHAPTER 30

Orla's bruises fade enough for her to go to church on Sunday. As per usual Da yelled after her as she left the house that she'd better be not to be late cooking his dinner.

They used to go to her aunt's house on Sundays for dinner but that stopped after Fiona yelled at Da one too many times about his drinking.

He's done with church anyway—and his sister.

Now he stays home and Orla goes to church with her cousins.

She walks into the small house across the river and her aunt holds her face in her hands and frowns. "It looks like you've healed up a wee bit."

"Yes, Auntie Fi."

"Don't worry my dear. Soon you'll be old enough to marry and you can leave your da's house for good."

Orla forces a smile. There's no way she'd ever follow her mother's footsteps and marry a drunkard like her father. Her poor mother. Buried before she was thirty with a string of dead babies in her wake. Orla was the fifth of eight and the only one to make it to age three.

The doctor said it was pneumonia that finally got her.

Orla wasn't so sure.

She seemed like she was just too tired and sad to go on.

After she died, Da started drinking in earnest. His eyes filled with contempt whenever he looked at his daughter. Anger at night gave way to sorrow in the morning. He would apologize for hitting her but did nothing to change his habits, so the pattern continued.

The Catholic church in South Berwick has no priest so they take the wagon to St. Theobald's in Dover. Her three small cousins play in the back as Orla sits between her aunt and uncle on the buckboard.

"What I don't understand is why your da didn't take you to the police. Didn't he believe you?" her uncle asks.

She shifts in her seat. "I didn't tell him."

"What? Why, Orla?" Fi asks.

"It just seemed easier not to, Aunt Fi. He'd only think I was lying anyway."

"Didn't he say anything about the shiner you had?" Fi asks.

"He thought he did it himself," the girl replies. "I didn't even have to lie. The morning after the attack he just started telling me how sorry he was."

"I think we should tell the police even if Colm doesn't know about it," her uncle Dan offers. "This man seems very dangerous. They should be told. What if he hurts some other girl? I mean, if you hadn't got away…"

They didn't need to warn her about the man.

Orla's nightmares were filled with what could have been.

She knew about rape.

She learned about it firsthand when she walked in on the priest and her dying mother.

Father Bligh just stared at her and turned back to what he was doing. Her father, drunk and absorbed in his own grief barely looked up from his bottle when she ran to him. Does he even remember it now?

At least Orla doesn't need to see that priest at church anymore. He was found dead soon thereafter and the South Berwick parish was closed until a replacement could be sent. Apparently, this is not a priority for the diocese as it has been two years since Bligh's death. The congregation has been trekking the five miles to Dover ever since.

"Orla, your father hasn't touched you in any other way has he?" Fiona asks.

Her face turns red. "No," she shakes her head. "Just the whippings."

Fi looks at her not sure if she believes her. "That poor Evelyn Shaunessey. Pregnant by her own da at age 13. You know you can tell me if anything like that ever happens, right?"

"I know," Orla says. "He's never done anything. I swear." And if he did she would pull the kitchen knife out from under her pillow and stick it in his eye. She was a fighter—not like that pale, lump-of-pudding Evelyn.

"I guess someone always has it worse. She was never quite right in the head that one," Dan says. "The whole Shaunessey family never seemed to be all there."

"At least Evelyn seems to have a happy demeanor," Fi adds.

"I just wish your brother could find his way out of this," Dan says. "He was such a fine young man—so much promise when he and Rosie first came from Sligo."

They pull up in front of the large brick church. The adults are whispering to each other on the steps as the children chase each other around the church yard.

"What's going on?" Dan asks Maeve Crowley as he unloads Brendan, Aidy and Maddie from the wagon.

"Oh Dan, it's awful," she replies holding an embroidered handkerchief to her eyes. "They found a body in Little Bay—a young woman. I heard that she was strangled."

"Holy mother of God!" Fiona exclaims. "When did this happen, Maeve?"

"Thursday. From what I hear Sheriff Allgood and Doc Churchill brought her to Dover."

Orla, Dan and Fiona all freeze.

"Why?" Maeve asks looking at their ashen faces. "Did you see something?"

"We'd better go to the sheriff," Dan says. "I don't care what Colm says."

CHAPTER 31

Sarah straightens the little boy's tie as he asks, "Why are we going to church? We never go to church—unless it's Christmas—it's not Christmas, is it? I mean you'd tell me, right?"

She smiles. "No Jonah, it's not Christmas. Your momma just seems to think it's a good idea for us to get some religious education."

"Isn't she your momma too?"

Sarah laughs. "I guess some days she is and some days she isn't."

"What do I get for going to church?" the boy asks folding his arms across his chest.

"You'll need to negotiate that with Momma."

"Negotiate what?" Jess asks as she emerges from the bedroom. She points to her back and Sarah tightens her corset.

"Nah thinks he deserves a treat for attending church today. I told him that being in the sight of God is enough reward for any of us." Sarah says as she smiles sweetly at Jess.

"Well ordinarily I would agree with your sister, Nah, but I was thinking that we could go to the waterfront and look at the boatyards. Maybe we could even get some scones afterwards."

"Yay!" He runs to get his best clothes on.

"Hmmm," Sarah says smirking. "Scones. Just like I thought. Maybe a little guilt going on this morning? You didn't mention a certain new member of our community."

"Oh, shut your mouth," Jess says laughing. "It's probably all for nothing anyway. You'd better get dressed if you're joining us."

"I wouldn't miss this for the world." She scurries into her room for her best Sunday dress—a yellow affair with small blue flowers embroidered around the neckline.

They walk together around the block to the front of the church on Piper Street. It looks like everyone in town is milling outside on the steps.

Mrs. Markwart greets them.

"Why is it so crowded?" Sarah asks.

"Apparently, everyone is as excited as we are to meet the future Mrs. Reverend Hobson," the widow replies.

Sarah winks at Jess. "Is that so, Mrs. Markwart?"

"Usually, there are half as many here on Sunday. I must confess that I myself have been known to attend at the West Church of late." She whispers, "Reverend Cheney is a far superior orator."

Sarah wonders if Cheney ever orates about birds.

They manage to get the last seats in the back row. Jonah sits between Mrs. Markwart and Sarah on the hard wooden pew. "Stop fidgeting," she whispers to her little brother.

"I'm so bored!"

"It hasn't even started yet," Sarah says.

Mrs. Markwart leans down and whispers in his ear. Sarah hears something about Jack and cookies. He's ramrod-straight all of a sudden and doesn't make a move until the service starts when he dozes off—his head in Sarah's lap.

Jess nervously plays with her gloves—pulling them further and further up her arms. "What the hell am I doing here?" she thinks.

The reverend introduces a smiling Maryanne to the crowd.

Their eyes meet and the stranger from Boston tilts her head. Jess swears that she even winks at her before seating herself in the front row.

The dowagers look askance at Jonah with his head in Sarah's lap but Jess is relieved that he's sleeping. Her face feels flush and she's certain that it must be bright red. This is all very confusing. She stares at the back of Maryanne's black bonnet and tidy bun at the nape of her pale neck.

Her mind swims and she barely hears the reverend's monotonous voice in the background.

"Once again it has been proven that a life outside of God—a life of debauchery and sin—results in horrible, painful, death. Suzanne, the prostitute, has reaped what she sowed. My soul lies in anguish over the many who have sinned and not repented the impurity in which they have indulged. Let it be a lesson to us all!"

Jess is jarred back to reality. Why is he saying this? Word spread faster than she thought it would.

"He's actually pretending to weep!" Sarah whispers to her. "It must be a show for the new wifey. What a holy poker."

The reverend drones on for an hour and even with this salacious material half the congregants are dozing off by the end. Jess's eyes stay glued to the back of Maryanne's head.

After the service, Maryanne and the reverend stand on opposite sides of the doorway to greet the flock. The dowagers linger and cluck over Maryanne—asking her all sorts of personal questions about her and the reverend.

Finally they dissipate and Maryanne takes Jess's hand. She looks into her eyes. "So kind of you to come today, Miss Jakes."

The smaller woman takes her other hand and Jess feels a piece of paper. She slips it into her bag as they walk away. She looks back to see Mrs. Markwart and the Springers greet the new resident.

The family makes their way around the block home stopping to say hello to Putt, at work fighting to contain the torrent of leaves in the wind.

CHAPTER 32

Dewitt Taylor's luck is starting to change. He makes it to Eliot and first thing catches a ride on a gundalow loaded with masts. The crew speaks a different language—something European. He doesn't speak anything but English—and some would even question his skill at that.

If the boatmen notice anything amiss about his ragged state or his smell, they say nothing. He sits downwind on a pile of timber for the short voyage to Portsmouth. The tide is running out and even before the sail is fully up the boat picks up speed along the Piscataqua River towards Portsmouth.

"There's no way that whore's body isn't in the middle of the ocean by now," he thinks as he watches the landscape sweep by. He hears the West Church bells ring one o'clock as they pull up to the dock at Chapman's boatyard.

He needs to find a safe place to stay so he can get cleaned up and maybe find something to eat. The Coxe Boarding House is out. He's sure the woman would scream bloody murder about her wagon, the horse and the money he owes her. She'd turn him into the police—or worse. Mrs. Coxe runs that house with an iron fist. He could see her pulling out a shotgun and shooting him on the spot. Maybe he should go to his favorite whorehouse, Sally Lightfoot's—hand jobs for a quarter—baths in almost clean water for five cents—but he doesn't have a quarter. He does have a dime! At least he can get a bath and maybe a drink. He puts his hand in his pocket and feels for the coin.

"Goddammit!" he squawks as his finger pushes through a hole. An elderly woman and her middle-aged daughter scowl and cross the street to avoid him.

He walks towards the South End where he spots a plump servant girl leaving one of the smaller houses with a basket. He watches as she crosses the garden and walks up the alley towards the center of town.

There doesn't appear to be anyone else around, so he slips into the kitchen through the back door. He helps himself to some of the loaf of crusty bread and cheese that must be the remainder of dinner. With a cup of ale in hand he heads up the stairs to find some clothes to steal.

"Miriam? Is that you? Back so soon from the apothecary? Did they have my tonic?"

Taylor stops short on the stairs.

An old woman.

He looks around the corner and sees her stockinged feet poking out from the blankets at the end of the bed. He's not likely to find any men's clothes in her room so he drops to the floor and scurries by the doorway.

"Oh, it must be the cat. That damn Miriam was supposed to let you out before she left."

Taylor slips into the second room. He catches a glimpse of himself in the mirror of a large carved rosewood wardrobe. His beard has patches of mud. He picks some twigs out of his hair. His scratch is now a festering wound. He'll need to wash up in the kitchen before the servant girl returns. He can't walk around Portsmouth like this.

He opens the armoire to find a rainbow of men's topcoats and vests. A drawer yields striped pants. He puts on the least brightly colored ensemble—a green coat and orange striped pants— and studies his image in the mirror. He looks ridiculous but at least these aren't covered in shit and dirt.

He hears the old woman snoring as he sneaks past her open door.

In the kitchen he pumps some water into the basin, washes his face and runs water through his hair. He wishes he could afford a shave. He unbuttons his pants to wash his privates.

"What are you doing wearing Mister Wilson's circus costume?"

The girl has returned.

"Oh, he said that I could borrow it."

She frowns. "Mr. Wilson has been dead for ten years. How could he have said that?"

"We'll I guess he won't care if I take them then," he answers.

"I don't think Mrs. Wilson would like that," she says clutching the basket.

"The old bat upstairs? She's fine with it. Say, what's your name?"

The girl looks down. "Miriam."

"And how old are you?" Taylor edges towards her.

"Fourteen."

"You're so pretty."

She turns red and hugs the basket rattling the small bottles of tonic.

"I'd better get this medicine up to Mrs. Wilson."

"Oh, don't worry about her. She's sawing logs up there."

"What? She's chopping wood?"

"No, she's sleeping. You never heard that before." He grins exposing a row of blackened teeth.

"I think you should go now. The Mrs. will be awake and wanting her tonic any minute.

Taylor steps towards her.

She puts the basket on the wooden table and backs towards the door. She's barely able to let out a yelp before he's on top of her—stuffing the wash rag into her mouth.

"Miriam? What's going on down there?"

CHAPTER 33

Mrs. Allgood opens the kitchen door and eyes Dan and Orla suspiciously. "May I help you?"

"Hello ma'am. My name is Dan O'Reilly, and this is my niece, Orla Flaherty. We need to report a crime."

The round woman wipes the flour off of her hands and sighs, "And what type of crime would that be?"

"My niece here was attacked by a man and tossed into a wagon," Dan says as he takes Orla's hand.

The heavyset woman's eyes narrow and she removes her apron. These Irish always have some urgent drama that causes her husband no end of grief.

She leads Dan and Orla into the small but tidy parlor. "The sheriff is having a nap. He'll be cross if I wake him up."

"I think perhaps you should ma'am," Dan says.

She rolls her eyes. "All right, if you think it's that urgent."

"We do. This happened on the same day they found that poor lady's body in the water."

Her eyes open wide.

"I'll wake him up now." She scurries up the staircase to the small bedroom. The sheriff snores—his head covered with the quilt. She hits him with the backside of her hand until he mutters, "Jesus, woman. What's the matter? Is the house on fire?"

She frowns. "No but I might just burn it to the ground unless you get up and come to the parlor. There's sheriff business afoot."

"All right! All right! I'll be right down. Can you cook me some eggs and beans for breakfast?"

"Breakfast came and went two hours ago. There's some bread scraps and butter if you like." She turns on her heel and leaves him looking dazed on the side of the bed.

After a few minutes Sheriff Allgood pads downstairs in his ragged socks. He looks different than usual—dressed in a plaid robe and rumpled work-man's pants. Orla tightens her grip on Dan's hand.

"So, you went away with this strange man?" These Irish girls were known to have loose morals—something in their upbringing—maybe it's all of those potatoes.

"No sir. He hit me and threw me in the wagon," she answers quietly leaning into her uncle.

"What were you doing to make him do that?" His eyes narrow and he blows his nose loudly into his red handkerchief.

"Um, nothing sir. I was walking with a basket of apples in Rollinsford—near the bridge to South Berwick."

"The Salmon Falls bridge," Dan offers.

"Hmmm." He looks Orla up and down. Red hair, freckles. Too skinny for his taste.

"Were you dressed like you are now?" he asks.

"Um, no sir. This is my Sunday dress." Actually, it was her mother's Sunday dress—two sizes too big. "I was wearing my regular clothes."

"I'm sorry sheriff but I don't see why any of this information matters," Dan says. "My niece was attacked, and we just want to report it. We thought maybe it's the same man responsible for the poor lady who was found in the bay?"

Mrs. Allgood hands her husband a paper and a pencil. "Maybe you should ask them to write down their names and addresses," she nudges. "It might be helpful if you need to contact them later."

He frowns but passes the paper to Dan.

"OK. Write your name and address here. If we need anything more, I'll let you know."

"Don't you even want to hear how she escaped?" Dan asks.

He scratches his belly and rolls his eyes. His wife clears her throat and pokes his shoulder.

"Oh, sure. How did she escape?" he asks.

Dan looks at Orla who shakes her head. She's too scared to speak.

"I guess the man ate too many apples and got the shits," he starts. "She ran away while he was crapping in the woods. It sounds like it was just beyond the edge of town."

"Oh really? The shits?" he chuckles. That detail will make for good fodder tomorrow when he's at lunch with his pals. Now all he wants is to get back upstairs and nurse his banging head. "Hm. South Berwick. That's in Maine so I guess this isn't my problem. Thanks for letting us know." The sheriff shuffles them through the kitchen to the back door.

"But she was kidnapped in New Hampshire—in Rollinsford like we said. Doesn't that mean anything?" Dan asks.

The sheriff looks to his wife. She shrugs in response.

"Don't you worry. We'll take care of it." He closes the door and turns back into the kitchen to see his wife frowning at him—her arms crossed over her apron.

"Do you think it's related to the murder?" she asks.

"The murder?"

"Yes Tom, the body you rescued the other day? The one we just talked about."

"Oh! Hadn't thought of that. Maybe so."

She smiles and rolls her eyes. Sometimes she thinks she'd make a much better sheriff than her husband.

CHAPTER 34

Taylor stops behind the privy and drinks two of the bottles of tonic. He feels much better now. The girl, the food and now the tonic. Two more bottles go down smooth as silk. He stuffs the rest into the many pockets of the bright green coat.

He stumbles out of the kitchen garden and into the alley where he collapses face first into a pile of horse manure.

"Mama, there's a clown in the alley."

"You're so funny, Janie. Now why would there be a clown in the road?"

"I don't know but I think he's dead," the young girl points to the colorful pile not twenty feet away.

Mrs. Couture turns around from her weeding and sure enough there's a man dressed in a green topcoat and orange striped pants lying in a mound of horse shit in the alley.

"Oh, dear God! Janie, run and get the police."

She walks to the body and pokes him with her lace up pointed boot. A groan. "Not dead after all," she thinks.

She hears weak crying from the house. "Mrs. Wilson? Where is her girl Miriam?"

Leaving the man where he lays, she crosses the garden and enters the kitchen.

Miriam is on the floor. Her eyes and mouth are wide open in a frozen expression of terror. Her skirt is up around her waist and her bloomers are ripped and bloodied beside her.

CHAPTER 35

After church Jess, Sarah and Nah return to the house to pack their picnic basket. With winter coming they know to take advantage of every nice day.

Putt is working in the yard of the rectory continuing his battle against the mass of orange maple leaves.

"Hello, Miss Jessamyn. Sarah. Jonah."

"Hi, Putt!" Nah says. "Can I help you rake the leaves?"

"OK."

Putt stands behind the small boy and helps him put the leaves into a wagon. "You're pretty strong there, Nah. I think you're much stronger than the last time you helped me."

Jonah beams.

They stop in a small park on Edwards Street to eat their dinner of cold chicken, cheese and bread. Jess even packed some cookies that Mrs. Markwart gave to her. There are a few other families enjoying the unseasonably warm weather and Jonah scurries off to play ball with a gaggle of small children. They hear him take over the game—making more and more complicated rules until chaos reigns and the youngsters are running around the park imitating farm animals.

"The captain's house looks so nice," Sarah says pointing to a brick structure with a courtyard across the street.

"It does. It must be one of the most elegant homes in town."

"Have you been inside, Jess?"

"No. He hasn't been home since it was finished three years ago," she replies taking a drink of cider.

"Who are you talking about?" Nah asks breathing heavily from running around and bossing the smaller children.

"Captain Pritchard. We live in his momma's house," Sarah says.

"Why do we live in somebody else's house?" the boy asks.

"The captain hired us to find some stolen things," Jess answers. "His momma died soon after we finished with the case and he gave us the house as payment."

"Is he a real sea captain?" Nah asks with his eyes open wide.

"That he is," Jessamyn replies, "He's gone a lot of the time—sometimes for years traveling all over the world."

"Is he having adventures?"

"Probably some," Jess laughs.

"I want to be a sea captain and have adventures," Jonah declares.

"I'm sure that you will, Nah," Jess says as she makes a futile attempt to smooth down his unruly curls.

"Did he know that other captain from that picture we saw at the library?" the boy asks grabbing a cookie and shoving it into his mouth.

"I don't know, Nah. Maybe you can ask him sometime. By the looks of all the activity he should be home any day now."

They watch the steady stream of workmen go in and out.

"You'd think that he'd have taken a wife by now," Sarah muses.

"Maybe he will now that he has the grand house. Maybe he'll court someone when he is home."

Jess stands and smooths her skirt.

"I'd better be off to see Odette. Let's meet back here in an hour. If you two could pick up the picnic, that would be wonderful."

Jonah moans at the request. He lets Jess kiss him goodbye before she turns towards the brothel.

"C'mon Nah," Sarah says. "We'll have this tidied up shortly and be on our way. Let's go to the water and look at some boats. Maybe we'll even see a selkie."

"Are selkies real?" Nah asks.

"You mean do they turn into humans and eat small boys?" she says. "I think they do."

"You're lying. Seals do not eat small boys, Sarah."

"Suit yourself, Nah. Just to be safe I'd stick close to me. You look pretty delicious."

He frowns at her but slips his hand into hers just to be safe as she picks up the basket.

Jess's thoughts keep returning to Maryanne as she walks down tree lined Mason Street.

Granny greets her at the door.

"Miss Jessamyn! Somebody killed Mrs. Wilson's girl, Miriam. Miss Odette wants me to go see what's happening."

The small girl starts to cry, her strawberry blonde hair sticking to her ruddy cheeks.

Jess gives her a hug and brushes her hair out of her eyes. "Don't worry, Granny. I'll go with you."

They hitch up their skirts and run the two blocks to the Wilson's. Granny struggles to keep up with her ill-fitting shoes.

In the melee around the house it's hard to see what's going on. The crowd circles around a man dressed in bright clothes.

Taylor.

It's him all right. Two of the Portsmouth cops hold him by the arms. He looks like a scarecrow—his legs not up to the task of keeping him upright. A few bottles of tonic fall out of his pocket and smash onto the ground.

Jess pushes her way to the front of the crowd and talks to one of the policemen, Gerald Emerson.

"Awful mess, Miss Jessamyn. A dead girl and this half dead suspect."

Jess picks up Taylor's chin. He's breathing heavily and barely conscious. The scratch Suzanne gave him is festering.

"Why would he be dressed like that?" Emerson asks her.

"Old Mr. Wilson owned a circus and animal show at one time," Jess replies. "His wife must have kept some of his costumes after he died. I guess Taylor was looking for clothes and stole them."

She turns to her young friend. "You wait outside, Granny. I'm just going to have a look in the kitchen." The girl whimpers but stands to the side as she was told.

Jess slips through the yard and into the house where she finds Miriam.

She bears little resemblance to the body the neighbor found earlier. Coins hold her eyes closed. Her hands are placed over her heart and her skirt is pulled down. "Some good Samaritan ruining the evidence," Jess thinks to herself. She sees angry purple bruising on Miriam's neck and chest. Opening her eyes, she sees the same blood that Doc. Churchill had showed her on Suzanne.

She hears a whimper from behind her. It's Granny at the door. "Is she really dead?" she whispers.

"I'm afraid so, Granny." She leaves Miriam and takes the Irish girl's hand. "Let's get out of here so the police can do their work."

After a much-heated discussion in the street it's decided that Balche and Palfrey will take Taylor to the jailhouse at Puddle Dock. Some of the residents are in favor of hanging him right there from the tree in Mrs. Wilson's garden. Cooler heads prevail, and the police lead him towards the waterfront.

Chief Skelton tells Gerry Emerson to remain behind to interview any possible witnesses.

Jess likes the affable cop even if he's only marginally competent. He was a frequent customer of hers back in the day. He seems shaken up by the morning. It was probably him who cleaned up Miriam.

"Gerry, you'd better keep a hold of him tight. He's a dangerous man with nothing to lose. That's two girls he's killed already."

"Two? You mean Suzanne? But wasn't that in Little Bay?" He seems to have just dawned on him that murderers can move from town to town.

"He was the last one seen with her before she died," she reminds him.

"Oh dear. That's right."

"Odette will need to visit the jailhouse if she wants to speak to Taylor now," Jess says to herself. She walks back towards her young friend sniffling at the edge of the crowd.

"Granny, you're very brave to come here with me. I'm proud of you."

She nods. "Yes, ma'am." The young girl tries not to sob.

"I'm meeting my daughter and son but can walk with you back to the house afterwards if you like." She puts her hand on Granny's shoulder.

"Thank you, Miss Jess. That man has been to see Odette. I can't believe he killed those girls. What if he tries to murder me?"

"You've seen him at the house? Recently?" Jess asks.

"Yes, a couple of times. He was there just last week."

Jess hugs her. "He can't hurt you now, Granny. The police will have him locked up soon."

They follow the crowd towards the water.

CHAPTER 36

N ah and Sarah wander towards the boatyards. The small boy pelts her with questions not waiting for her to respond. Finally he declares, "When I'm a sea captain I'm going to Africa and Antarctica and maybe even Portland."

"Wow! Portland even! That sounds very adventurous, Nah."

"Which one is farthest?"

"I think probably Antarctica."

"That's where they have the penguins right?"

"That's right," she answers as they dodge a wagon filled with pots and pans making its way down the alley.

"Do they have penguins in Africa, Sarah?"

"Nope—too hot there. Penguins need snow and ice—except for Galapgos penguins—but those are the only kind of warm water penguins."

Jonah stares at his sister.

"We have snow and ice, Sarah. How come we don't have regular penguins or those other kinds of penguins?" he asks.

"I don't know, Nah," she laughs. "I'll look it up and will let you know."

They turn a corner and see a man sitting on a lobster trap drawing.

"Stephen?"

He looks up from his notebook and his face flushes.

"Sarah!" He wasn't expecting to see her, and he's rattled. It takes him a minute to stop sputtering and speak. "I'm so glad you're here."

Nah wraps himself around Stephen's legs.

"Hey there, little man. I'm happy to see you too."

Sarah is puzzled. "I thought you were going back to the Goat Island Tavern. What happened to your job?"

"Well, that's a long story. I'm here looking for work at one of the boat builders."

"Oh." She seems wary. "What are you doing with that notebook?"

"I'm drawing the wharf."

"You can draw? Let me see." She snaps the book from his hands and pages through looking at his sketches.

"You didn't tell me that you could draw. Now I feel stupid for showing you my pictures. They must have seemed so amateurish."

"No, Sarah! No," he stumbles. "You're amazing."

She stops when she comes to his drawing of her complete with heart shaped birthmark and the beginning of cleavage.

"That's you!" Nah exclaims.

Now it's Sarah who's embarrassed. She quickly hands the book back to Stephen.

"Good luck with your job. Let's go Jonah."

"Wait! Wait a minute. May I buy you dinner? I'm staying at the Codfish and the food is really good."

"We've eaten," she replies.

Stephen searches for something that will make them stay. "They have cake for dessert today."

"Cake? Please Sarah!" Jonah begs.

She inhales. What's the harm in a little cake? "We only have a half an hour before we need to meet up with Jess."

Stephen smiles. "A half an hour is perfect."

The three make their way the few blocks to the inn and Stephen holds open the black-lacquered wooden door for them to enter.

Nah is beside himself with excitement. "I've never been to an inn before! Can I see your room?"

"Maybe later," Sarah says looking around. She's never been to an inn either. She's never really been anywhere except the Athenaeum and home—if you don't count Odette's or her life before that.

They sit at a sunny table near the front window. Trask emerges from the kitchen wiping his hands on a white cloth and gives them hand-written menus.

"Hello Stephen. Who do we have here? New friends?"

"No," he smiles patting Sarah's hand. "Old friends. This is Sarah and Jonah Jakes."

"We live on Holt Street," Nah pipes up.

"Jakes? Are you related to Jessamyn?"

Sarah looks at her menu. She hopes Trask doesn't know Jess from the whorehouse.

"That's our momma," Nah answers. "Sarah is adopted. That's why she's a different color than me."

"Miss Jessamyn helped me out with something once. She's a great investigator. Please send my regards to her. I'm Elias Trask."

"We will Mr. Trask," Sarah says with her eyes glued to the menu.

"Now what can I get for you?"

"Cake!" Nah exclaims.

"One piece will do," Sarah says. "We'll share."

"Nonsense," Stephen says. "We'll have one each of the apple, parsnip and the pound cake."

Sarah tilts her head and looks at him. After Trask departs for the kitchen she asks, "How is it that a tavern helper can afford to buy cake for three and stay at a nice place like this?"

"The Simpsons paid me," Stephen stops short. Maybe it's not such a good idea to tell Sarah about their arrangement and that his child will be born in a few short months. That might be off putting to some girls.

Sarah looks suspicious but doesn't say anything. After all, she has her own set of secrets.

"I brought some coffee and milk for you also," Trask says as he places the tray onto their table. Nah's eyes grow huge. He's never seen anything so fancy. Cake with buttery frosting. He lunges towards it with his fork nearly impaling Stephen's hand.

"Hold on, Nah. Wait until it's served to you," Sarah scolds him.

Too late. He already has a bite of the parsnip cake in his mouth. His eyes light up and a huge smile crosses his face.

"You should let Stephen choose first. He's the host."

"Why don't we have some of each kind?" Stephen suggests. "That way we all get to try them."

"Shall I bring you some more plates?" Trask asks.

"No, we'll just share these," Stephen says.

Sarah would prefer her own plate.

She sips her coffee and lets Nah and Stephen dive in. "Aren't you going to have any?" Nah asks as he drops a dollop of frosting into his lap.

"That's all right, Nah. I'm happy to watch you enjoy it."

"That's nonsense." Stephen scoops up a bite of the apple and holds it in front of her face. She opens her mouth slowly and he slides the fork in.

She stares into his eyes.

She starts to sweat even though they are nowhere near the fire.

"We really need to go," she says.

Stephen and Nah are crestfallen. "But we haven't finished our cake yet," Nah pleads.

"You finish and I'll wait outside on the bench." She moves to the door.

As she waits for Nah, she tries to collect her thoughts. Why is Stephen here? How come he drew that picture of her? How does he have the money to stay in a nice place like this? She inhales deeply. She still remembers his smell from the night they met. She licks her lips and tastes the sweet cake.

A crowd of people comes rushing from the east. In the front is a man dressed like a clown being dragged by two of Portsmouth's finest. He's having trouble keeping up and keeps falling on his knees.

It's Taylor.

She only saw him once—the day he tried to strangle Daisy. She'll never forget those cold eyes.

She sees Jess and the girl from Odette's towards the back of the crowd and waves to them.

"What's going on? Why is Taylor dressed like that?" Sarah asks.

"He's done it again," Jess whispers. "Another girl—Miriam."

"Miriam? Is that one of Wilson's circus costumes."

"It is. He must have stolen it. Maybe Miriam interrupted him—or he waited for her. I don't know."

She doesn't have time to elaborate as Stephen and Nah emerge from the inn.

"Stephen?" she asks.

"Hello, Miss Jessamyn. How are you?"

"We had cake, Momma!" Nah exclaims.

"Oh, my goodness. Cake." Her eyes move from Stephen to Sarah.

"Who are you?" Jonah asks as he points at the red eyed Granny.

"Um, this is Granny, a friend of mine."

The small girl smiles weakly. Nobody as important as Miss Jess ever called her a friend before.

Nah frowns but loses interest in the excitement. "What's going on?" he asks. "Why is that man dressed like that? Why does everyone look so cross?"

"Jonah, would you mind walking your sister home? I have a few more errands to run here in town."

"If Stephen comes too. Otherwise I'm not budging."

Jess tries to read her daughter's face. She would prefer it that the young man accompanied them—no matter how uncomfortable Sarah might be. Who knows what's likely to happen here?

"I'm sure Mr. Bailey has other important business to attend to," Sarah starts, "like drawing and other things he hasn't mentioned before."

"Who's Mr. Bailey?" Nah asks.

"That's me, little man," Stephen says as he points to his chest with his thumb. "I seem to have the afternoon free. I'd be happy to accompany you all home."

"Thank you, Stephen," Jess says. "I should be back soon."

Sarah scowls at her mother as she turns with the others towards Holt Street.

CHAPTER 37

They walk along the tree lined street towards the house. Granny says, "Thank you for bringing me back," as she trips over a root protruding from the brick walkway.

"Are your shoes a little big for you, Granny?"

"Um, yes ma'am. They were Suzanne's—you know the girl who died."

"I'll check at home. I may have an old pair of Sarah's that will fit you. In the meantime, just be careful."

"Thank you, Miss Jess. I will."

"Say Granny, do you like working for Odette?"

"It's not too bad. Mostly I help Moira in the kitchen. She's very nice and even gives me extra biscuits."

"That Moira is a miracle worker when it comes to biscuits."

Granny laughs and her smile returns.

"Do you know what the girls do upstairs?" Jess asks.

"They entertain the men."

"Do you know what that means, Granny?"

"I think so. I saw two dogs rutting out the back door and Moira told me that is what the girls get paid for."

"Sometimes, yes."

"I'm never doing that—for money or not."

"You'd be surprised what you'll do when desperate enough," Jess thinks to herself. "Let's hope it doesn't come to that."

They turn up the walkway and Odette stands waiting for them on the back porch. She spits a stream of tobacco across the porch and crosses her arms.

"It's about fucking time you got here." Jess isn't sure if the old madam is talking to her or Granny quivering beside her. "Was Mrs. Wilson's girl Miriam murdered by Taylor this morning?"

"Yes, Odette, he was caught leaving the house. More accurately he passed out in a pile of horse manure in the alley. Mrs. Couture found the poor girl on the kitchen floor."

"Miriam looked so scary," Granny starts to cry again.

"Jesus Christ, child! Go back to the kitchen," the old madam shrieks.

Granny looks at Jess.

"It's OK, Granny. I'll stop by and see you before I leave."

The girl moves towards the stairs.

"Odette, you really don't need to be such a bitch all the time—and you're really going to let that child run around in Suzanne's massive shoes? What is wrong with you? She'll trip and kill herself on the stairs."

"Never mind that shit! Where is he?" She looks outside the door checking left and right.

"He's in police custody."

"Pffft! That will do no fucking good at all."

"What do you mean?" Jess watches her pasty face turn slowly red.

"Um, I just mean that they're so incompetent—he's likely to be out within the hour."

She opens the door to the nearly empty waiting parlor. "Everyone get the hell out of here! We're closed until tomorrow."

"But I already paid," says Smitty Johnson. "Can I have a refund?"

"Come back tomorrow," Odette mumbles as she shoves him out the door.

"Granny, go upstairs and tell the girls that we're closed. Nobody is to leave the building."

"Yes, ma'am." She scurries up the stairs as best she can in her big shoes.

"You come in here with me." Odette drags Jess into the parlor. "Have you seen Taylor yet?"

Jess shakes her head. "No. I came here after Granny and I checked out the Wilson house. He was on his way to the station with the crowd."

"I need you to talk to him. I need to know why he killed Suzanne and what he learned," the madam whispers.

"What he learned about what, Odette?" Jess asks.

"I hired Suzanne and Taylor to retrieve some of my personal property. I have to know if they found it."

"Why would you send the two of them retrieve anything of value? I mean Suzanne was an opium addict and Taylor was—after all—Taylor."

She looks at Jess her face in a twisted grimace usually reserved for profound indigestion. "Suzanne had knowledge that she was unwilling to share. I thought Taylor would be able to get it out of her."

"Why would you trust a mutton nob like Taylor to come back with the property?"

"I didn't. I put certain safeguards in place." Odette puts a wad of tobacco in her cheek and pokes into place with her tongue.

"Ah. I see," Jess starts, "so that's why you hired me. To follow them and take possession of whatever it is and bring it back to you."

The older woman smiles showing her stained teeth.

"You didn't give a holy poker about Suzanne, did you Odette?"

"That's not fair. I let her stay here long after her usefulness—and her looks were gone from the opium."

"Only because she knew something. How did Suzanne come by this information anyway?" Jess asks.

"I sent her to the Shoals with a customer and she was supposed to come back and report what she learned. She returned and refused to tell me what I wanted to know."

Jess slumps into the worn settee. "You got her started on the opium when she came back from that weekend, didn't you?"

"I didn't have to try very hard."

Jess starts to lose her temper but changes the subject. "What are we talking about here, anyway? Some kind of jewels or coins?"

Odette sits heavily on the settee. "It doesn't matter. Just go talk to Taylor. He's a dumb ass. If he knows anything, you should be able to get it out of him."

"I'll talk to him," Jess says, "and after that, maybe I'll break him out of jail so he can kill your sorry ass."

"No, you won't," Odette smirks. "You're not going to risk your family for that waste of humanity."

CHAPTER 38

S tephen and Sarah walk back to Holt Street in silence. Nah yammers the whole way about his visit to the Atheneaum, the docks, and how the parsnip cake is the best thing he's ever tasted.

They arrive at the house and the boy runs off to help Putt with the leaves.

"So, when do you think you might start your job?" Sarah asks.

"I'm not sure yet. I'm supposed to speak with Trask's brother, Benedict, tomorrow. I don't even know if he'll hire me."

"Why did you quit working at the tavern?"

He touches her shoulder and says softly, "I think you know why, Sarah."

"Well that's just stupid." She hurries off towards the house—her cranberry shawl flowing behind her.

Jonah races after his sister leaving Stephen in the street. Putt stops his raking and stares at him. Stephen turns awkwardly and follows Nah to the house.

Sarah needs to get away from him. To think.

"I'm going to take care of the horses," she says as she grabs a few carrots on the way out the door.

Willie and Buttercup whinny in anticipation of their treat.

"Hello, Mr. President," she says to the gelding. Willie gives her a nuzzle.

"And you, Miss Buttercup, are the belle of the ball as usual."

She turns to see Stephen at the door with a mug of water in his hand. "I thought you might be thirsty."

"Where's Jonah?" she asks.

"He's gone to Mrs. Markwart's to get the dog."

"Sarah?"

"Don't say it," she says.

"I love you."

He puts the tin mug on the half wall.

She flies across the stall and kisses him. Their teeth smash together, and they knock the mug onto the floor where it clangs and bounces scaring the horses.

"Ow," he says. "That smarts a little."

"I'm sorry," she says and looks at the floor. "I don't have much experience with kissing."

"Let's try again," he says and guides her slowly towards him. He gently touches his lips to hers. She tastes the blood where she cut him with her tooth.

They are oblivious to the sounds of the small boy and dog running into the barn.

Jack barks and they jump apart.

Jonah's eyes grow wide. He races for the house and scurries up the stairs.

"Oh mutton nob!" she says.

"What's the matter?"

"Nah. He saw us and is scared."

Stephen pulls her towards him. "He'll be fine. Let's pick up where we left off."

She pushes him away.

"I need to go talk to him," she says as she walks across the garden towards the house. "Wait in the kitchen for me."

Stephen busies himself by stoking the fire. He almost has her—he's sure of it.

Upstairs Sarah finds the boy buried under the blankets with the dog.

"Hey Nah. What are you up to?" Sarah whispers.

A hand reaches out and grabs Mr. Soapy.

"Go away."

"What do you mean? Are you mad that Stephen and I were kissing?"

"He's my friend!"

"Wait—so, you're mad that I was kissing him because he's your friend?"

An affirmative moan comes from below the blankets.

"Well, I'm pretty sure he can be your friend and my friend at the same time."

The dog, tired of being buried in the blankets, wriggles his way from Jonah's grasp and darts out the bedroom door.

"Even the dog hates me," Jonah whimpers.

"Nah honey, we all love you. I'm sorry if we scared you. Kissing is something that grownups do sometimes."

"I've never seen you and Momma kiss like that. You're grownups."

"It's a different kind of kissing when it's your momma. You'll understand one day."

"Does Momma kiss anyone like that?" he asks.

Sarah's head is spinning. This is far too complicated for her to explain. She wishes Jess was back.

"I tell you what. How about you ask Momma about that tonight?" She tries not to sound frustrated.

A dissatisfied murmur comes from the blankets.

"Stephen, Jack and I will be downstairs playing cards. Please join us when you feel up to it."

She pats him on what she thinks is his head and makes her way downstairs.

Stephen has the dog in his lap and has put more water into the kettle.

"How's little man doing?"

"Miffed," she answers.

"At me?"

"Oh no. At me for tainting his friend."

Stephen smiles and grabs her hand pulling her onto his lap displacing an unhappy Jack who scurries from the room.

"Stop it," Sarah says sitting opposite him. She starts shuffling a deck of cards. "Jonah will be down any minute."

The cards fly in a graceful arch landing in a pile that Sarah knocks with her fist, indicating that he should cut them to begin play.

"Wow. You're really good at that," he says. "Where did you learn how to shuffle cards like that?"

"Jess taught me." A complete lie—Jess shuffles like a drunk monkey. She learned to be a dealer at Odette's—trying to avoid the upstairs work.

"You're the most beautiful woman I've ever met," he says.

"Who cares?" Jonah says as he sulks into the room with Jack.

"Should we play Rodeo?" Sarah asks Nah.

The lad seems to emerge a little out of his funk. "OK but I have some new rules. It's not going to be so simple this time."

CHAPTER 39

If Portsmouth puts little or no money into uniforms and salaries for their cops, they put even less into the jail. The town rents the granite basement of the Puddle Dock Warehouse to house criminals. There's no locked door, simply a ladder from the first level which they pull up once the prisoners are in place. It works fine most of the time except for especially high tides when as much as a foot of water seeps though the walls. It's usually occupied by troublesome drunks sleeping it off on one of the scattered wooden pallets.

Jess has been here before but has never actually descended the ladder into the cell.

Gerry Emerson calls to her as soon as she's on the first step. "Miss Jess, thank God you're here. Chief Skelton left me here alone and I have no idea what I'm supposed to do."

"Damned these church clothes," she says as she descends the ladder. "Don't worry, Gerry. I'm here to help."

Taylor looks to be asleep on the pallet. His clothes are filthy, and a pool of urine has formed around him.

"They let all the drunks go when we brought him in," Emerson reports.

"I see. It smells something awful in here," she says as she covers her nose with her handkerchief.

"I know, the chamber pots haven't been emptied. We can't get the woman to come to work since we put Taylor down the hole."

Jess walks across the room being careful to avoid any puddles of questionable origin.

Taylor is hog-tied with his arms and legs fastened together behind his back in the corner of the room.

She leans in for a closer look. He still has manure on his face. "Gerry, could you get me a towel and some water."

"I'm not supposed to leave the prisoner, Miss Jess."

"Don't worry. I'll be here," she says smiling.

As soon as Gerry ascends the ladder she whispers in Taylor's ear, "You evil piece of shit. I'll kill you for what you did to those women. Mark my word, you crupper, you'll never leave here alive."

The prisoner moans but doesn't wake up. He must have drunk a lot of Mrs. Wilson's tonic.

Gerry returns with the water and cloth. "I had to borrow it from next door. We got no pump here."

"Thanks." She bends down and uses the wet towel to roughly wash Taylor's face. "That scratch of yours looks like it is developing a serious infection."

He stirs a bit but doesn't wake up.

She dumps the rest of the water over his head. This has the desired effect and he looks bleary eyed up at her.

"What the fuck?" he asks. "Who are you?"

His eyes come into focus and his mouth widens into a black toothed grin. "Wait I know you. You used to be a whore and now you're some kind of copper."

"Hello Dewitt," she says quietly.

"Are you here to kill me for what I done to that scrawny bitch?"

"Not just yet. First I need some information from you."

Gerry observes the scene from across the room nervously looking up the ladder to be sure nobody is around.

Taylor spits at her.

"Spit all you want you donkey prong—you're still going to answer my questions," she says as she gives him a kick.

"Did that old crone send you?" he asks.

"Which old crone, Dewitt?"

"The painted sow—Odette? I know she's done all this to humiliate me. I'll fucking kill her when I get out of here."

"Ah, Odette," Jess replies. "She was laughing at you, Dewitt. She said you were too much of a dumb ass to ever find the treasure."

With that she steps on his hands.

"Fuck! That hurts! She's the dumb ass, not me," he cries.

"Suzanne told me right before she died that there wasn't any treasure. That it was all a trick to get me away from the girls. I showed that bitch. Fucked her hard as I squeezed the life out of her—right on the bridge."

Jess sees the faces of Suzanne and Miriam and kicks Taylor in his exposed belly.

Gerry yells from across the room, "Miss Jess! Miss Jess! Don't kill him. The Chief will be sore if he's dead before he gets back."

Jess takes a deep breath and steps away from the pallet.

She's shaking so badly that she needs Emerson's help to get up the ladder.

"Thank you, Gerry," she says as he pulls her into the main room of the warehouse.

"Miss Jess? Do you think you'll ever become a whore again?"

She laughs. "No. Those days are over."

Emerson looks sad. "That's too bad. You were nice and always smelled good."

"Thanks," she smiles at him. "How about we keep my visit here a secret?"

"Sure, Miss Jess. I'm not sure who would give a shit anyway. He's likely to be hung by morning once the word gets out."

"Take care, Gerry. He's a dangerous man."

As she walks out the door, she passes Frank Balche carrying the prisoner's meal—two lobsters. She cringes at the sight of them. Big cockroaches—they're only fit for the likes of Taylor.

CHAPTER 40

Jessamyn inhales the cool fresh air—clearing out the stench of the make-shift jail—as she walks the few blocks to Odette's.

Entering the empty kitchen, she sees a pot on the stove that's nearly boiled down. Moira must have stopped cooking supper midstream. Jess picks a cloth off of the wooden chopping block and moves the pot to the granite block near the door.

Noises come from upstairs. Talking? Singing?

She pushes open the door to the parlor. The girls have gotten into the liquor and Moira is leading them all in a singalong of sea shanties. Even Granny looks to be a little drunk.

Savannah sits on her own at a table in the corner slowly sipping her drink.

"Odette gave us the day off!" Essie yells.

Daisy runs over to her and hugs her. "Did you hear Jess, Taylor is dead!"

"That's not quite right. He's in the jailhouse," Jess replies.

"Oh," Daisy frowns. "Odette was screaming about Taylor being a dead man. We thought that meant he was really dead."

"Sorry, not yet," Jess replies as she looks around the room. "The old lady let you drink her liquor?" The madam is meticulous when it comes to dispensing spirits. Everything's marked and logged in her ledger.

"Well, sort of," Daisy giggles.

"Say, where is Odette, anyway?" Jess asks.

"She had Tot get the coach ready and then they headed off somewhere," Granny replies. "She looked to be having a fit. She even left her keys." She points to the open lock on the massive liquor cabinet.

The clock on the wall rings four times. "Granny, you better fill the bottles with water to make up for what you girls drank and get that cabinet back in order before Odette gets back. They'll be hell to pay if everyone's drunk and her supply is depleted."

Moira nods to Granny in agreement, "It was fun while it lasted, though."

Jess leaves out the front door and walks towards Holt Street. She spies Odette and Tot on their way back to the house.

"I hope Granny gets those bottles filled in time. Odette looks like a fisher cat in heat."

Turning the corner she sees Putt sitting on a log in the churchyard with his head in his hands. The leaves blow around him.

"Putt? Is everything OK? You seem out of sorts," she asks.

He shakes his head and wraps his arms around himself.

"Why don't you come with me for supper?" she asks patting his head.

"No, Miss Jessamyn," he replies. "The reverend says I gotta stay right on this log."

"Well at least go inside. You'll freeze to death out here."

She leads the giant of a man to his shed near the rectory, helps him off with his boots and stokes the fire for him.

"Putt, if you ever need anything you know to come see me, right?"

He nods as Jess closes the door to the shed and walks home.

Sarah, Stephen and Jonah have started dinner. Eggs, hot cakes and pan fries. Jonah steals bits of raw onion from the cutting board and feeds them to Jack.

"I can't believe how much that dog likes onions," Jess says as she enters the room. "He's going to have terrible breath."

"Worse than dead fish breath the mutt usually sports?" Sarah asks. "I doubt that."

Jess turns to Stephen. "Thanks for coming back with everyone today."

"Of course, Miss Jessamyn, anytime."

Sarah is unusually quiet throughout dinner. Jess sees her watching Stephen and occasionally blushing.

Jonah doesn't seem to notice and yammers on about the day.

"Don't you think it's time you took the dog back next door, Nah?" Jess asks.

"Awwww. All right. But only if Stephen comes with me."

"Sure, little man."

"He should be going anyway," Sarah says as she opens the front door.

"I'll see you Thursday," he says moving to kiss her. She turns her head so he catches her cheek.

"Thursday?" Jess asks once the door is closed.

"Stephen has asked me to dinner at the inn," Sarah replies.

"That sounds lovely."

Jonah runs back into the house.

"Sarah and Stephen were kissing in the barn," he reports, "and not like when you kiss me, Momma."

Jess looks at her daughter. "Is that so?"

"Yep," Nah answers before she can say anything. "I was mad about it because he's my friend, but Sarah told me all about grown up kissing and now

I understand. Do you kiss anyone that way, Momma?"

Jess stares at the two of them. "It sounds like quite the day."

"The cake was the best part. Momma, have you ever had cake at an inn?"

She smiles and puts the tea water on while Jess takes Nah upstairs and puts him to bed. She returns a few minutes later.

"That boy is going to have horrible teeth if I can't get him to start brushing them," Jess says.

The younger woman nods and pours the tea into the delicate china cups.

"Sarah, do you want to talk about all of this?" her mother asks.

"Not really, but I guess we should."

"You seemed so sure that you would never marry or even be with another man after Odette's. Have you changed your mind about concentrating on your studies and not let marriage and children get in your way?"

"I don't know. It's all very confusing. It was like I lost all self-control."

"Has anything else happened?" Jess asks.

"No. Just the one kiss, I swear," Sarah whispers.

"When are you going to tell him about your past?"

"I haven't figured that out yet."

Jess hugs her daughter. "I trust you, Sarah. You'll make the right decision. In the meantime, I still have some of Mrs. Goldstein's New York johnnies upstairs. You'd better put some in your bag."

Sarah looks horrified. "That's never happening! I'm never doing that again. I mean it. Never."

"Never is a long time. It's different with someone you love."

CHAPTER 41

Stephen has a restless night thinking about Sarah and wakes only when Trask knocks on his door.

"Bailey! Don't you have an appointment this morning?"

He jumps out of bed nearly knocking over the chamber pot on his way to his clothes. Five minutes later he's downstairs where Trask hands him a cup of coffee.

"No worries, my friend," the innkeeper says smiling. "You have ten minutes for a five-minute walk."

"Thanks so much, Trask—for everything."

"No problem. You're doing me and my brother a favor. Oh, and Stephen?"

"Yes, Trask?"

"You might want to wear a hat. Your hair is a fright."

Stephen catches his image in the mirror over the fireplace. He spits in his hand and tries to wrestle the locks into some semblance of neatness.

Trask laughs. "I guess they really won't care about your hair."

The younger man gulps the coffee and hands Trask the mug heading out the door.

It's gray, damp and blustery. He shivers and wishes he had worn his workman's coat over his nice clothes. Luckily, he turns the corner out of the wind and manages to get to the boatyard without being chilled to the bone.

He approaches one of the woodworkers shaping a rib for the schooner. "I'm looking for Benedict Trask."

The man points to a hut towards the water. Stephen's relieved to see the smoke of a fire emerging from the chimney.

"Hello?" He opens the door and steps into the warm building. Two men are looking at plans at a large table near the stove.

"May we help you?" the taller gentleman asks. He looks just like his brother the innkeeper.

"Are you Benedict Trask?"

"I am. Are you the young man my brother told me about? Dailey?"

"Yes, actually it's Bailey sir, Stephen Bailey."

"This is Reginald Chapman. He's the owner of the yard."

The shorter round man nods to Stephen.

"Would you like to stay and interview Bailey with me, sir?"

"No," Chapman smiles. "I think you have it well in hand. I'd better go check on that young lad, Flannigan. He'd chop off his own arm if I didn't keep an eye on him."

He grabs his coat and heads to the yard.

"So, Bailey, my brother tells me that you're an artist who's good with numbers? Is that so?"

"Yes sir. I did a year at the Philadelphia College of Art and before that a year at the University of Pennsylvania studying mathematics, oh and a year at Moravian College studying—well just studying—or sort of studying."

If Trask is concerned about his inability to finish a degree, he doesn't show it.

"We've got old Mr. Latouche on the books right now. He's set to retire in the spring. What I'd like to do is have you start working with him. When he leaves us you'll take his job."

"What does he keep track of?"

"Supplies coming in. Boats going out. It sounds easier than it is. You'll be checking every gundalow and counting every mast. Latouche is getting a bit old for the activity."

"How old is he?" Stephen asks.

"Nearly a half century. He's ready to retire and move to Massachusetts to be with his daughter."

"Sounds perfect. I can start today. Right now."

"You'll meet Latouche today, but it would be better if you could start next week. That will give us time to make space for you in the office." He waved around the cluttered small space. "We'll need to tidy up some."

Trask puts on his coat and leads Stephen to the docks where Latouche counts barrels of tar as they're unloaded from a flat bottomed gundalow. He marks the casks with chalk and makes a note in his ledger.

"Latouche, this is Bailey. He'll be working with you starting on Monday."

The older man grunts a hello and goes back to his counting.

"You'll report at the office at 7 a.m. We usually wrap up by 5 p.m. The pay is $15 per week to start. We pay every Friday. We mostly work Monday to Saturday but if we're on deadline we'll be working seven days. There are bonuses for the entire crew if we finish ahead of schedule. You'll be eligible for those after the first three months. Any questions?"

"I don't think so, sir—wait, maybe one question. I've been staying at the Codfish, as you know. I'm looking for more permanent lodging. Do you know of anything?"

"Coxe over there runs a house. More accurately, his wife does. They recently lost a tenant."

They wander across the yard ducking under planks being carried from the gundalow to the cutting station. The boat builder leans over a board and marks the length with a piece of chalk.

"Hey Coxe, did you find someone to replace that Taylor vermin yet?" asks Trask.

He looks up from is work and eyeballs Stephen before replying, "Not yet. You interested?"

"Yes sir," Stephen says.

Coxe looks him up and down. He turns back to his work and says, "See my wife, Lily, at the house—number six Dunwood Street."

"I will. Thank you," he replies before shaking Trask's hand and walking out the gate. He contemplates going back to the hotel for his usual mid-morning nap before seeing Mrs. Coxe but doesn't want to risk losing the room to someone else.

"Taylor. That name is familiar," he thinks as he crosses Water Street.

The boarding house is a light blue clapboard New Englander with a small yard in front. It's nicer than he was expecting. He passes a double swing on the front porch and knocks tentatively on the door.

A woman with curly blonde hair spilling out of her cap opens the door a crack. "Yes, can I help you?"

"I'm Stephen Bailey. I'm to be working at the shipyard with your husband. He sent me here to discuss the room you might have available."

"If my husband sent you what's his first name?" she asks keeping the door halfway closed.

"Uh, ma'am?" he replies.

"If my husband sent you then you should know his first name," she answers and starts to close the door.

"I'm sorry ma'am but Mr. Trask just introduced him as 'Coxe.' Do you want me to go back to the yard and ask him?" he asks. "I can do that if you like. I'll be back in fifteen minutes."

She looks him over through the cracked door before replying, "I guess you seem OK. Come in." She opens the door to a plain but immaculate entry way. Two decorated fire buckets sit by the door and a few coats hang on pegs on the wall.

"Thanks ma'am. About the room," he asks removing his hat.

"I'm sorry to be so unfriendly," she says. "Our last tenant just got arrested for murdering a servant girl. Everyone is on edge."

"Taylor?" he asks. "That's why his name was familiar!"

"Yes. Do you know him?"

"Not really," he starts, "but I think he may have murdered a woman at the tavern I used to work at. He had a different name."

"Terrible man. I tried to get rid of him right after he moved in, but he kept paying his rent, so the husband let him stay. He scared me something awful—his eyes were cold." She shivers. "Luckily he was only here for a month or so."

Stephen nods.

"Anyway. Let me show you the room. It's $5 a week," she says. "That includes breakfast and supper. Twenty-five cents more gets you a packed dinner to take to the yard."

"That sounds fair," he replies.

She keeps talking as she leads Stephen up the small stairway. A few cross stitch samplers adorn the walls. Nothing elaborate like he used to see at home but nice all the same.

"We change the sheets every two weeks. Baths are extra. They cost 10 cents and require 24-hour notice as I have to close the kitchen."

He nods.

She stops at the head of the stairs and looks at him, her eyes narrowing. "One more very important rule, Mr. Bailey. There are absolutely no female guests allowed in the rooms. On that note, if you want to whore around, you go to Odette's. We prefer that our gentlemen do not frequent the lower end Water Street houses."

"Don't worry ma'am. I hope to be engaged to be married soon," he replies smiling.

She raises an eyebrow. "Hope? What does that mean?"

"Well I haven't asked her yet," he replies blushing.

"OK. I meant what I said about lady visitors—fiancés or not," she replies as she turns.

Stephen follows her down the hall to the bedroom. A blonde tendril of her hair escapes her cap and flows down her back to her small waist.

"Right now we have Mr. Fitzgerald, Mr. Caron, and Mr. Simons all renting. You will be the fourth." She opens the door to a small but clean room with a bed, dresser and desk. A patchwork quilt covers the bed and a braided rug lies on the pine floor.

Stephen smiles. "This will be perfect. I'll move in tomorrow if that's alright. I'd like to give Trask a day's notice at the hotel."

She shrugs. "Suit yourself. You'll still owe for the full week. By the way, breakfast is at 6 a.m. if you want to eat here in the morning."

arah frowns as she continues her struggle with the prayer book. "I don't know Jess. I've been working on this for a long while now. I'm beginning to wonder if the marks have any meaning at all."

She hands Jess the volume and gets up to clear the breakfast table.

Jess pages through it. "Maybe it doesn't mean anything. When do you think your new friend, the right reverend, will be back in touch with the information about Mable?"

"I don't know," Sarah replies. "How long does it take for a letter to get to New Bedford and back?"

"At least three days, I'd imagine."

"Maybe tomorrow or Wednesday then."

"Are you excited about your dinner date with Stephen?" Jess asks as she puts the kettle on to heat water for the dishes.

"Scared mostly. It's one thing to be around and about in Portsmouth. It's quite another to be sitting at the inn with people at the other tables. What if I see someone I know from Odette's?"

"Sarah, there's no shame in what you did. You had to survive. We all did. Any man who comes into the inn and recognizes you will probably be with his wife. He'll be more afraid of you than you are of him."

"I suppose that's right," she replies.

"You know that you have to tell Stephen about your past if you are going to have any kind of future together, don't you?"

Sarah shrugs her shoulders. "I know. I just can't imagine how that's going to happen."

"You never know. He may have a story of his own to tell." Jess washes the dishes and rinses them in the hot water.

"Did you know that he's an artist?" Sarah asks picking up a dish towel.

"Uh, no. Did he tell you that?"

"No," Sarah shakes her head. "When we ran into him, he was drawing at the boatyard. He's pretty good too. I don't know why he didn't tell me that when we met. I mean we spent all that time talking when he brought me the prayer book."

"Strange. There may be other things you don't know about him."

"I suppose to," Sarah replies. "What are you doing today, Jess?"

"I only have until supper time when I'm supposed to pick up Jonah at Brodie's. I think I'll do a little more work on Taylor, maybe find out where he was staying and ask around a bit. I also need to visit the rest of the taverns and houses on Water Street. There may be more information to be found. As I recall, Taylor is a talker who can't hold his liquor."

"Do you think someone will bust him out of jail and hang him?" Sarah asks as she finishes wiping the dishes.

"The judge is coming from the county seat on Friday to arraign him and set a trial date. I would imagine that the sheriff will transport him to Brentwood for his own safety at that point."

"I don't know, Jess. I wish they'd just hang him and get it over with."

"I can't say that I disagree, Sarah."

"So, do we still have a client? I mean are we still working for the old lady?"

"I'm not sure. I collected a $25 retainer from her. As she obviously cares nothing about Suzanne, it's clear that what she really wants is the treasure or whatever it was she sent the two of them off for. I have to admit it's a pretty intriguing mystery."

"I'm curious about it too. Speaking of treasure, you don't suppose there's any connection with this and the one from the Concepción, do you?"

Jess pours them each some fresh tea and passes the jar of honey towards her daughter.

"Who knows? That was so many years ago—it doesn't seem likely."

"The official story kind of seems like malarkey to me," Sarah says.

"Really? What did you learn?"

Sarah pulls out her notes and starts to read. "During a storm in 1815 the Spanish galleon, Concepción, was wrecked on the rocks of Smuttynose Island at the Isles of Shoals seven miles off the coast of Portsmouth, New Hampshire. Donald Bentham, a local farmer, attempted to rescue the crew with the aid of a house guest. By the time the weather had calmed, and they could access the boat, the sailors were gone or drowned in the vessel. Several more lost souls washed up on shore and the farmer and the house guest buried them all. They marked the graves with simple stones. According to the farmer nothing was salvaged before the ship slipped off the rocks and into the sea."

"Speaking of that did you learn any more about the ship's cargo?"

"There was never an official report from Spain, but the rumors mentioned silver bars—payment for American made weapons."

"But what does all of this have to do with Suzanne?"

"Heck if I know," Sarah says as she shakes her head.

"You'll need to work on that language now that you're eating at fancy places like the Codfish Inn," Jess teases.

CHAPTER 43

Edward "Tippy" Prospect knows a good story when he hears it—and a dead beautiful whore found naked is a good story—even if it's in New Hampshire. Was she beautiful? He has no idea. She will be in his story, though.

Unlike many of his former colleagues at the *New York Tribune* he finds it to be helpful to go where the crime occurred and talk to people. Old Barney Boone hasn't left the Trib office in five years. In spite of that, he does have a talent for attracting readers and keeping them coming back. With only the slenderest grasp of the facts he spins salacious yarns about the latest scandal.

It isn't that Tippy possesses any kind of ethical standards—quite the opposite. He simply realized early on that truth can be stranger than fiction. He begged his editor, Clarence P. Smith, to let him take the train to New Hampshire to snoop around. When the old bastard said no, he quit and headed north. He'll be a stringer and sell the story elsewhere. His buddy, Stanley Huckins—newly appointed editor of the *Boston Standard*—is always looking for hot material.

Aside from all that, the time is right to change hometowns—New York is way too expensive—and of course, there was all that trouble with the landlady's daughter.

"This is kind of nice-looking countryside—maybe New England would make a good next stop," he muses as he strokes his short graying beard. The orange and red maples leaves get more and more vibrant as the train meanders north. He contemplates writing a first draft of the dead whore story but decides he'd better ask some questions first. He spends the time trying to make conversation with the pretty girl in the blue dress seated across from him. Finally, her mother drags her to another car.

The conductor calls for Portsmouth and Tippy collects his bag, hops off the train and starts walking downtown towards the harbor. "It really is a ratty old place, isn't it," he says to himself eyeballing the brick buildings and the row of wooden warehouses along the waterfront.

"Hey stranger!" he calls to a red-bearded man in a nice topcoat. "Where does a man go for a drink and some female companionship around this dump of a town."

The man scowls but points to a street across the square. "That's Water Street. They'll have what you're looking for."

He hears a lively—if out of tune—piano emanating from the dark interior of the Bladder Wrack, the first pub on the block.

There's a larger crowd than he would have expected for the middle of the day and everyone is buzzing with excitement. There's been another girl murdered and they've arrested a suspect. With the price of one round and half an hour of time, Tippy has pages of notes about the servant girl and the man in custody.

"We're thinking of killing the bastard tonight," a slight young man missing his front teeth whispers to the newsman.

"I'm not sure that is the best plan," the writer says. He doesn't want this story to be over for at least a month. He has a lot of milking to do. "You don't want to be strung up in his place, do you?"

The boy shrugs and puts his ale down on the rough wooden bar. "I guess not."

"What about the whore?" Tippy asks.

"Her name was Suzanne and she was one of Odette's girls," says a giant of a man in a big woolen sweater. "I never met her."

"That's because Odette doesn't let you dirty fishermen in the front door, Lars Peterson."

The toothless boy laughs at his buddy's comment.

Tippy has to admit that the large fisherman does have an alarming stench about him. The other patrons keep their distance.

"The devil is in the bathwater!" He laughs as he shakes his long red beard.

"Has anyone here ever been a customer of Suzanne?" Tippy calls to the rest of the bar.

"Odette's is kind of expensive," the toothless boy says. "Most of us go to Sally Lightfoot's or if we're really short of cash, the Randy Piddock.

"If you want to find someone who goes to Odette's, you best go right to the house. Most of her clients are uppity ups," he pushes his red nose up into the air. "They won't talk to you on the street. They have to keep their reputations intact."

"They're so pure!" a round man in carpenter clothes says laughing. "Like they don't enjoy a poke in the barley like the rest of us."

Wandering into the sunlight he makes his way the three blocks to the elite brothel. There's no sign out front but he was told to look for a lilac painted above the front door of a white clapboard house—just one of a dozen similar houses on a respectable street.

Going around to the back as he was instructed, he spies a discreet sign at the door. "Odette's, A Quality Men's Club. Ring bell for service."

A small, light-haired girl opens the door. Looking askance at his carpet bag she asks, "May I help you?"

He has a little trouble understanding her Irish brogue but responds, "Hello, my name is Tippy and I'm making inquiries about your colleague, Suzanne, the poor soul they found in the water recently."

The waif looks down at her oversized shoes. "I'm sorry, I'm not supposed to say anything about that. You should speak to Miss Odette."

"That would be most appreciated," he replies smiling.

The conservative façade of the house hides a gruesome baroque interior that mixes the worst of faux Louis XIV and Rococo.

"This must be New Hampshire's notion of what that palace Versailles looks like," he mumbles.

"I'm sorry, sir?" the waif asks.

"Oh nothing."

"Wait in here." She points to a door down the hall lined with dark flowered wallpaper. He opens it to find a few customers sitting on settees reading the *Portsmouth Chronicle*. The paper has a banner headline stretching across the top, "CHAPMAN'S LAUNCHES COLOSSAL SCHOONER." Below that there's a smaller headline, "COD PRICES UP!" On the lower left of the front page he sees the story he is looking for. "LOCAL WHORE FOUND DEAD."

"I would have gone with DEAD WHORE FOUND NAKED," Tippy chuckles to himself.

He tries to engage some of the waiting customers in conversation to no avail. Chit chat is apparently not popular at houses of ill repute.

"Miss Odette will see you now." The small girl leads him to a room at the front of the house. It's a nightmare of lace, gold and scarlet.

"Jesus Christ! It looks like a French wedding cake exploded," he mutters.

"Wait here. Miss Odette will be right in."

He's unprepared for the sight of the woman—her face painted in garish pinks and the dress—abundant apple green silk bedecked with embroidered dragonflies and praying mantis.

The fabric looks Oriental, the style is something vaguely Elizabethan—a tight fitting bodice complete with train and so many petticoats that her girth is amplified by a factor of six.

"You wished to speak with me," she says in an indeterminate European accent. It must be a put on. Nobody he's ever met speaks like that. Sort of French with occasional deeper dives into Boston elite.

"Yes, I'd like to learn more about Suzanne, the girl they found in the river."

"A tragedy. We're all devastated," she replies expectorating a brown stream into the brass spittoon at her feet.

"Could you tell me about her background? Where was she from?"

"I'm too distressed…" She holds her handkerchief to her nose.

"What about this Dewitt Taylor? Was he a customer of Suzanne's?"

"I have no idea. I've never met the man," the madam answers.

"What about some of the girls?" he asks. "Could I talk with them?"

"The ladies are all working. If you want to speak with someone, you'll need to purchase their time."

"OK." He almost wishes he was still at the Trib so he could turn in a receipt for this expense to old Baxter, the accountant.

"Go back to the waiting room. The girl will come get you when someone is available." She scrawls a note and hands it to Granny who runs up the stairs.

The waiting room is now empty so he takes a minute to read the abandoned paper. "Uninspired prose," he sniffs.

The girl returns after a few minutes and leads him upstairs where she knocks on the door and then scurries away.

A robust redhead opens the door. Tippy stares at her decolletage threatening to explode out of her tight corset.

"I'm Savannah."

CHAPTER 44

The warm weather has returned and Jess spies Putt painting the shutters of the rectory.

"Hi, Putt. Feeling better? You seemed out of sorts the other day."

Putt puts his head down. "I wasn't sick."

"No?"

"No, I was scared," he replies hanging his head.

"Scared? Who would you be scared of?" she asks.

"The witch," he whispers.

"The witch?" Jess asks. "And just what did this witch look like?"

"She had scary face paint on and a dress with bugs on it."

"Was her name Odette?" she asks.

"She didn't say her name," he answers as tears run down his face.

"Was she here on our street?" Jess asks. "Did she come to find me?"

"I don't think so. She came to the church—to see the reverend."

"Why would Odette come to the church? How long was she here?"

"Just a few minutes. She threatened to put a curse on me if I told anyone."

"Oh dear. It's OK, Putt," she reassures him.

"You don't think that's true—that she can put a curse on me? I haven't told anyone just to be sure."

Jess smiles and pats his massive hand. "There won't be any curse, Putt. She's something that rhymes with 'witch,' but she can't put curses on people."

"I hope not. I better not tell anyone just in case."

"That sounds like a good idea. I won't tell anyone either." Jess glances up at the yellow rectory and the freshly painted black shutters. "It looks like you're doing a really nice job. Maybe the reverend will let me hire you for some painting at my house."

"I'd like that, ma'am."

CHAPTER 45

Savannah turns out to be a wealth of information. Tippy pages through his book at the supper table reading his notes from yesterday. Trask brings him a meal of oyster stew, cod cakes and biscuits. He's really pleased by this inn. Not too fancy, but it's clean and the food smells delicious. He sits alone in the empty dark paneled dining room. It's a shame that he's the only patron. He's picked up many a story by making idle conversation with fellow travelers.

"Most of this seems like bullshit," he mutters as he motions to Trask to refill his ale. Still, bullshit has its place. At least Savannah will liven up the story quite a bit and she was outstanding as a whore—he'll leave that part out.

Southern belle my ass, he thinks. More like South Boston. She kept steering the conversation back to herself instead of the dead girl, Suzanne. It doesn't seem like they were very good friends. He did learn that a few of the girls called the victim "Sweetness," a name that may have been ironic if you believe Savannah's assessment of her. She was in her early thirties which seems a bit old for this kind of work. The years would have taken their toll.

The whore claimed not to know Taylor at all or anything about him.

Another guest comes into the dining room. Tippy nods and waves him over.

"Hi there. Care to join me?" He points to a seat at his table. "My friend's call me Tippy."

"My name is Stephen Bailey."

"What do you do, Bailey?"

"I'm an artist by training but I'm here looking for work."

"Ah. The artist type of work?" Tippy thinks to himself that he might need some illustrations to accompany his article. Maybe this kid could do that.

"Not right away."

"How's the search going so far?"

"Very well." He points at the innkeeper. "Trask there set me up with an interview at Chapman's Boat builders. I'm to start next week."

"What are you doing for them?"

"Clerking mostly. Counting things and marking them in a ledger."

"That doesn't sound very artistic."

"Well, I'd really like to learn about maidenhead carving. I think I'm a bit old to be an apprentice. I should have started ten years ago."

"You seem like a young enough fellow. What's the rush?"

"I need to start earning money sooner than that."

"Why? Do you owe a gambling debt?" Tippy says as he opens his notebook.

Stephen laughs. "No, I need money so I can get married."

"Ah! Young love. Who's the lucky girl?"

Stephen blushes. "Her name is Sarah."

"Tell me about her."

"She's beautiful. I have a picture of her." He pulls the loose drawing out of the sketchbook.

Prospect clucks approvingly noting the heart shaped birthmark and the suggestion of cleavage. "Ah. New love? That's the best kind. When do you plan on marrying?"

"Well, she hasn't actually agreed to marry me so far," Stephen says blushing.

"Does she live around here?"

"Not that far—Holt Street. It's just a few blocks to the east."

"What do her people do?" Tippy asks before taking another bite of crab cake.

"I don't know about her father. He doesn't appear to be around. Her mother is a detective—discreet investigations."

Tippy sits up in his chair. "A detective?"

"Yes—a lady detective. She's working on the case of the murdered prostitute and I guess now the murdered servant girl. Have you heard about that?"

"Why...no. What's it all about?" Tippy is a poor liar but the blonde fellow doesn't seem to notice and keeps talking.

"A woman's body was found in Little Bay. It was horrible."

"You sound like you saw it yourself."

Stephen shifts in his chair and looks down. "I'm sorry to say that I did. I can't get her face out of my mind."

Tippy leans in. "Oh, I can imagine. I've seen some drowning victims before. It's awful. Was she bloated from being in the water?"

"No, not really. The doctor said that the water was so cold that it prevented the bloating. The awful thing was that her left eye had been partially eaten away and the other was staring into space. Oh, and she didn't drown. Doc said that she was strangled."

"Oh dear," Tippy says as he wipes his chin and folds his napkin.

"Then the man apparently came to Portsmouth and killed some young servant girl. They caught him right after that."

"Oh, my goodness—sounds like some deviant behavior gone awry. What did the lady detective say about it all?"

"She seemed really upset about the first girl—I guess that she knew her."

"Hmmm." Tippy strokes his beard. "So, Stephen what's the name of this future mother in law of yours?"

"It's Jessamyn—Jessamyn Jakes."

Stephen's stew arrives and he dips a biscuit into the thick broth.

"She sounds very interesting. I mean, a lady detective—who ever heard of such a thing?" Tippy says chewing on the end of his pencil.

"Not me, that's for sure. She seems really smart—just like her daughter."

"And pretty too." Tippy points to her face. "Does her mother look like her?"

"No. I think Sarah must be adopted. She's not that much younger than her mother and her skin is darker," Stephen says as he uses his biscuit to wipe up the remains of the stew.

"So, what do you do, Mr. Tippy?"

"Just Tippy," the stranger replies.

"So, what do you do, Tippy?"

"Well, I'm a bit of a wordsmith—a writer."

"What do you write?" Stephen asks.

"Oh, this and that," Tippy says with a smile.

"Like novels and stuff?" the younger man asks.

"Sure."

Stephen pushes his chair back and starts to rise.

"Wait! Don't go! Let me buy you another ale," Tippy pleads.

Stephen shrugs. "Sure, I guess that would be all right. Thank you. I'll be back in a minute. I need attend to the privy out back."

CHAPTER 46

Mrs. Allgood calls upstairs to her husband, "They've arrested someone in Portsmouth for your murder."

"What kind of rubbish are you talking about?" the man mutters as he lumbers to the landing.

"The dead whore."

"What about her?" He scratches his belly.

"The man Taylor—the one they think killed the whore—was arrested in Portsmouth on Sunday after he murdered some servant girl."

"Well, I guess my work here is done. Sounds like I can sleep until I go downtown to meet the boys."

His wife stands at the bottom of the stairs. Her father was right. Tom Allgood is the laziest son of a bitch in all of Strafford County—maybe in all of New England. She yells up the stairs again.

"Seems a shame that they'll be getting all the credit for your murder." She stands with her hands on her hips on the bottom stair.

He pokes his head over the railing. "What do you mean, Doris? What foolish talk is that?"

"I mean with you rescuing the body and that poor Irish girl with the apples. Seems like the whole thing wouldn't have been solved without you. I'll bet the governor is there right now handing out commendations."

"Commendations? What's a commendation?"

"You know, Tom. You stand on the stage with the governor and he pins a medal on your chest," Doris explains.

"That sounds boring. Can't they just send it to me?" he whines.

"Think of all the well-wishers who might be inclined to buy a hero an ale?"

Allgood hadn't considered this. Even his friends here in Dover don't usually spot him a free drink. She smiles.

"Yes husband, perhaps you should go to Portsmouth to check this boy out and collect your commendation. Besides, wasn't the first murder in your jurisdiction?"

Tom Allgood is always a bit sketchy on things like jurisdiction. His primary qualification for the job is that he has ample time on his hands and lets the Megeso Mill detectives do whatever they want. Occasionally Mr. Beaudoin, the mill owner's lawyer, stops by and makes him sign some papers. For that he collects his paycheck every week. The best part of sheriffing is that it doesn't usually interrupt his lunch and nap schedule.

His eyes squint and his tongue slightly protrudes from the side of his mouth as he contemplates his wife's suggestion.

"All right. I'll head there tomorrow."

"Why not today?" she asks.

"Jesus Doris! Can't you cut a lawman a break? The day's almost over."

"It's noon—plenty of daylight left."

The large man grumbles as he retreats to the bedroom to change out of his bed clothes.

CHAPTER 47

Tippy manages to get his first story finished in time to send it to Boston on the nine o'clock train. It should just make it into tomorrow's paper. He writes a note to his contact giving background and the promise of more. It costs him $5 to send the boy with the story, but he doesn't want to spend the time himself. If this takes off like he thinks it will, money will be no object—he should be able to name his price for the rest of the series. It sure was lucky that he met that Bailey fellow. His information about the lady detective really added some spice to the story.

"Trask, my good man, when do the Boston papers arrive?"

"Usually on the early morning train. Would you like me to have my boy go after one for you?" the innkeeper asks.

"Thank you kindly, I'd appreciate that. It's the *Chronicle* I'll need. I'll read it over breakfast."

He brushes his top-coat and straightens his tie—smiling at his smart reflection in the entryway mirror before walking over to the house where the second girl was killed.

There's no getting in as the neighborhood hens are gathered in the kitchen watching over the old lady Wilson. A rodent-faced woman with mousy hair slams the door in his face before he can get the first question out.

The stone warehouse that doubles as the jail is nearby, but the detectives aren't allowing anyone in to see the prisoner. The only thing he learns from the guard was that Taylor was dressed in some kind of clown costume face down in horse manure when they caught him.

As he starts to turn away, he notices a paunchy bald man about six feet tall loitering across the street. He paces up and down the street taking his hat off and putting it back on.

"Hey friend, what's going on?" Tippy calls to the stranger.

"A very dangerous prisoner is being held here. A murderer," he pauses for dramatic effect then speaks quietly. "I pulled the blonde filly out of the water and then rescued the second almost victim."

"Second almost victim?" Tippy asks. "What does that mean?"

"The Irish girl that Taylor tried to steal from Dover."

"I haven't heard about her," the writer muses. "What's your name sir?"

"Sheriff Tom Allgood. I'm from Strafford County." He doesn't look much like a lawman to Tippy. He looks more like a baker—or a baker's best customer. His suspenders work overtime to keep his pants on over his belly.

"Strafford County? That's in New Hampshire, right?" Tippy asks.

"Well, um, why yes. Say, what's your name, stranger?"

"My friends call me Tippy." He pulls off his derby hat and bows slightly.

"What are you doing around here, Mr. Tippy?"

"Just Tippy."

"I'm just passing through and heard about the murder. You sound like you have a lot of vital information. May I buy you an ale? The Bladder Wrack is right across the street." A couple of libations poured into this jackass should render a flow of interesting facts. Another victim? That would be a great scoop.

"OK, sure." Tom Allgood is not one to turn down free ale. This trip to Portsmouth is already paying off.

The tavern is crowded for a Wednesday morning. It takes a few minutes to get their drinks and they settle in by the fireplace. The squeezebox player sleeps off last night's whiskey in the corner. Everyone's talking about the Portsmouth victim, Miriam. Nobody seems to know her last name.

"So, I heard that there was a lady detective around when you found the body," Tippy asks his new friend.

"Uh, yeah. I guess that she was a detective. She was kind of pushy." The sheriff takes a long draw of his ale.

"What did she look like? Was she pretty?"

"Hmmm. She was wearing men's work clothes. I didn't really notice her. She did have a long brown braid that ran down to her belt."

"Shit," Tippy mumbles to himself. "I knew I should have made her a brunette." He wishes now that he hadn't made up so many details. He'd wanted to get the story to Boston last night. No big deal, he'll just keep rolling with it. He'll just call her auburn in the next story and work his way towards brunette.

"So, I heard that the lady detective seemed very upset about the victim—like she knew her. Did you get that impression?"

Allgood thought hard about it. Truth was, he really didn't notice much about what was going on. His stomach was grumbling and he was meeting his pals for dinner. He just wanted to get the whole thing over with. He hadn't even wanted to be sheriff—the wife's cousin from the mill pushed him into running. Now here he is, feeling stupid talking to some stranger.

"I don't know. I was talking to the farmer and the tavern owner while the doc checked her out."

"Doc? Which doctor?" Tippy asks.

"Name's Churchill, James Churchill. Kind of a fancy pants. Thinks he's smarter than the rest of us. You know the type."

"Yes, I do Tom," Tippy says with as much sincerity as he can muster. He makes a note in his book about the doctor. "Another ale, sheriff?" He signals to the barmaid to bring another round. "So, tell me about the other victim—the one you mentioned from Dover."

"She was grabbed in New Hampshire but the address her uncle gave me was in South Berwick, Maine."

"Never heard of it."

"It's right across the river—the Salmon Falls River."

"Tell me more about her, Tom."

Tippy nods at the serving girl to fill up the sheriff's ale.

"She is just some Irish waif. Seems like we're starting to be overrun with them these days. Name's Opla or Ogla or some such nonsense." He takes a long swig of his ale draining half of the tankard.

"Orla?"

"That sounds right. Her last name was something like Reilly."

"Was it, Reilly or something like Reilly?"

"I'm pretty sure it was Reilly."

"How did you hear about her?" Tippy asks.

"She and her uncle came to my house after church on Sunday to report it," Tom says slurring his words a bit.

"What did she say?"

"Something about a man grabbing her and the load of apples she was carrying."

"Did Taylor rape her?"

The sheriff turns beet red.

"Well, I—I mean she didn't say anything about that. She got away."

Tippy nibbles on the end of his pencil and frowns. "She got away? How would a little slip of a girl get away from a hardened criminal twice her size?"

Allgood thinks for a moment. He'd been pretty hungover that morning and his grasp on the details is a little bleak.

"Shit!" he blurts spewing drink over the table.

"Pardon me?" Tippy asks.

"He had the shits from eating the apples and the girl ran off." He takes a gulp of the ale and smiles.

Tippy writes down the details. This Orla may be worth talking to. South Berwick can't be that big a town. Maybe he'll go over there tomorrow.

Allgood's eyes narrow as he watches Tippy writing in his notebook.

"So, what are you doing with that pencil?"

"I'm just interested in what you're saying. Maybe I can help write up your commendation. So, Tom, did you tell the police in Portsmouth about Orla?"

"That's why I was standing outside at the jail. The wife thought it might be important."

"Well, it doesn't seem very relevant to me. I tell you what. You can go on home and I'll speak to the authorities. I'll tell them everything you told me. I happen to need to see them on another matter."

"Really?" Allgood is so relieved that Tippy thinks he may cry.

"Yes, I'm supposed to be talking with them soon. I'll report it for you."

"Thanks Mr. Tippy. That sounds good. I'd like to be on my way home."

The newspaper man drops a quarter on the table. "Have another on me, Tom."

CHAPTER 48

Jess stares at the note for so long that Sarah finally snatches it from her hand and reads it aloud.

The body of the deceased has been delivered to our location. Please advise on disposition of remains. Should we arrange for a pauper's burial? —Sincerely, Cyril St. John, funeral director.

"That cold, calculating mutton nob. He shot his milt in Suzanne at least a dozen times," Sarah says. "How can he be so callous?"

Jess sits in silence at the breakfast table.

"Don't you worry, Jess, I'll take care of this. We're going to have a service for that girl if I have to dig the grave myself."

Her mother nods.

"I'll speak to Reverend Cheney about it tomorrow. I'm sure he can help."

CHAPTER 49

Stephen wakes early on his last morning at the inn. He rubs his eyes as he makes his way down to the dining room. He smiles at Trask, ready with a cup of coffee.

"Breakfast this morning, Stephen?"

"Thanks, Trask. I'll miss staying here. Your food is so good."

The innkeeper smiles. "Don't you worry. Lily Coxe is a hell of a cook."

"She's tantalizing, that's for sure."

Trask rolls his eyes and pours the younger man a coffee. "She's a married woman and you're about to be a married man. I suggest you keep your eyeballs off her."

"No harm in looking, I say."

Trask shakes his head and returns to the kitchen,

Tippy arrives just as he's finishing his eggs. "Good morning, Bailey."

"Good morning, sir." The newsman settles in at the table.

"How's the writing going, Tippy?"

"Excellent, my fine furry friend, excellent. Thank you for asking. What have you been up to now that you've secured employment?"

"Drawing mostly—on the wharf." He opens his notebook and shows the smaller man.

"Hmm, very nice. Not as good as your drawing of your lady love, though—very pretty, that one. Speaking of Sarah, have you seen her around? Or perhaps her mother?"

"Not since Sunday. They were downtown when the excitement was happening and we had cake here. I was able to make a date to take Sarah to dinner on Thursday."

"Where does a young man take a special girl in this town?" Tippy asks.

"I was thinking of here. She's never eaten dinner at an inn before."

"That sounds very romantic." The writer makes a note in his book.

"I hope so," Stephen replies. "Well, I better be going. I need to pack up my things."

"Leaving so soon?"

"Yes. I've found a room at the Coxe Boarding House. I'm moving in tomorrow morning."

"Ah, that sounds fine. Good luck to you Stephen," Tippy says as he flags down Trask to order breakfast.

"Thanks, sir. To you as well. I can't wait to read that novel of yours."

The newsman smiles as the younger man goes up the stairs to his room.

Trask stops by the table pours coffee and drops the *The Chronicle*.

Tippy unfolds the newspaper, smoothing it as he goes and looks for the story. He was hoping for above the fold, but it's landed in the lower left corner of the front page. The headline reads, "LADY DETECTIVE INVESTIGATES WHORE'S MURDER."

He smiles. He can milk lady detective for a whole series. In the story, he teases the fact that there is a second murder and a suspect who might be connected in custody. No reason to give all the details in the first installment. He wants people coming back for more.

Retiring to his room he spends most of the day writing. He fusses over the description of the lady detective's clothing so much that the boy has to run to make the train to Boston.

It's nearly 4 p.m. and his stomach is grumbling.

He retreats to the dining room where he feasts on two bowls of clam chowder and an adequate bottle of French wine. He lights his pipe and his thoughts turn to Savannah. Maybe she can get more information about the victim. Perhaps she even knows Jessamyn Jakes.

He's certainly looking forward to burying his face in those tremendous, soft breasts.

Maybe he'll do a separate feature on the statuesque redhead. He's heard that racy stories sell well in France. He could write something about her customer's peccadilloes and have someone translate it for him—or maybe he'll just tell her that he will. That seems like it would go a long way with a girl like Savannah.

He leaves the inn and wanders along Wren Street. A wagon pulls up in front of a brick house and servants begin to unload the contents. Exotic statues and fine furniture are unwrapped and carried inside. "It must be a sea captain's home," he thinks. "They're always carting back a bunch of crap from places like Africa and China."

He'd once been to a brothel in New Orleans that was filled with carved phalli of all sizes—from the massive to the diminutive. Someone mentioned that the owner had been in the British Navy and had picked them up from all over the world.

All this thinking about erotic statues gets him revved up for Savannah.

He walks up to the back entrance of the house and rings the bell until the small Irish girl opens the door.

"I'd like to see Savannah please."

She leads him to the waiting area and then disappears returning after a few minutes.

"I'm sorry sir, but one of the other girls will need to help you," she says looking at the floor as she speaks.

"What? Savannah is unavailable? What do you mean? Where is she?" he demands.

"I'm sorry sir, but she isn't available on Wednesday evenings," the small girl answers.

"Why not?" His eyes narrow. "Where is she?"

"I don't know sir," she replies. "One of the girls just told me that she is in church every Wednesday evening."

"Church, my ass," he thinks. He paid double last time he was in. There must be something interesting going on that she would refuse a good customer like him.

"Say little miss, you sound Irish," he observes.

"Yes sir, from Killarney. Have you been there?" she asks, her eyes brightening .

"Uh, no," he replies shaking his head, "but do you know an Irish girl named Orla. She lives in South Berwick."

"Where's that?" Granny asks.

"In Maine."

"Sorry, sir. I've only ever been to Portsmouth."

Tippy settles for a scrawny girl with a beak-like nose named Daisy. She has a raspy voice which he kind of likes, but she's no Savannah.

"Did you know the girl who was murdered? This Suzanne?" he asks as he mounts her from behind. She seems to ignore him—focusing on the bottle he brought.

"Everyone knew her," the girl answers taking a swig.

"How did she get her name?" he asks getting momentarily distracted by the conversation.

"Sir?"

"Sweetness. Wasn't she called that?"

"I don't know. I didn't really talk to her much. She was kind of out of it all the time."

Tippy stops poking her and flips her over, spilling the bottle all over the bed.

"What did you say?" he asks.

"It's just that she was on that opium," Daisy answers wiping her face with the clean part of the sheet.

"Wow! She was on opium? Did she have any friends at all?"

"Not since Anastasia left," she answers collecting her clothes. "Odette is going to be some pissed about the wet bedding."

"Anastasia? Russian girl?" Tippy grabs his notebook and starts scribbling.

"No, that's just the name that Odette gave her when she started here."

"Do you know this girl's real name?" he demands.

"No," Daisy answers pulling on her robe. "Nobody tells their real name. It's kind of a rule. She did start going by another name when she left, though."

"What was that name?" he asks.

"Jessamyn Jakes."

"The lady detective? Holy shit! She worked here?" Tippy writes furiously.

"She and Desiree both did until five years ago. Say mister, your time is up. You'll need to pay for another hour if you want to keep talking."

"Wait. Sure, I'll pay. Desiree? Who's Desiree?"

"Suit yourself." She shrugs dropping her robe and gets back into the bed avoiding the spreading red wine stain. "Sarah's her name now. Jess adopted her. Why are you asking? Everyone knows this."

Tippy has the feeling that one bearded rube knows nothing about any of this.

CHAPTER 50

The note had said to come to the rectory at 5 p.m. It's five minutes of and Jess stands on the outside of the large, freshly painted wooden door with her hand on the simple bronze knocker.

"What the hell am I doing here?" she says aloud.

"I hope having a cup of tea with your new friend." Maryanne comes up behind her. "I was in the church polishing the pews. They were a mess."

She opens the rectory and leads Jess inside. The room is gloomy with coals barely glowing red in the fireplace. "Toss some wood on the fire and I'll get these cleaning supplies put away."

"I've never been in the rectory before," Jess starts. "It's…"

"Awful is what it is—dark and awful," Maryanne replies. "The first thing I'm doing is disposing of forty years of clutter. The man never threw anything out. You wouldn't believe the basement. It's like the catacombs of Paris down there. I keep expecting to find a wall of skulls."

"Isn't there a maid?" Jess asks.

"Yes, Amelia—she's really more of a cook. She comes every day—except Wednesdays—and makes meals for the reverend—and now me. She only cleans the kitchen. She'd probably quit if she had to scrub anywhere else."

"It's so dark in here," Jess notes. "You can't really do much about that, I suppose."

"My room upstairs gets better light. Would you like to see it?"

Jess tugs at her tight collar and shifts nervously. "Um. Sure."

"The reverend sleeps downstairs," Maryanne says smiling leading her guest up the compact stairwell.

The room has a simple bed and dresser. A tiny desk and chair sit in a dormer. The white walls glow pink with the late afternoon light.

"This is very nice," Jess says as she runs her hand across the smooth desktop.

"Yes, Putt just painted that for me. In fact he just painted the whole room. He did a wonderful job. Between you and me, I don't like the way the reverend treats the boy. That's one of many things I'd like to change."

Jess nods. She strokes the desktop nervously.

"Be careful or you'll wear a hole in that." Maryanne laughs as she sits on the bed and pats the space next to her. Instead of taking the invitation Jess pulls out the desk chair.

"You've got to be dying to ask me questions," the smaller woman says.

"I guess I am. How did you get here?" Jess points around the room.

"How did I get here and why did I agree to marry the reverend?" Maryanne laughs.

"Something like that."

"Let's just say that my family and I don't get along well and it seemed beneficial to relocate."

"How did you meet?" Jess asks.

"My brother is also a clergyman. They met at a meeting. Apparently, the higher ups told Silas that he was unlikely to rise in the church as an unmarried bachelor—too many questions being asked."

Jess laughs "If they're concerned about him preferring men, I'm pretty sure that he doesn't. It's the women he gives the lascivious eye—especially my Sarah."

She stops talking and her face flushes.

"Um, I'm sorry. I didn't mean to offend you," she says quietly.

"No offense taken," Maryanne answers. "I barely know the man at this point. As you can see," she says as she waves her hand around the room, "we are not exactly sharing the conjugal bed. I'm not sure if we ever will unless we attempt to have children."

"Then why marry him? Why not marry someone you actually love?"

"There's no marrying of that type allowed. This is more of a business arrangement—at least for me."

Jess looks down from her gaze. "Oh, I see."

"Tell me about Sarah," Maryanne says.

Jess smiles at the name of her daughter. "I adopted her four years ago. I've known her since she was ten or so."

"She's not like you? Us?"

There it is. Maryanne said it out loud.

Jess has never had this type of frank discussion outside of Odette's. Even she and Sweetness never really spoke about their love—or whatever it was. She shifts in her chair.

"No," she says shaking her head. "Sarah is not like us."

"How did you find her?"

Jess takes a breath. "I met her when we were both working as prostitutes at Odette's." She wipes the tears from her eyes.

Maryanne moves to Jess and holds her head against her chest stroking her hair. "And that's how Jonah came to be?"

"Yes, but the reverend didn't tell you all of this?" Jess replies. "I'm sure he's heard the gossip."

"For some reason, I don't talk to him about you—or about brothels," she laughs, lowers to her knees and gives Jess a soft kiss on her lips. Jess smells the faint traces of the pine cleaning oil on Maryanne's hands as she strokes her face.

The kissing becomes more intense and they struggle with the many layers of clothing.

"Next time wear your workman's pants," Maryanne demands, "so we only have one set of nonsense clothes to remove."

CHAPTER 51

Sarah insists on meeting Stephen at the inn so that she can check in with the right reverend and visit the Athenaeum beforehand. She closes the door behind her and spies Putt across the street filling the wagon with neverending debris from the yard.

Her feet crunch on the leaves as she walks towards the rectory. "Hi, Putt. Are you better today? Jess was worried about you."

"I'm better. Thanks, Sarah." He turns red and keeps his eyes on the rake.

She's glad of her shawl as the wind whips down the street and blows Putt's work all over the street. "Snow will be here before you know it. You'd better get this mess all cleaned up before that," she teases.

The tornado continues—the wagon is soon empty and he sighs.

"Don't worry, Putt. The wind will die soon. Why don't you take the afternoon off? I'll be back soon and you can play with Jonah and me." She makes a note to bring him a piece of cake.

Crunching through the fallen leaves along the tree lined street she turns to wave at her big friend before turning the corner.

She's so distracted by thoughts of Stephen and their date that before she knows it, she's arrived at the West Church's formidable wooden back door.

A small, hunched-over woman wrapped in a plaid shawl responds to the knocker. "May I help you, dear?"

"Hello, I'm looking for the right reverend. Is he here?"

"I'm Mrs. Carbunkle, the reverend's cook. He's across the street at the Atheneaum. You can wait here if you like. I just pulled some muffins out of the oven. Blueberry!"

"Thank you, ma'am, but I think I'll try to find him next door. Have a nice day," Sarah says.

"You too, dear." The older woman strains to close the heavy door. Sarah reaches out and helps her and the door closes with an authoritative thump.

Market Square is deserted at this time of day and she slips around the corner to the back and opens the door to the reading room. Only Mr. Dunwoody—asleep in the corner—and the right reverend are in attendance. Cheney's nose almost touches the surface as he peers at the portrait of Grievance Collins.

At the sound of her footsteps he turns. "Miss Jakes! I was about to send word to you. I'm so glad that you're here."

"Did you hear back from your sister church in New Bedford?" she asks.

"I did in fact. It turns out that your Mable is the daughter of this gentleman here." He points to the portrait.

"She is? What happened? Did he used to live in New Bedford?"

"That he did," he replies.

"Did he move to Portsmouth and abandon his family?" she asks.

"It would seem so," Cheney says. "My colleague remembers that when the daughters were young, the captain left one day without explanation. The mother was granted a divorce due to abandonment and died soon thereafter. The children were sent to live with an aunt in Boston. A few months later the captain turned up in Portsmouth,"

"Daughters?" she asks.

"Yes. Mable had a sister named Agnes."

In the corner the newspaper on Mr. Dunwoody's lap drops to the floor stirring him briefly. He smacks his lips and resumes snoring.

"What happened to the girls?" Sarah whispers.

"My colleague lost touch with them when they moved away." He reaches into his breast pocket and pulls out a folded paper. "Here's his letter with the church address if you'd like to ask further questions. His name is Right Reverend Bernard Smithee. I mentioned that you might be in touch."

"Thank you so much for your help, sir."

He smiles. "My pleasure. This is the most fun I've had in a while. Perhaps once you get this sorted, you can come for tea and tell me the full story of this mystery. If I am not mistaken, this all has something to do with the shipwreck depicted in the picture."

"Maybe, sir. We're not sure. I will definitely tell you the whole story."

"That sounds perfect. Have a nice day, Miss Jakes."

"You too, sir."

She starts to walk up the stairs to George's office and turns back to the older gentleman. "Oh, sir?"

"Yes, Sarah," he smiles.

"I have another favor to ask."

"What do you need? Something else about the Collins family?"

"Sort of. In a way," she looks down.

"What is it, my dear. I will certainly try to help."

"Sir, I am going to speak plainly."

"I would hope that you would," the right reverend says.

"Sir, it's about Suzanne, the dead working girl."

"What about her?"

"Sir, she needs to be buried," she says quietly.

"Ah. I see," he nods.

"I wouldn't ask sir, but Reverend Hobson spoke so unkindly about her on Sunday that I dare not ask him."

"Oh yes, Hobson." He thinks for a moment and tugs at his chin. "I tell you what Sarah, let's plan on a small service on Saturday at 2 p.m. I've a wedding at 9 in the morning. Does that sound all right?"

"Yes, sir! Thank you so much!" She nearly hugs him but then reaches her hand out instead. "We'll have St. John, the undertaker, deliver her coffin to you at around 10 a.m. Saturday morning if that's alright."

"Certainly. I may have a few others delivered that day. Tell Cyril to put your friend directly in the church near the altar."

"I will, sir."

With that he tips his hat and exits out the front door. Now he just needs to figure out where he can bury a prostitute in the graveyard without the dowagers raising a stink.

"Was that the right reverend?" George asks as he enters the reading room.

"Yes, it was," Sarah replies. "He's been so nice."

"Really? He never speaks much when he comes to the reading room. I always thought he was a bit of a curmudgeon."

"I always thought so too, but he's actually been very helpful. He found out that Grievance here is the father of Mable." She points at the painting.

"Mable of the prayer book?"

"The very same."

"Speaking of our captain friend, I found another book that might be of use to you," George says.

"A book about the shipwreck?"

"Yes," he smiles, "but I think you'll like it for another reason."

He hands her a volume. Her face lights up when she reads the title.

"*The Birds of the Shoals.*"

"Yes. The author, Katherine Mary Holden, lived on Star Island during the time of the events of 1813. She mentions the wreck and even talks about Donald Benthem, the farmer that buried the dead crew members. Miss Holden frequently rowed over to Smuttynose to observe the terns during mating season. There's even a picture of the carved cane she used to protect herself. The local gulls can be quite aggressive, apparently."

"Wow!" she exclaims. "How did you find this?"

"I asked Mr. Quimby about the Concepción after you were last in. It turns out he purchased the painting because he was interested in the shipwreck. He also has some newspaper clippings from the time if you'd like to take a look. They aren't very compelling, truthfully."

"That's fine, I'll take a look all the same."

She spends thirty minutes reading the clippings and making notes. "There's no mention of the treasure in the stories. There's a list of the dead crew members and an account of the storm from the farmer. Not much information here."

"It's a fairly uninspiring news report," he nods.

"Do you have any idea of how the rumors of the treasure emerged?"

"I think you'll find the answer in the book. I marked the page."

She shuffles through the book admiring the bird sketches throughout until she reaches the marked page.

The clock strikes two.

"Oh dear! I'm late. I'll need to read this at home. Thanks, George!" She gives him a hug and runs out the door.

He staggers to his chair as Mr. Quimby enters the room. "You have a silly grin on your face, George."

CHAPTER 52

S arah runs towards the water and is out of breath by the time she arrives at the Codfish Inn.

Stephen is pacing in his new clothes in front of the door.

"Hello!" He rushes forward and hugs her. "I'm so happy that you're here. We're going to have a wonderful dinner."

They step though the black heavy door into the blue dining room. She looks around—relieved to see an empty dining room.

"Thank you for asking me, Stephen," she says as she slides into a seat at a table in the dark corner.

"Wouldn't you rather sit by the window? There's more light over there."

She shakes her head. "No. This will be fine."

"OK," Stephen shrugs and sits next to her—dragging his chair so their knees touch. Sarah edges away but she can only go so far—now regretting picking this table in the corner.

"I told Trask you were joining me, and he said that he would make something special."

"That sounds very nice. Could I order a piece of the parsnip cake to take with me?" she asks.

"Sure. I guess that would be OK. For Jonah?" Stephen asks.

"Actually, for Putt. He's been a little under the weather."

Stephen frowns. "He's an odd one—but big. I've never seen such large hands." He holds his own hands out for inspection.

"He's really a sweetheart," she says. His size scares people but he wouldn't hurt a fly."

"I'd be happy to buy cake for any friend of yours, my darling."

Her mouth widens to a stiff smile. He clutches her hand with both of his. She wishes Trask would come to the table.

"Sarah. I'm just so happy to be here with you," he says as he inches closer.

Blushing, she carefully extracts her hand and changes the subject, "When do you start at the shipyard?"

"Monday. They even helped me find a place to live, the Coxe Boarding House. You won't believe who their tenant was before me?"

"Dewitt Taylor?" she asks.

"How did you know?"

"Jess told me," she says looking towards the front door.

He leans in closer, "I heard from Tippy about the servant girl being Taylor's lover and how he murdered her in a fit of passion."

She raises her eyebrow. "First of all, her name was Miriam. Second of all, that's plain stupid. She was just a girl."

"Um, yeah. Miriam," he says quietly. "So it wasn't just some deviant behavior gone bad like with the whore?"

She furrows her brow. "That's a strange thing to say. "Did your new friend tell you that as well?"

"I guess he did. Speaking of Tippy, here he comes," Stephen says looking out the front window. "He'll be so glad to meet you."

The tidy newspaper man opens the front door, waves and makes a bee-line for their table.

"You must be Sarah—complete with heart shaped birthmark. Stephen, you were so right. She's as pretty as a chocolate pie."

"Uh, hello," she says.

Trask brings two small bowls of clam chowder and pitcher of ale.

"I see your food is arriving," the writer says. "I'll retreat to my usual spot. Have a succulent dinner."

She watches him as he settles in across the room and drops his stack of newspapers onto the table.

"Sarah," Stephen says drawing her attention back. "I want you to know that you've really inspired me. I've been drawing a lot lately. I finished that sketch of the boatyard. Mr. Chapman may use it for a pamphlet he wants to get printed Would you like to see it?"

She nods and he opens his sketchbook to the drawing as Trask brings the main course, a partridge stuffed with oysters. The innkeeper gives her a warm smile as he takes away the chowder bowls.

"This is very nice, Stephen. I like the way you sketched the workers as kind of blurry. It really looks like they are moving."

Stephen beams.

"Thank you. I was hoping for that. May I draw you sometime?"

"Um. OK. Show me again the other drawing you did of me. I won't be posing half naked like in that picture."

"Oh, that's the thing," he says. "I can't find it. I looked for it yesterday and it was gone."

"Missing? From your sketch book? How can that be? I would be embarrassed if other people saw that? I mean it looks like I am not wearing any clothes." She shrinks away from him and closer to the wall.

"I don't know, Sarah. I must have dropped it when I was drawing on the docks. It was kind of windy. I wouldn't worry about it. It's probably halfway to Portugal by now."

"Hm. Maybe."

She looks over and sees that the writer keeps stealing glances at her. "Why is your friend staring at me?"

Stephen waves to Tippy. He waves back, turns and focuses on his paper. After a minute or so he leaves his belongings and half eaten dinner and moves to the back door. "Probably headed to the privy," she thinks.

Trask brings out coffee. "How was the partridge?"

"Delicious, Mr. Trask," Stephen says.

"I have some parsnip cake that was baked just this morning. Would you like some, Sarah?"

"Could I order a slice to go?" Sarah asks.

"Of course!" Trask smiles at her as he begins to clear the table.

"Better make that two," she says. "If Nah finds out I brought one for Putt and none for him, there'll be hell to pay."

Stephen frowns but nods.

"I'll pack them up for you," Trask says and walks past Tippy's table where he clears a few things on the way back to the kitchen. He returns and hands her a paper sack. "Have a wonderful evening."

Sarah is relieved that Tippy has not returned from the privy. No more small talk with the annoying man.

They walk in silence in the fading light.

"Sarah."

"Yes," she whispers.

"I think you know how I feel about you."

She nods.

"Do you think you might feel the same way about me?"

"We're only just getting to know each other, Stephen. There's a lot of things you don't know about me."

"I don't care about that—I just know I love you," he says as he grabs her hand.

"Well, I'm sure that there are things I don't know about you. We need to take this slow," she offers, peeling his hands away.

"I don't know, Sarah. It seems like everything that happened before I met you is meaningless. Let's just start fresh."

She frowns. "That doesn't seem like a good idea to me."

"We can take it slow if you like." He's disappointed. This meandering approach doesn't conform with his plans. Surely, if she was his fiancé—even a proper girl like Sarah—would be willing to let him love her. Then who knows what might happen.

Sarah takes the cake from him as they reach the back of the rectory. He waits in the street as she crosses the lawn and knocks on the shed. The large man opens the door. He looks sleepy.

"Miss Sarah?" he asks.

"Hi, Putt. I have a present for you."

"A present? Nobody ever gave me a present before."

"It's parsnip cake." She reaches into the bag and pulls out the first piece wrapped in newspaper. She unwraps the treat and hands it to Putt.

"Cake made out of parsnips?" he grimaces. "Those things like carrots? Those don't taste like cake."

"Trust me, Putt, it's not a cow patty! You're going to love it," she says.

He sticks his tongue out and just touches it to the frosting. His eyes light up and he takes a big bite.

Sarah laughs.

"Don't eat it too fast or you'll get a belly ache," she warns.

Putt watches as she joins Stephen in the street and they walk towards the front stoop of the house.

"Good afternoon, Stephen. Thank you for dinner." She holds her hand out.

He wants to kiss her but feels awkward when he notices the big idiot boy staring at them. He settles for her hand and looks into her eyes. "Goodnight, Sarah."

"Um, bye," she says as she twists out of his grasp, opens the door and enters the house leaving her suitor on the front steps.

CHAPTER 53

A knock at the front door disrupts Nah's adventure with Mr. Soapy. "I'll get it!" he yells as he abandons their search for a kidnapped princess.

He opens the door to a tall, dark-haired man.

"You must be Jonah," the stranger says.

He nods slowly.

"I'm Captain Pritchard. I'm a friend of your mother."

Nah's eyes grow wide. "Are you a sea captain?"

"That I am, young man."

The boy stares up at him.

"Do you think it would be OK if I came into the house? We seem to be letting all the heat escape."

Nah nods and opens the door wide.

Jess is humming to herself in the kitchen—distracted by thoughts of Maryanne.

The stew on the stove starts to boil over.

"Holy poker balls!" she exclaims grabbing a towel to remove the cover.

A male voice says, "such nasty language from such a genteel lady."

"Bart?" She runs across the kitchen and hugs him. "When did you get back? It's been so long!"

"I just got in yesterday," he answers. "They're still getting things together in my new house. Have you seen it yet?"

"Of course! In fact, we had a picnic across the street from it the other day. It's beautiful."

"Thank you. It's been a long time in the works. They broke ground right as I was leaving."

"I remember. Five years ago," she replies. She looks around the room and smiles. "Right when we moved in here."

"How are you're settling in?"

"I should think that we'd be pretty settled by now," she laughs.

"I brought you a housewarming gift. It's a case of that Spanish wine you're so fond of." He retrieves the wooden crate from the front stoop.

Her eyes light up. "Thank you. You shouldn't have."

"Of course, I should. Besides, I have a cellar full at my house. Speaking of houses, it doesn't look like you have changed very much. It looks exactly like it did when I was a child."

"Only in Sarah's workspace. Your mother had impeccable taste. There didn't seem to be much reason to redecorate—and it's not our forte."

He laughs. "She would have liked that—and you. She definitely would have liked you." He smiles.

"Well, I'm sorry that I never met her. I do feel like I know her from living here. We get great enjoyment from the house—especially the dictionary and globe she left."

"Mother always tried to expand her vocabulary even in her dotage. I gave her the globe so she could see where I was sailing."

Jonah emerges from behind the pie safe and sits staring at Bart. Jess smiles at him and squeezes his hand.

"What do you say, Nah? Should we ask the old captain to share our dinner?"

He nods slowly and asks, "Is this your momma's house?"

Bart smiles. "It was, but she went to heaven, so now it's your house."

Jonah sighs. "Well that's good."

"I'm pretty sure that he's relieved about the house and not glad that your momma passed," Jess says.

He laughs. "I understand. Where's Sarah?"

"She's out with a young man."

"His name is Stephen," Nah interjects. "He's my friend."

Bart smiles. "So, you approve of him?"

Nah nods.

"Is it serious?" Bart asks Jess.

"Hard to say. They've only recently met. He's starting work for Chapman next week and boarding with Coxe."

"Ah, as a shipbuilder?"

"Not really. As I understand it he'll be keeping the ledgers."

"I see," Bart says. "What does Sarah like about him?"

"She should be back soon. You can ask her yourself."

"She must have changed a lot in the last five years. How is she doing?"

"She's thriving. She helps me with the business, but she's really interested in art and birds. You wouldn't believe how she soaks up knowledge."

"She always has her nose in a book—at least when she's not boiling bird bones," Nah offers.

Jess laughs, "She does read at least three books a week. It was so good of you to give her access to the Atheneaum. I'd be broke if I had to keep her in books."

"What about mother's books?" He waves his hand around the volume lined walls.

Jess laughs. "She reads mostly science books. Although, her friend George is trying to get her to read novels."

"She's done a million drawings of birds. I help her by keeping the dog away," Nah says proudly.

"Do you have a dog?" the captain asks.

"Nope." With that, the small boy runs up the stairs.

"OK. I'm a little confused, but it's wonderful to hear that she's doing so well. I look forward to seeing her and some of her million drawings."

Jess laughs. "You've got a lot to catch up on."

He nods towards the stairwell. "Especially our boy there. He seems to be a delight."

She smiles. "That he is, Bart. I'm happy that you'll have the chance to get to know him."

He squeezes her hand. She rises and fills the tea kettle.

"I suggest we crack open a bottle out of the case I brought, Jess. Leave the tea for the dowagers."

Jess shrugs and goes to the cabinet to retrieve a pair of crystal wine glasses. He opens the wine and fills the glasses to the brim.

"How is your investigation company doing?" he asks. "Is there enough detective work in Portsmouth to keep you busy?'

"Yes, and it keeps building. Sarah and I've enjoyed a respectable flow of cases. It seems there is always a wife tracking a cheating husband or a businessman tracking a cheating partner. We even get the odd missing person case. I may even need to hire a secretary at some point."

"I have a few more items I'll need your help with while I'm home."

"Of course. It will be like old times," she says. "I don't know if I ever thanked you for believing in me and spreading the word about my new venture. We never could have left Odette's without your help."

"You built the business, Jess. You saved me a lot of money and headaches with your fine work. I was happy to recommend your services to others— your detective services that is."

She laughs as she stirs the stew.

"Speaking of work, Bart, I was wondering if you might know a sea captain named Grievance Collins from years back?"

"Ah yes," he strokes his beard and answers. "What a battleaxe. I only crossed paths with him a few times. He had a brittle disposition."

"Did you know anything about his family?"

"There were rumors that he left people in New Bedford. Sadly, that's fairly common for men in my trade."

The boy returns to formally present Mr. Soapy.

"A fine companion and adventurer to be sure," Bart says inspecting the stuffed doll.

"So, where did you adventure to?" Nah asks.

"All over the world—mostly Asia."

"What's Asia?"

"It's a continent, Nah," Jess says. "Get the globe and Bart will show you exactly where it is."

"OK, but you'll need to watch Mr. Soapy. He needs constant watching as he's a 'rapple rouster.'"

"He looks like it," the captain laughs.

The lad shrugs and runs to get the oversized globe. He's barely able to carry it to the kitchen without dragging it across the floor.

"Let me give you a hand there, Nah," Bart offers.

"So, where's this Asia place?"

"Right here," the captain points.

Nah's brow furrows. "But that says China. Where's Asia."

"China is part of Asia," Bart answers.

"That doesn't make any sense."

"We're nearly ready to eat, Nah," Jess interrupts. "How about we save the geography lesson for after dinner?"

They sit down at the table as they hear Sarah opening the front door.

"Capt. Bart!" She runs and hugs him. "We saw all the interesting things being loaded into your house. Where were you this trip?"

"All sorts of places. Bali, Malaya, India. I even saw the emperor of Japan."

"What's an emperor," Nah asks.

"It's like a king," Sarah answers.

"Do we have one of those in New Hampshire?"

Sarah roll her eyes. "Nah and I have been talking about government of late."

The boy spies her bag. "What's in there?"

"It might just be some parsnip cake for a certain boy."

"Yay! What's all this paper." He pulls the newspaper out of the bag and tosses it to the side.

"Now don't have the cake before you finish your dinner, Nah," Jess warns. "You need to eat your stew."

"Speaking of food and other exotic things, I can't wait to show you what I collected during my travels. You're all invited tomorrow evening if you're free. I'm sure that's enough time for Cook to have sorted the kitchen."

Jess smiles to see the excitement in her children's eyes. They've never been to a house as nice as Bart's—and certainly not for supper.

"Oh, and please bring your gentleman caller, Sarah," he adds.

Sarah blushes, her eyes avoid his. "I guess he's my gentleman caller."

"How about six o'clock?" he says. "I can leave word for him at Coxe's. I understand that he's staying there."

"Um, well, OK. His name is Stephen Bailey. Do you know Coxe's?"

"I do. My ship's boy lived there before we took off five years ago. It would be nice to say hello to Lily."

"I just thought of something," Jess says as she passes the rolls to Bart. "Sarah and I want to be at Taylor's hearing tomorrow and I'm not sure how long it will take. How about we bring Nah over to visit with you during the afternoon. You can get to know each other."

Bart asks the boy, "What do you think Nah? Want to spend a few hours with an old sea captain?"

Jonah's eyes grow wide. He nods.

"It will be right before 2 p.m." Jess says.

"That's perfect. We can continue our discussion about Asia."

Jonah savors his cake while the rest finish the bottle of Spanish wine.

"Wanna see my room, Captain Bart?"

"Sure, Nah. That would be stupendous. But then I should probably be going. I have some work to do before my first guests arrive tomorrow."

The boy leads Bart up the stairs.

"This is mine," he points to his small bed. "and that's Momma's."

"Your mother is a very special lady, Jonah," Bart says as he looks longingly at the lacy quilt.

The boy frowns. "She's just Momma."

The captain laughs.

"Let's go say goodnight. We'll have fun tomorrow. I have lots of things to show you at my house too."

Sarah turns Nah around on the stairs. "Time for bed, little brother."

He frowns but allows her to lead him up to his room.

"It's wonderful to have you home, Bart," Jess says opening the front door.

"I've missed you, Jess," he says as he envelopes her in his barrel chest and kisses the top of her head.

After a moment she gently pushes him away and smiles. "Have a good night. We'll see you tomorrow."

"Do you think it's time to tell the boy?" Sarah asks as soon as Bart leaves. "I mean he looks just like him."

"Maybe you're right. Let's see how tomorrow goes. I'm going upstairs to say goodnight."

Sarah picks up the glasses and moves towards the kitchen. She scoops up the newspaper and is about to toss it into the stove when something catches her eye.

"Mutton nob!" she yells and falls against the kitchen table.

"What is it?" Jess races into the room. Trembling, Sarah hands the paper to her mother.

"Oh, cruppers."

CHAPTER 54

S avannah takes a drink from the goblet and pours Tippy another glass. This new client seems to enjoy listening to her talk as much as the basket making.

"Then there was the fellow from Japan who wanted to eat raw fish from between my paps and down to my hoohaw. The fish looked very pretty all rolled up with bits of seaweed on top. He used these wooden sticks to slowly eat each roll until he got to my mossy treasure. I had to bite down on a rag to keep from giggling."

"Did you eat the raw fish?" Tippy asks.

"Hell no. Why would I do that? Disgusting."

Savannah regales Tippy with more stories of her career in between glasses of wine and rump riding. Occasionally the reporter makes a note in his book.

"Tell me about the old lady—the one with the makeup."

"Odette?"

"Yes. How did she start this business?"

"The rumor is that she began as one of the low rent girls on Water Street. At some point she gathered enough money to move in here and open up. There were only a few girls at first. She slowly built up the business."

Tippy frowns and bites the end of his pencil. "How would a Water Street whore have enough money to open up this place?"

She shrugs. "Nobody knows. There were a few old timers here when I started. One said that she thought Odette had a benefactor who was looking for a little class and discretion."

"How long have you worked here, Savannah?"

"Ten—I mean five—years or so."

Tippy smiles. She's not fooling anyone. He changes the subject.

"Was Suzanne addicted to opium the whole time?"

Savannah rolls her eyes. "Why do you give a crumpet button about that bitch? She was unpleasant and wasn't much of a whore."

"You really didn't like her much, did you?" He laughs.

'Truthfully, she was a snob. She didn't speak much to the other girls and didn't carry her weight after she started on the drugs."

"I thought she had one friend," he says, "someone named Anastasia. Wasn't that her name?"

"I guess you could call them friends," Savannah rolls her eyes.

"What do you mean?" he asks, taking a swig of wine.

"I mean I can put on quite the show with another girl for a paying customer but those two did it on their own time."

Tippy's eyes open so wide Savannah's worried that they are going to pop out of his head.

"Are you telling me that Suzanne and Jessamyn Jakes were together—in that way?"

"You really are a chowder head at times, Tippy. What did you think I meant?"

Tippy laughs. "You should be a star, Savannah."

She smiles. She's heard this malarkey before from richer men.

CHAPTER 55

Scoot Massey slowly rolls off the girl and lights his pipe. Commodore Beauregard gives him his choice of the field girls every time he returns another escaped slave to Pullyhawly, the largest plantation in Rooster County, Virginia.

Cilla, Mrs. Beauregard's personal maid calls through the door, "The commodore wants to see you."

"He can wait. I'm busy now." The slave catcher slaps Ruth's naked behind and takes another puff of his pipe.

"He says right now," she insists. She'll get hit if he doesn't come immediately. The master doesn't take no for an answer—about anything.

"For Christ's sake it's only just past dawn. All right."

She walks back to the house.

"One day that asshole better let me fuck that Cilla," he says to Ruth as he pulls up his pants.

"You know only the commodore is allowed to touch her. Not yet eighteen and she already has two babies by him."

The walleyed, scrawny slave catcher pulls on his ratty shirt and hat. "We'll see about that."

"Maybe if you'd brought Esther and Ada back years ago, you'd have gotten to poke all of them," Ruth says laughing pulling her cotton shift over her head.

"Shut the fuck up!" He backhands her across the face and walks out the open doorway towards the house.

"What a fool that man is," Ruth says to the yellow cat licking his paws in the corner.

Esther and Ada.

Cilla's mother and sister.

He chased them all over for years and then they disappeared. He finally had to abandon the hunt when a mob of abolitionists ran him out of the north. By then the trail was so cold, he'll figured he'd never find them.

Massey crosses the grand porch of the main house. Mrs. Beauregard always tells him to use the servant's entrance in the back. "I may not be able to fuck that Cilla, but I sure as shit am using the front door," he grumbles as he passes the master's dogs.

The two white poodles, Fantine and Lola, lie in the shade next to the wicker chaise lounge where mistress usually has afternoon tea with her dotty old friends. The dogs growl at him as he crosses the threshold. "I hate you fucking Frenchie mutts," he grumbles.

The house feels cool compared to the early morning heat. The dark wooden floors gleam and Scoot makes his way to the front parlor. The petite mistress scowls at him as he tracks mud across her fancy flowered rug.

"Glad you could finally join us Mr. Massey," the plantation owner sneers at the younger man.

"Uh. Yeah, sure," the slave catcher responds. He's pretty sure the commodore doesn't mean it.

The gray-haired, stooped man rolls his eyes at Massey and asks, "Have you seen this?" He holds up a tattered newspaper.

"What's that?" Scoot asks.

"It's from up north, the commodore answers.

"Why would I read some Yankee trash?"

Massey's reading skills aren't top notch so he's unlikely to be perusing anything with words—Yankee or not.

"One of my business associates in Boston sent it to me. It's about some whore that was murdered in New Hampshire." He hands the younger man the paper as he takes a drink of his morning bourbon.

"Why would I care about that?" the slave hunter asks as he settles himself on the settee. Mistress covers her nose with a yellowed lacy handkerchief.

"It's not the dead whore that interests me," the commodore says. "It's the adopted daughter of the lady detective working on the case."

Massey looks at him with a blank expression. He's confused about why he was pulled out of Ruth's bed at such an early hour.

"Christ!" Beauregard snatches the paper from his hand.

"Language, commodore. Language," Mistress says as she moves away from him to a chair next to the marble fireplace.

He smiles at his wife, nods and starts reading, "Not only is she intelligent, but the fiery redheaded detective outsmarts the local authorities every day of the week. Her lovely adopted mulatto daughter, Sarah—with the heart shaped birthmark on her cheek—calls Jessamyn Jakes the 'smartest filly on the east coast.'"

"Sound like anyone you know?" Mrs. Beauregard asks.

"Heart shaped birthmark?" Massey scratches his sparse beard. "Wait! Esther's girl, Ada?"

The commodore nods and points to the paper. "Look at the picture."

"Jesus," Scoot says. "She looks just like her mama."

"Yes, she does. Esther must be dead if she was adopted by someone else," Mistress observes.

"We want you to go up to this place called Portsmouth, New Hampshire, and find out if this girl is our missing Ada," the old man says as he fills his glass again with the crystal decanter.

Massey can't believe it. After fifteen years, he'll finally bring her home.

Cilla, pressed against the hallway wall covers her mouth with her hands to keep from crying out.

Her sister is alive and living somewhere named New Hampshire.

CHAPTER 56

They sit on the settee drinking tea in the early morning. A square of pink light travels across the floor illuminating the globe and finally the wall of leather-bound books.

"But how did this happen?" Jess asks shaking her head holding the newspaper in her hand.

"Stephen," Sarah says as her eyes fill with tears. It's hard to believe she has any more to shed after the last sleepless night.

"What? Why?" Jess asks.

"The writer of this story—this Edward Prospect—must be his new best friend, Tippy. He was at the inn when we had dinner. Stephen said he was a writer."

Jess lays back on the settee and closes her eyes. "This can cause us a lot of problems."

"I'm aware of that," Sarah says. "Don't you think I know that?" Tears run down her face.

"We have to put a stop to it," her mother says as she paces back and forth. "This reporter can't keep writing about us."

"But how do we do that?" Sarah pleads. "How do me make him stop? We didn't know he was doing it in the first place."

"I don't know, Sarah. I don't know," Jess says as she rubs her temples. "How did he get that drawing of you, anyway?"

"Stephen drew it of me after he was here the first time," she answers. "He sketched it from memory."

"So, you didn't pose for it?" Jess asks.

"No!" Sarah shouts. "I would never pose for him that way. I can't believe that he made me look like I was naked. I'll never talk to him again."

Jess sighs and gives her daughter a reassuring caress to her cheek. "It's all right, Sarah. I know you didn't sit for him." She remembers her own time before Odette's where she posed for worse.

"I saw it when we ran into him at the waterfront. When I asked to see it again at the inn, he told me that he lost it—that it blew away to Portugal. That mutton nob was lying to me," Sarah says.

"Maybe this Prospect stole it—or maybe Stephen sold it to him," Jess says.

"Yes, that could be," Sarah replies.

"What I don't understand," Jess starts, "is why would the newspaper publisher put a drawing of you near a story about Suzanne's murder? It just doesn't make sense."

"I don't know," Sarah says. "I'll never understand journalists."

They sip their tea as Sarah wipes the latest tears from her face.

Jess breaks the silence with a whisper, "Sarah, have you told Stephen about your past yet?"

"No," she replies, "and I won't—I'll never tell him. As far as I'm concerned, he can drop dead."

"He's bound to find out sooner rather than later," Jess offers, "especially with this reporter around."

"I don't care. It's over." Tears flood her eyes and she slumps back on the settee wrapping her shawl tightly around her shoulders.

"You don't think he did this on purpose, do you?" Jessamyn asks. "It seems like this Tippy person may have tricked him into revealing things about us."

"That just means that Stephen is soft in the head," Sarah exclaims. "I'm not sure what's worse, that he's malicious or that he's as dumb as a bucket of clams."

"Hmm," Jess says. "How do you suppose that the newspaper got into the cake bag, anyway?"

Sarah thinks for a moment. "Well, Tippy had a stack of papers at his table at the inn. He left the room when Trask was clearing the dishes. Elias must have seen the story, picked up a paper and slipped it into the bag."

"To warn us?" Jess asks.

"Maybe. I suppose it could have been happenstance."

Jess furrows her brow. "I doubt it was a coincidence. Elias Trask is a smart, kindhearted man. He must have done this deliberately."

"Maybe so," Sarah says.

Jess continues, "Whatever happened, it's better that we know—no matter how painful it is. It being a Boston paper we're unlikely to have seen it. Until, of course, the Portsmouth paper picks up the story—that's bound to happen sometime."

"Oh God," Sarah says. "My life is ruined."

"Don't worry, we'll figure something out. With any luck the whole thing will blow over soon and they'll be onto the next scandal. There's always something dreadful happening in New York or Boston."

"It would be good if they'd hang Taylor quick," muses Sarah. "Not only to kill this story but also because he's a sadistic jelly bag."

"I agree with that."

Sarah wipes her tears as Jonah pads into the room with Mr. Soapy.

CHAPTER 57

Mistress requires an extra dose of laudanum before she'll settle in her darkened bedroom for her usual nap. All the excitement of the morning has brought a return of her vapors. Cilla struggles to remove the old woman's stockings and petticoats trying not to wake her. She'll be out for at least two hours. The young woman opens the curtains to let air into the stagnant room before slipping down the hallway to the back stairs.

She runs down the hill to the slave quarters looking through the open doorways to be sure that Massey isn't lurking somewhere. She finds her friend chopping carrots and okra for soup.

"Cleo! My sister is alive."

The older woman looks up from her work.

"Ada?"

"Yes," Cilla replies. "There was a Yankee newspaper. It says that she lives up north in a place called New Hampshire.

Cleo frowns. "Why would Ada be in a newspaper? Do they list escaped slaves in the papers up there?"

"No. At least I don't think so," Cilla replies. "Anyway, it doesn't matter. What matters is that Massey is going up there to get her."

"Oh shit," Cleo says shaking her head. "That's no good."

"I need to warn her."

"How?" The older woman frowns. "How can you do anything about it? In case you've forgotten, we don't have any power around here."

Cilla nods. "I know that. I have to try. I cannot sit back and do nothing."

The older woman whispers, "Even though Esther and Ada left you here all those years ago?"

"I can't blame her for that," Cilla shakes her head. "She was only five."

"Do you even remember her?" the older woman asks.

"Barely, but she's still my sister. I remember what a three-year-old remembers, her smell, the heart shaped birthmark on her cheek, her soft hands. All I know is that I need to get a letter to her."

Bonnie and Delilah crawl in from the yard and Cilla plops them on her lap. She nuzzles their necks eliciting giggles. "Hi babies. You know your mama loves you."

Cleo watches the younger woman cuddle the children. "No, it's too dangerous. Remember the last time the master caught you writing? You couldn't walk for a week."

It was true. Mistress had taught Cilla some letters. It was one of the few times that the old couple had fought bitterly in front of the slaves—the commodore insisting that no good could come of it. He beat Cilla and sent her back to Cleo. The exile was as much punishment for his wife as anything else. It was two weeks before the old lady could convince him to send for her. He gave in mostly because it took too long for Cilla to come to his bed in the middle of the night.

Even though the reading lessons stopped, Cilla kept learning in secret. Dusting the books in the commodore's dark paneled office was a task that took five minutes but now takes a half an hour. At night, she uses a stick to write words in the dirt floor. She also steals the old newspapers that she's supposed to use to wrap fish and reads them by candlelight in the small shack that she shares with her quiet, new roommate Alice. The paper seems to be mostly about the price of cotton and something called the Crimean War.

Occasionally there will be something about people who are headed west. A topic of debate seems to be whether slavery should be legal in these new territories. Cilla reads these carefully even though she doesn't know a lot of the words.

The main reason Mrs. Beauregard wanted Cilla to read in the first place was so she could help with her correspondence to her sisters and aunt in Gandersburg County. As time goes by, the older woman struggles to see. Her handwriting now looks like that of a child.

Even though she can't help the mistress write letters, Cilla is still responsible for bringing the mail the post office.

"I have an idea," Cilla says. "I can slip an envelope into the letter pile as long as it looks like the mistress wrote it. The postman should just send it."

Cleo shakes her head. "I don't know, Cilla."

"I have to risk it," she says. "First I need to see the newspaper that Mr. Beauregard showed Massey."

The young woman kisses her children and returns to the house before she's missed. She keeps her head down for the rest of the morning fussing over the old lady's clothes. The last thing she needs is to get in trouble for something today. Before Mistress rises from her respite, Cilla makes her way to the commodore's study to look for the newspaper.

She desperately wants to see the picture of her sister.

It's nowhere to be found.

There is, however, a map of the United States open on the desk. She's heard of Portsmouth, Virginia, but not Portsmouth, New Hampshire. She runs her finger up the coast until she finds another Portsmouth, but it appears to be in Rhode Island. Finally, her finger lands on Portsmouth, New Hampshire.

She makes a note of the spelling in her head.

She continues cleaning until Benjamin, the head of house, comes in. "What the hell are you doing? You just dusted in here yesterday. You know you're not supposed to loiter."

"Mistress asked me to tidy up while she naps. She's upset about the ash coming from the fireplace."

"That's the washer girl's problem, not yours."

"Yes sir."

She curtsies and backs out of the room hoping that she hasn't caused a beating for poor Alice.

Luckily, Mrs. Beauregard's writing desk is in the front parlor—a room Cilla has reason to frequent. The basket where she puts outgoing mail has a couple of letters in it already. She should be sent to the post office any day now.

CHAPTER 58

Everyone is packed into Cheney's church for the hearing. It's the largest space in town and the only one that can accommodate the crowd. Sarah sees Tippy slink in, but he quickly disappears. He must have gone up to the balcony.

"Judge Ichabod Minke presiding!"

The booming voice comes from a robust bear of a man ringing a bell next to the altar. A titter of giggles emerges from the crowd as the petite judge steps on an apple crate to reach his chair.

Savannah, looking radiant in a new peach dress and hat sidles up to Jess. "You think his roly poley is child sized too?"

Jess rolls her eyes. "Show some respect, Savannah. He's a man of the law."

"Whatever," she replies twirling her matching fan.

The gavel bangs and the judge speaks. "Order in the court! We're here today to conduct a preliminary hearing regarding the pending charges against one Dewitt Isadore Taylor for murder in the first degree and rape in the first degree against one Miriam…" He fumbles through his papers. "What the devil is that girl's last name?"

The bailiff leans over and whispers in the judge's ear.

"It seems that nobody knows the last name of the deceased. We will use the name of her final employer until such time as her actual name can be discovered. What is that name?"

"Wilson!" the crowd shouts.

"What about Suzanne?" Daisy, Essie and a few of the other girls from Odette's call out. "Doesn't anyone give a shit about Suzanne?"

"Order in the court!" The judge bangs his gavel.

"He's got a big voice for such a little guy," Daisy whispers.

"Shh!" Sarah scowls at her.

"Ladies. As this is Rockingham County and Miss…what the hell is her last name? What is wrong with you people that you don't know anyone's last name around here?"

"She was a whore," someone from the upper balcony yells as if that is explanation enough.

The judge rolls his eyes. "Well, whoever she was, she was killed in Strafford County and not Rockingham County where we sit today. Mr. Taylor will be charged and tried separately in Dover at the conclusion of these proceedings. Which brings us to today's hearing. Please bring the prisoner before me."

Taylor looks rough. He's still dressed in the colorful clothes he stole from Mrs. Wilson. His wound has scabbed over and festers. He has two black eyes and his nose has a new angry twist.

Jess gasps as he turns his head to face the crowd. "Cruppers."

"What?" Sarah asks.

"I think I did that," Jess whispers.

"What, beat him up? He looks like a pig on slaughter day."

"I don't remember hitting him. I kind of lost control but I think I just kicked him in the belly. He looks terrible."

"Did you do that?" Savannah asks leaning in. "I hope you did. Essie offered to lollipop the guard so Daisy and I could get in there with a bull whip. Emerson wouldn't even let us in the door much less down the ladder."

"Mr. Gadney!" the judge booms. "Are you here representing the defendant Dewitt Taylor?"

"Yes, sir." Archibald Gadney, moves to Taylor's side at the temporary dock.

"Old Gadney," Savannah says loudly. "He stopped coming around a few years ago. Someone said he found religion."

"Shhhhh!" Sarah scolds. "Christ, Savannah, everyone's looking at us."

The redhead smiles to the crowd. "That's why I'm here—advertising."

"So, Mr. Gadney," the judge says. "How does your client plead on count one, the murder of Miriam Wilson?"

"Not guilty, sir."

"Count two, the rape of Miriam Wilson?"

"Not guilty, sir."

"Count three, burglary of the Wilson household."

"Not guilty, sir."

The gavel bangs.

"As Mr. Taylor has been deemed a flight risk it has been determined that he be held without bail in the Portsmouth City Jail until the trial date of December 5 at this location. We'll start promptly at 9 a.m. Court is adjourned." He bangs the gavel.

The two prosecutors rise from the first pew, shake hands with Gadney and exit out the side door.

"That didn't take very long." Sarah says to Jess. "And they aren't taking him to the county seat."

Jess shrugs, "Maybe they're worried about lynching along the way."

"They don't give two bullocks in this town for quality working girls," Savannah starts in. "I even heard that Sally's on Water Street is thinking about bringing new talent up from Boston every two weeks. There's no respect for professionals anymore."

Jess and Sarah nod.

"Say, can I talk to you two—alone?" the tall redhead asks.

Sarah frowns as Jess replies, "Yes of course, Savannah." The three women exit the church and walk towards Odette's.

"What can we help you with?"

"I'm thinking of changing my line of work and was curious about how you were able to do it without a man. I mean I think I could convince one of my regulars to put me up for a while but beyond that..."

"Are you talking about the Wednesday regular?" Sarah asks. "I mean I wouldn't count on him too much if he's too afraid to even show his face in public."

"No, not him. There's a new client that just came in. He's a newspaper man. He seems very interested in my story and my other services—even paid double."

Jess and Sarah exchange glances. "Just who is this newspaper man?"

"Goes by Tippy but I saw his story in the paper. His real name is Edward Prospect. Didn't you meet him? I mean, he wrote about you. I thought he must have talked to you."

"No, he didn't," Jess frowns. "I'd be careful of him, Savannah. I don't think I'd put all my eggs in that basket."

CHAPTER 59

Tippy enters the church and is able to slip by the crowd of women. He spies Savannah as he retreats up the stairs to the balcony shoving a few dowagers out of his way as he goes. They make disapproving clucking noises at him.

Hidden by a column, he looks over the crowd. If he cranes his head just so, he can see his favorite redhead talking to Sarah and a tall brunette with a long braid.

"I wonder if that's Jessamyn Jakes, the lady detective herself." He probably should be more careful about what he tells the red-haired whore. She may still be on friendly terms with her former coworkers.

Ah Savannah! He'd like to take a big bite out of her. That outfit makes her look like a ripe peach. She definitely needs to keep that hat on when he fucks her next.

She comes back on duty at 5 p.m. today. He wants to be there promptly so he can spend the whole evening with her. Things are going so well, he feels like he can splurge for the night. "Maybe I'll even book a bath," he says to himself. "I wonder how much it would cost to have Savannah blow my grounsils in the tub?"

He knows what he should do today. He should go to South Berwick to track down that Orla Reilly. "Oh, forget it," he mumbles. "I'll just finesse it old style." He has the basic details. That's all he really needs. "It will take too long spend a couple of days searching out the girl."

After the final gavel, he waits for the room to clear and slips out the back to head to the inn. He'll write up the hearing and send it on the early evening train to his editor in Boston. Luckily for him, the lady detective and Sarah showed up so he can write them into the narrative.

The question remains, when does he reveal the new facts to his readers?

Their former lives as whores.

Jessamyn Jakes and the first victim were lovers.

He can't believe his luck with this story. It just keeps getting better. No need to reveal those shocking details yet. He has plenty of material for now.

After the hearing he walks towards the inn and catches sight of Savannah, Jess and Sarah talking in Market Square. He darts behind a bush and makes his way back to the Codfish.

The dining room is quiet but for an elderly couple eating by the window.

"Trask, how about some of those excellent cod cakes, my good man."

"The kitchen is closed, Mr. Prospect," Elias responds.

"But yesterday, I came in around the same time and you didn't have any problem serving me."

The innkeeper shrugs with a slight smile. "Sorry, sir. That was yesterday. Today is different."

"But, aren't those two eating?" Tippy points to the couple.

"Kitchen closed as soon as we served them." With that Trask marches out of the dining room. Tippy can smell the cakes frying in the back room.

"That's strange." the newspaper man says. "I wonder what's eating him."

The reporter spends a few hours in his room writing up the proceedings with the judge. The trial update is complete with detailed descriptions of Jess and Sarah's clothing—except now Jess is wearing what Savannah had on and her daughter is wearing what the beak-nosed girl wore. He uses a little creative license to relay their reactions of shock and horror at the pretrial event. He adds lots of made-up details about Miriam and her gruesome ending. As an afterthought, he adds that after the trial in Portsmouth the prisoner will be transported to Strafford County to face charges in the whore's death.

He has time to kill before Savannah will be on duty, so he writes the Orla story. Without interviewing her he doesn't feel the constraint of sticking to the actual facts. The words flow and he scribbles with abandon. He reviews his work and doesn't bother with a second proof before he packs the two stories up and drops them at the train station.

The pretrial update will run tomorrow, and the Orla story will run on Saturday. That gives him a buffer day to gather more material. He'd like to do something big for the Sunday edition.

As the sun drops behind the nearby warehouses, he wanders downstairs and spies some new guests eating an early supper.

"Is it serving time now, Trask? How about those cakes?"

"Sorry, sir. We're fresh out." Elias smiles as he drops off a full plate to the new guests. "Oh, and Prospect, we have a big party coming in tomorrow for the boat launch. They reserved the room in advance. I'm afraid that you'll need to check out by 11 a.m.

Tippy knows he's getting the bum's rush. It's not worth the fight. He'll find another room tomorrow.

He stops in at the Bladder Wrack for a drink and orders the supper special. It's some kind of gray soup. He pushes the bowl away from him and eats the bread while finishing his watered-down ale. He only has a few minutes before Savannah comes on duty.

CHAPTER 60

N ah is so fascinated by Captain Bart that he doesn't even notice that he's been at the house for hours before Jess and Sarah arrive.

"Momma! Look at these!" He holds up a carved ivory bead the size of a walnut. "They're rats trying to get in a bag of rice!"

Sarah grabs the carving out of Nah's hands. "Oh my! It really is. What is this thing?"

"It's called a netsuke," Bart replies. "They are used to fasten purses to kimonos in Japan."

"It looks like you must have been collecting them for a while. There has to be at least 20 here," Sarah says

"I started collecting them this voyage. I confess that I may have won the majority of them in a card game. It seems that my opponent was more used to sake than whiskey," he chuckles.

"Look at this!" Jonah picks up one of the intricate carvings. "It's a snake wrapped around a monkey."

"They're incredible, Bart." Sarah gets out her sketchbook and starts to draw the figurines.

A mahogany desk with burlwood inlays gleams in the candlelight against the blue silk wallpaper. Jess is overwhelmed by the richness of the surroundings. It's too much. She prefers the simplicity of the house on Holt Street.

"What is that shiny black box?" asks Sarah, pointing to a large chest in the corner.

"It's lacquer from Japan," Jess answers as she runs her hand across the smooth cool surface. "Inlaid with abalone. This looks to be of the highest quality."

Sarah wonders, "How does Jess know so much about Japanese furniture?"

"Jess is right," Bart says. "It is indeed a lacquered Japanese wedding chest. It was part of a collection on a ship bound for Malaya."

"It's beautiful, Bart. All of it," Sarah says.

"Purists would not appreciate that I'm mixing all of these cultures together in one room. The rugs are from Turkey, the wallpaper is from China and the mahogany furniture was made in western Massachusetts."

"I think it's all amazing," Sarah declares. "But the netsuke are my favorites."

"That's my favorite," Jonah says pointing to a sword hanging above the fireplace.

"You have fine taste, my young friend," the captain says. "That is the prize of my collection. It's a fifth century Samurai sword."

"What's a Samurai?" Sarah asks.

"A great Japanese warrior," Jess answers.

"I'm going to be a Samurai when I grow up," Jonah declares.

"Me too!" Sarah laughs.

"Cook has been experimenting with some of the spices I brought back from Asia. I hope you're feeling adventurous."

"It smells lovely." Jess follows Bart and Jonah out of the parlor. "Come on

Sarah. Those netsuke will be there after supper."

The formal dining room is a vision in purple. The walls shimmer. Sarah runs her hands along the surface. "What is it? How did you make it sparkle so?"

"They're glass beads," Bart answers. "It's supposed to increase the brightness in the room by reflecting the candlelight from the sconces."

"It's magical," Sarah says. "I've never seen anything like it before."

There's a knock at the door.

"Ah, yes," the captain says. "Your friend Stephen must be here." He moves towards the hallway.

"Crupper juice! I completely forgot that he's coming tonight," Sarah lunges for the door. "He needs to leave."

Bart looks confused but lets her pass by as they slip to the kitchen.

"What are you doing here?" she yells at the blonde man holding a bottle of wine. "How can you think of showing your face here after what you did?"

"What do you mean?" Stephen says. "What did I do?"

"Did you see the Boston paper?" she asks.

He shrugs. "Why would I see the Boston paper? I don't even read the Portsmouth paper."

"Your little friend, Tippy, has taken it upon himself to write about Jess and me. He only could have gotten the information from you."

"What? Tippy is a reporter?" He takes a step backwards toward the door.

"He told you he was a writer. What did you think he wrote?"

He shrugs. "I guess I thought novels."

"Well no, you mutton nob, he writes salacious news stories." Sarah pokes her fingers into his chest. "Do you have any idea how bad this is for Jess and me?"

"I don't understand. What did the story say?"

"It said that Jess is a good detective," she starts, "and that I am pretty with a heart shaped birthmark on my cheek."

"Um, I'm confused," Stephen says. "Aren't those good things?"

"Don't you understand? It's only a matter of time before he finds out about our time at Odette's and where I came from. Don't you get it? They'll be coming for me."

"You worked at Odette's—as a whore?" he blurts.

"Yes, Stephen, I worked as a whore. Jess and I left when I was 15."

"You slept with men for money?"

"Yes, Stephen. That is what whores do."

He collapses on the settee. "But you said you were a virgin."

"I never said that," she shakes her head, "I said that I didn't have a lot of kissing experience. I never kissed any of the men who paid to be with me. Aside from that I think that you're missing the larger point here."

He looks up at her dazed. "What point?"

"The point is that I am an escaped slave and some crupper prong slave catcher probably knows where I am—and, to top it all off they even have a picture of me!"

"What? What do you mean?"

"I mean Tippy printed your drawing of me with the story," she replies gulping for air trying to hold back the tears. "The one where I look naked."

"My drawing? But how?"

"You didn't sell it to him? Is that how you got the money for dinner?"

"No! Oh, my God. I'm so sorry, Sarah. He must have stolen it from me when I was distracted."

Tears run down her face and onto her yellow dress.

"Please just leave," she says quietly.

She points to the street and he walks down the granite steps and through the courtyard. He doesn't look back as he wanders away.

Jess and Bart lead her back inside to the settee. Jonah starts crying and crawls onto Sarah's lap. He clutches her and they rock back and forth.

The evening repast is cold by the time they sit down—Cook is furious.

In silence they pick at their food—a mushy mass of meat and vegetables on rice.

After a while Bart speaks up, "I think she's still getting a handle on how to use the spices. The main dish was supposed to be a type of lamb curry that I had in India."

"I can't really taste anything," Sarah says sniffling.

"The bread was excellent, Bart," Jess offers.

"It's called roti. It's also from India. In fact, the whole meal is from that region. We have a rice pudding for dessert. I tasted it and I believe we're in for a treat. It's flavored with a spice called cardamom."

The servant girl, Maude, clears the dishes while Cook shuffles around the table with crystal bowls placing them in front of each of the guests. Jess dips her spoon in first and smiles. "It's delicious."

Cook smiles and retreats to the kitchen.

Even Sarah manages to eat a second bowl.

After dinner they retire to the parlor with glasses of port for the adults and hot chocolate for Jonah.

"Jess, I have some business I'd like to talk over in my study if we can leave Nah and Sarah for a few moments."

"Of course." They walk through the dining room towards the study.

Jonah sits on Sarah's lap with his arms tightly wrapped around her neck. "Sarah, is someone really going to come steal you?"

She looks down at him. "Oh Jonah, no. I was just upset. Nobody's going to steal me." She squeezes him tight—wishing she believed what she's saying. She hasn't been this scared since her real momma died and Odette picked her up off the street.

Bart slides the doors closed behind them as Jess asks, "What is it? Do you have another ship gone missing? Another accountant skimming off the top?"

"Pretty much always but that's not why I called you in here."

She furrows her brow. "Hmmm. Then what is it?"

"Jess, I think you should marry me."

CHAPTER 61

C illa tosses and turns all night on her pallet. What good is a letter going to do if Massey gets to Ada before it arrives?

By morning, she knows what she has to do.

"You're plum crazy," Cleo says as she listens to the plan. "You won't get fifty yards, much less all the way to Portsmouth."

"Mama and Ada managed it. There must be some way—and besides, I don't have to make it to New Hampshire. I just need to get far enough for the letter to reach Ada before Massey goes after her."

Cleo frowns. "So, you're betting that they'll chase you and not her."

"Why would they chase her first?" Cilla asks. "As far as they know, she's not going anywhere."

"But how? You can't do it on your own," Cleo shakes her head.

"There's those church people," Cilla says.

"You mean the Quakers?"

"They've helped others," the younger woman replies.

"Not from this plantation. Besides that's 100 miles over the mountains from here."

"Still, I've got to try," Cilla says smoothing her plain yellow dress.

"What about your babies?" she says as they watch the two toddlers fight over the corn cob doll that used to be Cilla's.

"I thought about it all night. I need to show them that some of us can escape and build a new life. Ada has done that. Even if it means the beating of a lifetime."

"Or worse," Cleo whispers and hugs her close.

"Yes, or worse."

Cilla slips back to the house before her mistress notices that she's missing. Luckily, her master left at dawn for a business meeting. He'll be gone for hours. He usually stops by the Broomstick Tavern on his way home and arrives home late—if at all.

She thinks she's figured out the writing and the address part but then there is the problem of the expensive postage. She'll need a whole dollar to mail the letter. Luckily, today is also dry goods day so she'll be entrusted with cash to do both errands. Maybe she can squeeze the dollar out of that.

What she needs now is to have some time alone in the parlor to write and address the letter using the old lady's inkwell.

It has to match the others as best as she can manage.

Mistress takes her first nap every morning after breakfast. She's fast asleep and Cilla takes her clothes downstairs to freshen them up. Her mind races as she lays out her lady's dress. She needs to write the letter before she is to go on the next post office run. Noticing a small food stain on a lacy collar she goes to the kitchen to retrieve a damp cloth. Blotting the garment, out of the corner of her eye she sees the blur of Fantine running through the house with a fisher cat on her tail.

"Benjamin! Benjamin! Help! Help!" Mistress yells. Cilla runs to the bedroom just in time to see the animal rip a gash in the dog's neck. The old lady faints as Benjamin kills the predator with a shotgun splattering blood all over the walls and floor. By this time, the whole household has gathered in the bedroom.

"Oh, dear God," Benjamin says as he kicks the fisher cat to be sure it's dead. "How did that vermin get into the house?" He yells at the timid washer girl, "Bring a bucket and some rags and clean this bloody mess up!"

"You!" he points at Cilla. "Get mistress's laudanum. She'll need a triple dose today." Cilla nods and runs downstairs, meeting Alice in the hallway on her way with the bucket and rags. The small girl whispers to her "Go! Now! Get what you need for the letter."

Cilla's eyes open wide. She says softly, "Was it you? Did you let that fisher cat in here?"

The girl's eyes twinkle as she smiles.

"Thank you, Alice," she whispers.

Cilla runs to the pantry for the laudanum and slips into the front parlor to retrieve the inkwell, paper and quill pen stashing them in her skirt as she enters the bedroom to delivers the medicine.

"Cilla!" the old woman cries. "My poor Fantine." She clutches the girl's arm. Despite being frail, the woman has a tight grip.

"It's all right, Mistress. You just take some of this," Cilla whispers. "We'll fix Fantine up while you sleep. Everything will be fine."

The woman drinks the laudanum and lemonade out of the small cordial glass and lays back against the silk pillows.

Benjamin notices Alice scrubbing up the bloody mess with a big smile on her face. "There's something not right about that girl," he whispers to Cilla as they walk into the hallway. "Mistress will be out most of the day," he continues. "Let's leave for town as soon as you get your morning chores done. The sooner we leave, the sooner we're back so you can help with the pickling—and I can get my nap in."

She nods and smiles before racing to finish the letter.

CHAPTER 62

Bart insists on taking them home when Jess refuses to stay the night. If Jonah weren't so scared about his sister, this would be the most exciting night of his life. Sarah brings him into the house and upstairs while her mother and the captain linger in the doorway.

"Remember, Jess," he says. "If you need anything at all, please send word."

"You've been a great help already," she replies. "Thank you for spending the day with Jonah and for walking us home."

"Don't forget about the awful dinner," he adds laughing.

Jess smiles. "It really wasn't that bad. We're just not used to the spices."

"Jess, please consider what I've asked you," he says taking her hand. "You know I love you—and of course I love Sarah and Jonah. You're the only family I have left, now that my mother is gone."

Jess hugs him. "Don't worry Bart, I'm giving it every consideration. Thank you again for everything."

He kisses her gently on the forehead and turns back to his home.

She locks the door tight and walks upstairs where her family is already curled up in her bed asleep. Nah has Mr. Soapy in a death grip. "No wonder that doll needed surgery."

She smiles, realizing there is no room for her so she retreats to Sarah's bed. It's amazing how much space a small child like Jonah can take up.

After tossing and turning for hours she goes downstairs to the parlor and curls up on the settee. She lights the oil lamp and starts to read one of Mrs. Pritchard's novels—something about a family called Usher. She doesn't get far before she blows out the lamp and falls asleep. It seems like just a few minutes later when she wakes to the sound of a soft knock on the kitchen door. Wrapping herself in her shawl she finds her way in the dark to the kitchen.

"Jess? It's me, Maryanne."

She opens the door, smiles and envelops the smaller woman in her arms kissing her in her sleepy daze.

"I had to see you." Maryanne says returning her kisses and rubbing her hands along Jess's body through the thin shift.

"We need to be careful," Jess whispers. "Jonah and Sarah are right upstairs. What time is it anyway?"

"I think it's around 4 a.m. I couldn't wait until Wednesday to talk to you—and so when I heard the reverend leave the house an hour or so ago, I slipped out."

"I'm glad that you came." Jess leads her to the kitchen bench. "I've been thinking about you all week."

"Even with all the excitement?" Maryanne asks.

"Even with all the excitement." She kisses Maryanne behind the ear. "You smell wonderful—like lavender."

"That's nice but I came here because I need to tell you something."

"What?" Jess asks.

"The reverend and I are to marry."

"That I know," Jess laughs. "He did introduce you as his fiancé."

"I mean today," Maryanne says, "this morning."

"What? Why so soon?"

"I'm not sure. We were supposed to marry in the spring. A friend of his from seminary was to come and officiate at Silas's church. For some reason he arranged for us to marry at Cheney's church at 9 a.m. today."

"At Cheney's church?" Jess asks, "But they hate each other. That makes no sense. This is so strange."

"I know." She nods. "I thought I would have a little more time to adjust."

"Are we still on for Wednesdays?" Jess asks quietly.

"I think you know the answer to that." Maryanne slips her hand under Jess's shift and up her thigh.

"We'd better stop," Jess says. "I can't think of how I'd explain this to Nah."

"I'd better be going anyway. The cook arrives at 5 a.m. It wouldn't do for me to be coming in after her."

Jess kisses Maryanne goodbye and watches her slip through the kitchen garden to the alley.

"I didn't tell her about Bart's proposal," Jess thinks.

She hasn't told Sarah either. She needs some time to contemplate it herself before getting other people's thoughts.

The truth is she doesn't know herself what to make of the captain at this point. He visited her frequently at Odette's and was her first customer as a detective. He had made a good case to her. Security for her family. Could he really protect Sarah? Be a father for Jonah? She told him she would think about it but this new relationship with Maryanne has her head spinning.

She wouldn't be able to cheat on Bart the way Maryanne is doing with Hobson—she respects him too much. She even loves him in a way—more like a brother than a lover. She could pretend to love him but that seems like a giant step backwards. Doesn't that just make her another type of whore?

She makes tea, wraps herself in her shawl and watches the sunlight rise up the side of the barn.

A busy day lies ahead—burying one lover while another gets married.

CHAPTER 63

She keeps it simple. Cilla addresses the letter to Ada's adopted mother—making a guess on the spelling of her name.

Jassamin Jaxe

General Dilivery

Portsmouth, New Hampshire

She sneaks into the Commodore's office to confirm the spelling of the name of the town and she copies the return address from the mistress's latest letter to her sister Arabella. It looks just like the others in the stack waiting to be posted. With the old lady's five, she now has six letters to mail. Now, she just has to see if O'Leary notices the Yankee address and says something. Master writes to northerners all the time as part of his business dealings, but his wife has never written to anyone outside of Virginia and North Carolina. If the postmaster notices anything, she'll be dead.

Mistress has left a long list of items for purchase at the dry goods store with cash for both errands. She counts the money and reviews the list. There isn't a spare dollar for the postage.

"Oh well, I guess Arabella won't be getting her cross-stitch update," Cilla says as she tosses the letter into the outside kitchen stove on her way to meet Benjamin and the wagon.

It's an hour-long ride to town on the dusty road. The excitement of the morning has made Benjamin more talkative than usual. Cilla sits quietly as he rambles on and even sings in his deep baritone. She gets the feeling that he hates the dogs.

Her mind keeps going back to the postmaster. She almost abandons the mission as she's sure he'll question the Yankee letter. Where can she hide it? She needs to burn it. Too late now. They've arrived in Buttonhole—the seat of Rooster County.

Main Street seems quiet for a Saturday. Usually the shops are full of farmers, wives and slaves doing errands. Benjamin stops the wagon in front of the post office. "I'll meet you at the dry goods store when you're done here. I have a few errands on my list. Don't take too long. Remember you have those pickles to help with when we get back."

"Yes sir. I remember the pickles," she says dropping the few feet to the dusty road.

Her hands are sweating, and she almost pees herself as she pulls opens the door of the small post office.

"Hello Miss, what can I do for you?"

A strange man with a pleasant grin and short beard stands behind the counter.

"Where's Postmaster O'Leary?" she asks shyly.

"Gone to the coast," the bearded man replies. "His mother is poorly—not expected to live through the night."

Cilla relaxes a little and lets out a sigh. "That's too bad," she says as she walks across the creaky floor.

"Do you need to mail those? He points to the letters in her hand."

"I do, yes. Thank you," she replies. "Also, my mistress wants to know when the next coach comes through. Her letter to her auntie has some importance."

"This afternoon at 2 p.m. You're lucky, you got here just in time," he replies. "You tell your mistress the letters are on their way."

"She'll be glad to hear that."

"That'll be five dollars," he says as he stamps the letters and tosses them into a canvas bag at his feet.

"Thank you, sir," she says as she hands him the coins.

"You're welcome, girl. Have a nice day."

She considers running, but realizes that she'd be walking on the same road that she traveled, and adding five miles to an already long journey through the mountains. She says a prayer that the Quakers are there and that they will help.

"It doesn't matter—as long as Ada gets the word," she tells herself as she enters the dry goods store and starts to fill her basket. Usually she reads the list before entering the store. She gets a strange look from the shopkeeper.

"Oh, Mrs. Mullaney!" she exclaims.

"Sarah," the older, rail-thin woman says with an eyebrow raised. "What do you have there?" She points to the list.

"Oh, could you read this for me? My mistress is under the weather today and she sent me along with it without telling me what is on it."

The frowning woman takes the paper from Cilla and begins to collect items from around the store.

"That'll be $2.75."

Sarah looks at the money in her palm. "Mistress only gave me $2.50."

"I told the Commodore there would be no more credit," the sharp woman snaps. "You'll need to put something back."

"She'll be upset if I don't have everything when I return."

It occurs to her that she doesn't care what the mistress thinks and she pulls the ribbon and thread out of the basket and places them on the wooden counter.

"Here's your nickel change," the older woman says as she drops the coin in Cilla's hand.

"Thank you, ma'am," she responds as she bows her head.

Benjamin pulls the wagon up just as she walks out the door. She climbs aboard and settles next to him on the buckboard.

Her mind is racing. What does she need for her journey? Food for sure. Warm clothes. Water. A map. Is there such a map? Money? Where the hell would she get money?

She doesn't know where she is going.

"You're awful quiet today," Benjamin says eying her. "What's got you all tongue tied?"

"Nothing," she responds. "Just feeling poorly, I guess."

"Nothing about that newspaper that Mr. Beauregard had yesterday?"

"I don't know anything about that."

"I think you do," he says as he snaps the reins on Esmerelda's spotted brown back.

"If you say so," she closes her eyes and pretends to doze off.

Benjamin hums the whole way down the dusty road to Pullyhawly.

CHAPTER 64

B art picks them up in his coach midday for the funeral. He knew Suzanne from Odette's, but he never used her services. In fact, Jess is hard pressed to remember him ever paying for one of the other girls.

Jonah is spending the day with Mrs. Markwart and Jack so he won't ask a lot of unanswerable questions. At some point, they'll tell him the truth about everything—but not today.

As they turn the corner into Market Square, they see a crowd milling about outside the church.

"What the hell is going on?" Jess asks. "I thought Cheney and you agreed to a small service, Sarah. What are all these people doing here?"

The right reverend greets them as they enter the church.

"This is my mother, Jess, and our friend, Captain Pritchard," Sarah says. "Thank you again for agreeing to perform the service right reverend. I'm sorry about the crowd. I know we said to keep it small."

"No worries, Sarah. We'll sort it all out. It seems that the newspaper story has generated a lot of interest. Word spread like wildfire."

Noticing Sarah's red eyes he asks, "Are you feeling all right, my dear?"

She tears up, but she nods, "Yes. I'm fine, sir."

He pats her hand and turns his attention to Jess.

"Miss Jakes? Do you have a few moments to speak to me about your friend Suzanne? I ordinarily try to mention an anecdote or two about the deceased. Do you have any stories to share?"

Jess thinks for a moment. All of her stories involve sex and none of them are appropriate for church. It occurs to her that she really didn't know Sweetness at all.

Sarah watches her struggle and blurts, "Her most prized possession was a prayer book."

"Ah, OK," the clergyman smiles but looks confused. "Thank you."

They enter the church and spy a bevy of women—the entire local whore population has turned up dressed in brightly-hued finery.

"Do you see Odette?" Jess asks Bart.

He looks over the ladies' hats and replies, "No. I don't think she's here."

"That evil bitch," Jess whispers. "Not even showing up at the funeral after she caused Suzanne's death."

The colorful ladies giggle as Cheney ascends the chancel to the pulpit.

"This is the strangest funeral I've ever been to," whispers Bart, "and I've been to a Famadihana death ceremony where they dance with corpses."

"Shh!" Sarah raises an eyebrow at him.

"We are here today to lay to rest one of God's children, Suzanne. May she rejoice in the arms of the lord, finally at peace…"

Lars Peterson bursts though the heavy wooden church doors. "The Puddle Dock Warehouse is on fire!"

Jess, Bart and Sarah stay in their seats as the crowd stampedes to the exit.

"Well, I guess the service will be small after all," Cheney says.

CHAPTER 65

Stephen watches the warehouse burn before pitching in to help the fire brigade keep the flames from torching the whole waterfront. It feels good to do something other than sulk in his room.

The brigade takes a while to set up the pump to douse the flames with water from the harbor so the volunteers pass buckets to try to keep the flames from spreading. They cheer each other on as the buckets are emptied onto the flames. Stephen sees Coxe and the Flannigan boy in the line but loses them when the pump finally arrives.

The fire brigade douses the structure which collapses in on itself. By dusk the flames are out, but the warehouse and the two souls inside are assumed lost.

Stephen's new clothes smell like smoke but he's proud to have been part of the effort. At least the ever-present dead fish odor near the water has dissipated.

They drag Emerson's body from the flames. A few minutes later, another brigade member emerges from the hole shaking his head.

There's no sign of Taylor.

Rumors quickly spread across the crowd that Taylor escaped by lighting the fire that killed the policeman, Gerald Emerson.

Stephen doesn't know and really doesn't care either way. He starts to walk back towards the boarding house thinking about Sarah and imagining her naked with other men. How many of the fire brigade and volunteers has she been with?

He turns the corner and spies a tidy Tippy walking out of the Bladder Wrack—no firefighting for him. He must be on his way to pick over the remains of the tragedy.

CHAPTER 66

Early the next morning, Gerald still lies the near the smoldering shell of the building. Jess lifts the tarp covering him and looks over his body. He has a gash across his chest. His face frozen in the throes of final agony.

She calls over to the policeman guarding the scene. "Balche? Did anyone ever find Taylor's body?"

"No ma'am—although there isn't much left of the basement. If he was in there, he's as likely as not a smudge of charcoal. The fire brigade searched but didn't find anything."

"Hm. Thanks, Balche."

"Sure, Miss Jakes. Have a good day. Miserable mess this is."

"That it is," she agrees.

She moves along towards Odette's as they load Gerald's body into a wagon and drive him towards Cyril St. John's funeral home.

There's a hastily made paper sign on the door of Odette's. "Closed until further notice."

Jess rings the bell.

Nobody answers.

She walks around to the kitchen entrance and catches Granny headed to the oven with a tray of biscuits.

"Is everything all right, Granny? Why is the house closed?"

The girl whimpers a reply, "Miss Odette closed it yesterday as soon as the girls came back from the funeral."

"May I see her?" Jess asks.

"She said not to disturb her. She's been holed up in the waiting parlor."

"I think I need to see her," Jess insists. "Don't worry, Granny. I'll tell her I ran around you."

The small girl looks scared. "Thanks, ma'am. She was scary last night. She slapped me hard when I went to collect her chamber pot. It spilled and she wouldn't let me clean it up. I've never seen her like that before."

Jess makes her way up the stairs to the parlor. Knocking on the door she asks, "Odette? It's me Jess. Are you in there? We need to speak."

She knocks harder. Nobody answers. "Now come on Odette, open the door!"

Finally, she goes back to the kitchen. "Moira? Do you have a spare key for the parlor door?"

"Sorry, Jess," the cook answers. "Odette grabbed her keys and took them into the room with her. There aren't any others."

"Well, we need to get in there. I'll grab a ladder from the shed."

Jess crosses the back garden towards the outbuilding. The shack door is wide open.

She looks inside. "The ladder is missing," she says aloud.

"No, it's not."

She turns. It's Savannah. "Look there, Jess." She points to the south side of the house. The ladder sits against the now broken parlor window.

"Oh, cruppers!"

"You got that right," Savannah replies.

"Have you looked in yet?"

"No, but it can't be good," she replies.

"Did you hear anything, Savannah?"

"No, we were in the dormitory after the funeral and everyone was crying and carrying on about Taylor."

Jess climbs the ladder in her dress and uses her gloves to wipe the broken glass off of the sill. She can see something from behind Odette's desk. A beaded slipper lays on the floor. Gnarled toes emerge from a ripped green silk stocking.

She crawls through the window and onto the Oriental rug.

Circling around the desk she gets a full view of her former boss.

The madam's tongue protrudes from her mouth and her eyes bulge. Strangled with a silk garter belt. Her green dress and myriad of petticoats are torn exposing heaps of gray flesh and blue veins.

Jess won't clean her up like someone did for Miriam.

She has her hand on the doorknob when she remembers something.

The map of the Shoals is still on the wall. She wraps it in her shawl before she opens the locked door to Savannah's waiting figure.

"I guess we know for sure that asshole isn't fried chicken like we hoped," the redhead says.

A few of the girls peer into the room. Daisy runs down the hallway and almost makes it to a planter before vomit splatters the wall and floor.

"Essie and Granny. You run to get the police—or whoever is left of the police now that Gerald Emerson is dead," Savannah commands.

The redhead doesn't notice that Jess is holding her shawl in a strange manner. Her eyes are fixated on the ring of master keys lying on the floor near Odette's gnarled foot. She snatches them up and flies downstairs to speak to the rest of the girls. Jess closes the door behind her and walks down the front staircase and out the door.

Jess knows that she should wait for the police but instead she makes her way towards Bart's.

"Maybe I should marry him. This detective work is getting a bit grim."

CHAPTER 67

Benjamin puts the horse and wagon away as Cilla carries the full basket into the house. Cleo has been waiting for the spice packages for pickling. The kitchen is full of cucumbers, beans and okra.

"Thanks, Cilla. Did you eat any supper?"

"No ma'am," the younger woman replies.

Cleo hands her a chicken drumstick and an apple which she eats out on the back step. "This may be the last food I have for a while," she thinks to herself. She has to leave tonight. With the mistress out like a light and the commodore drinking in town this may be her last opportunity.

Cleo puts her to work until dark with the pickling. When they finish, the older woman hands her a small bundle and shoos her out the door towards her cabin.

Alice stands in the dark next to two additional bundles, waiting for her.

"I'm coming with you," the quiet girl says.

"Alice? You can't. You're too small. We'll probably be killed."

"I have food, a knife, some extra shawls and most important, this." She hands Cilla a large piece of paper. She holds the map near close to her face to better see it in the dark. There's no writing except an arrow pointing a large N for north. Hills, farms and streams are depicted.

"What do you have?" Alice asks.

"Just some food," she says pointing to the bundle at her feet. "How did you get this map? It's incredible."

Alice grabs it back from her.

"A friend." She holds out her hand. "He also gave me this." Six silver dollars glimmer in the low light. "I don't know if he stole it or not but it's ours now."

Cilla looks at the small girl's feet. "But you don't have any shoes, Alice. How far are you going to get without shoes?"

"We don't need to worry about that. Come with me."

CHAPTER 68

A knock on the door wakens Stephen from his restless drunken sleep. He moans and rolls over pulling the patchwork quilt over his head. He ignores the throbbing and the knocking sound. His head feels like an anvil fell on it and his mouth tastes like he's been eating mothballs.

"Mr. Bailey! I need to speak to you immediately! It's nearly noon. Get out of bed!"

He crawls to the door and opens it. A scowling Mrs. Coxe stands there with her arms crossed.

He realizes that his pants are on backwards and hopes the landlady doesn't notice.

"Mr. Bailey. When you moved in here, I told you that we were a respectable boarding house. Respectable does not mean coming home drunk and sleeping half of the day. I'm of a mind to throw you out, but the mister insists on giving you another chance."

Stephen can barely remember anything from last night. "Um, thank you ma'am. I assure you that it was an aberration. It won't happen again."

"It had better not." He starts to close the door pushing her out. She sticks her foot in the door. "One more thing. I believe that I told you firmly that

Odette's is the preferred brothel for our tenants. Mr. Fitzgerald has told me that he spied you on his way to church this morning emerging from Sally Lightfoot's on Water Street."

It comes flooding back to him. He was on his way home when he ran into Tippy. He took a swing at the scrawny reporter who easily ducked his shot and retaliated with a surprisingly strong left hook. He fell to the ground and was picked up by a few onlookers. The group retreated to the Bladder Wrack and the whiskey started flowing. The bars were crowded, and everyone was talking about the fire, Taylor and the dead servant girl. At some point they left the Wrack and wandered down Water Street.

He's not sure if it was his idea or Tippy's to go to the brothel.

They ran into Mr. Fitzgerald who was definitely not on his way to church. His fellow boarder had a blonde on his lap with her hand down his trousers. He's a little fuzzy about the details after that except he does remember a naked Tippy riding a robust girl around the shabby parlor. At some point he poured out the whole Sarah story to his former friend—not quite remembering that talking too much was what got him into trouble in the first place.

"Sarah. Oh God! Sarah." He puts his head into his hands and collapses onto the braided rug.

How could he have been so stupid? Did she even care for him? A whore. He can't believe it. He should have stayed with the Simpsons. At least there he knew where he stood. Matie may not have been exotic but she certainly tried to please him.

He fixes his pants, combs his hair and walks down the stairs. He's starving. It's nearly dinner time. He stops in the kitchen doorway but retreats out the front door when he sees the angry look on the woman's face.

"I guess I'll need to find sustenance somewhere else," he mutters as he walks in the cold towards downtown.

The bars on Water Street aren't open yet so he beats a familiar trail to the Codfish Inn. The dining room is filled with customers in Portsmouth for the schooner launch.

"Jesus, Bailey. What happened to you?" Trask inquires as he pours him a cup of coffee.

"I found out that the love of my life was a whore," Stephen laments.

"You mean Sarah Jakes?" Trask asks, his eyes narrowing.

"Yes. Did you know that already?" Stephen blurts as his face reddens.

"Everyone knows that," the innkeeper replies. "There aren't many secrets in this town."

Stephen looks around at the other diners. How many of these men had been with her?

"What about you, Trask? Did you fuck my Sarah?" He starts to rise out of his chair.

Trask swats him with his kitchen towel. "Listen here, Bailey. Sarah and Jess are good people. They did what they had to. You don't look to me like you have ever had to do much to survive. Ever been desperate, Stephen? Have you ever even missed a meal?"

"Except for breakfast this morning, I guess not," Stephen replies slumping down in his chair. Even when his father threw him out after all those years at university, he gave him money. He even let him keep his horse, Leonardo. It was just two nights later that he landed at the Simpson's.

"To answer your previous question Bailey—even though it doesn't deserve the dignity of a reply—I never met Sarah until you brought her here for lunch. I only met Jess when I hired her to track down some missing papers for me." He takes a deep breath then continues quietly, "Believe it or not, there are a few gentlemen in this town who don't visit whorehouses—no matter how classy they are supposed to be."

Stephen starts to cry. The other patrons steal glances at him. He doesn't seem to notice or care.

The innkeeper sighs and pats him on the shoulder. "Say Bailey, why don't you come into the kitchen and I'll cook you some eggs and bacon."

CHAPTER 69

Tippy has so much material that he doesn't know where to start. Between the funeral, the fire, Taylor's possible escape, Odette's murder and the treasure trove of details from Stephen he has enough to generate stories for the next week.

He's had to relocate to the more expensive Rockingham Hotel, but he feels he deserves the added grandeur. Future stories will bring even more money as other papers pick them up. The piece on Orla was in a handful of outlets today after running in Boston yesterday. The escape/fire story he's filing now should be in twice that many by the end of the week.

He may even buy a new suit.

Maybe he'll bring Savannah here for supper. Although she seems kind of preoccupied now with getting Odette's under control. She had the place open for business just two hours after the police took the old madam's body. The house has been swamped with paying visitors who want to see where Odette died. Savannah pulled Daisy off of whore duties so she can walk people through the room and describe the gruesome details.

All of this is annoying to Tippy—not only did Savannah refuse his company but she made him pay the $1 entry fee for the tour.

He's not sure he likes this new version of his favorite redhead.

It was a good thing he ran into Bailey. The night turned out to be all right in the end. Maybe he'll bring that girl he was riding at Sally's here for dinner if Savannah doesn't have time for him anymore.

He looks around the wood-paneled lobby at the well-dressed patrons. "Hmm. Maybe that girl wouldn't fit in here. I'll need to get her a better dress."

CHAPTER 70

J ess rises at dawn and watches her children cuddled together under the quilt. Three in her small bed made for a restless night. She doesn't disturb them as she retrieves the shotgun from the floor.

She makes her way down the stairs, stashing the weapon in the pantry before pumping water for tea and stoking the stove.

A noise from upstairs jars her.

"I need to get a hold of myself. Taylor is probably long gone by now and Massey can't possibly be here yet," she says to herself.

"Let's hope so," Sarah says, wandering into the kitchen. "I don't think I can spend another night sleeping with little kicky boy up there."

"Nice to hear you sounding more like yourself, Sarah. I was worried about you," Jess says as she hands her daughter a cup.

"I'll be fine. Let's just sort out this treasure business and move along. I'm ready for a new case." She drops the book from the Atheneaum onto the table next to the map of the Shoals and wraps herself tightly in her shawl sipping the steaming tea.

"We need to talk about a few other things while Jonah is still sleeping," her mother says, settling next to Sarah at the table.

"Like Bart's marriage proposal?" she asks cocking one eyebrow.

"You guessed?" Jess laughs and after a few moments responds. "I'm considering his offer."

"Really? What about Maryanne?" her daughter asks.

"That's one of the reasons I haven't accepted yet."

Jess rises to feed a log into the stove. "I like our lives the way they are—without a man telling us what to do."

"Bart doesn't seem like he would be that way," Sarah says.

"I don't know. Men change when they get married," she muses. "Although, I suppose he would be gone a lot."

Sarah laughs. "That's a funny reason to marry him. I mean, usually wives want their husbands around—at least at first."

Jonah comes running in the room sobbing. "Momma! You left me alone."

She strokes his hair and kisses him softly calming him down.

"Say sweetie. Let's look at this together." He crawls onto her lap and they all look at the Shoals map from Odette's office.

"What's that?" Jonah points to a very small marking on the east side of Smuttynose Island.

"It looks like someone made a mark in pencil," Jess says.

"Can it be?" Sarah asks.

"Can it be what?"

"Wait a minute." Sarah opens her bird book about the Shoals to a page with a map of the islands.

"Right there." She points to the words "Wreck of the Concepción. 1813."

CHAPTER 71

Mirabelle seems to be as happy to be leaving Pullyhawly Plantation as the girls. She keeps up a rapid clip on the ride north. Cilla holds on as tightly as possible to Alice's tiny waist.

"I can't believe we stole the master's best horse," the older girl says. "This is crazy! I never should have let you talk me into this."

"You just have to trust me," Alice says. "I know we haven't known each other that long—I mean it's only been six months since I got here."

"Why did you get shipped over to Pullyhawly anyway?" Cilla asks ducking her head to avoid a branch.

"I just got into a little trouble at Mistress's sister's plantation, that's all. Besides, we're likely to hang anyway. Might as well not walk to our destiny," the smaller girl notes.

They ride Maribelle hard for a few hours through the dark wooded terrain finally stopping at a stream just as the sun is peaking over the treetops.

"Here's where we lose the horse. We walk in the stream for a day north over this mountain."

They hit the horse on her rump sending her west.

"You don't suppose we'll be so lucky as to have Massey follow that horse all the way to California?" Cilla asks.

"California?" Alice asks. "Where's California?"

"The newspapers call it a paradise where gold rocks can be scooped up by anyone with a basket."

"Sounds like pig shit to me," Alice says. "We're meeting someone."

"Meeting someone?" Cilla asks. "I thought we were looking for Quakers."

"That Quaker story is all lies. If they were around once, they sure as hell ain't anymore," Alice replies. "We're meeting my brother's people."

"Your brother?" Cilla asks. "You have a brother?"

"Yes. He escaped from Evangeline's plantation six months ago. When they couldn't find him, they whipped me and sent me to Pullyhawly."

"How do you know he escaped for real?" the taller girl asks raising her eyebrow. "I only know my sister and mama escaped for real."

Alice sighs and replies, "My first week with you I went to the privy at night and someone tossed a pebble at me from the woods."

"Was it him—your brother?"

"I don't know. I came out of the privy and couldn't see very much in the dark. I tripped over a package on the ground. It was wrapped in the shirt he escaped in. In it was this map, the knife and these coins." She holds out her hand with the silver dollars.

Cilla's eyes open wide. "You'd get strung up for having any of these things. Where did you hide them?"

"I buried them in a burlap sack near the privy in the woods."

They consult the map to be sure they are on the right track. There are no words on the paper, but Cilla sees detailed drawings of landmarks and the author even used a clever sun symbol to indicate how long to walk. She looks up and there's Sassafras Mountain, right where it should be.

CHAPTER 72

Stephen thinks about getting on his horse and leaving Portsmouth. Tossing and turning all night, he obsesses about Sarah. "What do I have to stay here for? The love of my life is a whore who hates me. Why do I even want a job anymore?" He finally gets up and goes down to the kitchen at about 5 a.m. for a cup of water.

The smell of freshly baked bread reaches his nose. He sheepishly bows his head to his landlady. She looks up from her potatoes, wipes a tendril of hair out of her eyes and greets him with a stern nod. "Up early for your first day of work. That's a good sign."

"Mrs. Coxe, I want to apologize once again for my behavior. I had received some shocking news and went a little insane afterwards." He sinks slowly into a chair at the table where she works.

She raises an eyebrow and keeps chopping. "What kind of news makes a man go a little insane?"

He holds his head in his hands. "I just found out that the woman I am in love with was a prostitute. You can see what that might do to a man."

She frowns and commences chopping a stack of carrots. "Is this lady friend of yours still a prostitute?"

"No, of course not," he answers.

"Then what's the problem?" Bits of carrots fly across the table and hit him in the face.

"Well, what—what do you mean?" Stephen starts blustering. "I mean I can't possibly marry anyone who was a prostitute—I mean what would my mother think?"

She puts down her knife and stares at the young man. "Talk often to your mother about prostitutes?"

"Well, no," he answers, "I really don't talk to my mother much about anything anymore."

"Hmmm. So, let me get this straight," she says as she picks up the knife and points it at him. "You decided that the best way to solve this little problem of your lady love having been a prostitute is to get raging drunk and hire a prostitute yourself?"

Stephen turns red. "You just don't understand."

"Where was she a prostitute? That Sally Lightfoot's that you were in?"

"Oh no, she was at Odette's," he sputters.

"But she's not anymore?" Lily crosses her arms over her chest.

"No. She hasn't been there for five years."

A frown comes across the woman's face. "Are we talking about Sarah Jakes? Is she your lady love?"

"Yes. Do you know her?" he asks.

"Of course, I know her. My husband and I hired her mother to help us evict a problem tenant. Sarah is a great girl. Lick smart and sweet. Don't be such a jackass, Bailey. The girl was not even fully grown when she had to work there."

Stephen slouches down in his chair. "I guess she was pretty young."

CHAPTER 73

Massey has been following their tracks since early Sunday morning when Benjamin first rang the alarm bell. He'd gone out to find the washer girl when she didn't show up with the wood for the cook. He'd have been out there earlier, but he tripped over the prone body of the Commodore in the front parlor. The master of the house came home so drunk that he left his horse wandering in the front yard.

At least that's where he thought he left her—Mirabelle was nowhere to be seen.

Massey may be as dumb as a palmetto bug, but even he could see that the girls had stolen the master's horse. The trail led north and by the sight of the tracks, they were riding Mirabelle pretty hard. He'd have to pick up speed if he was going to catch them before dark. Once he did, he was going to take his time bringing them back to Old Battle Axe Beauregard. He would fuck that Cilla until she begged him for more. He'd show both her and the old man who was boss.

He'd probably even fuck that little skinny girl, too.

It's pretty easy to follow the tracks at first. Massey stops to take a break and to eat some of the bread he'd coerced Cleo into giving him. He takes a swig off his bottle of whiskey and sits down on a rock near a stream. Storm clouds are rolling in—he's in for a long night. He takes another bite of the bread and notices some human footprints amidst the horse hooves near the riverbank.

"The girls must have gotten off Mirabelle and started walking in the stream. Dumb shits. I should catch up with them in no time."

Massey flips a coin into the air.

"Upstream it is," he says as he tosses the empty bottle into the woods, smashing it against a rock.

CHAPTER 74

Latouche grunts in Stephen's direction indicating that the younger man should follow him to the waterfront. A shipment of boards has come in from the sawmill in Eliot and needs to be counted and logged.

The yard is cranking up for the day. A few of the men drinking coffee from hot tin mugs generate a cloud of steam as they exchange stories from their day off. The tide is low and as Stephen approaches the water's edge, he can smell the stink of the outfalls from the city.

The wood is neatly stacked by thickness on the dock and Latouche hands him the log, a pencil and the chalk. He counts each stack and makes a notation in the book as the older man sits on a crate, smoking his pipe.

Stephen's mind keeps wandering back to Sarah. "Oh, dear God. What am I to do?"

He also keeps thinking of his new landlady and her small waist and pretty hair. "I wonder what she looks like naked? Blonde curls flowing over those white shoulders."

"Excuse me?" Latouche grumbles at him.

"Oh! Sorry! My brain is elsewhere I'm afraid. Here." He hands the ledger to his mentor. Trying to keep warm, he blows into his cupped hands. "This seems pretty easy. I think I'm done."

The older man grunts again as he reviews his work. After a minute of cross checking he hands it back.

"Try again."

"What?" Stephen asks. "What do you mean?"

"Try thinking about your work and not about some hen you're chasing. You got half of these wrong. Start over."

Stephen looks at the ledger in disbelief. He crosses the numbers out and starts counting the boards again trying to keep Sarah and Mrs. Coxe out of his head. It takes most of the morning to finally get the numbers right. "This Latouche is going to be a pain in the ass about this counting," he mutters as he sits eating his lunch. "Maybe I should look for something else where the boss is less of a stickler."

CHAPTER 75

Cilla and Alice walk in the stream until the clouds cover the moon and it's too black to see. The terrain turns to hills and then mountains. Raindrops hit their faces as they scramble over boulders and up cliffs.

"We're going to fall off a cliff in this dark. Let's pull to the side and find somewhere to hold up," Alice says.

Cilla is scared to stop but, knows Alice is correct. "It's starting to rain harder. We need to get somewhere dry for a few hours."

The terrain is rocky so at least they won't be leaving tracks. Clutching tree roots they make their way to the top of a hundred-foot waterfall. A small outcropping provides some shelter from the wind and rain.

"Maybe the water will wash away our scent," Alice says.

"Massey isn't one to use dogs to track," Cilla responds. "Lucky for us, he hates dogs. Ruth said he was attacked by one as a child and never got over it. That's why he has the scar on his jaw—some mutt nearly took half his face."

"Too bad it didn't kill him," Alice says wistfully.

"It would just be some other slave catcher following us if it weren't him. They're all the same, the white men."

"Aren't there a lot of white men where we're headed?"

"I guess so," Cilla nods. "They're supposed to be different in the north."

"We'll see," Alice says frowning.

The rain picks up and the girls huddle together. Alice is careful to protect their bundle from the water as they doze in and out.

A crack of lightning splits a tree towards the waterfall jarring them awake.

They clutch each other as the woods light up around them.

Cilla whispers prayers into Alice's ears as the girls push their backs into the rock.

"What's that noise?" Cilla asks.

"It sounds like a train coming through," Alice says.

"I've never heard a train. I don't know what they sound like," Cilla admits. "There's no train in Rooster County."

A lightening flash reveals a torrent of water rushing not five feet from them. The innocent stream is now a deadly river carrying limbs and debris over the waterfall and towards the valley.

Cilla takes off her dress and uses it to tie them to a root emerging from the rock. They secure their precious bundle between them and pray.

CHAPTER 76

A knock at the front door startles Jess as she cooks breakfast. She holds her breath—too scared to move. What if it's Taylor—or Massey? Finally she slips through the parlor and opens the door. Jimmy, the postmaster's boy stands on her stoop with a handful of mail.

"Hi, Miss Jakes. I have a couple of letters for you. This one had your name misspelled. Luckily, I was there and saw it. The postman almost sent it back to Virginia."

"Virginia?" she asks her eyes growing wide.

He smiles. "Yes, somewhere named the Pullyhawly Plantation. That's a funny name."

"Cruppers!"

"Excuse me, ma'am?" he asks.

"Oh, sorry, Jimmy. Thanks for bringing these." She gently shoves him out the front door.

"What's got you swearing so early in the morning?" Sarah asks sleepily.

Jess hands her the letter. Sarah's eyes grow wide as she reads the envelope. She rips open the letter.

Massey. Run.

Sarah sinks to the floor.

"But who sent it?" Jess asks.

"I don't know. The writing is childish. Maybe it was my little sister."

"Cilla?" Jess asks.

"Our worst fears have been realized," Jess thinks as she rocks her shaking daughter in her arms.

Jess lifts her up off the floor and leads her to the settee. "Don't worry Sarah, I'll figure something out. I always have before." Wrapping her shawl around her daughter, she takes the letter and puts it on the side table just as Jonah walks in, rubbing his eyes. "What's happening? Why are you sitting in the fancy room? We never sit in here."

Jess can't help but smile as she waves the boy over and drags him onto their laps.

"Today, we are going to have an adventure, Jonah," Jess says trying to sound cheerful.

"An adventure?" he asks suspiciously.

"Yes, but first you need to go upstairs and pack a bag. Just Mr. Soapy, pajamas and your Sunday suit. Sarah will be up to help you."

"Where are we going?"

"To Bart's," Jess replies.

"Captain Bart's! Is he taking us on an adventure? Yay!" Jonah runs up the stairs.

"What's the other letter? More bad news?" Sarah says noticing an envelope by the door.

Jess picks it up and rips it open and reads it to herself. "It's from Savannah. She wants to see me. She says it's a business matter. I'll bring you over to Bart's and make sure you're settled before I go by the house."

"Aren't you staying with him also?" Sarah asks with tears in her eyes.

"No sweetie, I have some things to clear up here. I must see Maryanne and I also need to sort out our Taylor problem. Don't worry. This is all temporary, I am sure."

Sarah looks skeptical but nods.

Jonah drags a bag big enough for a month-long excursion down the stairs. His blocks bang on each step as he descends.

"I don't know, Nah. That's a lot of stuff," Jess says. "Why don't you take a few things out?"

"OK, Momma." He pulls one block out of the bag and drags the bag towards the door.

Sarah laughs in spite of her nerves.

In no time Sarah and her mother are ready to leave the house. They exit through the front door and Jess locks it behind her.

It's quiet except for the leaves rustling and a few crows cawing as they make their way to the Captain's house. Putt emerges from his shed and waves to them as they walk past.

They knock on Bart's back door and Cook opens it.

"Miss Jessamyn? Why are you here so early?" the older woman asks.

"Could we see Captain Bart please?" Jess replies.

"Of course," she answers smiling. "I heard him stirring upstairs. Let me tell him you're here. In the meantime, help yourself to a scone. They're hot so be careful. They just came out of the oven."

She disappears while Sarah and Jonah dive into the cranberry scones. Melted butter runs down the little boy's chin.

Cook returns with the captain in tow.

"Jess? Has something happened?"

"Yes. Can we speak privately?" she whispers to him.

"Of course. Come back to my study."

He leads her to the back to the office and closes the sliding French doors behind him.

"Yesterday we received an anonymous letter from Virginia," Jess starts.

"Uh oh. That can't be good," he says as he settles into the red wing back chair, motioning for her to sit on the settee.

"No, it's not," she agrees. "The letter indicated that Scoot Massey, Pully-hawly's favorite slave catcher, is on his way here."

"You think the newspaper article is responsible for this?" He reaches for his tobacco bag from the side table.

"We think so," she nods. "The timing is suspicious."

"You've been so careful and have built such a paper trail. Can he even come get her legally? Can he prove who she is?" he asks as he lights his pipe.

"She's still Beauregard's property no matter what we've done. He'll just grab her and hightail it back to Virginia. He certainly won't be contacting law enforcement while he's here. Even if he did, there'd be nothing they could do. The Fugitive Slave Act requires them to cooperate." She slumps back on the settee and closes her eyes.

"What are we going to do, Jess?" Bart asks. "Sarah can't hide in the house forever. She's certainly welcome for as long as necessary, but that's not a long-term solution."

"I only can think of one answer," she says as she opens her eyes. She's so tired and it's not even 8 a.m. "I haven't discussed this with her yet, but it seems to me that she should go to Europe with you at the end of the month. I'd like to find a school where she can study art and ornithology. Maybe in France?"

"I know of several colleges that would meet that criteria," he says rubbing his bearded chin. "Do you think this is what Sarah wants?"

"I don't know. She's certainly bright enough. She can only learn so much from the Atheneaum. I thought I should check with you first—to see if it was even a possibility."

"Of course, it's a possibility," he smiles. "We can even leave sooner than that and arrange for her schooling when we get there. The boat will be ready ahead of schedule."

"Thank you, Bart. I'm prepared to pay for her voyage and schooling."

She rises and smooths her skirt wishing to end the meeting.

He raises an eyebrow. "Does this mean that you have decided against my proposal?"

"Truthfully, I haven't made up my mind about that yet," she answers. "I don't want to combine the two issues."

"But you're still thinking about it?" he asks quietly as his stands and takes her hand.

"Yes, I am." She hugs him. "I really am."

"I noticed that you don't have a bag with you. Are you not staying here as well?"

"Not now if you don't mind. I need to wrap up this recent case and should be at the house to not appear suspicious in the event Massey shows up in the next few days."

"But you'll visit?" he asks.

"Of course, I'll be by every day. I'll need to be discreet. I don't want to lead Massey here." She turns to him and lays her head on his chest. "Thank you, Bart."

He holds her tight. "You know I'd do anything for our family, Jess."

Her tears threaten and she smiles. "We'd better join the others in the kitchen."

He slides open the doors and leads her by the hand to the other room. They hear Sarah and Jonah laughing. Jess knows she has made the right decision bringing them here.

"Cook," Bart starts, "Miss Sarah and Master Jonah will be my guests for a few days. Could you see that Maude makes up their rooms when she arrives to work?"

"Of course, sir," Cook says smiling. "It will be nice to have young people around."

Sarah takes Jonah into the parlor to look at the netsuke while Jess slips out the back and returns home.

CHAPTER 77

The early morning sun streams though the trees as Massey kicks his soggy bedroll away and surveys the landscape below him.

"Fucking water everywhere."

The floodwaters dissipate quickly leaving a wake of destruction. By mid-morning only puddles, dead animals and downed trees remain.

He leads his horse down the muddy hill back to where he lost the girls last night and looks to see if he can find any trace of them. He slips and he and the gelding slide twenty feet through the mud before coming to rest in a soggy heap. The landscape is so different that he's not exactly sure where he is.

"That rock looks familiar."

Only it's not a rock. It's the bloated body of the commodore's prize horse.

"Shit. He's is going to be some pissed," he says as he sits on a fallen tree trunk eyeballing the corpse.

"Well, Mirabelle. If you're dead then those girls are probably drowned too. I could stay here and see if I can find them," Massey says. "On the other hand, I also know where I can find a real live escaped slave right now—at that place up north."

"I know what you're thinking, Mirabelle. I didn't have an easy go at it the last time I went north. This time, I'll keep my trap shut."

He makes his way back to Pullyhawly through the flooded landscape and arrives just before nightfall.

The house is in an uproar. Mistress is in a fit of rage as Fantine doesn't seem to be recovering from her encounter with the fisher cat.

"Benjamin! Where's my laudanum?" Massey can hear her shrieking.

"I'm looking for it, ma'am. It's not where it usually is," the old man replies.

That's because Alice poured it into the master's bottle—the same bottle that the commodore is slowly draining of bourbon. He barely looks up as Massey enters.

"Sir?" the slave catcher says quietly.

"What do you want, Massey? You find those girls who stole my horse?"

He takes off his hat and replies, "I think they're dead, sir. Drowned."

"Why would you think that?" the older man asks.

"Flash flood came through. Took out trees and all sorts of stuff."

"I repeat—you shit for brains—why do you think they're dead?"

"Well, sir…It pains me greatly to report to you that I found Mirabelle in the water—all bloated up like a balloon." He hands the old man the horse's bridle and reins. "I got her saddle outside. I thought you might want it."

The commodore springs up from his chair, grabs the reins and wraps them around the younger man's neck. "And how is it that a weasel like you managed to survive while my Mirabelle perished?"

"Sir! Sir! You're choking me." Massey can smell the bourbon as he struggles to speak. "It was dumb luck sir! I mean it. I happened to camp on the top of a rise and when I woke up the river was all around me."

The commodore drops the reins, falls backwards and passes out before he lands on the settee.

CHAPTER 78

Alice's eyes open to the red sunrise. She and Cilla are still tied to the root with their precious bundle between them.

"Wake up. It's morning and we're still alive."

Cilla stirs.

There is devastation below them where the water came through. Miraculously it stops about four feet from their shelter.

"Let's untie your dress and see if it's fit to wear," Alice says. "These knots are so tight. It doesn't help that they are wet. Should I cut them open?" Alice pulls the knife out of the bundle.

"No, I can untie them. I can't be running around with a shredded dress."

Alice shrugs and puts the knife back.

Cilla finally undoes the garment and shakes it loose.

"It looks OK. Only a few small tears."

"That's good. I'd hate to have to make you a shift out of leaves."

Cilla laughs as she puts the damp cloth over her head. She looks across the valley to where they came from since yesterday.

"Alice."

"Yes, Cilla."

She takes the smaller girl's hand. "This is our first day of freedom."

Alice smiles. "Let's hope it isn't the last."

The girls eat some of their precious food along with some berries they find in the woods as they walk along the ridge line.

"The map says we should be at the meeting spot by sundown."

CHAPTER 79

J ess looks for her door key in her saddle bag. The old lock sticks but eventually gives way and she enters the quiet parlor. The eerie silence doesn't last for long, broken by the familiar scratching of the dog at the back door.

"C'mon in, Jack. Jonah's not here but I think I can manage a treat before I take you home."

The dog jumps up and down at the word treat and Jess laughs pulling a pig's ear out of a crock. "We really should train you to do a trick for this sometime."

The terrier follows her to the barn where she feeds the horses a few oats and a carrot. First, she walks Buttercup to the fenced yard so she can graze and get some exercise. Jack nips at the horse's heels until she stamps her feet and whinnies at him. Back in the barn, Jess unhooks the latch on Willie's stall as she hears a thump.

"Hmm. It must be the dog and Buttercup," she reassures herself even though it sounded more like it was coming from upstairs.

She leads Willie out of the barn and ties him in the kitchen garden on her way to their small corral. The dog runs circles around the gelding until he is panting and takes a long drink from the bird fountain.

"C'mon, Jack. We need to get you home," Jess says.

Feeling uneasy she takes the time to lock the house up before bringing the dog next door.

The pup runs ahead, and Jess glances behind at the barn.

"Calm down. It was probably nothing," she whispers to herself.

"Excuse me dear, what was that you were saying?"

"Oh! Sorry, Mrs. Markwart. I was just talking to the dog. I'm afraid that Jonah is away for a few days. He won't be able to play with Jack."

"Where is he off to?" the older woman asks.

Caught off guard she says the first thing that pops in her head, "Um. He's visiting my family in Manchester by the Sea."

"Oh! Is that where you're from? What a lovely place! My cousin lived there for many years. Juliette Lawson was her name. Did you know her?"

"Oh, cruppers," Jess thinks. She should have thought this out more carefully before blurting out her real hometown. The aforementioned Juliette Lawson was her family's next-door neighbor. "I'm afraid not. You're speaking of her in the past tense. Has she passed on?"

"Yes, sadly. Five years ago, now," the older woman responds.

Relieved, Jess responds, "So sorry Mrs. Markwart. Were you close?"

She can't stop asking questions even though she wants out of this conversation. It must be frazzled nerves.

Mrs. Markwart leans in close. "Truth be told. I couldn't stand her. What a gossip! She used to tell me all these stories about her neighbors, I think their name was Fawcett. I'm pretty sure she made up most of the yarns. You wouldn't believe what she said about the goings on in that house." She clucks as she shakes her head. "She should have been a novelist."

Jess stares at the older woman unable to speak.

"Are you OK, Miss Jess? You look a bit pale," Mrs. Markwart reaches out and holds her hand to Jessamyn's forehead.

"Oh!" She snaps out of it. "Thank you. I'm fine. I'll see you soon."

Jess is so rattled that she leaves Willie tied in the garden, grabs her bag and walks to Odette's. She doesn't even hear the sound of glass breaking as she makes her way up the street.

She stops when she sees Putt sitting on a log. He stares at the ground and he has a few burlap bags at his feet.

"Hello, Putt. Are you going on a trip?" she asks.

"No ma'am," he whispers. "The reverend told me I was fired."

He starts to cry.

"What? Why?" she asks.

"Don't know, ma'am. He just told me to get the heck out today. Only he didn't say 'heck.'"

"Really?" She looks at the poor boy in front of her.

"Well, Putt. Today is my lucky day. It just so happens that I have a position that you would be perfect for. I can use some help with the horses and such."

And that was exactly when she knew that she wouldn't marry Bart. Her life is headed in a different direction. She knows that she won't be Mrs. Pritchard. She makes her own decisions.

"Move your belongings into Sarah's workshop and tend to the horses. I'll be home for supper, and we can discuss your wages."

"Won't Miss Sarah be mad that I'm in her room?" he asks.

"She'll be fine as long as you don't mind sharing it with her birds."

Putt laughs. "I don't mind, ma'am." He picks up his bags and marches away from the rectory. She watches him close the garden gate before she turns onto Pulpit Street.

Jess enters the whorehouse through the kitchen expecting to sense tension in the air, but is greeted by a flurry of activity.

Moira is piling what looks like a hundred cucumber sandwiches on a pewter tray and Granny runs up and down the stairs with buckets of water.

"What's going on?" Jess asks as the cook flies by her with the platter.

"Savannah's got us running around like rabid foxes today. She's throwing a two-for-one sale. We've been busier than I've ever seen it here."

"Hm. That's smart. Where is the budding businesswoman anyway?"

The cook points to the stairs. "She's upstairs in what used to be Odette's bedroom. She's been waiting on you."

"Thanks, Moira. Don't work too hard, Granny."

"I won't, ma'am," the young girl giggles.

Jess knocks on the door. "Savannah? Are you in there?"

"Enter!"

Jess looks around the room. The furniture has been replaced by a table surrounded by a few chairs from the kitchen.

"Oh my! It certainly looks different in here."

Savannah lifts her head from her work. A stack of papers takes up most of the table. "I needed a place to make plans for the house. Besides, nobody wanted Odette's furniture. Everyone thinks her ghost is lurking."

"I see the line to visit her office is still out the door. I even noticed some women and children in the mix."

"Yes, we've been playing up the ghost story. It seems to be driving a lot of attendance. I've got Essie dressed up as Odette—it took nearly all of our bed pillows to flesh out the dress. She jumps out of the closet when Daisy gets to an especially gruesome part of the story."

Jessamyn laughs. "I may need to buy a ticket myself. In the meantime, you wanted to see me?"

"Yes. Thank you for coming in, Miss Jakes."

Savannah is dressed in a tasteful dress of medium blue silk. Her red hair is in a tidy bun at the back of her head.

"You really are formal these days," Jess observes.

"Please sit down." The redhead waves to one of the chairs.

Jess sits opposite Savannah across the table and accepts a cup of tea and cucumber sandwich.

"As you are probably aware," Savannah begins, "I have taken charge of the business here."

"I can see that," Jess says. "It seems like you are doing a wonderful job."

"Thank you. Anyway, what I am saying is that I've taken over for Odette. I hope to make improvements and increase the profitability of the house over the coming months." She takes a delicate sip of her tea and replaces it in the saucer.

"That all sounds very ambitious. How can I help you?"

Savannah pulls a letter from the stack of papers. "This is a notice from five years ago regarding past-due property taxes." She hands the paper to Jess. "This is the only thing I've found in her files with any clue as to ownership of the house. There are no statements from landlords regarding rent and nobody has come to claim her property."

Jessamyn nods as she puts the paper back on the pile.

"I want you to find out if Odette had a will and if there is there an heir who'll inherit the house."

"Hmm. I suppose you could move if necessary, right Savannah? I mean the house isn't the only asset."

"I could move, but that doesn't seem like an optimal solution. The dowagers in town would make it difficult for me to relocate to another respectable neighborhood. It's important that the business remain as far away from Water Street as possible."

"I can see that," Jess agrees.

Savannah leans over the table to speak. "Please find out who inherits the estate and help me to negotiate a quick purchase."

"I can check into it for you, Savannah. Most likely it will take only take a day or two."

"That sounds fine. I assume you will want a retainer. How does $20 sound?" she says as she pulls the cash out of the libee chest resting at her feet. The lacy sweet nothings lie in a heap in the corner.

"Perfect," Jess says as she takes the money. "I must say, you are very impressive, Savannah."

"You learn a few things over the years rump riding bankers, businessmen and lawyers."

"That's certainly true," Jess laughs. "My best training for detective work occurred within these walls—reading people—sussing out what they're hiding."

"I suspect we know more about these men than their wives do," the redhead says.

"I'll bet you're right about that. I'll get started on this project today. I'll let you know when I have an answer."

"Thank you, Miss Jakes."

Jess works her way through the crowd on the stairs to the door.

CHAPTER 80

It usually takes a few minutes to walk to Bart's house from Odette's, but Jess takes a meandering route to avoid being followed. When she thinks it's safe, she darts down the alley and in through the kitchen door where Cook is struggling with a large clay pot. "The captain told me it's a tandoori pot. I'll be damned if I can figure out how to use it."

"Good luck with it. I'm afraid I can't offer any insight. My culinary skills are somewhat limited. Where is everyone?"

"In the front room I believe. They've been running amok all day."

"Oh dear. Sorry, Cook."

The older woman laughs. "It does my heart good to hear so much joy in the house."

Jess walks down the hall towards the parlor when Nah jumps out from a wardrobe and pretends to attack her with a loaf of French bread.

"You scared me half to death!" she says hugging the small boy.

"Good! I'm a samurai pirate!" he yells.

"That sounds wonderful," she says evading the sword which makes lethal contact with the mahogany sideboard shattering the loaf into a thousand crumbs.

"Oh dear. Jonah, go to the kitchen and get a whisk broom from Cook so we can clean this up." She looks around the entryway. "Where is Sarah? Is she a damsel in distress?"

"Nope. She's a pirate too! We're making Capt. Bart be the girl."

Jess peers into the front room to see her suitor dressed in an elaborate silk kimono with white makeup on his face.

"Wow! What have we here?" she says as she enters.

"Momma!" Sarah jumps across the room and hugs her.

"That's some pirate costume! Complete with eye patch no less."

She turns towards Bart and stares.

"He's a geisha," Sarah offers.

"A Japanese courtesan?"

"See, Bart. I told you Momma was smart," Nah says. "She knows everything."

"I'm not sure about everything. I try to learn as much as I can—reading helps," she says winking at her young son.

"How was your trip back to Holt Street?" the painted lady asks.

"Uneventful, thankfully. Except for one thing. Hobson has fired Putt. Told him to get out today."

"Why would the old man do that? He'll never get another worker like that boy," Sarah says.

"True. That's why I hired him," Jess says.

Sarah and Nah stare at her.

"For the time being he'll be staying in your workroom, Sarah. As I will be paying him real wages, he'll soon have enough to get a room of his own."

"Well, I for one think that's great," Bart says. "I'll feel better with him nearby until all this unrest gets settled."

"Putt wouldn't ever hurt anyone," Sarah says. "He wouldn't be much good in a fight."

"His size alone should scare some off," the captain observes.

"Momma, can I go home with you so I can help Putt move in? I want to show him how to light the stove." Nah pleads.

"No, sweetie. You'll see him soon enough. Now run along and get that whisk so we can clean up before I have to say goodbye."

"I wish you'd stay," Bart says.

"I'll be back soon. Thank you so much for being such a good host and a great sport. I mean this," she says pointing at the kimono, "this is incredible."

"I kind of like it. I may wear this more often. Why should you ladies have all the fun?" he says.

"You can have all of my girlie clothes if you like," Jess says. "Big pain in the ass."

"Good thing you look so beautiful in men's work clothes," he smiles at her cracking his white face paint.

"Um, oh well. To each his own. Pirate Sarah? If I could have a word with you in the study? I have some information about our latest client."

"Sure. Jonah, you keep guard of our prisoner. Don't let her get away."

"I won't." Jonah waves the remains of the bread at Bart's made up face.

"So, what's up?" Sarah asks as soon as Jess closes the sliding doors.

"Savannah wants to hire us to find out who inherits Odette's house."

"That should be fairly straightforward. If she has a will it's probably on file with the city clerk. I can go this afternoon and look it up."

"I'd rather that you didn't leave the house if it can be helped. I'll go over there myself. Anything else I should look for?"

"The registrar's office will have the name on the deed right now. It may be Odette, or it could be under her real name."

Jess makes notes on her paper sheet.

"Why does Savannah want this information—to see who her new boss is going to be?" Sarah asks.

"Actually no, she wants to take over. She's doing a great job already. Apparently, she has an undiscovered knack for business."

"Savannah?" Sarah frowns. "Bosomy, red-haired whore who specializes in wrinkled keisters?"

"The one in same," Jess laughs.

"Who would have reconnoitered that?" Sarah asks adjusting her eye patch.

"Life is full of surprises," Jess replies. "I'd better go if I'm going to visit both offices on the way home."

Cook has already cleaned up the mess by the time they return to the others. She waves goodbye to Geisha Bart and Pirate Jonah and makes her way towards the Portsmouth City Hall.

CHAPTER 81

She finds the registrar's office in the basement after wandering around the tombs of the building for what seems like an eternity.

A bell rings as she opens the door, startling the bespectacled bald man sleeping at the front desk.

He yawns and waves her in. "May I help you with something?"

"Yes. I'm looking for information related to the ownership of this house." She hands him a piece of paper with Odette's address on it. "The owner—at least I think she's the owner—is recently deceased."

"Give me just a minute. That record would be in the back."

She looks around the dingy office. She hears rustling and assumes that the clerk is coming back when a large orange tabby emerges from a bin of tax receipts. "Hello there, cat. Where did you come from?"

The animal rubs along her boots and looks up at Jess with beautiful green eyes. She reaches down and scratches underneath the feline's chin.

"I see you've met Savannah," the clerk says as he returns.

"Savannah? Is she your cat?" Jess asks.

"Well, technically she lives here to keep the mouse population down, but I did get to name her."

"Hm. Pretty name. Where did it come from?" she asks.

He hesitates, "Oh…an old friend."

Jess shakes her head to get rid of images of Savannah and the clerk.

"So, what did you find out about the house?" she asks.

"The property is owned by the Staff of Life Trust Company. It has a manager listed here—a lawyer named Ignatius 'Justice' Tompkins, Esq."

"Do you happen to know where I can locate Mr. Tompkins, Esquire?"

"I believe he lives at the Rockingham and uses that as his office as well," the clerk replies pointing in the direction of the hotel.

"Thank you. You've been very helpful." She smiles on her way out the door.

Her next stop is the office down the dark hallway.

There's a line of customers waiting to speak to the rattled clerk, a woman with frizzy black hair and a sour expression.

"May I help you, Miss?" the woman asks.

"Yes, thank you," Jess replies. "I'm looking for a will for a recently deceased person. A Miss Odette…"

"Last name?"

"I don't think I know her last name," Jess answers.

The woman rolls her eyes and sighs. "I need her last name."

"You can't look her up under Odette or her address?"

"Sorry, no. I need the last name." She starts to wave the person behind Jess to the front.

"Try Smith," Jess blurts.

The clerk raises an eyebrow. "Smith? Really? Come back when you have the last name."

CHAPTER 82

The tailor sees the tidy man looking in his window and calls to his assistant in the back. "Charlie! We've got a live one! Bring out the rack of that mutton cloth we've been trying to get rid of."

Tippy is feeling so pleased with himself that he decides to treat himself to a new cravat. He enters Sheffield's Tailor Shop and is greeted by a well-dressed older gentleman. "Hello, sir. In the market for a new suit? I can tell by your bearing that you are a man of exemplary taste."

Tippy smiles. "It's nice to be recognized as such in this god forsaken town. Thank you kind sir, but I had a cravat in mind. Something silk and festive, I believe."

The assistant wheels in the cart with fabric in deep blues and grays. Sheffield rubs his hands along the row. "Ah, it's a shame sir. I've just received this shipment of the most exquisite Australian Merino wool. I fear that it will go to the moths as I have very few customers of your caliber. Perhaps I could offer you a suit at a discount?"

"Hm," Tippy touches the wool. "I suppose that I should have a suit that better meets my new station in life. Let's do it."

Thirty minutes later, Tippy has a suit on order and a new overcoat to boot. It seems that Sheffield made it for a customer exactly the writer's size who came to an untimely end before he could take possession. The arms are a little long but Tippy takes it anyway. He feels good that he was able to talk the tailor down another few dollars and the old man even threw in the cravat for free.

He wears his new coat to the hotel where he orders a bottle of Mouton 1845 to have with dinner. He has a stack of newspapers to review while he enjoys his rack of lamb. The hotel carries the Boston and New York papers—a day late of course—but who is he to complain?

The first two articles have been picked up by everyone. Even his old employer, *The Tribune*, is running the picture of Sarah Jakes and the story on the front page. It looks like Barney Boone has done a little bit of rewriting making all the characters a bit more risqué. That Jessamyn Jakes would get arrested if she wore the outfit Boone described. He's glad to see that most of the other papers have stayed true to the original stories. He saves *The Chronicle* for last looking for the Orla story.

He unfolds the paper and smiles. The banner headline at the top reads, "BEAUTIFUL APPLE GIRL ESCAPES TAYLOR."

"OK so far," he mumbles.

CHAPTER 83

The girls reach the top of a rise and are greeted with a few misty clouds drifting into a valley green with rhododendrons.

"That's the waterfall," Alice says pointing to the west.

Cilla looks at the map. "It could be that one," she says pointing east.

"I say west."

"I say east."

"West."

"East."

"You're both wrong. It's south."

They jump around to see a young man coming out of the woods.

"Robert!" Alice runs and jumps into his arms. He's just a few inches taller than her but much bigger in the chest and legs.

"I knew you'd come, Alice. You always were the smartest of us all. I knew you'd find a way."

"I'd never have made it without Cilla here," she replies.

Robert turns to Alice's travel companion who despite the mud on her face and the twigs in her hair, is the sweetest thing he has ever seen.

She shyly plays with the knot on her cloth bundle.

"Cilla meet my brother. Robert, this is Cilla, my friend."

Robert tips the remains of what used to be a fine straw hat. "Hello, Cilla."

"Hello," she says quietly.

"Cilla taught herself to read, Robert. She's smart—and she's brave."

"And pretty too," he says as he winks.

Alice rolls her eyes. "Smart's better than pretty, Robert."

"Pretty doesn't hurt," he replies.

Changing the subject Cilla asks, "So, what are we doing now?"

"Tonight, we'll sleep at my camp and in the morning make our way to the next spot," he says. "We're to meet friends that can help us."

"How long have you been here, Robert?" Alice asks.

"Since I tossed that rock at you in the privy. I followed the wagon from Arabella's plantation to Pullyhawly. I hid in the woods until I saw you take the package. After that I came here and waited."

"But that was months ago!" the small girl exclaims. "You've been here since then?"

"I knew you'd come sooner or later," he says.

"But how did you survive?" Cilla asks.

"There was a stash of beans waiting for me and I fished, tracked turkeys and scrounged for berries to add to my meals. It's been lonely. It was all worth it now that you are here." He picks her up and swings her around.

The camp is hidden in a patch of rhododendrons not far from the meeting place. They make no fire, but Robert has plenty of blankets that are almost dry. They have cold beans with turkey jerky for supper and Alice falls asleep almost as soon as she takes her last spoonful.

"What did you do during the storm?" Robert asks Cilla. "It was bad here. I managed to get to higher ground just in time."

Cilla takes a bite of the turkey and replies, "We hid in a cave—well, it was sort of a cave—more like a bit of shelter under a rock outcropping. It was scary. We had to use my dress to tie us to a root so we wouldn't get blown away. That's why it looks like this." She smooths the front of her tattered clothing.

"It looks fine to me," he says smiling.

"I can't believe that you've been waiting all this time for Alice—I mean us."

"Of course, I did," he replies. "That's what family does."

Tears start to roll down her cheeks.

"What's the matter, girl?" He puts his arm around her shoulder.

"I'm so glad to be here…it was so scary…and to top it all off I left my babies behind."

He lets go of her.

"Babies? Are you promised to someone?"

"No. They're my master's babies," she says quietly.

"I'm sorry, Cilla—about all of it. Those babies are still yours. Our momma had to do that with the master when Alice and I were small. She almost had a baby by him."

"Almost had?" she asks. "What does that mean?"

He sighs. "Our momma died trying to have the baby—they both died—momma and the tiny little girl."

Cilla reaches out her hand to his. "I am so sorry."

"It was ten years ago. I tell you, the screaming was something awful. You never forget that especially when it's your mother. The old women knew that the baby was pointed in the wrong direction. The master refused to send for a doctor even though the child was his."

He shakes his head at the memory.

"Let's hope that where we are going is kinder to mothers and babies," she says.

"It can't be any worse," he replies. "If all people in the north are like my friends that you'll meet tomorrow, we will be looking at sunshine from now on—even in the snowy north.

She laughs and shivers at the cold.

He squeezes her to him and wraps the blanket around her shoulders. They fall asleep as the moon rises above the treetops.

CHAPTER 84

I t's nearly dark when Jess walks back to the house. The horses are in their stalls, fed and happy. She hears a noise from upstairs.

"Putt? Are you up there?"

Nothing but a muffled moan comes in reply. She runs up the staircase to find him lying on the floor with a gash on his head. The bust of Darwin lies beside him in a sticky pool of blood.

"Cruppers! Putt? Are you OK?"

He rolls over. "Miss Jess? Is that you?"

"Oh, thank God." She pulls him close to her and helps him sit up.

The gash on his forehead bleeds down his face and onto her clothes. Jess takes off her shirt and wraps it around his head.

"We have to get to Doc Springer's. Let's go downstairs. Hold onto me, Putt."

She leads the large man down the stairs and starts towards the wagon. Changing her mind, she helps him down the driveway. "It'll take too long to hook up the horse. You can make it Putt, it's just up the street."

Like two drunks they sway back and forth until they are nearly to the blue clapboard house two doors up from the rectory.

"Help! Doc Springer!" she yells from the yard. "It's Putt. He's been hit on the head. He's gushing blood. Doc, are you in there?"

The doctor and his wife run out of the house and across the garden and meet them in the street.

"We've got you, Putt. Just take my arm," Mrs. Springer says as she grabs him around the waist. She's half his size, but doesn't even strain as she and Jess lead him to the door.

"He'll need stitches for sure, Doc," Jess says. "His head's bleeding like a milt shooter—um, sorry Mrs. Springer—no offense."

The small woman laughs. "Not to worry, my dear. I've been a nurse for a long time and am well acquainted with a vast array of bodily functions."

They settle Putt on a chair in the parlor and the doctor brings an oil lamp closer to look at the wound. Using a damp rag he cleans the blood squinting through his spectacles in the dim light. "I suspect that you are correct about the stitches, Miss Jakes."

The doc goes to work on the young man and Mrs. Springer walks Jess to the door.

"Why don't you go home and get yourself cleaned up. You come back tomorrow. We'll stitch him up and put him to bed."

"Are you sure?" she asks shivering in her bloody shift.

"The wife's right. I'd like to keep him under observation for the night," the doc adds. "You can never be too careful with noggin injuries."

"OK. Thank you both. I'll be back tomorrow." She kisses Putt on the cheek and hurries up the street home.

CHAPTER 85

Jess shakes off the cold as she crosses the dark kitchen garden feeling her way to the back door. There's a noise in the bushes and she swings around. "Who's there?"

"It's me, Jess. Maryanne."

"Oh my God. You scared me half to death. What's going on?" Jess asks.

"I need to see you. Are you alone?"

"I am."

Jess can just see the glimmer of Maryanne's smile in the inky darkness.

"Let's go inside and make a fire. It's freezing out here."

Jess pulls out her key and notices some broken glass by her door.

"Maryanne? You didn't by any chance break a windowpane, did you?"

"No," she replies. "I've done a lot of things in my life but breaking into houses is not one of them."

In the kitchen Jess grabs the poker by the stove. "You wait here. I'll check out the house."

She lights a lamp and slowly makes her way room by room opening wardrobes and closets, even going into the root cellar.

"There's nobody here," she says as she puts the oil lamp on the table.

"When I first came over about 30 minutes ago, I knocked on the front door. I thought I heard someone inside. I assumed that you must be home. When you didn't answer I came around back to wait."

Jess lights another lamp and Maryanne finally sees her shift.

"Holy Jesus! What happened? You're covered with blood!"

"Someone attacked Putt. That may be what you heard when you came over."

"Putt?" she asks. "That sweet boy? Oh Jess, there's so much blood everywhere. How is he?"

"Doc says he'll be fine. They're keeping him overnight."

"Oh dear." Maryanne slumps into a kitchen chair dropping her carpet bag next to her on the pine floor.

"Why were you hiding in the bushes?" Jess asks.

"Because I'm supposed to be in Boston at my brother's. At least that's what the Reverend thinks," she answers removing her cape.

"Why?" Jess asks. "What's going on?"

"I'm not sure. He's been acting very strangely since the old painted lady came to see him last week. He even canceled prayer night on Wednesday. Then, of course, he fired Putt."

"Wait. Old painted lady? You mean Odette?"

"I never caught her name. He rushed her into the study and told me to stay in my room. Wait! Isn't Odette the madam you worked for?"

"Yes, she ran the brothel downtown where Sarah and I worked—at least she used to," Jess replied, "until she was murdered."

"Oh, dear God. Promise me you'll be careful, Jess. Don't put yourself at risk."

"I won't," she cups her hands around Maryanne's face and lightly kisses her lips. "I have too much to live for," she says as she shivers with cold.

Maryanne wraps her in a blanket. "Get out of those clothes. I'll light the fire and give you a bath. Just sit by the fire until it's ready."

She puts several pans of water on the stove and stokes the fire. She fills the small tin tub and says, "OK. That's enough. Get in."

Jess barely fits in the small tub and her knees break the surface of the water.

Maryanne wets a cloth and slowly washes the blood off Jess's face. She moves to her neck and finally to her chest.

Jess stands up in the bath and picks Maryanne up setting her on the kitchen table. Water drips onto the floor.

She takes off the inner layers first. The bloomers and the petticoats. She leaves the stockings and works her way up to Maryanne's soft white thighs. She stops between her legs. The smaller woman nearly falls off the table.

After a few minutes they lie on the floor wrapped in blankets near the stove. Maryanne whispers, "I'm guessing that Sarah and Jonah are not due home at any point soon."

Jess laughs. "That's right. They'll be back in a few days."

Maryanne sighs. "Let's make some supper. I'm famished."

They find a rasher of bacon, carrots, potatoes, an onion and some eggs.

"Perfect for a frittata," Maryanne says. "Hand me that cast iron pan."

"A frittata?" Jess frowns. "What is that?"

"It's Spanish or Mexican. I'm not quite sure which."

Jess smiles. "I have just the Spanish wine for that."

She opens one of the bottles that Bart brought and pours them each a crystal glass.

Maryanne begins chopping vegetables as the oil heats up on the stove.

Jess makes herself busy by nailing a board over the broken window. Satisfied, she takes another sip of wine and asks Maryanne, "How was the wedding?"

"I was wondering when you were going to ask," she replies. "It was strange and short—very short. It's clear that Silas and the right reverend hate each other. I'm still not sure what the rush was."

"Did Hobson try anything with you when you got back to the house?"

"That's another odd thing. He ignored me—told me to stay in my locked room until my train to Boston. He seemed preoccupied."

"At least there's that," Jess says caressing Maryanne's thigh.

"Be careful or you'll ruin the frittata."

The smaller woman takes a break from the stove and picks up her wine. She turns the delicate crystal glass in her hand. "You have a lot of prissy things for a not so girlie girl."

Jess laughs. "I know. Actually, the house came furnished."

"With your captain friend's belongings?" Maryanne cocks her head to the side and twists her black hair around her finger.

"So, you know about him. This was his mother's house. He only lived here as a child."

"I do know about Captain Pritchard," Maryanne says. "Mrs. Markwart can be very chatty. She said he was by for supper the other night."

"He was my first client—I mean as a detective. That's how we got the house."

"She also said that Nah is the spitting image of the captain as a boy."

"Did she now?"

"Yes. Any particular reason for that?" Maryanne asks.

"I think you can guess the reason," Jess says laughing.

"I think I can. Is there anything there? A spark or is he just a friend?"

"Just a friend…at least from my point of view. Although, he did ask me to marry him."

"So what are you going to do?" Maryanne asks.

"Don't worry," Jess says. "He doesn't know yet, but I'm telling him no."

CHAPTER 86

Stephen is halfway through his second day shadowing Oswald Latouche in his duties at the shipyard. The older man remains quiet except for the occasional grunt in response to his trainee's questions.

Stephen fills the silence with nervous banter about his childhood, family, his artwork—eventually winding his way around to telling the older man all about his dilemma with Sarah.

More grunting and counting. First it was masts—now it's wooden pegs.

"So Latouche, what do you think I should do about Sarah?"

"Sorry for eavesdropping. Are you talking about Sarah Jakes?" Coxe jumps onto the gundalow to help unload the shipment.

"I am. Do you know her?" Stephen asks.

"No, but the wife does. Thinks very highly of the girl."

"Yes, she was talking to me about her yesterday morning. Your wife is a very opinionated person."

Coxe laughs. "That she is. Lily certainly keeps me in line."

Stephen spends the rest of the day obsessing over Sarah.

Finally, at nearly 5 p.m. Latouche pipes up. "Why don't you just get your ass over to Holt Street and talk things over with this girl instead of bending my ear about it all day?"

"I suppose you're right Latouche. Sorry if I've been bugging you."

"One word of advice, Bailey," the older man grumbles.

"Yes, sir?"

"Try keeping your bone box closed more. Listen to what the girl has to say. You might get farther."

"Yes, sir. I will." He slinks out for the yard and away from the water. It's dark by the time he turns onto Holt Street.

Mrs. Markwart is out with Jack in the yard.

"Hello, Mr. Bailey. Are you here to see Sarah?"

"I hope so. Do you know if she is around?" he asks.

"I'm not sure. There's a fire in the stove. I do know that Jonah is off visiting relatives for a few days."

"Hmm. Well, I'll try the door. Have a good evening, Mrs. Markwart."

"You too Mr. Bailey."

He wanders past the barn to the back garden. The warm candlelight illuminates the steps. Stephen can see a figure peering into the window.

"You there! What are you doing?"

The figure turns. "Shit! You're Taylor!"

Stephen picks up a rake and moves towards the man. The fugitive jumps over the fence and is gone.

Placing the rake on the ground he walks up the steps. He's about to knock on the kitchen door when he spots two figures in the kitchen.

"Oh my God!" Bailey takes a step backwards and nearly trips over the rake as he runs from the yard.

CHAPTER 87

Alice smiles to herself as she wakes to find Cilla and Robert curled around each other in the early morning light.

"We must have slept for twelve hours," she says nudging them. "We should get going."

Cilla wakes with a start and rolls away from Robert.

They pick up their belongings and sweep the area with a branch to get rid of any sign of the camp.

"My friends are a half day's walk from here. They are at the same location for the full moon each month. We should be there in time for dinner." He hands them some more of the jerky as they walk through a clearing. The grass is wet from dew. It soothes Alice's bare feet.

Cilla's stomach grumbles. "It will be nice to have a hot meal."

"What happens next?" Alice asks.

"We'll meet up with my friends and then we need to decide where we're headed," Robert answers.

"We get to decide?" Cilla asks taking another bite of the turkey.

"Yes. They'll take us wherever we want to go."

Cilla can't quite believe it.

"We've got that figured out," Alice says. "Cilla needs to go a place called Portsmouth, New Hampshire and I want to go with her."

"Where is that?" Robert asks shifting his bundle to the other arm.

"Up north," Cilla replies. "It is where my sister Ada lives."

"Your sister?" he asks.

"It's a long story," Alice answers.

"Portsmouth it is. We have a lot of time as we walk to the meeting spot—plenty of time for a few long stories."

CHAPTER 88

Massey rubs his hands along his new brown coat and eyes his reflection in the mirror. He's dressed like a northerner—or at least what the commodore thinks a northerner dresses like. He has a vest and a white shirt with a tie. He insists on keeping his brown hat in spite of the protests of the tailor and Mrs. Beauregard.

Just yesterday, he thought the old man was going to kill him and now here he is on his way to someplace called Portsmouth to finally bring that Ada home.

He's not used to the movement of the train and has a hard time getting back to his seat.

The last time he was north of the plantation he rode his horse the whole way chasing that bitch Esther and her daughter. They always seemed to be one step ahead of him.

That time he only made it as far as New Jersey.

His balance probably isn't helped by the fact that he used some of the travel money to buy a bottle of whiskey. The commodore didn't spend enough to get him a berth, so he'll be traveling overnight in his seat. He doesn't mind as he usually sleeps outside on the ground or on the floor of some saloon or whorehouse. He's getting a bit woozy from the motion and the alcohol. He sure is hungry. Cleo said she was too busy to pack him a picnic. She's getting too much of an attitude these days as far as he can tell.

As the train rattles north, he takes the occasional sip off the bottle, garnering fierce looks from a pug-nosed lady in a black bonnet. She eventually picks up her basket and moves to the next car. She must have had fried chicken in there because the good smell follows her as she moves away.

His stomach growls.

He wakes up and his neck is so stiff that he can barely move his head. The blood red sky on the left side of the train tells him it's evening. His stomach is killing him. He has to get something to eat.

"Hartford! Hartford, Connecticut!" The conductor walks through the car.

He'll be in Portsmouth early Friday morning. That is if he can figure out how to change trains in Boston. He can't wait that long to eat.

"I'll bet I can hop off the train in this Hartford place and get a bag of boiled peanuts."

The conductor calls again for the station and Massey disembarks with the other passengers.

As he enters the street, he hears the whistle blow and his train departs the station.

"Shit!"

He finds out that the next train to Boston isn't until tomorrow morning. He goes looking for a tavern to get a meal and then maybe a whore or bed for the night.

CHAPTER 89

Walking over a rise, they see the caravan in the valley below. Wagons are circled around a campfire. The light flickers revealing brightly colored pictures on the sides of the wagon—horses and riders with feather decorations, strange animals bearing sharp teeth and menacing looks, women in colorful underwear flying through the air.

"What is this?" Cilla asks.

"One step towards freedom," Robert answers as they make their way towards the strange apparition. "Come meet my friends."

A child comes running towards them. As he gets closer, Cilla realizes that he isn't a child at all but a very small man.

"You're back!" he yells nearly out of breath. "We're pulling out tomorrow. You almost missed us this month."

Robert and the man embrace and he turns back to his traveling companions.

"Leopold, I'd like you to meet my sister Alice and her friend, I mean our friend, Cilla."

The man sweeps his arm up and bows low.

"Ladies, I am delighted to make your acquaintance. Welcome to Peculiar Penny's Traveling Circus and Animal Show. I am your most hospitable host, Leopold Q. Isendorph."

The girls' eyes grow wide.

"What's a circus?" Cilla asks.

"You're in for a treat, my lovely ladies, nothing beats the circus life. We'll see what roles you shall play in our ensemble."

"What roles we will play?" asks Alice. "What does that mean?"

"It means that for the next few days we are in the circus," Robert answers.

"But what is a circus?" Cilla repeats.

"Oh, my dears!" the short man says. "The circus is the greatest show on earth. Acrobats! Wild animals! Gravity defying stunts!"

The two girls shrug.

"But first things first," Leopold says. "Let's get you some hot dinner and some clothes to wear. Best that we burn the ones you have on. See my lady love, Penny, in the first wagon and she'll set you right up."

A six-foot tall woman with almond shaped eyes opens the caravan door. She wears a blue suit cut for a man with a fancy silk cravat at her neck. Her silky dark hair is in a bun held together with sticks. "One of you must be Alice."

The smaller girl nods looking up at the taller woman.

"We've been waiting for you—and who is this?" She takes Cilla's hands.

"My friend Cilla."

"Welcome to you both. Come inside and we'll sort out some everyday clothes for you. Later, we'll worry about costumes."

They enter the tightly packed wagon. One wall is filled with hanging clothes of all types and sizes.

"Pick out a set of traveling clothes first," Penny instructs them.

The girls stay where they are and stare at her. Alice finally speaks. "What are traveling clothes? We only ever had one set of clothes. Unless you count

Sunday clothes which are only a little better than our everyday clothes."

Penny smiles.

"Tania should have a bath ready for you outside. Why don't we start there? I'll pick out some things for you to choose from. Does that sound OK?"

The girls look at each other. "I guess so," Alice answers.

The girls find a tarped area near another campfire. Inside a tin bathtub sits filled with warm water.

"Welcome ladies," a round woman with a neatly trimmed goatee says pouring another bucket into the steaming tub. "Who'd like to go first?"

The girls shrug.

"Cilla can go first," Alice says after a pause.

The taller girl takes off her dress and steps into the tub. She is so thin— Alice can see each of her ribs. She lowers her body into the water. Dirt of all colors is washed away.

Tania scrubs Cilla until the water is a murky reddish brown.

"You look like a brand-new woman," Penny says as she enters with a stack of clothing over her arm. "Looks like we'll need some fresh bathwater or Alice is likely to come out dirtier than when she went in."

"I've never had fresh bathwater before," Cilla says quietly.

"We don't always either but today is special," Penny says. "Wrap yourself in this towel while we wait for Alice's bath to be drawn. Let's get you some clothing. First, we'll start with the shift, corset and petticoats. Then you'll pick out a dress."

Alice watches Cilla struggle with the layers of undergarments as she soaks in the warm water. "I think I'll skip all that. Since I look young can I just wear what a girl might?"

"Of course, Alice. I have just the thing. I'll be back in a moment."

Alice closes her eyes as Tania scrubs her down with pleasant smelling soap and warm water. She wishes she could stay here forever.

"Tania?" she asks. "Where did you all come from? You don't look like any people I've seen before."

The bearded lady erupts with a squeaky laugh as she dumps a cupful of water over the girl's head.

"All over the place! Penny was born in Minnesota. Her father was a Chinese railroad worker. Her mother was a Norwegian beauty. I was born in Boston. I come from a long line of bearded ladies."

Alice mulls this over as Tania ladles the warm water over her. She's never heard of Minnesota, Norwegian or Boston.

Tania wraps her in a towel and leads her to Penny's costume trailer.

Cilla picks out a cream-colored dress with small orange flowers and Alice puts on the child's sailor-style outfit that Penny has found for her.

"You look perfect," Penny says admiring the two women.

"How old are you really, Alice?" Tania asks.

"I think I'm almost 16 years."

"Before we join the others for dinner there's another matter to discuss," the tall woman declares. "What shall you call yourselves?"

"We need new names?" Cilla asks.

"Yes, you will need to pick out new identities for yourselves. Your old selves need to be left in Virginia. Robert is now Simon."

"My master named me, so I don't care about keeping my name," says Alice.

They sit in silence thinking.

"Any ideas, Cilla?" Penny asks.

"No. I never thought of a name before. Even my babies were named by the master—or by the mistress."

"I know what name I want," Alice says.

"What name is that, Alice?" Tania asks.

"Tulip."

Cilla laughs. "That's a silly name, Alice!"

"That's what my mother called me until she died."

"I think it's grand," says Penny, "It suits you. You can always change it again later."

The tall woman turns her gaze to Cilla. "And how about you my dear?"

"I have no idea," she says

"Who was your favorite person in the bible?" Alice asks.

"Moses."

"Hm. Well," Penny says.

"Wait! I know the perfect name for you," Alice says. "Eve."

"She was the first woman on earth," Penny says. "Talk about a fresh start."

"So, Tulip and Eve. Very nice," Tania smiles and hands the girls each a shawl.

"And you'll need a last name," Penny says. "Robert, I mean Simon, already picked out Freeman. Would you like to share that name?"

"I will," Alice says. "That sounds perfect."

"Eve?" Penny asks.

"Jakes—my last name is Jakes—Eve Jakes."

"That sounds lovely," Penny says.

The bell rings for dinner and they step down the stairs of the caravan and approach a long table with twenty of the strangest people Eve and Tulip have ever seen. A mixture from all over the world, wearing strange costumes. One fellow is a half a foot taller than Penny with the darkest skin they have ever seen. He wears a costume made of leather and string and carries a spear. Over his shoulder is a blanket with bright designs on it. Eve averts her eyes as he is nearly naked. Tulip can't stop looking at him. "He's so beautiful," she whispers.

Penny smiles.

"May I introduce Nhial of the Nuer people. He was born where the Nile meets the Sobat River in Africa. His people are warriors."

Tulip smiles shyly. Nhial looks straight ahead ignoring the girls.

Penny whispers to her lover and he jumps up onto the table.

"It is my great pleasure as Leopold Q. Isendorph, the ringmaster of this paltry circus, to introduce our guests. Ladies and gentlemen, may I present Miss Tulip Freeman and Miss Eve Jakes, the latest additions to the motley group of talent that is the Peculiar Penny's Magical Circus and Traveling Animal Show."

"Are there animals here?" Tulip whispers to Penny.

"No, we haven't had animals since they died of anthrax years ago," she whispers back. "He just likes the name."

"So, my dearest friends, we shall make our way to Washington D.C. where we will load the wagons on to a train. Our eventual destination is Portsmouth, New Hampshire. We leave at dawn."

"It will be nice to be back in Portsmouth," Tania whispers to Nhial.

CHAPTER 90

Jessamyn sighs and rolls towards Maryanne. "The only time in my life that I've been this happy is when Nah was born." She strokes Maryanne's hair as they watch the sun rise from Jess's bed.

"I've never been this happy, ever."

"But you've had other lovers, Maryanne?"

"Yes, but nobody like you," she curls her arms around her new love.

"How long can you stay?" Jess asks.

"Probably just one more night. I do need to get to Boston. My brother corresponds with Silas on a frequent basis. It won't do well to have him asking after me."

"I have to go check on Putt and then work on a case," Jess says. "I'll bring food back for supper. What will you do all day, Miss M?"

"Miss M? I like it," she says kissing Jess's fingers. "As a woman of leisure, today I was thinking of baking something and starting on one of the thousands of novels you have in your parlor."

"We're not much for the baking. You might have a hard time finding the necessary ingredients."

After a lengthy goodbye involving dressing and undressing, Jess finally makes it out the door. It's a sunny day, so she puts the horses into the corral so they can enjoy the warm weather.

She greets her neighbor, "Hi, Mrs. Markwart. How are you today?"

"Fine Jess. It's a beautiful day, isn't it?" the older woman replies.

"Yes ma'am, it is."

"Were Sarah and Mr. Bailey able to work out their differences last night?"

"Last night?" Jess asks.

"Yes, I was out with Jack and happened to chat with him for a moment when he was on his way to your house. Did you not see him?"

"No, I didn't," she answers, her face flushing.

"Hmm," says the older woman. "Perhaps I was mistaken. I thought he was going to your place."

"Oh, well Sarah is with Jonah so he couldn't have seen her." She starts to walk away. "Have a nice day, Mrs. Markwart."

She turns her head and sees Putt waving to her from the doctor's porch where he sits swaddled like a giant baby. Mrs. Springer sits on a chair and feeds him some scrambled eggs and toast.

"Hi, Miss Jess!" he yells to her as she walks along the path to the porch.

"Are you feeling any better, Putt?"

"Much better. Thank you, Miss Jess. I can come back to work today."

He starts to get out of his chair, but Mrs. Springer holds him down. "That's not a good idea my boy. You need to stay here another night. Doctor's orders."

Jess laughs. "Don't worry, Putt. There will be plenty of work when you're better. You rest up and come back when the doctor says you're ready."

"OK, ma'am," he replies and takes another mouthful of eggs.

Jess pats his cheek and leaves him in Mrs. Springer's capable hands. The doctor and his wife never had children of their own. The woman seems to enjoy coddling the patient.

Her next stop is the Rockingham to track down the attorney. The fancy, new hotel opened last year, and Jess has never been inside before today. She walks up the grand steps stopping to admire the cast iron lions guarding the entrance.

Stained glass windows and rich, dark wood paneling line the lobby area. It's hard to believe it is only a few blocks away from the seediness of Water Street. Portsmouth really is changing.

"Excuse me ma'am? Would you like a room?" the young clerk asks. He tugs at his bow tie and tails.

"No, thank you. I'm here to see one of your residents, a Mr. Tompkins. I believe he's a lawyer?" she asks.

"Yes, that is correct—as a matter of fact that is him right over there enjoying breakfast." He points across the dining room.

The furriest, red-haired man Jess has ever seen sits by the fireplace delicately cracking open a soft-boiled egg.

"Mr. Tompkins?" she asks.

"Yes," he replies. "To whom do I have the honor of speaking?"

"My name is Jessamyn Jakes. I'm a private detective representing Savannah West of Odette's."

"Ah yes—the esteemed brothel." He extracts a bit of egg from the shell and slips it into his mouth. "And what does the fair Miss West need from me?"

Jess sits opposite him at the table. "You are the trustee for the corporation that owns the house where the business is located. Is that correct?"

"Yes, that is true." He motions to the waiter to bring Jess a cup for tea.

"Miss West is interested in buying the house now that Odette has passed on."

"Ah yes, the murder. What a tragedy. I didn't know her well, but she seemed like a force of nature."

"She certainly was that," Jess agrees.

"I'll need to consult with the remaining shareholder and get back with you," he replies pouring the tea into Jess's delicate china cup. "He had an arrangement with Odette that he may want to continue with Miss West."

"As opposed to selling?" she asks dropping a sugar cube into the hot liquid.

"I will be happy to present the various options to the shareholder and let you know what he decides. Is Monday soon enough? I'll be seeing him on another matter early that day. How about we meet here at 3 p.m. and discuss it then?"

"Monday it is," she replies taking a sip of her tea. "Thank you for your help, Mr. Tompkins."

"Call me Justice," he says.

"Thank you, Justice." She rises leaving her hot tea.

A large doorman with a top hat nods goodbye as he opens the grand door for her. "Have a lovely day, ma'am."

"Thank you. You as well."

She hums to herself as she walks in the sunshine to the whorehouse.

A workman takes down Odette's name from the side of the building. A sign that reads, "Savannah's: A Quality Establishment" sits on the ground nearby.

She knocks on the door and her small, Irish friend answers.

"Miss Jessamyn!" Granny exclaims.

"Granny, is that a new dress and are those new shoes?"

"Yes ma'am. Savannah bought new clothes for everyone. Says it's time we classed the place up," she giggles.

"Well, it's very pretty and it must be so much easier to walk around with shoes that fit. Where is Miss Savannah?"

"She is talking to one of the workmen upstairs in the blue room," the girl answers. "She left word that you should just go up if you visited."

"Thanks, Granny."

She hears Savannah's voice as she reaches the landing.

"I want just new curtains and paper in here. We'll be replacing the furniture at some point but that's it for now. You'll start here and work your way room by room until the whole house is done. I don't want to disrupt business so just do one project at a time."

"Yes, ma'am," he replies. "I'll bring some curtain samples for your review."

"Thank you, Douglas." He turns and passes Jess in the hallway tipping his hat on the way.

Savannah greets her. "Hello, Jess. Let's retreat to my office to discuss business."

Jess passes Daisy leaving the blue room. She remembers her last time with Sweetness. It was in that room.

"Are you all right?" Daisy asks her. "You look a little pale."

"Oh, I'm fine," she says as she hurries down the dark hallway.

"What did you find out?" Savannah asks as she closes the door behind her.

Jess starts right in. "The house is owned by a corporation. I spoke to their lawyer and he promised to bring up the potential sale to the remaining shareholder on Monday. We should be able to start negotiations then if he agrees."

"Excellent. I have drawn up an offer." She hands Jess an envelope.

"The lawyer also felt that there was a good chance that even if they don't want to sell, they'd still be interested in maintaining the relationship that they shared with Odette."

Savannah frowns. "I'd rather buy it outright. I'm tired of having a boss."

"Trust me, I understand," Jess says. "We'll know more on Monday."

"Sounds good. Say, what do you think of this?" She holds out a sample of wallpaper to Jess. Flowers in mostly yellow and cream.

Jess frowns. "I don't know. You wouldn't want it to look like a dowager's house, do you?"

Savannah laughs. "I suppose not. I just want to move as far away from Odette's style as possible. I shouldn't overreact and end up with the opposite extreme."

"That's true. Odette may have had her faults, but she did run a successful house for many years."

"I just want a classy establishment where we ram objects up old wrinkled fannies in a carefully appointed environment," Savannah says with a smile.

Jess laughs. "I understand."

"Hm," the redhead muses. "Maybe I should ask some of my customers what they would like for decorations?"

"That sounds like a good idea. Speaking of customers, are you still seeing clients or are you just managing the house these days?"

"Right now, I'm just managing the house," Savannah replies adjusting the brooch pinned to her blue dress. I don't really have the time for clients."

"Even your regular?" Jess asks.

"That seems moot as he was a no show this week. He may be spooked by all the activity."

"Interesting," Jess replies rising to her feet. "Well, I best be off. I'm meeting with the lawyer at 3 p.m. Monday. I'll stop by here immediately afterwards."

"Thank you Jessamyn."

"You're welcome, Savannah."

CHAPTER 91

T he three guests take turns riding in different caravans. Today they ride with Penny and Leopold. They tell them stories of the circus from the old days when they had animals and twice as many people.

"The children would run out from the towns to greet us," Leopold says. "We were the most exciting thing they had ever seen. You haven't lived until you have a sea of little faces looking at you in awe."

"So when will we get to see a performance?" Tulip asks.

Penny laughs. "Oh, my dear—that's just the thing—we don't really perform anymore. We answer to a higher calling."

"A higher calling?" Eve asks. "Do you mean Jesus?"

Leopold laughs, "Something like that."

The tall woman hands the reigns over to her lover. The girls retreat to the back to pick out costumes.

"If there's no real circus then, why do we need costumes?" Eve asks.

"In case we're stopped by any authorities, you'll need to look like performers. Besides, everyone should wear sequins and feathers at least once in their lives."

The girls giggle as they try on the clothes. Most are too large for Tulip and bag to her knees.

"Oh dear, that won't do," Penny frowns. "Wait! I have just the thing."

She pulls out a fancy men's suit. "It's one of Leopold's. It will be just perfect for you."

They're finally dressed.

Eve is in a blue trapeze artist bodysuit with crystal sparkles. "I don't know, ma'am. This seems kind of small. I feel like I am in my underwear. Do people really wear these?"

"Of course! Trapeze artists especially. Now let's practice some flourishes."

"Flourishes, ma'am?" Tulip asks.

"Yes, you saw how Leopold bowed deeply to the audience. Half of what we do is flourishes. I'll show you one."

With one hand on her hip she swishes her arm in a graceful arc and curtsys to the girls.

Tulip and Eve try to mimic her but can't stop laughing.

"Don't worry ladies, you can only get better," Penny says.

They wander outside to show Simon their costumes and flourishes.

The sound of horses announces the strange men's arrival.

"It will be OK. Just try to keep quiet," Penny warns.

"I am Leopold Q. Isendorph, the ringleader of this troupe. What can I help you with?"

"Routine inspection. Everyone out of the wagons and line up."

Tulip takes Eve's hand and they jump to the ground.

One of the two scruffy men dismounts and walks towards the group. Penny turns up her nose at his stench as he turns to speak to her.

"So, you're some kind of freak show, is that it?" he says spitting as he talks. She's easily 8 inches taller than him so most of it lands on her chest.

"In a manner of speaking, sir," she replies. "We're a traveling circus."

"Oh. Where are you traveling to?" he sneers.

"To Frederick, Maryland," she answers.

"Where's that?" the other man asks from atop his horse.

"North of here. We disband in the winter and take jobs for the cold months. It's our understanding that there is work in Frederick."

"Hm." He absorbs this information as he walks along inspecting the troupe.

He passes right by Nhial in his African finery and stops in front of Eve.

"What's your name?"

"Eve," she replies softly.

He looks her up and down in her sequins and licks his lips.

"And what's your act, pretty girl?" He pushes up her chin with his whiskey bottle.

"My act, sir?" she asks averting her eyes.

"Your act? Or do you just suck the little one's cock?"

His friend laughs so hard he almost falls off his horse.

She looks at Simon who nods slightly to her. "I..um…can show you. I just need my props."

She darts into Penny's wagon and emerges moments later with a broom.

"This will have to do as my props are packed away."

Remembering what she learned about flourishes she starts with a graceful spin with broom, dancing with it like a partner.

"Whatever. This is boring," the man on the horse says. "Make her take her clothes off."

"Now, now Elliot, you shut your mouth and let the lady finish. Then maybe we'll make her take her clothes off."

She tosses the broom between her hands finally flipping it and balancing it on her nose with the bristles high. After ten seconds she flips it up and catches it in her hand finishing with the best flourish she can manage.

The troupe cheers.

"I don't know, Elliot, I think I'm still going to need to see her naked."

Something catches the sunlight and the man falls to the ground. A knife. Someone has thrown a knife right though the man's neck.

"That's my act," Simon says.

Elliot seems to be catching on that something bad is happening. He hasn't quite gotten to a gallop before he's knocked off the horse.

Penny walks over to him and bracing his body with her foot, she pulls Nhial's spear out of his back.

Within an hour, the men are buried, their saddles and clothes are burned, and the horses are tied to the back of the last wagon to be sold once they cross the state line.

CHAPTER 92

T he sunlight through the window makes no dent in the darkness of the tavern. Colm snores until Fiona slams a riding crop on the bar next to his head.

"Wake up, Colm!" she yells.

"That's not going to help, Fi," her husband says. "We have to wait it out. Let's get him into the wagon and take him to our house."

She turns towards Dan. "But Orla's there. I thought the purpose was to keep him away from her—to finally protect her."

"We need to face him together. It would be far worse for him to have one of his drunken arsehole friends show him the article. Maybe we can control the situation this way."

Dan waves to the barkeep, "Thanks for letting us know he was here, Patrick."

"No problem, Dan. You're saving us the trouble of tossing him out." The young bartender smiles as he opens the door.

They guide the drunken man into the bright sunshine. The streets of Dover are deserted as the mills have a couple of hours left until shift change.

"Why would that reporter make all that up about Orla and what happened that day, anyway?" Fi asks as they roll Colm into the back of the wagon. "I mean, who even told him about it?"

"It must have been that piece of shite sheriff, Tom Allgood. He's the only other person who knew."

"You're right," she answers shaking her head. "We should have made her stay with us when Rosie first died."

"Colm said no," he says.

"We shouldn't have listened." She starts to cry thinking about Orla living with Colm all these years.

"He had the law on his side, Fi," Dan replies.

Colm's eyes start to flutter as they reach their small cape on the outskirts of town. "What the fug…where are ye taking me?"

"Calm down, brother-in-law. We're just taking you to our house to sober you up."

"It's time we had a heart to heart conversation, Colm," his sister says.

"Orla?" Fi calls for her niece as she enters the house.

The girl enters the room carrying the baby, Brendan, who smiles a gummy grin at his mama.

"Orla, darling, take the children to the Tasker's farm to look at the animals. We'll need an hour to talk to your da."

The slight girl looks beyond her aunt to her father lying in the back of the wagon. She takes the hand of two-year-old Aidy and tells five-year-old Maddie to follow along.

Once the kids are out of earshot Fi turns to her husband. "Dan, do you think we should tie him to the kitchen chair?"

"Sounds prudent to me," her husband agrees.

He retrieves some rope from the barn, and they secure him to the chair just in time.

"I'll kill you for this, Fi!" Colm yells. "Stop your fuckin' meddling."

"Aye, shut your pie hole, Colm. I'm gonna make you listen to me. I should have done this as Rosie lay dying." She crosses herself.

"You know nothing about that, Fi," Colm says.

"What do you mean by that, brother?"

"Never mind," he says as he shakes his head. "Why are you talking to me now?"

"Something's happened—to Orla," she replies.

He looks confused. "What do you mean? I didn't mean it! Whatever it is. You know I love that girl."

"Not you this time, Colm," Dan says.

"What? What happened?" the drunken man asks as he struggles to free himself from the chafing ropes.

"Do you remember the day that Orla came home and told you she had lost the apples?" Dan says.

It comes back to him. He'd woken up in the morning and saw the empty basket. Orla's eye was blackened and her cheek was purple. Guilt raced through him and he just mumbled an apology. He didn't ask for details. He assumed she hadn't gone for the apples and in his drunkenness, he had beaten her for it.

Even now the shame causes his face to flush.

"I guess I remember."

"Orla didn't lose the apples, Colm," Dan says. "She was attacked by that rapist and murderer, Taylor."

"Who?" Colm asks.

"Jaysus, brother!" Fi says exasperated. "You really are a disaster. He's killed two girls already. Orla could have been one of them. He smashed her face and tossed her in his wagon. It was only the apples that saved her."

"The apples? How?" Colm is confused.

"This Taylor got sick from eating them and she was able to escape," Dan says.

"Where is this arsehole now?" Colm asks.

"He's in jail in Portsmouth. He raped and murdered a servant girl there."

"So why are you telling me this, Fi?" he asks. "It sounds like Orla is safe."

"I'm telling you because there's a story about it in the newspaper."

"Newspaper?"

"Yes, the Portsmouth paper. Front page. It's a few days old."

She holds up *The Chronicle*. The headline reads, "BEAUTIFUL APPLE GIRL ESCAPES TAYLOR."

"Unfortunately, this reporter got pretty much every detail wrong," Dan says. "He made it seem like Orla is some kind of prostitute and she lured Taylor into the woods."

"What?" Colm's eyes narrow. "My Orla a prostitute?"

"He even got her name wrong. He called her Orla Reilly."

Fi takes her brother's face into her hands. "Even in that rotted soul of yours, Colm, you know that Orla is a good girl."

He starts to cry. The hole in his gut creeps slowly back as he sobers up.

"Orla will live here from now on, brother," Fi whispers. "I've never said anything before because I thought what happened to Father Bligh was God's justice—but if you bother her again, I'll tell what I know to the police—and I don't mean that ridiculous arse, Tom Allgood."

He's never seen that cold look in his sister's eyes. He believes what she says.

"I'll take you home now, brother-in-law. I'd suggest that you stay on the Maine side of the bridge from now on."

Colm says nothing as he gets into the wagon. All he can think about is how he is going to Portsmouth to kill that bastard Taylor.

CHAPTER 93

After Jess leaves, Maryanne tidies up the house taking the time to study the small portraits of Jess's predecessors on the wall. "Hm," she thinks, "Mrs. Pritchard was a formidable woman." She pulls a novel off the shelf and reads the first few pages before putting it aside. Feeling restless she goes in search of ingredients for a cake. She finds apples, flour, butter, eggs, baking powder and sugar in the larder.

"The only thing that's missing is cinnamon. It just won't be the same without the spice," she says to herself.

The clock strikes 11 a.m.

Silas should be at the church preparing for the noon service and as he sent the cook away the rectory should be empty.

"I can slip right in there and get what I need," she thinks.

Donning her bonnet and cape she walks out the back door and cuts through the kitchen garden to the street behind the house. She takes the long way around the block so she doesn't walk by Mrs. Markwart's yard. The street is deserted and she's able to get to the rectory without anyone seeing her. She goes directly to the spice cabinet and picks out several cinnamon sticks. As soon as she has them in her bag, she hears a noise.

Stopping in her tracks she whispers, "Silas?"

More noises emerge from the basement. Maryanne doesn't stop to investigate. She bolts out the door and runs as fast as she can to Jess's house. Panting, she locks the door behind her.

"Calm down, Maryanne. You're too old to believe in monsters." She reassures herself that it was probably a raccoon who got trapped in the basement. Silas can deal with it when he gets home.

CHAPTER 94

Jess whistles a tune to herself as she makes her way from Savannah's towards Bart's house. The sun shines, warming her shawl as she walks through the residential neighborhood south of town. The clapboard houses give way to the palatial homes of the shipyard owners and successful sea captains.

Bart must be told soon that she won't be marrying him. She knows it will hurt, but it must be done. She feels sad for him but realizes that she can't build a marriage on a lie.

Slipping in the back door, she hears Sarah reading something aloud to Jonah in the front parlor.

"Momma!" Jonah almost knocks her over.

"Hello, Nah. Is Sarah reading to you?"

"Yes," he answers, "but it's really boring. It's a book about birds."

"Surprising," Jess says laughing.

Sarah rolls her eyes.

"Hi, Jess," Bart says as he walks into the room. "I'm so glad you are here. I've done a little research on schools in Paris,"

"What do you mean? What about Paris?" Sarah asks.

"Sarah," she turns to her daughter. "Bart and I have been speaking and we think that you should travel with him to Paris in December and attend school. You need to be away from here for a while."

"Because of Massey," Sarah says.

"Yes—it's no way to live being afraid all of the time—always looking over your shoulder," Jess replies. "I'll feel better if there is an ocean separating you from him or any other slave catcher."

The younger woman shakes her head. "I don't know. This is my home and there's the additional problem that I don't speak French."

"It won't be forever," Jess says. "Just for a year or two—until things quiet down. You can study art and birds. You'll pick up the language quickly—you're good with words."

"I'll visit you, Sarah," Jonah says. "I'll be a sea captain soon and I'll drive my boat to see you."

Sarah's eyes well up. "What do I need to do?"

"We'll need a few letters of reference about your academic prowess, an essay from you about your life and your best drawings," Bart says. "We can start work on it today if you like."

"Who would you like to ask for a reference?" Jess asks.

"Well, I think George or Mr. Quimby would give me one. They certainly know about every book I've read in the last five years. Mrs. Markwart, I suppose. Aside from that I'm not sure—maybe Reverend Cheney."

"They all would be perfect," Jess says.

Bart goes to the kitchen to ask Cook to bring tea.

Sarah looks at her mother. "I think I'll go upstairs and lie down for a while. This has given me a lot to think about."

"Sure, my darling. We'll work out a plan for gathering the documents you need."

"Would you like Cook to send something up for you?" her mother asks.

Sarah shakes her head. "No thank you."

Bart and Jess make a list of the documents needed for Sarah and then they play cards with Jonah. He has a new game which involves hiding the cards all over the house.

"I don't know, Jonah," says Bart. "This may be the end of this deck. I'll be finding escapees until May."

"It's been a while since Sarah went upstairs. She's awfully quiet," Jess says. "I better go see if she's OK."

She wanders up to the guest room and knocks.

No answer.

"Sarah?"

She opens the door expecting to find her daughter asleep on the bed. Instead she finds a note.

I'm at the Athenaeum. I need to get out of the house. I'll be very careful and will be back soon. —S

"Oh, cruppers!" Jess cries.

"What's going on?" Bart asks as he and Nah climb the stairs.

"Sarah's gone to see George."

"Don't worry, Jess. She's a smart girl. She'll be fine," Bart reassures her.

"All the same, I think I'll go over there to be sure."

"I think that's a mistake, Jess. You could lead Massey right to her. If she's not back soon, I'll go over there to look for her. Why don't you go back to Holt Street and come back tomorrow morning so we can work on her applications and paperwork."

"I don't know..." she says. "I guess you're right. You'll send word if she's not home soon?"

"Of course, I will," he replies.

He hugs her and is close to kissing her on the lips. She turns and kisses his cheek before walking out the back door.

Jess turns towards the water to purchase some fish for supper and nearly runs into a small man with a bowler hat.

"Excuse me, Miss Jakes. Do you have a minute?"

"Who are you?" she asks.

"Name's Edward Prospect," the man replies.

"You're that cretinous reporter who is making up all of those stories."

He ignores the insult. "Ma'am. I'd love to get your perspective on the Taylor escape," the reporter asks. "Would you like to make a statement?"

"I've nothing to say to you. You're worse than he is."

CHAPTER 95

The conductor announces the train to Boston and Massey boards. He settles himself on a bench near a mother and daughter dressed in black. He nods to them and the mother gives him the hairy eyeball. It must be the smell of last night's whiskey and the girl. He must admit that the whores in Hartford are much better than the slaves he used to get for free in Virginia. He just barely made it to the train on time and is nearly out of money.

He'll grab that Ada quickly and get the hell back to Virginia. He doesn't have any extra cash for a long stay in Portsmouth. He's also freezing and he's not even out of Connecticut yet. He watches the bright leaves out the window and starts to see patches of snow in the woods. He should have made the old man buy him a better coat.

The commodore—not being a fool—purchased the train tickets for both he and Ada in advance. He gave Massey only a little bit extra for the journey. The way he figures it if he stays out of the pubs and whorehouses he should have just enough to buy some food for the return journey—the girl can go hungry. He wishes he had been able to find a boiled peanut vendor in Hartford before he got on this train. He'll be plenty hungry by the time he gets to Portsmouth.

He settles into his seat and notices a sign above him. The words are unfamiliar but there is a drawing of a muffin and a drumstick with an arrow pointing to the back end of the train.

"Excuse me, ma'am," he asks the woman in black. "Sorry to bother you. What does that sign say?"

She turns to view the sign. "It says 'Café Car.' It's where you buy food on the train."

CHAPTER 96

Sarah sneaks in the side entrance of the library. George is alone in the reading room, restocking the shelves. He smiles at her from his ladder perch.

"Sarah, I've missed you," he says. "You didn't come by last week. I found that book on the mating habits of the night heron."

She nods and sits in the sunshine at Cheney's usual table. "Thank you for finding it for me. I really appreciate it." She starts to tear up and pretends to be studying the portrait of Captain Collins on the wall so he doesn't notice.

"Sarah, is everything all right?" George asks, descending the ladder.

She shakes her head no. She can't speak for a few moments for fear of bursting into tears. Finally she says softly, "George, I have something to tell you and a favor to ask."

"Anything for you, Sarah. You know that." He sits down next to her and takes her hand. "I don't think it's any secret that you are very special to me." He looks down as his face reddens.

Sarah's eyes well up again. "You're very sweet George. I'll miss you."

"What do you mean miss me?" he asks.

"I'm leaving soon to go to France."

"What? Why?" he asks as tears fill his eyes.

"Because I'm an escaped slave and my owner found out where I am. There's a real danger that I'll be sent back to Virginia."

"Oh dear, Sarah." He grabs her hand. "I'll help hide you! You don't need to go to France."

"I have to, George, it's the only way. Jess and Captain Bart are arranging for me to go to school in Paris. I'll be studying art and ornithology." She wipes her nose on her sleeve and George hands her his handkerchief.

"Oh, Sarah. How long do you think you'll be gone?"

"I don't know," she replies. "Two, maybe three years? If nothing changes here, I may never be able to come back."

George falls back into his chair.

"You said you needed a favor," he says softly. "What can I do to help?"

She sits up and leans across the table. "You know that I don't have much of an academic record. Would you be willing to write a letter for me about all the books I've read since we became friends? You're the closest thing to a teacher that I've ever had." She starts to cry again.

"Of course, I will Sarah. I'll do anything for you."

She hugs him and rises from the table.

"I'd better get back," she says. "I slipped out without telling anyone. We're hiding out at Captain Bart's. They're bound to have noticed."

"I'll walk you back," he says. "Let me tell Mr. Quimby."

"Do you speak French?" he asks as he leads her out the rear entrance.

"No. I guess I'll learn when I get there."

"I can tutor you until you go. My mother was born in Quebec. I grew up speaking two languages."

"Really?" she says.

"Oui! We can start today. I'll be over after work."

CHAPTER 97

Latouche hates listening to Bailey yammer on, but this silent brooding is even more irritating. "How did your talk with your lady love go the other night?" the older man reluctantly asks his young apprentice. It's been two days since the meeting and Bailey hasn't said a word about it. He hasn't said a word about anything—truth be told.

"Fine, sir. Can we talk about something else?"

"Suit yourself. I was just asking to be polite." Latouche turns back to counting the shipment of pegs.

They work the rest of the day in silence. Bailey seems to be getting the hang of things and has his first day without any errors.

He takes a detour walk through the square on his way back to the boarding house. At least he's distracted by Lily there. At night lying in bed he thinks about her on her knees washing the kitchen floor.

Even with the distraction Sarah keeps entering his mind.

He carefully hides his handkerchiefs so he can wash them out on his own. He doesn't want Lily to know what he spends his evenings doing in his room.

Sometimes he thinks that Sarah lied to him all along.

The only thing he knows for sure is that this is all Jessamyn's fault.

It doesn't help matters that Sarah seems to have vanished. She's not at her house that he can see—at least not in the morning or after work when he walks by.

He can't take another evening listening to that idiot Fitzgerald talk about millinery, so he wanders to the inn after work to have an ale with Trask.

As he walks though Market Square, he sees a bespectacled young man locking up the library.

"Didn't Sarah mention some friend of hers who works at the Athenaeum? George somebody?" he asks himself as he flags down the young man.

"Say, aren't you a friend of Sarah's?" he yells across the square.

"Who says?" George looks at him like he's the devil. "Who's asking?"

"My name's Stephen. I was—I mean am—a friend of Sarah's. I'm looking for her. Do you know where she is?"

He doesn't look much like a slave catcher, but George still doesn't trust the bearded blonde man.

"I don't know who you're talking about. I suggest that you move along, mister." George turns on his heels and walks in the opposite direction of the Bart's house.

Stephen follows him at a discreet distance. The librarian seems to be trying to lose him by darting into alleyways and hiding behind pillars.

It's nearly seven o'clock by the time George knocks on the kitchen door of the captain's house.

"George! We were worried," Sarah says. "We expected you an hour ago. You look a fright! What happened?"

"Massey!" he stammers. "I, I think I saw Massey—at the Athenaeum."

"What? What happened?" Sarah asks.

Bart and Jonah come in from the dining room.

"What's going on?" the captain asks.

"I think I saw Massey," George says. "I mean he pretended his name was something else, but I saw through that."

"Calm down, George," Sarah says. "Cook, could you take Jonah into the kitchen for dessert while we sort this all out?"

"I'm not going anywhere," the little boy exclaims. "This is exciting! I don't know who Massey is, but this is better than playing pirates."

"No pudding for small boys who don't do what they are told," says Cook.

Jonah frowns and follows her into the kitchen as a knock comes on the door.

"Don't open it," George cautions.

Sarah motions to Bart to open the door as she hides behind the large shoji screen.

"I know she's in there, Bart," Stephen yells. "Let me in."

"Get away from here, Massey!" George shouts as he grabs the samurai sword and opens the door.

"Excuse me?" Stephen exclaims. "Who are you?"

"Keep away, Massey!" George shouts.

"That's not Massey," Bart says taking the sword from the librarian's hands. "George, meet Stephen Bailey, a friend of Sarah's."

"Stephen! What are you doing here?" She barrels out from behind the screen.

"I knew you were here!" the blonde man exclaims. "Why are you hiding from me?"

"Stephen, you damn fool. Get inside before anyone sees you," Bart says as he pulls the blonde man into the house and looks up and down the street.

Stephen and George stare at each other until the captain speaks.

"I think perhaps it's time that you and Stephen sort all this out. George and I will join Cook and Jonah in the kitchen. Please retire to the study where you will have more privacy."

"What are you doing here, Stephen?" Sarah says wearily after she slides the study door closed.

"I had to see you! I've given it a lot of thought and I now realize that it's not your fault."

"What's not my fault?" she says.

"You know—your p-p-p-past," he sputters.

"Go on." She crosses her arms and sits on the red wingback chair.

"I mean you were so young and all," he says.

"OK. What are you trying to say, Stephen?"

"I mean, I know everything now," he says.

Sarah frowns. "What do you mean by 'everything?'"

"I know how your morals have been corrupted by living with that sapphite, Jessamyn. I mean it's a small wonder that you turned out the way you did. I just want you to know that I forgive you and would be honored if you would be my wife. Of course, we'd need to move from here—somewhere far away from anyone who knows about your past and away from Jessamyn. The sooner the better. Why don't you get your things and we can be on our way right now?"

Sarah sits in stunned silence.

CHAPTER 98

He leaves the house at dawn and walks the five miles to Eliot to catch a gundalow. With any luck, he'll get to Portsmouth by noon and be done with the whole sorry business by early afternoon.

What happens after that?

He doesn't care.

Taylor will be harder to kill than the cowardly priest—especially since the murderer is locked up in the Portsmouth jail. He carries a shotgun and his hunting knife—one of those should do the trick. He just needs two minutes with the prisoner.

As luck would have it, a gundalow loaded with lumber is ready to depart from the pier as soon as he arrives. On another day he would be happy to learn that the crew are fellow countrymen. Their familiar Irish language is music to his ears—until he realizes what they are saying.

"Liam, to think we had that murderer on our boat!"

"And now he's escaped."

"He needed a bath, but he kept to himself," says the taller man as he turns the wheel to guide the boat around a bend in the river.

"I thought he was just down on his luck." Liam shakes his head.

"Are you talking about Taylor?" Colm asks in his rusty Irish.

"Aye! He murdered a policeman and burned down the jail. Liam and I gave him a ride to Portsmouth without knowing who he was."

"What day was this?" Colm asks.

"Saturday. Nearly a week ago," the taller one answers.

"Why are you just talking about it now?"

"An article in the newspaper said that he nearly killed some whore in South Berwick last week. Liam and I realized then that we'd seen him."

"A week ago?" Colm asks. "And nobody has heard from him since?"

"Well, the paper said that he killed another lady in Portsmouth," Liam says. "She ran a whorehouse."

"When was this?" Colm asks.

"I'm not sure. I think it was Sunday or Monday," Liam answers.

"Shite," Colm says to himself. "This will be harder than I thought."

CHAPTER 99

Apple cake made for a delicious supper in bed. They stayed up until the wee hours of the morning. Jess told Maryanne all about Suzanne, Odette and the Shoals treasure. Maryanne told Jess about her upbringing and her favorite brother. They are close despite the fact that he is a man of the cloth.

Jess rolls over in the morning light and caresses Maryanne's chest.

"Your breasts are perfect."

"I always thought they were too small," she yawns. "I wanted ones like yours."

"I suppose everyone wants what they don't have," Jess says.

Maryanne asks, "So, has Savannah been working at the house for a long time?"

"Years and years. She has a regular that pays extra for her discretion. That has helped to keep her as the big earner in the house."

"Interesting. But not as interesting as you." Maryanne rolls over on top of her pinning her to the bed.

Jess laughs. "We should get up, my dear Miss M. The horses need to be cared for and I have some documents I have to prepare for Sarah."

"You're right. Besides now I think I require a visit to the privy."

"I'll fix us some tea," Jess says as the two women rise and slip their shifts over their head.

"Maryanne, I wish we could stay naked all day."

"Might be a tad chilly in the privy."

Jess laughs and wraps a shawl around Maryanne.

"Don't dilly dally," she says as she kisses her nose.

Jessamyn heats water for the tea and unwraps the leftover apple cake to eat for breakfast.

She makes the bed and uses water in the pitcher to wash her face.

"Where the hell is Maryanne? The privy can't have taken that long."

She puts on her boots and wraps herself in her shawl and heads out into the garden. It's then that she hears it.

Taylor's voice.

"You dumb fucking bitch. Think you can parade all around naked and not get what's coming to you. I'll kill you and that cunt lady detective. We all saw you."

Jess grabs the rake and smashes it into Taylor's head. At least she aims for his head but at the last minute he rolls, and it catches his shoulder. Maryanne scurries out of his reach and Jess swings for him again. He manages to stagger up and comes towards her in a rage. He's dripping blood everywhere. He grabs the rake and tosses it to the side putting his hands around her neck. They struggle and crash through the grow box, shattering the glass.

She stares into his eyes as he tightens his grip.

He releases her and falls to the ground.

Maryanne stands behind him with a shovel.

She drops to her knees and Jess holds her.

"I think I killed him," Maryanne whispers. "He was strangling you."

Out of the corner of her eye Jess sees Taylor charge at them. She picks up a shard of glass and drives it into his eye. He spins around and falls to the ground. After a few gurgling breaths he quiets.

The women stagger to the door.

Maryanne sits, rocking at the kitchen table.

"It's OK," Jess says holding Maryanne close. "We had to kill him. Good riddance to bad rubbish. What I want to know is where has he been these last few days?"

"I think I may know," the smaller woman says softly. "I thought I heard something in the basement when I went back to the rectory yesterday."

"What? You went to the rectory?"

"For the cinnamon."

"Oh, dear God, Maryanne. He could have killed you!"

"Silas must have known about Taylor. He must have been helping him."

"But why?" Jess asks.

The two women cling to each other.

"What was he saying? What did he mean? Who else was spying on us? Silas?" Maryanne asks.

"Oh cruppers—although that seems kind of minor compared to this." She points at Taylor's body through the open door.

"Maryanne, you need to go get cleaned up and get out of here. I'll get Mrs. Markwart's kitchen boy to run and get the police."

"Wait. You don't want me to talk to the police?" she asks.

"No. It'll be easier if I tell them. Nobody has to know that you were even here."

"Jess, what was he was saying about someone else seeing us?"

"He was probably lying to make us nervous. We'd have known if there was someone else and besides if Silas has been helping him, he's not going to say anything to the police."

"I have to go to the rectory. I need to ask Silas if it was him," Maryanne says.

"There will be plenty of time for that. Just get dressed and go to the train station. I'll send word to you at your brother's."

Jess runs to Mrs. Markwart's house in her shift and tells her that Taylor is dead in her garden. Maryanne washes her hands as best she can. She then dresses, throws her bloody clothes into the stove and walks around the block. She starts to turn left towards the train station but instead turns right and walks to the rectory.

She finds Hobson in the church.

"Hello, Silas."

He turns suddenly. "Maryanne? You're home?"

"Yes, Silas."

"What are you doing here? I thought you were at your brother's. I wanted you to stay there until this all blew over."

"Silas, why have you been harboring a fugitive in the basement?" she asks calmly.

"What do you mean?" he sputters. "I have done no such thing."

"You don't have to worry about him anymore, Silas. He is lying dead in Jess's garden."

A look of shock mixed with relief crosses his face.

"How did he die?" the clergyman asks.

"I hit him in the head with a shovel after he tried to rape and strangle me."

"Why were you at Jessamyn's and not at your brothers?" he asks.

"I think you know, Silas. Didn't you and Taylor spy on Jess and me as we made love in Jess's kitchen?"

"What?" The old man seems genuinely surprised.

"Anyway, it doesn't matter anymore."

Silence.

"Thank God you're all right." He embraces her as she stiffens.

"Why would you protect a man like that, Silas? Why would you help him escape? Does it have something to do with the madam who came here to see you?"

"I…can't. I can't tell you."

"You'll need to tell the police everything," she says.

"I can't. I just wanted to keep you safe." He starts crying.

"Why did you insist on getting married last Saturday?"

"Because I was afraid if you went to your brother's and we weren't married yet you wouldn't come back."

"Silas."

He looks down.

"But Maryanne, I gave up Savannah for you."

She smiles. "Ah, Wednesday prayer night. You're the regular."

"Yes," he says quietly.

"That doesn't matter, Silas. I could have forgiven a sexual relationship but harboring Taylor, that's going too far. Did you help him to escape?" she asks.

"I didn't think he was going to kill that guard and burn the place down! I swear. I just gave him the knife when I offered to pray with him. He was supposed to threaten Emerson and run away. Nobody was to ever see him again. That's what Odette said anyway."

"We're done, Silas," Maryanne says as she turns to the door.

"Please don't leave!" he cries.

She shakes her head, turns and walks down the street as the neighbors fill Jessamyn's driveway.

Jimmy Palfrey of the Portsmouth police has arrived and before Jess can open her mouth Maryanne says, "I hit him with that shovel, then I stabbed him with a piece of glass. He was trying to rape and strangle us."

Jess starts to protest but Maryanne stops her.

Palfrey sighs. "Well, Mrs. Hobson, we'll need to take Mr. Taylor and yourself to the police station and talk to the chief to sort this out."

"I understand," she says.

They load Taylor into a wagon and Maryanne is about to step into a coach when they hear screams from across the street.

Mrs. Markwart runs towards them.

"The reverend has hung himself in the church."

Maryanne sighs, gets into the coach and is driven away.

It's then that Jess feels the throbbing of the slice on her hand from the broken shard. She looks down to see a pool of blood forming at her feet.

CHAPTER 100

He manages to change trains in Boston with the help of the old woman and her daughter. They seemed to soften towards him once they found out he can't read. There was no way he'd have been able to navigate the station without their help. They wave goodbye as they board their train for Montréal.

The café car makes all the difference and for the first time in days, Massey has a full belly and is reasonably sober. He ran out of whiskey in Hartford and the train didn't carry anything harder than cider.

It takes two hours to reach Portsmouth and Massey steps onto the platform and takes a look around. After Boston and Hartford, this seems like a small town. It's still much larger than anything he experienced in Virginia.

He wanders through the town square. The commodore said to look for a library with a fancy name that was mentioned in the newspaper. He asks a pack of boys for directions—it turns out he's right in front of it. He'll stake it out. She'll come here at some point.

Tomorrow will be soon enough to start his watch.

"You there!" he calls to a group of young men smoking outside the big church. "Where does a stranger find a drink and a whore in this town?"

A boy with a toothless grin responds, "Are you looking for highfalutin?"

Massey has no idea what that means. "Just a whore and a drink is all."

"The Randy Piddock is fine if you only have two bits or so. Otherwise Sally Lightfoot's is good."

"What about the one where the whore was murdered?"

"Odette's," the boy snickers. "You don't look like the type for that place."

Massey looks down. After five days of travel, his new clothes look just like his old ones.

The boys point him towards Water Street, and he walks through the square. He'll have to be careful with his money as he only has a few dollars left. The Randy Piddock it is. He walks down the street as the sound of laughter emanates from the open doorway. It looks like a tavern. "I'll bet there ain't gonna be decent food at the whorehouse. Probably should stop in here for something first."

His eyes take a moment to adjust once inside the dark room. A single musician plays somber tunes on a squeezebox in the corner. A bar to the left is filled with men wearing dirtier clothes than his own. A man in a hat with a clean suit seems to be holding court.

The tidy man tells a joke and the crowd laughs. He turns towards Massey and beckons him over.

"What's your name, stranger? I'm Tippy. Buy you a drink?"

CHAPTER 101

Tulip and Eve have never seen anything like the train yard in Washington, D.C. Steam spewing engines strain pulling too many cars to count. They look like they might collide at any moment. Men dressed in uniforms direct the traffic. The cacophony of the engines, the shoveling of coal and the constant squealing of livestock on their way to the abattoir creates a din that leaves Tulip, Simon and Eve numb.

A whistle blows and jars them awake.

"We're really riding on one of those?" Tulip asks Penny.

"Yes," she replies. "We're taking the wagons, the horses, everything."

The caravans are loaded onto flatbeds and the horses into special cars complete with stalls. The three sit and watch the excitement while eating the remains of the breakfast.

"This biscuit tastes so good," Tulip says. "In fact, everything Tania makes tastes delicious."

"It tastes like fresh air and freedom," Simon says.

Eve laughs and crumbs spew onto the floor of the porch.

Penny approaches. Everything is loaded.

"You three will ride in your own wagon with the three beds for the overnight journey," the tall woman says. "We should be in Boston by tomorrow evening. It's pretty difficult to walk between the cars so I'll make sure that you have everything you need before we get rolling."

They watch as the workmen tie the caravan to the flatbed car.

Penny hands Simon a new basket. "There's plenty of food and water in here and there's a chamber pot in the wagon that you can empty over the side of the train. You'll be 20 feet off the ground but don't get scared."

"Thanks, ma'am," Simon says.

Penny and Tania help the three climb into their wagon.

"Now get yourself settled," Penny says. "We leave in a few minutes."

Tulip and Eve try not to look outside the window to the ground far below as the train pulls out of the station. The wagon lurches from side to side .

"You suppose that we're tied on tightly enough," Eve asks. "It feels like we could fly off at any moment."

Simon hugs her and smiles. "It's fine. I'm sure," he says even though he isn't sure at all.

CHAPTER 102

Jess and Sarah sit alone in Bart's front parlor. Trying to lighten the mood, Cook has brought them a tray with tea and a selection of small brightly colored cookies.

Sarah takes a sip of her tea and asks, "What did he mean, saying that you're a sapphite? Did something happen?"

Jess shakes her head. "I'm not sure, Taylor said that someone else was spying on us at the house. It must have been Stephen," Jess answers. "Mrs. Markwart mentioned that he had been by."

"He was? What were you doing in the house?"

"I was with Maryanne," Jess whispers.

"Oh mutton nob," Sarah says and reaches out for her mother's hand forgetting about her stitched up wound. Jess cringes at the touch.

"We thought that Taylor was talking about Silas. It turns out the old man was harboring the fugitive in his basement. It must have been Stephen he was actually referring to."

"We'll it doesn't matter anymore," Sarah says curling her legs under her on the settee. "I've told him to go and to never come back."

"I'm so sorry, Sarah. If only we had been more careful."

"Jess. It's not your fault. I'm sorry about what may be next for you and Maryanne once this gets out, but I am not sorry to have learned about his true colors. Thankfully, it was before I did something I regret."

Jess smiles and takes a bite of one of the cookies. "These are delicious. They are so light."

"They're French. Cook says that they are made with egg whites. She called them macarons or something like that."

Jess laughs, "Everyone is trying to get you ready for Paris."

Sarah laughs, "I suppose so. On that note, you'd better go along. George will be here soon for my French lesson and he'll be cross if I don't have my homework done."

"If I stay, will I finally get to meet George?"

"Well, he'll be here in a few minutes so I guess so. He's really a good egg. You should have seen him with the samurai sword when he thought Stephen was Massey." She laughs at the memory.

"Does he know everything?" Jess asks.

"About me—yes. I felt that I owed him an explanation after he defended my honor."

"How did he take it all, Sarah?"

"I'm pretty sure that he already knew about Odette's, but he listened quietly as I told him the whole story—then he hugged me."

"What about the Stephen part? Did you tell him that whole story?"

"I did. I think he was a little jealous at first. I'm pretty sure that he regrets not running him through with the blade."

Jess laughs. "He sounds like a good one, that George."

"A true friend," Sarah says nodding. "Oh I forgot to mention it, but there are a few books that belong to the library on my table at home. Do you mind bringing them back to the Athenaeum?"

"Of course. I have a meeting Monday afternoon about Savannah's case at the Rockingham and can slip over afterwards."

"You don't mind?"

"Not at all. It's about time that I saw the inside of the place that you've spent so many hours."

"Thank you Momma," she says as she hugs Jess.

"I love you, Sarah."

They hear Cook answer the back door and George appears at their door.

"George, this is my mother, Jessamyn Jakes," Sarah says.

The bespectacled, dark-haired man removes his hat and takes her hand.

"I am honored to meet you, Miss Jakes. I think very highly of Sarah and Jonah. You are to be commended for your parenting skills."

Sarah swats his shoulder. "George! That is the silliest thing you've ever said."

"Thank you, George," Jess replies winking at him. "Regardless of what my daughter says, I appreciate it."

"Enough of this *absurdité*," Sarah says. "Let's start my lesson."

Jess leaves out the back and walks around Portsmouth before heading home in case anyone is following her. As she passes Sally Lightfoot's, a familiar figure emerges.

Stephen.

Their eyes lock. He's clearly inebriated and stumbles towards her.

"You! It's your fault that she doesn't love me. You ruined everything!"

"Stephen, calm down," Jess says softly.

People cross the street to avoid the two of them as he splashes down in a muddy puddle.

"Stephen? Why don't we walk to the Codfish and get something to eat?"

She helps him up and they stagger around the corner to the inn.

He sits at a table with his head in his hands.

"Anything other than the coffee, Miss Jess?" Elias asks.

"Perhaps some bread, Trask. That might help soak up the alcohol in his system."

The innkeeper retreats to the kitchen.

"Stephen, I'm sorry that things didn't work out with Sarah. That has nothing to do with me. I never even told her about your child with Matie."

He looks up groggily. "What? You know about that?"

"Yes Stephen, I do. You see, we all have secrets—even you."

He starts to cry.

"It didn't seem like anything bad," he lays his head on the table. "I mean she wanted a baby so much."

"And now they'll have one," Jess says.

Trask delivers the bread and hands Jess the latest newspapers.

"Oh dear. More from that crupper Tippy?"

"I'm afraid so. Sorry about all of this, Miss Jess."

"Thanks for being such a good friend, Elias. I'll take these to read later."

"Tippy! He's the asshole responsible for all of this," Stephen mutters.

"Now, Stephen, it's time to stop blaming others for your problems. Grow up, my boy," Trask says as he leaves the table.

The young man's eyes narrow. "He's right. It's time I did grow up and took responsibility for something."

"What do you mean, Stephen? Don't do anything stupid." Jess says.

CHAPTER 103

George leans forward across the table and points to the text. Sarah reads a bit of text then looks at her tutor.

"You've almost got the pronunciation correct, Sarah. It's 'Calay' and not 'Calayz.'"

"I'll never get this. How will I survive in Paris without speaking French?"

"Don't worry." He takes her hand. "You'll get better and better. It will be easier once you're there. It won't just be words on a page."

"I guess so," she says doubtfully. "I can't believe I'm leaving next week."

"I know." He looks down. "Sarah, you know that I care about you deeply."

She looks away. "I know. I care for you as well."

"It's my hope that when you return from France, we might be able to explore some of these feelings," he says.

"I don't know, George. I'll be gone so long. You shouldn't wait for me."

"I'll wait."

"You don't understand, George. I've taken a vow."

"A vow? Like a nun?" he asks slumping back in his chair.

"Not exactly. After I left Odette's I realized that I need to make my own way in the world. That means no babies, no husband."

"Oh," he sighs.

"I need to wake up each day and be able to work on my studies and my art. If I have a husband and babies, I'll only be able to work for them."

He nods. "But what about Stephen. You almost let him in your life."

"I know. I was out of control. I can't let that happen again. I'm sorry."

All George can think about is how out of control he feels with her right now.

"You never want children, Sarah?"

"My mother—my real mother—didn't have a choice about having children. She was the master's property and she had two babies by him."

"But that was slavery, Sarah. This would be your choice and babies born out of love," he argues.

"It's different, George, but it amounts to the same thing. It means a life spent in servitude."

"But what about your little brother, Jonah? Do you think Jess regrets having him?" he asks as tears come to his eyes.

Sarah shakes her head. "She didn't make any vows when we left Odette's. She still believes in love."

George nods.

"I mean, I love Nah, but I've also seen how hard Jess has had to work to keep up with the detective agency and be a mother."

"I understand. My mother raised me alone, don't forget. If it wasn't for the Atheneaum, I don't know where I'd be. I pretty much spent all my days there, after age ten."

"I guess it helped raise us both," she says laughing.

She reaches out and takes his hand.

"You are my best friend, George."

He hugs her to hide the look of disappointment on his face.

CHAPTER 104

J ess spends Sunday morning cleaning the house and fixing up Putt's room over the barn. She moves the bird skeleton and the Charles Darwin bust into the house and makes the couch up with fresh linens and blankets. The doc has said that Putt can come home on Monday and even do some light labor for the first few weeks. Mrs. Springer is sending him home with a new knitted blanket and a supply of canned peaches.

She is to be at Bart's at 2 p.m. for dinner with the family. Apparently, Cook has figured out how to use the tandoori oven and is determined to get Indian cuisine correct.

Today is the day Jess will tell Bart that she won't marry him. She can't put it off any longer. On account of Sarah's troubles, he's pushing the departure date to next week instead of the end of the month. She must talk to him before they leave.

She puts on her Sunday dress and says to herself in the mirror. "It seems strange to put on my nice clothes to decline a marriage proposal."

Finally, at 1:30 p.m. she leaves the house and meanders to Bart's. She stops in front of Carbew's to get some pastries for Sarah and Nah, but nothing looks good in the bakery window. She sighs and turns towards the captain's house.

"Wait! I know what I can bring." She turns back to Holt Street and knocks on her neighbor's door.

"Hello, Mrs. Markwart. Is Jack available to play today?"

The older woman adjusts her bonnet and laughs. "Feeling a little lonely without the boy? I must confess Jack and I miss him also."

"Something like that," Jess says covering her bandaged hand with her bag. He'll be home soon, though, and we'll be back on our usual schedule."

"That will be good," Mrs. Markwart says. "I'm up to my eyeballs in cookies. Speaking of treats, let me pack some for you to give to Putt."

Jack follows along behind Jess as they make their way through Market Square. A drunken man lies on a bench with his brown hat covering his face.

"At some point the dowagers are going to scream loud enough to clean this town up," Jess says to the pup. "The Water Street party will be over."

The dog barks in reply and wanders over to sniff the prostrate man. He starts to lift a furry leg, but Jess grabs him.

"Leave him alone, Jack. He's just a harmless drunk."

They finally reach Bart's back door and the dog starts barking. Nah runs from the front parlor. "Jack!" he yells and chases him through the house.

"Sorry Cook, I had to bring him for a visit," Jess says.

The red cheeked woman rolls her eyes.

"Sarah and George are in the study and the captain is upstairs," Cook says handing Jess a cup of tea.

"How is the Indian cooking going?" Jess asks.

"Good, I think Miss Jess. Never having had tandoori chicken before I'm not sure it is accurate, but it seems tender and tastes lovely."

"Wonderful. I look forward to dinner. I'll go upstairs and say hello to Bart."

Cook has turned back to her bread dough and waves her away.

Jess lingers outside his door unsure of what to do next.

"Are you going to come in or stand in the hallway all afternoon?" a voice asks from inside the room.

She laughs and opens the door to Bart's bedroom. It's a grand room with a balcony that overlooks the courtyard at the front.

"Wow Bart, this room is beautiful. The silk wallpaper is stunning."

"It's from China. It could all be yours—or if you want you could have the room down the hall. I understand that you might want your own space."

She sits on the jacquard bedspread. "Bart, I can't…"

"I knew it was folly," he says turning towards the balcony. "I was just hoping it might work out."

"I do love you," she says, "but it wouldn't be right. You deserve a woman who loves every bit of you."

"I was thinking that it might evolve into that," he says quietly.

She smiles and kisses him on the cheek.

"Of course, you'll always be Nah's father, Bart."

The captain smiles. "He is an amazing boy. You have done a wonderful job raising him."

"Sarah and I both. He's a family project," she laughs. "Perhaps we should tell him today who you really are."

"Hm. Are you going to tell him how that came about?" Bart asks.

"Eventually yes—when he's older. There will be no secrets in my house. How about we go down and see if we can get his attention now? On second thought I probably should talk to him alone for a few minutes."

They hug and Bart kisses Jess on the top of her head. "I'll always be there for you."

"You're family, Bart. Please remember that."

As soon as they open the bedroom door the dog bounds into the bedroom. Nah comes barreling in after him.

"We're playing pirate!" he shouts. "I'm the pirate and Jack is the scalawag British Navy."

"Yep—pretty sure you're the father," she whispers. "Hey Nah, sit down with me for a few minutes while the captain takes the British Navy to the yard for a privy visit."

Bart closes the door behind him and gets halfway down the stairs before he hears Nah.

"Woohoo! This is better than Christmas! Brodie is going to be so jealous! His father is just the mayor."

CHAPTER 105

Maryanne has not returned from the police station—if she ever will. Jess's whole life has caved in quickly. A week ago, she had a beautiful daughter, a wonderful son, a thriving business and a new lover. Now she still has Jonah but who knows about the business after word gets out about her and Maryanne.

Maybe they should all go to France next week with Sarah—or maybe just Montréal.

She should be able to wrap up this Savannah business today and that is her last official client—she needs to get more work if her agency will survive.

Luckily, the meeting is only a few blocks away at the Rockingham. It's starting to snow, and she wants to visit with Sarah and Jonah before it gets really bad.

Walking along Holt Street towards the hotel, she takes stock of her other case. It seems that she'll never know the truth about the treasure. Odette, Suzanne and Grievance Collins are all dead. Mable and Agnes are nowhere to be found. Maybe the secret disappeared with them.

She climbs the steps to the hotel and pauses to wipe the dusting of snow off the bronze lions guarding the door. "I should bring Nah to see these."

The dining room is dark. The candles and the winter light coming through the small windows can't compete with the mahogany paneling.

Justice Tompkins waves her over. "Miss Jakes! I'm so glad that you're here. There have been some developments." He stands and motions for her to sit.

"Really, Mr. Tompkins? What kind of developments?" she asks. "Did the shareholder decide to sell to Savannah? I have a written offer from her." She pulls a folded paper out of her bag. Jess is in a rush and would like to finish this errand.

Tompkins's red beard shimmies in the firelight as he shakes his head. "The original shareholder has recently passed away, so the corporation is now in the hands of his next of kin."

"Next of kin?" she asks.

"Yes. She requested a meeting to consider your offer and go over the estate. She will join us here shortly. As a matter of fact, here she is."

Jess turns towards the door.

"Maryanne?"

"Oh, do you two know each other? Mrs. Hobson didn't tell me that."

"Yes, Mr. Tompkins, we are friends from way back," Maryanne says. "Jessamyn was a parishioner of my late husband."

"Such a tragedy, ma'am. I'm sorry for your loss," he says.

"Thank you, sir," she replies removing her bonnet and settling in next to Jess.

"Before we start, Mrs. Hobson. May I offer you both a cup of tea?"

"I'd like a glass of whiskey please," Jess says.

"Make that two. We're in mourning," Maryanne says smiling.

The bushy lawyer looks them over. They don't seem very sad. "All right. Whiskey it is."

He signals the waiter, orders the liquor for the women and a fresh pot of tea for himself. He pulls documents out of his leather satchel.

"Here's a complete listing of the holdings of the Staff of Life Trust Company." He keeps pulling papers until he has a stack in the center of the table.

The women's eyes widen.

"Oh my. I assumed it was just the house," Jess says quietly.

"Oh no. The reverend's partner in the company, a Miss Odette La-Francaise…"

"Ahhh. LaFrancaise," Jess says. "I should have thought of that."

"Excuse me?" he asks.

She shakes her head. "Nothing. Go on."

"As I was saying, the reverend's partner in the company, a Miss Odette LaFrancaise, nee Lucinda Bentham, was an astute investor. She multiplied their initial investment fifty fold."

The whiskey arrives and Jess downs hers in one gulp.

"Did you say Lucinda Bentham?" she asks.

"Yes Miss Jakes. Why? Did you not know Odette's real name?"

Jess shakes her head. "No, I did not."

"Well, anyway. The investments were varied—truth be told most of them are just this side of legal. For example, she owned a controlling share of a business in Brooklyn called Goldstein's Notions and What Nots—apparently it is a manufacturer of prophylactics."

Jess bursts out laughing.

"What is it, Jess?" Maryanne asks taking a sip of her whiskey.

"Nothing. I had no idea Odette was such a savvy investor."

"So, how did this corporation start?" Maryanne asks.

"Silas Hobson provided the seed money from an inheritance twenty years ago," Tompkins says. "The madam ran the company and periodically sent the reverend a large donation to his church."

"Astonishing." Jess shakes her head.

"And now that Odette has died without heirs and the reverend has also perished. That just leaves you, Mrs. Hobson."

"I don't know what to say. This is all so overwhelming," Maryanne says. "I didn't realize it would be so much money."

"No worries, Mrs. Hobson. I will help you sort it. Which brings us back to the reason Miss Jakes has joined us. Would you like to sell the disorderly house to Savannah West, the current operator of Odette's?"

Jess unfolds the offer and hands it across the table to Maryanne.

She shrugs. "It seems fair. What do you think Mr. Tompkins?" She hands the paper to the attorney.

After a few minutes he says, "Yes. I agree. This is a very well thought out offer and is more than fair."

"So how does this work?" asks Jess.

"Mrs. Hobson, do you want to finance the loan to Miss West or should she see a banker?" Justice asks.

"Savannah has seen all sides of many bankers over the years," Jess offers. "I don't know if they'd loan her money, though,"

Maryanne laughs. "Then so be it! I'd be happy to loan her the money. I do have one question, though."

"What is that?" Tompkins asks.

"Is she going to be a good boss to the women who work for her. From what Jess has said Odette was not nice."

"You should ask her yourself," he replies. "You could make it a condition of the loan. I can help you draw up a list of requirements and will set up a meeting."

Jess thinks of Granny. There will be no auctioning off of her cherry.

CHAPTER 106

The women feel the warmth of the whiskey as they leave Tompkins and go out into the heavy snow. The lions are now lumps of white guarding the stairs. The doorman tips his hat as he takes a break from sweeping the snow.

"You know," Maryanne starts, "I think I'll take some of our money and open up a place where desperate women can have better options than ending up at a whorehouse."

"That sounds like a grand idea. Our money? No Maryanne, it's your money," the taller woman says.

"No, my love, it's our money."

Jess cringes as Maryanne takes her injured hand.

"Oh dear God, Jess! Did I hurt you? Was that from the glass shard?"

"Yes, I'm afraid so," she replies. "I didn't even notice it until Doc and Mrs. Springer helped clean me up after the police left."

Maryanne unwraps the bandage. "It looks like they did a very nice job stitching you up. "I am sorry that it hurts so much." She kisses it lightly.

"Why did you tell the police that you stabbed Taylor?" Jess whispers.

The smaller woman smiles. "I had to, Jess. I couldn't let anything happen to you. You have Sarah and Jonah to think about. I have nobody to protect. It all seems to be moot now that they've released me."

Jess kisses her hand as they walk towards the Athenaeum. The square is full of snow covered figures rushing to do their errands and get home.

"Jess, I just thought of something," she says. "I don't understand why Odette cared so much about the Shoals treasure. I mean, she was rich."

"I think I might know," Jess answers. "I'm pretty sure that she was the daughter of Donald Bentham."

"The farmer?"

"The one and same. Her father and Grievance witnessed the shipwreck and found the treasure. I suspect that Collins stole it after the fact."

"Now I see why she was so obsessed," Maryanne says.

"Yes. These wounds run very deep, I suppose," Jessamyn says. "I can't wait to tell Sarah. She was worried that we wouldn't crack the case before she left."

"One more piece of the puzzle," Maryanne says. "You'll need to teach me more about this discreet investigation business of yours."

Jess smiles. "Of course! Most of it is pretty dull, though. Rifling through old records and such. Sarah did a lot of that for me."

"How is she, Jess?"

"She's fine. She leaves for Paris to go to school on Monday," Jess's eyes tear up. "They were trying to beat the weather. It looks like they didn't quite make it."

"I'm so sorry, Jess. I know that you will miss her terribly,."

Jess wipes her tears with her bandaged hand. "It had to be. It's safer to keep her away from Massey."

"It must be so frightening for her." Maryanne shakes her head.

"It is. I can't protect her anymore. Now that her owners know where she is, there will be no end of slave catchers on their way—even if Massey fails."

"Now that we have money," the smaller woman says smiling, "we can visit her in France."

"I'd like that, Maryanne."

They stop in front of the library.

"This is the Athenaeum," Jess says. "I have some books of Sarah's to return. Would you like to come in?"

"Of course," Maryanne says. "Am I allowed to? Isn't it a private library?"

She shrugs. "I actually don't know if we can. I've never been inside either. This is Sarah's place."

She opens the door for Maryanne and follows her into the reading room.

A familiar figure sits at one of the tables, smoking a pipe and perusing his paper. He waves to the women as they enter.

"Hello, Right Reverend," Jess says. "You remember Maryanne, I mean Mrs. Hobson."

"Yes, of course. I'm so sorry for your recent loss, Mrs. Hobson."

"Thank you, sir," Maryanne replies.

"I'll just be a minute," Jess says as she pulls the books out of her bag. "I need to run these up to George."

"Oh, George isn't here today," Cheney says. "His boss, Mr. Quimby is in, though. His office is the first one on the left at the top of the stairs."

"I guess I'll give them to him then. Thank you."

The clergyman nods and goes back to his reading as Maryanne looks around the library. Her eyes are drawn to a painting on the wall.

She leans in for a closer look. There's the ship all right and the map of the Isles of Shoals—just like Jess had described.

"That must be the portrait of Grievance Collins," Jess says as she enters the room.

She stops dead in her tracks halfway across the floor.

"Oh my God."

Cheney looks up from his newspaper. "What Miss Jessamyn? What is it?"

CHAPTER 107

The train takes them as far as Boston. They unload the wagons and the horses and slowly wind their way north. The circus caravan keeps moving despite the snow until after midnight, when they make camp outside of Portsmouth.

Simon and the girls play in the soft snow while the others make a fire and put some stew together for a late night supper.

"It's magical," Eve says as she opens her mouth to catch the soft flakes in her mouth. Tania shows them how to make a snowman even though the snow is too fluffy. Finally, about 1 a.m., they retreat to their bunks to curl under their many blankets.

Penny knocks on their guests' wagon lightly at first dawn. "Time to go," she whispers.

They emerge sleepily and Tania hands them each a cup of hot tea. "Have some breakfast and meet Penny back here in 15 minutes. Be sure and use the privy as you won't have the chance for the next few hours."

The woods are a winter wonderland. The pink sunlight glows on the snow. Eve can't keep staring at it. Tulip is less impressed. "It's too damn cold!" She claps her mitten-covered hands together.

As they walk to the campfire, Penny rolls up the carnival signs transforming the colorful wagon into somber black.

She enters the caravan, removes the mattresses and hands them to Nhial waiting outside.

What were beds are now coffins.

She pulls her black suit out of the first casket and dresses in the dark.

Nhial hitches the horses to the wagon just as Eve, Tulip and Simon return from their hot breakfast.

Penny opens the door, beckoning them in and they enter the caravan and settle into the caskets. She tucks blankets around them each for warmth.

"This is scary, I know," Penny says softly. "It won't be very long. Just an hour or so."

Eve whimpers a little bit and the taller woman takes her hand.

"You're very brave to have come all this way. This is the end of the journey."

With that she closes the caskets and makes her way to the driver's seat.

They ride in the early morning light through the outskirts of town. The wagon wheels cut through the light snow and they make short work of the journey.

Sometime later they stop in front of the church where the right reverend waits with some local men—pall bearers.

She tips her hat and smiles at the clergyman as the men unload the three coffins and bring them into the church.

"Be sure not to open those, gentlemen," Penny warns. "Cholera—very nasty business."

CHAPTER 108

Massey, still drunk from last evening's frivolities watches as the black caskets are carried into the church. The scene sends a shiver up his spine. This waiting for Ada to show herself is getting really old and expensive—he's almost out of money. Spending his nights at The Randy Piddock is getting pricey even if it is the cheapest house in town. That Tippy fellow was plenty generous when he was talking about Ada and her mama. Once he ran out of stories, the man wouldn't even spring for a whiskey much less a milt shooter.

Now it's starting to get really cold. It snows in Virginia but not like this. As far as he is concerned, the north can keep it. He wants to get back south as soon as he can.

He was able to track down the house where Ada lives with her mother, but the neighbor told him that the girl wasn't around so he decided to stake out the library some more.

He watches the undertaker shake hands with the pastor, climb aboard the wagon and drive away. Hunger starts to gnaw at him. Maybe they have some food in the church they'd be willing to share. He hates preachers, so he takes another approach.

"Hey boy!" he calls to a youngster walking through the square. "Get me some whiskey and food." He hands him a quarter and a bit later the lad returns with whiskey and a loaf of bread. Massey dives into right away. There's no more action in the square and the whiskey makes him sleepy so he curls up on the bench for a nap.

He wakes to find the boy and his friends kicking him and stealing what's left of his dinner.

They run off laughing down the street.

"God damn it!" he yells. "Where is hell is that little bitch?"

CHAPTER 109

George arrives for their French lesson right after work. As soon as he closes the study doors, he whispers to Sarah, "The right reverend requests our company at the church."

"We'll need to sneak out. Luckily Bart is seeing to the ship and Jonah is in the kitchen with Cook," she replies.

They carefully make their way through the darkened snowy alleys to the West Church.

Sarah finds the front entrance locked so they go to the side entrance and knock. A wrinkled eye appears in the peep hole. The door springs open and the right reverend ushers them inside.

"Come with me—down these stairs."

"Is everything OK, sir?" she asks. "Why are we going to the basement?"

"Everything's fine, Sarah. I have some people I would like you to meet," Cheney replies.

"In the basement?" the younger man asks.

"Yes. George, would you mind waiting upstairs for a few minutes?"

He looks unsure but sits on a bench in the hallway. "I'll wait up here for you, Sarah."

They walk to a fireplace and the right reverend turns one of the stones. The wall opens and Sarah enters what appears to be a parlor with bunk beds on the side. Standing in the middle of the room are three people. The girl in the middle looks familiar to her.

"Oh mutton nobs," she whispers.

The right reverend speaks, "Sarah, this is your sister, Cilla, now known as Eve."

Sarah stares at the girl.

The girl stares at Sarah.

Nobody speaks.

Finally, Cheney introduces the other two people in the room, "this is Tulip. She escaped with Eve from the Pullyhawly Plantation and this," he puts his arm around the young man, "this is Tulip's brother, Simon."

Sarah starts crying.

Eve starts crying.

Everyone is crying.

Mrs. Carbunkle arrives in the doorway,

"I have scones and tea!"

Laughter.

Sarah and Eve cling to each other. Each telling tales of their lives in spurts.

Eve is underwhelmed by Sarah's stories from Odette's.

"Seems like you had it pretty easy—at least nobody beat you."

Sarah has to concede that point. "And the food was pretty good."

"So, who is this white woman who adopted you? Jessamyn?" Eve asks.

"She saved my life. She rescued me from the whorehouse. She gave me everything," Sarah says.

"A white woman gave you everything?" Eve raises her eyebrows.

"She taught me so much," Sarah replies. "How to be a person and not property. How to read, for crupper's sake."

"She taught you to read?" Eve perks up.

"Yes, as soon as we met. I was 10 years old."

Tulip pipes up, "Eve taught herself to read. She didn't need some white lady."

"Shh, Tulip!" Eve says. "Do you think she could help me with reading? I have started, but have a long way to go."

Sarah nods. "I'm sure she would. Where will you be?"

"The right reverend has a house for us in Greenland until we can get on our feet," Simon says.

Sarah asks quietly, "Did you send the letter, Eve?"

"Yes," she nods. "Then we escaped, hoping that Massey would forget about you and follow us. We never thought we would make it this far."

Tulip pipes up, "I always knew we would get this far."

"Your plan might have worked. I haven't seen Massey. All the same, I'm leaving for France soon."

"France?" Eve asks.

"Yes. Jess doesn't think I'll be safe here, so I'm going to school in Paris. The right reverend helped with that as well." She smiles at Cheney. "Speaking of my mother, I need to get back to Captain Bart's. I'm already really late. They will be worried."

"Worried?" Eve asks. "Not angry?"

"No, not angry," she replies. "Worried. I'll be back tomorrow, and we can talk more."

She gets up to leave when a figure darkens the door.

"Lookie what we have here? It's my lucky day."

They swing around and Massey stands smirking at them with a Colt 45 pistol in his hand.

"I'll be fucking you girls for the next 40 years once we get back to Pully-hawly—if you live that long," he sneers.

Simon lunges for Massey who fires his weapon hitting the younger man in the shoulder.

They struggle. The gun flies out of Massey's hand and lands at Eve's feet. She picks it up and points it at the slave catcher who shields himself with Simon.

"Now you won't shoot this boy, will you?" he sneers.

Eve stands there holding the gun unsure what to do. She sees something move out of the corner of her eye.

A crash.

Massey falls to the floor. George stands behind him. The gilded cross from the alter in his hands. He starts to shake and sinks to the floor.

"Holy Jesus Christ," the right reverend says under his breath.

Eve rushes to Simon who's bleeding from his wound. She removes his shirt and holds it over the wound.

Tulip kneels by Massey and pokes him with her finger.

He groans and moves his head.

"He's not dead, yet." She pulls out her knife and sticks it into the slave catcher's neck.

"He'll be dead now," she says as she wipes the knife on his jacket.

"The bullet just grazed you, Simon." Eve says as she rips a strip of his bloody shirt and wraps it around his upper arm.

Sarah takes the cross out of George's hands and helps him to the settee in the corner. "Are you all right?" she whispers.

He manages a weak smile but starts to shake. Sarah holds him until he calms down. "It's all right George, you had to do it."

They sit in silence looking at the bleeding body of the slave catcher in the middle of the floor.

Finally, the right reverend speaks. "I take it that you all know our recently departed guest, Mister Scoot Massey?"

They turn to him.

"Yes, but how do you know him?" Sarah asks.

"Mr. Massey and I met years ago in New Jersey when he was chasing another group of slaves—a very unpleasant fellow."

"What are we going to do? We have to call the police," George says. "I mean we just killed a man." He drops his head into his hands.

"Perhaps George is right," Sarah says. "You all should leave, and we'll call the police. Nobody will ever know that you were here."

Simon, Eve and Tulip all start to protest.

Cheney holds up his hand.

"Silence please. Confession is good for the soul, George, but in this instance, I feel that it may be unnecessary."

"What do you mean?" George asks.

"He was threatening our lives with the gun and you simply defended us. The Lord works in mysterious ways."

"Shouldn't we just tell the police that?" Sarah asks.

"I think we have witnessed in recent days that the police in this town are not very competent. If we report his death then his bosses in Virginia will not only know where you all are, but will also know about our operation here. That can't happen. Does anyone know if Massey was likely to send any reports back to Virginia?"

Eve responds, "No, sir. He couldn't read or write and he wasn't the type to ask anyone for help. I would say that he would not have sent anything back to Pullyhawly."

"That's good news," he replies. "I have another plan for the eternal slumber of Mr. Massey. Not to worry anyone."

They look at each other and shrug.

"George, Sarah and Tulip. If you would be so kind as to assist me."

CHAPTER 110

T he girl's eyes are wide open. She stares at the bejeweled, silk clad matrons enjoying an expensive meal in the rich wooden interior of the Rockingham Hotel.

"Try not to look like you're going to throw up, dear," Tippy says.

"I'm sorry, sir," she says pulling at the neckline of her fancy dress. "I've just never been to a place like this. I usually don't leave the house unless we're short of pickled eel or bread."

"It's OK, my dear," Tippy says. "Rich people are just like the rest of us. Just keep your mouth shut and I'll order."

This girl is no Savannah. Tippy tried to make an appointment with his favorite redhead so he could bring her to the Rockingham, but she spurned him again. Something about her needing to meet with her new financiers about the house.

He was definitely tired of her newfound dedication to entrepreneurship.

He finds himself with the girl from the other night at The Randy Piddock. He's pretty sure her name is Trixie, but just to be safe he calls her "dear" or just "you."

He orders a nice bottle of wine, a 1840 Chateau Mangouste, to celebrate his latest article. The story of the death of the murderer at the hands of the lady detective's female lover was rejected at first until he toned down the nature of the two women's relationship. He called them "friends" and left it to the reader to look between the lines.

The new revelations about Sarah—or Ada as the slave catcher called her—will be great fodder for the next week or two.

Trixie looks happier after she swigs the first glass of wine. The waiter pours her another from the bottle. Prospect makes a mental note to order swill next time for the girl. The wine is clearly wasted on her.

He had to buy her a respectable dress after he realized all she had for clothing is tattered, cheap lingerie. She looks presentable in her blue satin. The neckline isn't as low as he would like it and he can barely see the curve of her cleavage. He'll have the seamstress fix that once he takes it back after their date is over.

God, he misses Savannah.

Most of all he misses her funny stories about the men she's serviced over the years. What he wouldn't pay for another hour with her. That's what he needs to do. Offer her triple her old rate. She's a businesswoman. She'd go for it. Maybe after he drops the girl off he'll stop by Odette's for a night cap and a late night basket making session.

He orders the fillet mignon for himself and cheap skirt steak for the girl. She can't read so she doesn't know she is getting a lesser cut of meat. Considering the food at The Randy Piddock, she should be thrilled.

As he cuts the first bite of beef, he sees Old Tompkins across the way and waves at him. He heard from the waiter that the hairy lawyer met with two women matching Jessamyn Jakes and Maryanne Hobson's description on Monday. He's dying to know what that was about. All the waiter knew was that they ordered three rounds of whiskey in the middle of the afternoon and that the two women left together—information hardly worth the dollar he slipped him.

"I'm sure that man knows ninety percent of the secrets in this town. I just need to figure out his weakness."

He orders another bottle of wine—the cheapest they have—for the girl and a glass of Vieille Moufette for himself. He swirls the green liquid around the glass and observes the other guests in the dining room. An elderly couple—the woman dripping in diamonds—sits nearest to him. The old gentleman must be deaf as his wife periodically yells something into his ear trumpet.

The girl is getting drunker and he starts to think he needs to get her up to his room if she is to be of any use. He flags the waiter down and looks to the lobby where he spots a frowning Stephen Bailey watching him—seated on the couch by the door.

Something about Bailey's face makes him nervous, so he orders another drink and a piece of cake for the girl. As soon as the cake arrives the girl passes out and smashes her head into the dessert with a loud thump. The waiter suggests that perhaps Mr. Prospect might want to make his way out of the dining room.

"There, there, dear," he says. "Time to wake up. We need to retire upstairs for a bit before I take you home."

She raises her head, frosting drops off of her face. She dips her finger into the cake and licks it.

Tippy and the waiter manage to get her to the lobby. They walk right past Bailey whose eyes never leave the reporter. The girl has never seen an elevator before and starts to scream as the operator closes the door.

Trixie looks like she may throw up at any moment.

"Can't you get this contraption to move any faster? Tippy yells at the poor young man.

"Sorry sir! This is as fast as it will go."

Tippy harrumphs as they finally make it to the third floor and he drags the girl towards his room.

CHAPTER III

T he men struggle and the box groans as they lower it into the ground. The snow has melted over most of the churchyard—another sign that God is on their side. Ordinarily, the ground would be so frozen that there would be no burial until springtime.

"Jesus Christ. I knew this woman was big, but this coffin weighs more than a bull moose," the toothless boy says to his friends.

"I know. It means extra money for us, though. This pall bearer work seems to be coming fast and furious these days."

"Aye. Better than the fishing, Lars?"

The coffin is lowered into the grave. The bearers outnumber the mourners by half a dozen.

Only Jess and Sarah are at the grave side.

"May she rest for all eternity in the loving arms of her benevolent master," the right reverend says.

Sarah covers her giggle with a cough.

"Amen," the small group responds.

The three of them watch as the pall bearers cover the coffin with dirt.

When the last shovel of dirt is emptied, the men take their tools back to the shed. Jess leaves Sarah with the right reverend and walks to retrieve Jonah.

They stand in silence for a moment looking at the fresh dirt covering the grave. Then Sarah asks, "Right Reverend Cheney, may I ask you a question?"

"Of course, Sarah. Anything," he replies.

"That first time I came into the church, you were on your knees."

"Yes—I was atoning."

"Atoning for sins like what we committed," she whispers.

He smiles. "Yes, and other things."

"Don't you think the lord will forgive you for what happened. I mean forgive all of us?"

He smiles. "I learned a long time ago that it's best to be flexible about the scriptures. I try to do what I can for the people most in need and ask for forgiveness later."

She holds out her hand. "I am very happy to have known you sir. Thank you so much for helping me and my sister."

"Thank me by coming back so we can have that conversation about birds," he laughs.

She hugs him quickly goodbye and walks towards Bart's.

CHAPTER 112

Bailey hasn't moved an inch when Tippy emerges hours later with the whore. The same cold expression. The same stature with his arms crossed. The writer feels a chill run down his spine and it's not because he has loaned the girl his new topcoat to cover her nakedness.

She wasn't much good just lying there passed on the bed so he'd had to improvise. Taking the dress off of her was enough of a challenge so he took a knife to her undergarments.

"Like fucking a corpse," he mutters. He had to keep his eyes closed and his thoughts focused on Savannah's breasts to finish his work.

After an hour she woke up enough to send her on her way.

Tippy does his best to ignore Bailey.

The girl staggers and Tippy holds her up as he leads her to the front door. Luckily, the doorman seems to be on break so he pushes the door open and leads her past the lions and down the stairs. The snow wakes her and she starts to mumble to him. There are a few people out in the street who look his way. She has slippers on her feet and there is no dress emerging from the bottom of his coat.

He nods at the people and makes jokes to them about how she can't hold her liquor.

"Oh shit, I'll need to walk her all the way back to the Piddock if I'm going to see my coat again," he mumbles. At least that Bailey should be gone by the time he returns.

He makes it to the Piddock which is still hopping at this late hour. The sounds of laughter and the drunken piano player stream into the street as he approaches the door.

He shoves her into the fray in her nakedness and retreats with his coat back to the hotel.

CHAPTER 113

Colm Flaherty stares at the ashes of the former Puddle Dock Warehouse and Portsmouth city jail shaking his head.

"Where the hell am I supposed to go now? That arsehole could be anywhere," he mutters.

He spent last night at the new Young Men's Christian Association on Pulpit Street. He thought about staying at one of the taverns on Water Street but—for the first time in his life—he craved sobriety.

He would find Taylor and kill him. Then he would find that reporter, Edward Prospect, and kill him.

It doesn't matter what happens to him. It's the one thing he can offer his daughter—his life for her honor.

A man watches him and approaches.

"Hi, stranger. A tragedy to be sure." He clucks his tongue and points at the smoking wreckage.

"Aye, it is," Colm responds.

"Sad about the policeman that was killed," the stranger says.

"Where do they think Taylor is now?" the Irishman asks.

The other man raises an eyebrow and says, "You haven't heard?"

"Heard what?" Colm asks.

"Taylor's dead. Killed by a woman wielding garden tools."

Flaherty can't hide his disappointment. "What do you mean he's dead?"

"Yes, I am happy to report to you he was killed last Friday. Say, what's your name, friend?"

"Flaherty. Colm Flaherty."

"I'm Tippy. Nice to make your acquaintance, stranger. Care for a drink?" He points towards the Bladder Wrack.

"No. I'm not a drinker," the Irishman replies.

Tippy shrugs. "Suit yourself." With that, he loses interest and wanders off towards Water Street.

Now that Taylor is dead, Colm knows what he needs to do.

Find this writer Edward Prospect and kill him.

He's unsure how to proceed. Is he even still here in Portsmouth?

There was a lady detective mentioned in the article. "If I can find her, I can ask about the writer's whereabouts. She's bound to know."

He pulls out the tattered article and looks for her name. He yells to a boy in the street, "Do you know where I can find someone called Jessamyn Jakes?"

"That's her right over there coming out of the church."

He sees an attractive woman with brown hair emerge from the church.

"Excuse me Miss. Are you Jessamyn Jakes?"

She looks around nervously and replies, "I am. What may I help you with?"

"I'd like to hire you to find this writer," he says as he points to Prospect's name in the paper.

"You don't need to hire me to do that, sir," she replies. "From what I understand, he's staying at the Rockingham Hotel. It's five blocks that way."

CHAPTER 114

E ve throws another log onto the fire and settles next to her sister. Picking up her sewing, her eyes strain to see the small stitches as she mends a small tear.

"I can't believe that you're leaving tomorrow," she says to Sarah. They sit in the small front room of the white clapboard cottage. Just a parlor, kitchen and a simple bedroom. A sleeping mat sits tidily rolled up in the corner.

"Even after a few days together, I'll miss you. I'm so happy to have a sister," Sarah says hugging Eve. "We can write each other. How are the lessons going with Jess?"

"We've just had a couple," Eve answers. "She even brought me a bag full of novels! I'm teaching Simon too."

"What about Tulip?" Sarah asks.

"She has no interest—her brother has been showing her how to throw daggers. She cares more about that."

Sarah laughs. "I can see where she would."

"Did you tell Jess about what happened in the church basement?"

"Yes—actually George did. Right when we got back to Bart's. Don't worry. She keeps other people's secrets. She'll never tell anyone what happened."

"I'm not worried," Eve says picking up her sewing.

"How do you like living in Greenland?" Sarah asks poking the fire.

"It's nice. The people are friendly. Mrs. Johanson brought us over soup and bread for dinner yesterday. With Jessamyn dropping in to help with our reading, it's been a bustle of activity around here."

"Have you found work yet?"

"I've been able to pick up this sewing work. This is Mr. Johanson's shirt." She holds up a well mended white blouse.

"What about Simon?"

"He was a blacksmith on the plantation. A pretty good one as I under-stand. The local man offered him a job as soon as he met him."

"With the area growing, they'll need all sorts of tradespeople," Sarah says.

"The extra work will help us get on our feet and into our own place," Eve says wistfully.

"The three of you?"

"No. Just Simon and me. Tulip is leaving," Eve says.

"Leaving? But she just got here!" Sarah says.

"She wants to go back and work with Miss Penny's group."

"That's honorable. Her new dagger throwing skills might come in handy," Sarah laughs.

"I think it has more to do with a certain tall African man," Eve whispers.

"The Nuer tribesman?"

"Yes, Nhial."

Sarah laughs. "The thought of little Tulip with a six-foot five husband."

"They aren't married yet," Eve says.

"I'm pretty sure Tulip gets what she wants."

"That's true," Eve says laughing. "Heaven help that man if he resists."

"So that just leaves you and Simon," Sarah says raising one eyebrow.

Eve looks down shyly.

"Until we have little ones. We're to be married."

"That's wonderful! Hopefully, I'll be home before your babies get to be having babies of their own."

"I hope so too," Eve says.

They sit enjoying their tea and company. Sarah drops a log on the fire and warms her hands in its glow.

"Sarah?" her sister asks.

"Yes, Eve?"

"What happened to Momma?"

Sarah looks down and tears well up in her eyes.

"Truthfully, I don't know. We were living in the outskirts of town with some people like us—just scraping by. I was the only child—the next oldest was a 13-year-old boy who had run by himself from South Carolina. One day we heard that a boat was offering free transport for work in New Brunswick and everyone signed up. On the day we were to leave, Momma sent me to return some pots and pans from a neighbor. It was about a twenty minute walk each way. When I came back to the house, everyone was gone."

"What?" Eve asks. "Did you run after them?"

"I did. When I got to the waterfront I asked about the boat to New Brunswick and nobody knew what I was talking about."

"I just don't understand," Eve says shaking her head. "Where were they?"

"I always thought it was a slave catcher's trick and they were shipped south but since you said momma never came back to Virginia, I don't have any idea."

"So, what happened to you?" the younger girl asks.

"I was sitting on a lobster trap crying when Odette spotted me and talked me into coming to her house. I didn't know what to do, so I followed her."

Eve hugs her weeping sister.

"Ow!" Sarah exclaims laughing.

"Oh, sorry! I forgot about my sewing needle! Are you OK?"

CHAPTER 115

Sarah unpacks her clothes and puts them into the built-in drawers in Bart's cabin. Inside her trunk she finds a small package wrapped in paper and tied with string.

She opens it to find ten carefully packaged johnnies from Goldstein's.

Maybe you can have love AND freedom. I love you Sarah. —Jess

She laughs through tears. "She's such a romantic."

Bart emerges in the open door and asks, "Are you settled in, Sarah? It's not often that we have such a fine lady aboard. We're about to pass the Shoals. It's the last land we'll see for a while."

"Bart, thank you for giving up your cabin for me. I just have a few more things to do and I'll come up on deck."

"Sarah, you'll like it in France, I am sure," he says patting her hand.

"I hope to be back someday. I don't know what I'll do without the Athenaeum," she says wistfully.

Bart laughs. "I have it on good authority that there are libraries in Paris."

"True—but there's no George there," she says.

He smiles.

"Are you sad to leave so soon?" she asks. "You were supposed to have another few weeks in your new house."

"It worked out well for me leave early. It seems prudent to get to Europe before the winter weather hits in earnest—and I need a little space between Jess and me right now," he says sadly.

"I'm sorry that she turned you down. She likes her independence."

"That's for sure. Oh well. Maybe I'll ask again in a year or two."

He changes the subject. "Do you have everything you need? Your letters of introduction? Your drawings?"

"All packed up and safe. I can't believe that I'm to go to school."

"Hopefully, by the time you're done with your degree, slavery will be illegal here," he says.

"I don't hope for that anymore," she says sadly.

"Sarah, there's something else I need to tell you."

"What's that?" she asks.

"We have another passenger on board."

"Oh, knackers." She rolls her eyes.

"Sorry. I'm a romantic at heart. When he begged me, I relented. If you don't want to see him, I can arrange for him to stay below decks."

"For eight weeks? That moron Stephen can't stay below for eight weeks."

"Oh. It's not Stephen," he says with a smile.

"No? Then who?"

Bart opens the door. George smiles holding the Audubon portfolio.

"I thought you could use some more work on your French. Your pronunciation of 'plumes de heron' is almost there."

She hugs him and cries, "But what will they do at the library without you? Who will take care of your mother?"

"Mother's the one who insisted I come," he says.

CHAPTER 116

Tippy lies in a pool of blood on the expensive Oriental carpet. His notes and papers burn brightly in the fire. The poker has been cleaned and now sits by the hearth ready for duty.

He slips down the stairwell rather than wait for the elevator. He nods to the angry bearded man sitting in the lobby and exits out the front door into the early morning snow.

He makes his way back to the docks. Hopefully, he'll be back in South Berwick before dark.

There's a lot of work to do to get his life back in order and repair his relationship with Orla.

It will be several weeks before he'll hear that another man, one Stephen Bailey, was arrested and subsequently confessed to the murder of the writer.

He said that he did it all for the love of a runaway slave.

Newspapermen from all over the country flooded into Portsmouth to cover the affair.

Spring 1855

CHAPTER 117

Jess sees the fiddleheads and makes a mental note to pick some for supper. She stops to look at the demolished bridge to Cedar Point. "I can't believe that the ice took it out—after 80 years."

She circles back to the front of the tavern and hops off Willie.

She's surprised to see a wagon filled to the brim with a lifetime of belongings waiting out front.

Matie comes out the front door carrying a baby.

"Jess, we're so happy to see you. We're just finishing up our packing."

"Where are you headed?" she asks.

"To Danvers. They just decided last week that the bridge will not be rebuilt. There really isn't a tavern without the bridge. With Max here and hopefully another on the way soon we figured that I'd need some help so we're moving to be closer to my sister."

"Another on the way?" Jess says.

"Yes," she replies sheepishly.

A handsome, brown-haired young man walks out of the tavern carrying a rocking chair.

Jess smiles at Matie.

424   Bridget Finnegan

"Mrs. Simpson, where do you want this?" he asks.

She blushes and she averts her eyes.

"Congratulations, Matie," Jess says. "I'm thrilled for you."

Samuel comes out of the building carrying a carved cradle.

"Hello, Miss Jakes. We were happy to receive your letter. You almost missed us. When you said you'd visit in the spring we didn't realize we might be gone."

"I'm sorry about the bridge. It was here for so long. I can't believe the ice took it out."

"Nature always wins," he says. "It's good to see you looking so well."

"What is the reason for your visit?" Matie says. "It seemed like a matter of some importance."

"Oh, yes." She pulls out the prayer book and hands it to Matie. "If I am not mistaken, this belongs to you."

She hands the baby to Samuel as tears well up.

"What is it?" he asks.

"It's my prayer book from when I was a child."

"But how?"

"It's a long story," Jess answers. "I have to ask. What are the markings on the pages?"

"Oh! I'd forgotten those." She flips through the pages. "It was a game my sister and I used to play during church."

"A children's game?" Jess asks.

"Yes. We pretended that we could communicate through the spirits. I would mark a letter or number and Agnes would try to guess which one it was," she says as she caresses the cover of the small volume. "It used to drive my father to distraction. He said we were disrespecting God and inviting Satan into our lives. He finally got so angry that he pulled the book out of my hand and ripped the cover. I never got it back. I thought he threw it away."

"And now here it is," Samuel says.

"There's something else that belongs to you here," Jess says.

"What do you mean?" she asks.

"Do you have a couple of shovels?" Jess asks.

Samuel and Jess take turns digging up the trash heap. After about an hour they have a pile of broken bottles, crockery and some chicken bones.

"I don't understand what we're doing here," he asks.

Jess is beginning to have her doubts until she hits something that feels different than the bits of crockery.

A box.

More accurately a wooden chest about the size of a small coffin.

Jess and Samuel strain as they heave it out of the hole onto the ground at Matie's feet.

"What is it?" she asks.

"I believe that we are looking at the remains of the missing treasure from the shipwreck Concepción," Jess says.

There's an old rusty padlock on the box. One hit with Samuel's axe and it crumbles away.

Inside wrapped in burlap are ten tarnished bars.

"Silver?" Matie asks.

"Yes. From Spain—and now I think they belong to you."

"But how? Why?" Samuel asks taking Max from his wife's arms.

"Matie, your father was Captain Grievance Collins, correct?" Jess asks as she hands her a bar.

"Yes. But I haven't seen him in years. He abandoned us when I was about ten—in fact, soon after he took my prayer book. I heard that he lived in Portsmouth until he died."

"And yet you kept a portrait of him," Jess says.

"Yes. The wedding portrait is all I have of my dead mother. It was deemed worthless by the state when they took everything else."

"If it wasn't for that portrait you never would have known about this." Jess points to the pile of silver.

"I'm confused, Matie says. "I still don't understand how you found this all out and how this relates to me," the young mother says.

Jess explains, "Your father was on Smuttynose the night the ship smashed on the rocks in 1813."

"How do you know this?" Matie asks as she turns the bar over and over in her hand.

"News reports mention a house guest of the farmer on the night of the wreck—I believe that house guest was your father."

"What? My father was witness to a shipwreck forty years ago?" She sits on a stump and wraps her shawl around her shoulders.

"Yes, the newspapers say that the two of them tried to rescue the sailors. Sadly, their efforts were in vain as all souls were lost. At least that's the story they told after the fact."

"What do you mean, 'at least'?" Samuel's eyes narrow.

"It seems that some of the sailors may not have been quite dead when they were buried."

"Oh, dear God," Matie sucks in a breath.

"Anyway, the farmer died leaving his wife and daughter destitute. He never told them where the silver was. The wife died soon thereafter, and the girl disappeared into the squalid nightlife of Portsmouth."

"How did the treasure get here?" Samuel asks.

"At some point, Grievance Collins must have returned to Smuttynose and retrieved it."

"But how did it get here?" Matie asks pointing to the junk heap.

"It was some time after you married that your father brought it. He probably did it at night when the household was quiet. I'm not sure what his intentions were or exactly when he buried it."

"How do you know this?"

"When he was in failing health, he took my friend, Suzanne, to the Shoals for the weekend. He had used her services over the years and I suppose she was the closest thing to a friend that he had. I believe that he told her what he had done and where the treasure was before he went into the sea. He gave her your prayer book that weekend."

"Why?" she asks.

"Maybe he felt remorseful and wanted her to make things right with you," Jess replies. "Part of that was returning the book."

"But she didn't bring it to me. I mean it was five years ago that he died."

"Actually, she did. Do you remember that I found your small bean pot when I was here?"

"Yes." She nods.

"The prayer book was inside."

Matie laughs.

"I didn't realize it was yours until I saw the portrait of your father in the Athenaeum and recognized him from your painting," Jess says.

"So, she was trying to bring it back when she came here?" Samuel asks.

"I think so," Jess answers.

"But why not just give it to me?" Matie asks.

"I believe that she thought Taylor would kill everyone once he found the treasure. Placing it in the pot near the scrap heap was her way of telling you. She thought you would find it the next time you went to the throw something away. But instead I picked it up. If it weren't for the portrait I never would have known it was yours."

"That poor woman." Matie turns the bar over and over in her hand.

"I don't understand why you think we should have the silver," Matie asks. "Shouldn't it be returned to the Spanish? I mean it was theirs to begin with."

"Well, Spain is in such disarray now it would be hard to know where to even start to return it. There are no Benthams left—not that they deserved it anyway—and that leaves your father's descendants or more accurately you—and your sister."

"I think I'll choose to believe that my father wanted me to have it and not that hiding it here was just one of his schemes," Matie says.

"That's probably wise," Jess says.

CHAPTER 118

The voyage takes a few hours. This is Nah's first sail and he's beside himself with excitement. The captain and first mate take turns answering his questions and letting him help as they guide the boat to the Isles of Shoals.

Maryanne and Jess lounge on supplies destined for the hotel on Smuttynose. They watch the gulls chase the boat hoping for a handout. There are flowers for the sailor's graves and a picnic lunch nearby. The May sun warms them as the stiff breeze propels the boat forward.

"Perfect day for sailing," Jess says.

"You've done this before?" Maryanne asks.

"Yes, as a child we sailed all summer."

"As a child?"

Jess smiles. "Yes. When I was growing up in Manchester by the Sea."

Maryanne takes Jess's hand.

"That was long before Odette's, Sarah, Bart, Jonah, Taylor, Massey and, of course, you—a lifetime away—back when my name was Emma Louise Fawcett."

DISCLAIMER

This is a work of fiction. Any resemblance to any persons, living or dead, places, business establishments or events is entirely coincidental.

THAT BEING SAID...

These actually exist or existed, but probably not in the way I have imagined them.

The Goat Island Tavern, Newington, NH
There were two bridges linking Goat Island to Durham and Newington and there was a tavern. The draw bridge on the Durham (Cedar Point) side was taken out by the ice in the winter of 1855.

The Rockingham Hotel, Portsmouth, NH
This landmark of Portsmouth still stands today and houses the Library Restaurant and private condominiums. Unfortunately, it wasn't built until 1885—thirty years after the fictional Jess met Justice Tompkins there.

The Wreck of the Concepción from Cadiz
There was a ship that crashed onto the rocks of Smuttynose in 1813 killing all aboard. As to there being a treasure of silver...Who knows?

Water Street, Portsmouth, NH
Water Street was the red light district complete with whorehouses and taverns.

The Athenaeum, Portsmouth, NH
This historic library was founded in 1817 and is still located in Market Square. As to the number of tomes that they have on birds I can only guess.

READ MORE!

The following books provided inspiration and background information for this novel. Additional information has been provided by numerous online articles by J. Dennis Robinson.

J. Dennis Robinson. *Mystery on the Isles of Shoals: Closing the Case on the Smuttynose Axe Murders of 1873*. New York: Skyhorse, 2014.

Jeffrey Bolster. *Cross-Grained and Wily Waters: A Guide to the Piscataqua Maritime Region*. Portsmouth: Gundalow, 2002.

Erika Armstrong Dunbar. *Never Caught: The Washingtons' Relentless Pursuit of Their Runaway Slave, Ona Judge*. New York City: 37 Ink, 2017.

Henry Louis Gates Jr. *The Trials of Phillis Wheatley: America's First Black Poet and Her Encounters With the Founding Fathers*. Civitas Books, 2009

Made in United States
North Haven, CT
14 May 2024

52487842R00262